PERNICIOUS PURSUIT

A Howard Knight Escapade

Gary D. McGugan

For Kristy!
Warm Wishes
Gary 05-13-23

ISBN

978-1-9995656-4-0 (Paperback)

978-1-9995656-5-7 (eBook)

1. FICTION, THRILLERS

Also by Gary D. McGugan

Fiction

Three Weeks Less a Day

The Multima Scheme

Unrelenting Peril

Non-Fiction

NEEDS Selling Solutions
(Co-authored with Jeff F. Allen)

What People are Saying About Books by Gary D. McGugan

"Gary McGugan skillfully crafts an intricate tale of suspense, thrills, and non-stop drama, and I was thoroughly captivated by *Three Weeks Less a Day*." ~ *Sheri Hoyte, Reader Views*

"If his audience thought crossing the finish line in *Three Weeks Less a Day* was epic, they better fasten their seatbelts and get ready for another thrilling ride to be had in *The Multima Scheme*. Bravo Mr. McGugan. I am a fan and am thrilled with the momentum of this series!" ~ *Diane Lunsford, Feathered Quill*

"The challenge that McGugan faces in creating this second novel is to stay true to the more significant plot-line of the series. There is also the added problem to create a sequel that would be complete enough that readers could just read the follow up without being lost. It becomes a balancing act, which McGugan has admirably pulled off." ~ *Norm Goldman, Bookpleasures.com*

"Thoroughly enjoyed *Unrelenting Peril*, the third installment in the story of the Multima Corporation. It is definitely the best of the three books! I was so absorbed in the story it was difficult to put the book down. The author's writing style, which was excellent already, keeps getting better which each book. I can't wait to read the next one!!" ~ *GoodReads Reviewer, Mary*

This book was published during the COVID-19 Pandemic. I salute all who are doing their part in the battle against the virus and express heartfelt condolences to families and friends of those who made the ultimate sacrifice.

ONE

A chime jolted Howard Knight awake. The doorbell? It rang again and he slid groggily from bed to peer through a narrow slit in the Venetian blinds. Three floors below, two men in uniform stood waiting. Official caps on their heads, hands at their sides, they stared at the front door.

Howard peeked farther down the street. An unfamiliar large dark van parked next to the curb in a neighbor's space three doors down. He shook off his twinge of unease as an all-too-automatic mental reflex. Police officers, after all, still have work to do at three o'clock in the morning.

As he pulled on a pair of jeans, a third chime sounded, suggesting impatience. They held the doorbell button down for a second or two longer than necessary. The effect produced a louder, longer clang and Janet stirred in her sleep. It would probably take a tornado to wake her though. She'd had an entire bottle of white wine before they made love for a second time last night.

"Don't worry. I'll be right back," Howard whispered as he set off barefoot down the two steeply pitched flights of stairs.

The bell rang out yet again as he reached the ground floor. Before opening the door, he looked out the tiny peephole to be sure they were indeed police officers. Both had badges prominently displayed on their chests. Neither smiled nor showed any other emotion, though both appeared a little startled by the sudden flash after Howard clicked on the light over the outdoor entrance. One officer reached reflexively to his holstered gun before catching himself and relaxing.

"Who's there?" Howard called out in English through the still-locked door.

"*Wij zijn politieagenten Jansen en De Vries van het Haarlem-kantoor,*" a voice called back, then paused and switched to English. "It's an urgent police matter."

Warily, Howard opened the door only the couple inches a recently reinforced security chain permitted. "How can I help you, gentlemen?" he asked.

"May we come in?" the older one asked. "I'm afraid there's been a tragic occurrence in the neighborhood this evening. We must ask you a few questions."

The man's tone was polite and reassuring. Still, Howard sensed something amiss in the deliberate calm delivery. Looking for any clue, he hesitated and glanced inquisitively from one to the other. Neither said another word, implying they were prepared to wait as long as necessary.

The older man suppressed a cough and raised his hand to cover his mouth. In the time it took for Howard's eyes to follow the man's hand to his mouth, the younger one lashed out with a wooden club and violently struck the exposed security chain, splintering it from the doorframe and launching a chunk of wood past Howard's head.

He ducked and the older officer forced the door open with his shoulder, slamming it into Howard. He staggered from the impact, then fell backward against the stair railing. The younger one grabbed Howard by the neck and pressed hard on a sensitive nerve, forcing his knees right to the ground.

Howard tried to resist but his hands, arms, and legs refused to function. A wet stain spread on his jeans as his bladder voided, and the piss puddled under him.

"Quiet," the younger man growled. The older one jerked a cloth from a pocket, then mashed it hard against Howard's nose and mouth in one deft motion. The stench of chlorine or something similar filled his nasal passages. After a short struggle, Howard succumbed.

When consciousness slowly returned, he was in a moving vehicle, lying on his right side, his hands bound behind his back. Cable zip ties secured his wrists to the back of his knees. His hands could move only an inch up or down. He could wiggle them and move his feet, but the cable joining his hands to his knees restricted further motion in any direction.

He could breathe, but only through his nose. Adhesive tape covered his mouth and much of his face. He felt no pain, but he was groggy and struggled to keep his eyes open for a few seconds at a time.

The vehicle was a large van. Perhaps the same one Howard spotted earlier from the bedroom window? Its ride was quiet and he concluded they must be traveling on an expressway. His body rolled from side to side, gently but involuntarily, following the swaying motion of the vehicle and occasional dips in the roadway. No one talked. Rock music played on the sound system, but the volume was low. His captors probably wanted to hear movement should Howard try to free himself.

The first glimmer of light confirmed they'd been traveling for a while, possibly several hours. The sun usually rose about seven at this time of year, so they were outside the borders of Holland. From Overveen, four hours driving in any direction would put them in Belgium, France or Germany. Clearly, it wasn't the Dutch police transporting Howard in the back of the van.

Was it possible they'd grabbed him for someone else? Howard's spirit deflated as that possibility registered. And where was Janet? There was only room for one person in the van's storage area. However, if they'd snatched her as well, was it possible she was in the vehicle's rear seating area? Or did they leave her sleeping in Overveen?

The van slowed. Howard took a deep breath as they swerved from the expressway onto a bumpier paved surface and gradually rolled to a silent stop. He closed his eyes. It was better they think he was still sleeping. Otherwise, they might apply something even stronger to knock him out again.

Doors of the vehicle clicked open and shut, but no one came to the back. Howard no longer heard sounds or voices coming from his captors, even muffled ones, so he opened his eyes again. Glowing light standards in a parking lot confirmed it was not yet fully daybreak. Occasionally he heard the hums and swishes of vehicles, but the reverberations suggested the traffic was mainly trucks. As time passed, from boredom, Howard dozed off again.

"Wake up," a gruff voice said. "Christ, you stink."

Howard opened his eyes.

Two men stood outside the van. Neither face was familiar. Neither wore a uniform. They dressed casually in jeans and bulky sweaters, and one wore a cap. Both were older, large men. One was tall and physically fit, the other even taller but obese. Enforcers. With their shaved heads and scarred faces, they looked like the kind of guys The Organization used to settle scores and protect its leaders.

The new noiseless surroundings weren't a parking lot next to an expressway like before. Instead, only yards away, a small forest skirted the opposite side of a narrow two-lane paved road, making the location isolated. The sky looked brighter outside the vehicle but was partially shrouded with fast-moving clouds. The air was uncomfortably chilly, and rain threatened.

"Come with me," the fat one commanded as he cut loose the zip ties around Howard's feet, then dragged him out of the van and across the roadway toward the wooded area. Tiny pebbles and bits of broken glass punctured the bottom of Howard's bare feet, and he gritted his teeth against the sharp jabs of pain. He hopped and danced gingerly to protect the vulnerable soles of his feet as he tried to keep pace with the hulk rushing toward the forest.

They stepped over a dangling break in a fence with the brute shoving Howard roughly as he tried to protect his exposed toes from barbed wire on the ground and scramble over without injury.

On the other side, they strode quickly, snapping dead twigs and rustling leaves on the ground. Apparently, the big man wanted the cover of the forest before any cars came along. Howard tried to slow down to ease the pain on the bottoms of his feet, but with one massive hand, the thug shoved his captive's shoulder, causing him to trip and fall again. A rough yank on the waistband of his jeans hauled him to his feet. More pain.

They barged through trees, shrubs, and debris for a few hundred feet until the road was no longer visible. An engine started in the distance and broke the absolute silence of the forest. The vehicle accelerated in a spray of gravel at the shoulder of the road and sped off. Seconds later, the growing roar of an approaching truck was followed by a loud swoosh of air as it rumbled past before stillness returned.

"Take off your cruddy jeans," the fat one ordered in perfect American English. There were no formal introductions, so Howard decided he'd call him Jumbo. "Then do your business. No more pissing or shitting in your clothes from now on."

Jumbo released the remaining zip ties securing Howard's hands with two forceful snaps. He rubbed his wrists before following the other instructions. He dropped his eyes in humiliation as he first urinated and defecated while his captor gawked with a sneer of derision. Satisfied, the thug removed some items from a plastic bag. Then, with an outstretched arm, gestured to Howard.

"Use the bag to wipe your ass."

Jumbo tossed a few more pieces of clothing on the damp ground as Howard followed his instructions and wiped up as thoroughly as one could with a slippery, non-absorbent plastic sack. *Couldn't the bastard at least have asked for a paper bag from the store?*

"Put on the underwear and jeans first," the thug commanded, pointing to the clothes lying on the ground. Howard had trouble bending over. His more-than-middle-aged body was stiff from the extended confinement. Jumbo yanked him upright when Howard momentarily lost his balance and tumbled forward.

With the jeans in place, another order followed. "Shoes next."

Howard responded to the instructions slowly. Perched on a damp fallen tree trunk, he slipped on the sneakers and took an unusually long time to methodically tie the laces. He glanced around as he slowly completed the task, doing his best to avoid creating the impression he might be wondering about the chances of escape.

"Don't even think about it, Knight. I'm supposed to keep you alive 'til the boss gets here, but he didn't say nothin' about rearranging your face or other body parts," he growled. "Just give me an excuse."

The guy looked powerful but didn't appear to be carrying a weapon. Guns weren't as readily available in Europe and even a recently arrived goon might have had trouble getting one quickly.

However, he surely outweighed Howard by more than a hundred pounds. In contrast, Howard's six-foot-tall frame was trim, the product of dedicated exercise. Over the past two years, he walked, ran, or rode a bicycle virtually every day. His stamina and energy were probably the best they'd been since hiking through the mountains of Bolivia almost four years earlier.

Howard took a long, lingering look around him as he got to his feet. Slowly, he bent over, picked up a T-shirt from the ground and slid it over his head. Before he could pull it all the way to his waist, Jumbo grabbed his forearm with one massive hand and squeezed forcefully, causing a twinge of pain.

"Let's go," he muttered, still holding on firmly.

Howard listened for the sound of a returning vehicle, but the forest and surroundings remained silent except for the subtle crunches created by two men trudging across shriveled leaves and twigs on uneven ground.

"I need to adjust my shoe. It doesn't feel right." Howard suddenly declared, stopping. "A pebble or something is in it."

Jumbo looked around, listening for some indication of a returning vehicle. Satisfied time was not an issue, he loosened his grip on Howard's arm, and allowed him to bend over and touch the ground. Howard emptied the shoe but nothing came out. He inserted his hand and fiddled about theatrically for a few seconds, then gestured that he couldn't find anything after all. He put on the shoe again, tied it up, and then told his captor he needed to piss again.

"Do it right here, and no funny stuff," the big man responded as Howard opened his zipper and relieved himself.

He took as much time as possible. To make a show of finishing, he shook himself twice. As he made an exaggerated motion to pull up the zipper, Howard suddenly pivoted just beyond the man's reach and ran furiously, zigzagging toward a more densely wooded area. His obese captor gave chase while loudly spouting curses and threats.

Within a few hundred yards, Howard discovered a dirt path with tracks from a tractor or some other equipment and ran on it with longer strides and greater speed. He glanced back once to see a gap of at least fifty yards between the thug and himself. And that gap was growing.

Jumbo probably weighed three hundred pounds and had started to labor already. Howard pushed his body to its maximum. His heart pumped furiously, but his breathing stayed controlled and measured. His legs were strong, and his body warmed with the activity. He ran at breakneck speed for at least ten minutes.

Short of breath, but confident in the growing gap between the thug and himself, Howard left the track to take refuge in the more densely wooded area. Escape looked promising, so he found a large rock to rest on and gather his thoughts.

The first reality to register was that he had no money, no credit cards, no identification. He needed all of them to survive for any length of time. Without money, food, or water, his situation was dire.

Overhead, the sky turned darker and dense clouds threatened. The wind picked up and the air cooled. Howard shivered as his breathing slowed and his heart rate returned to normal.

He weighed his chances. They were low, at best. He'd need to find a farmhouse and break in to steal some food and water. With any luck he would find a coat, some gloves, and some money. But it could take hours to find a place and scout it for possible entry.

A twig broke loudly behind him. He turned to find his pursuer, now just yards away. The approaching thug held a broad stub of a tree branch in his large hand and waved it menacingly above his head.

As Howard jumped up from the rock and twisted his body to run off again, he glimpsed only the outline of another shadow just as it delivered a painful, surprising wallop to the side of his head. Then darkness.

TWO

Janet Weissel heard a commotion downstairs around the front door of their three-story home and lurched upright in bed. Howard wasn't in the room. She didn't hear voices, but something had broken. Muffled noises suggested movement, maybe a struggle. She breathed deeply to avoid panic as her heart raced and hands trembled.

Janet tiptoed over to the door of the bedroom. By the time she reached the top of the stairs, the struggle had stopped, but something unusual was going on. She craned her neck to hear better but deciphered only muffled tones.

Who was Howard talking to outside at this time of night?

Janet resisted a temptation to call out to him because she sensed something terribly amiss. Instead, she crept along the outside wall toward the window, taking particular care to avoid those areas of the wood floor that usually creaked.

She peered from the window and spotted two police officers lugging Howard along the sidewalk in front of their house, headed toward a dark van parked beside the curb. Howard's body was limp, and they were half dragging, half carrying him. He wore jeans, had no shirt on, and his feet were bare.

What is friggin' going on here?

She recoiled in horror as one of the men in uniform glanced up at the window. The next time she peered out, they were roughly hoisting Howard into the back of the van.

What to do? Who to call? If these guys were really officers, it wouldn't help to call the police. If they were thugs dressed in uniform, they'd probably be from The Organization and looking for her next.

Janet scrambled across the room and pulled on the panties, jeans, and top she'd worn the night before. Then she dashed to slip on a pair of running shoes off the closet floor. From the dresser, she grabbed a

13

fistful of euros, her phone, and Howard's credit card tucked in a corner between the wooden frame and mirror. From another drawer, she snatched a cap and the running belt she used to carry water bottles and stuffed everything inside.

After tearing a sheet off the bed, Janet rushed out the door to a small balcony at the back of their house. She swung closed the bedroom's glass doors and frantically tied one end of the sheet through the door-handles and into a knot around the wood railing.

It had been Howard's idea to practice this maneuver. "Just in case we ever need to leave in a hurry," he once said. They both worried continuously about The Organization finding them even though they'd successfully eluded the dreaded criminal element for nearly two years.

Deftly, she swung her long legs over the waist-high wood railing, grabbed the sheet, tugged it hard to be sure the knot would hold, and then lowered herself as quickly as possible. After she hit the ground, she ran a few steps to a tiny opening in the fence behind the shed where Howard kept gardening tools. The opening was on the left, beside an old oak tree.

The previous occupants had agreed with the neighbor behind them to leave the tree ample space to grow in the corner they shared. Janet had barely squeezed through that tiny gap when they did an earlier trial run, and she silently prayed she hadn't gained any weight in the ensuing months.

She dropped to the ground and pushed her head and chest inside the opening. It was tight and she needed to give her left breast a nudge to stuff it through before she inhaled deeply, wiggled and squeezed her hips into the gap. It pinched as she forced her lower body into, then through, the tiny space.

Almost out of breath, she hauled herself into the neighbor's yard. On her hands and knees, she crept along the wooden fence and away from the tree. From the other corner of the confined backyard, she looked up.

Sure enough, a man on their balcony stared down into the darkness. He wore a uniform. In one hand, he held an end of the sheet she'd used to escape. In the other, he spoke into a phone and was probably relaying his discovery to someone else. Janet couldn't hear what he was saying because his tone was barely a whisper, and a breeze carried his voice away into the night air.

His body language didn't look encouraging. He took deep breaths as he spoke, shaking his head in frustration or angst as his eyes darted in multiple directions looking for her.

A light came on in the neighbor's bedroom above her. She had to move. With her knees bent and her back against the fence, she slid along it toward the neighbor's house, hoping she wasn't visible to the man on their balcony. Fumbling in the darkness, she found a chain-link gate that opened from the neighbor's yard into a narrow grassy patch between the two houses.

The damned gate squeaked—just like theirs—even though she tried to open it as delicately and slowly as possible. She glanced up. The guy on the balcony looked right at her, then dashed into the house, still with a phone to his ear.

Janet rushed from the neighbor's backyard as quickly as she dared on the wet, slippery grass. She needed to get away but didn't want to alert the neighbor or take a tumble. The guy in the uniform could never squeeze through the same opening and looked too short to easily scale the fence. He'd need a couple minutes to drive around to this side of the street. Howard had timed that drive. She had two minutes to run down the first side street from the house and into a schoolyard the next street over.

Glancing from side to side as she ran, she watched for any signs of movement. There was no traffic. But streetlights seemed to glow brighter than usual as she sprinted with every ounce of energy she could produce. A fenced walkway into the schoolyard sat partly open and she ran through it, but at a slower pace to compensate for the new walkway's darkness. No light from the streets spilled into that area. A good thing, perhaps, but it increased the risk of a fall.

She circled the school to its front entrance, running warily until she found the exit she needed. The Dutch thoughtfully created walkways to the yard from every nearby street. Just like Howard and she had practiced, she found the one leading toward the village road that eventually headed away from town and past the sand dunes.

As she prepared to step out, the night lit up with flashing blue lights. She ducked behind several large shrubs. Seconds later, a police car swept past, headed in the direction of their home, so she waited behind the bush and checked to be sure no others were following. In the distance, three more cars soon sped toward her, and she hunkered down deeper into the shrub.

The cars zoomed past with lights flashing but no sirens. Janet gave them a few more seconds to clear out before she dared move from her hiding spot, taking care to avoid the possibility some hawk-eyed policeman might detect movement from a rear-view mirror.

Satisfied no more cars were coming, she tucked as much of her hair as possible into a wad under her cap, then ruffled her top to make her breasts as inconspicuous as possible. Satisfied she looked more masculine in the darkness, she started jogging again, gradually increasing her speed to a measured pace.

Janet wasn't a natural athlete, but she took care of her body and was fit. Her regular runs with Howard taught her to hold her elbows high and pump rhythmically with her stride for minimum effort and maximum running efficiency. She knew how to control her breathing, using her nose instead of her mouth to retain as much oxygen as possible.

Wary but confident, she needed about twenty-five minutes at a steady jog to reach the massive—but eerily solitary—sand dunes next to the North Sea.

THREE

The pain was excruciating. Howard opened his eyes. A sharp stabbing at the side of his head spread to his neck with only the slightest of movements. He breathed deeply for a few moments to wake completely. The ache in his head was the worst, but he had pain or discomfort in several parts of his body.

He could barely move. His captors had tightened the zip ties around his arms and legs securely, leaving him lying in the fetal position on his right side. They'd bound his hands to his feet, forcing his body to hunch forward and making it impossible to stretch out his legs or lift his hands.

"I need to piss," Howard shouted, much feebler than he intended.

Can they even hear me over the drone of tires at a high speed on an expressway?

The music suddenly stopped.

"Are you awake back there?" a voice shouted.

"Yes. I need to stop, or I'll piss my pants again."

"Hold on. We'll take the next exit. It'll be about five minutes," the other voice called out.

Without a watch, it was impossible to judge the accuracy of the captor's claim, but the vehicle soon left an expressway and continued some distance farther before coming to a complete stop. They shut off the engine, then opened the door at the back of the van. They hauled him out, released the zip ties around his arms, and stood Howard somewhat upright at the side of the vehicle, deliberately outside the view of passing vehicles.

"Okay, Knight. We were careless before. Must have been the fucking jet lag. This time we take no chances," the more fit of the two said. Howard dubbed him String Bean. "Felt good to wallop your head back there, but my fat buddy here wasn't impressed. You made him bust his ass trying to catch you." They both laughed as though a brilliant comedian had just delivered the punch line to a raucous joke.

When their laughter subsided, they wrapped a rope around Howard's neck, tied a knot, and squeezed it tightly right below his Adam's apple. String Bean jerked it harshly, pulling Howard off balance. They caught him just before his face hit the ground. The intimidation left him warily stroking his neck where the coarse strands of the rope had scratched his skin and left an unpleasant burning sensation.

"Try to escape again and I'll give this rope a real yank the next time." He laughed, his face an expression of menace. "Giancarlo wants you alive. He said nothing about us having a little fun along the way. Pull down your zipper. Get your little dick out. Do whatever you have to do. Try to escape and I'll decorate your neck with a scar you'll regret for a long time."

Howard turned away from them to urinate, and the rope tightened again. The mention of Giancarlo removed any remaining doubt about who his captors were.

As he stood at the side of the road relieving himself, Howard's shoulders sagged and his head hung low in humiliation. He looked spent and beaten. He slowly pulled up his zipper with an aimless movement and furrowed brow.

"Where are we?" he mumbled as he turned to face his captors. Their faces were hard, unsmiling, and grim.

"No concern of yours," Jumbo replied. "We're still in Europe. That's all you need to know. When we get where we're going, Giancarlo will decide if you need to know your location or not. I'm guessing not." His snarl transformed his face into a scowl of disgust.

"Where is Janet?" Howard asked.

"Your whore? No idea," String Bean muttered with a dismissive wave of his hand. "By now, they've probably got her displayed in a window servicing the sex-starved tourists of Amsterdam."

"Have some water," Jumbo added. "But not too much. I won't stop again until we're out of this lousy country. Another three or four hours." He also offered up a piece of baguette. "That should hold you until we cross the border."

They stared at Howard with cold, unfeeling expressions while he silently chewed bits of the baguette. The thugs remained silent, leaving Howard to mull over his plight. He realized how The Organization dealt with those who turned against them, and Giancarlo Mareno was the worst. He didn't become the boss because of his people skills.

And his displeasure with Howard undoubtedly surpassed his irritation with most of those he punished. Millions of dollars had disappeared while Howard was in charge of the financial side of The Organization. Mareno ranked among the wealthiest men on earth, although his name never appeared on the Forbes list of billionaires, and he'd never miss the lost money in practical terms.

But greed consumes men of his ilk, and they never forgive.

After a few moments, String Bean motioned for Howard to hurry up with his bread and dragged out the cable zip ties and tape. Jumbo snatched the remaining morsel of baguette from his hand and tossed it casually aside.

"Bend over while we prepare for departure," he laughed. When Howard hesitated, the thug kicked Howard in the joints behind his knees. He crumpled, writhing in pain. Jumbo stomped on Howard's left hand as he tried to push himself up. They all heard an audible snap as pain worse than the wallop to the side of his head shot from his little finger up his left arm and into his shoulder.

The pair wrapped the zip ties tightly around Howard's legs. Then Jumbo roughly clenched his captive's hair and yanked forward, bringing his face almost to his feet. To complete their task, the thugs secured Howard's wrists and attached one end to the cable connection around his bound feet.

Wordlessly, both jerked him up from the ground and casually tossed him like captured game into the back of the van. Howard landed on his left hand and screamed out in pain. Another bone cracked on impact. One of the thugs jammed a rag over his mouth and nose, pressing forcefully until his struggle ended.

FOUR

The small cavern was unoccupied whenever Janet and Howard had visited. In the continuing quiet darkness before sunrise, she located the isolated and forlorn site and found it empty now too.

Still puffing hard from her run and climb over the summit to the side of the dunes facing the sea, Janet reached for a gulp of water, only to remember her bottles were empty. She had two plastic bottles in the pouches attached to the belt she'd grabbed from her bedroom, but there'd been no time to fill them as she ran from the house.

As usual, it was raining. Janet was sheltered inside the cave, but the humidity was uncomfortable. Incessant rain this time of the year was the only thing about the Netherlands she truly hated. She found it ironic that Americans knew all about the insufferable amounts of rain in England and typically avoided trips there during the winter months. Yet she had no idea before she got here that the Netherlands received even more precipitation. And it created the damp, cold air that penetrated deeply into the bones of even a young person. Janet detested it.

But for once she saw opportunity in rainfall. Scooping up both bottles, Janet slipped out of the cave, removed the lids, and buried the bottom half of the bottles in the sand to keep them upright. Within seconds, gentle tinkling on the bottom of the bottles affirmed she'd soon be able to quench her thirst. If it lasted long enough, she might manage throughout the day.

Resigned to the reality that she'd be there a while, she tried to divert her attention away from the cold by gathering her thoughts. Several months before, Howard had mentioned that the real police in the Netherlands would probably have little interest in either of them. They both made sure they obeyed all laws and traffic regulations, and their immigration papers were up to date. She thought then he was merely paranoid about the danger they were in, but this bizarre incident validated his fears.

Those strangers in the middle of the night were almost certainly people associated with The Organization. Howard had told Janet about a rogue element of the police he once dealt with in nearby Haarlem during his life with organized crime.

"There's only a couple of them and they're real police officers, but corrupt ones," he had warned. "They're on The Organization's payroll and are reputed to be absolutely ruthless."

They had designed a plan. In the event of an unwelcome visit, it would be essential to avoid the hundreds of cameras positioned around the town to combat petty theft and more serious crimes. To accomplish that, she needed to get out of Overveen. The sand dunes and the tiny secluded cavern on the side facing the North Sea assured she was well out of the range of any security camera, and she intended to hide there until it was dark again.

Their decision to cooperate with the FBI and testify against The Organization had enraged its kingpin, Giancarlo Mareno. Janet's testimony had been of limited value to the FBI compared to Howard's because she knew too little about the criminal element's activities to make a great difference. He, however, knew everything about their operations and shared information with the authorities that filled volumes.

"If The Organization ever gets to me," he told her during one bout of unusual melancholy, "assume I'm dead. They'll let me live only long enough to take whatever satisfaction Mareno gets from torturing and dismembering me. Try not to think about it. Follow the escape plan we devised with my friend Klaudia in Germany. Forget all about me and get on with your life as best you can."

Back then, Janet shrugged off the message as a moment of vague despair. Now, she shuddered at the thought of Howard in the hands of sadistic enforcers for The Organization, and tears welled in her eyes. She wasn't prepared to accept his despondent forecast as fact just yet, but the situation wasn't good.

He was the best human being she'd ever known and didn't deserve this end. They'd had only two years together, and those full of uncertainty, but at that moment she'd gladly trade the pain she felt for all his uncertainty and paranoia. The void left by his loss would never heal. Janet couldn't recall him actually using the word "love" during their time together, but his thoughtfulness, care, and passion all seemed like love to her.

The concept of love had always been ambiguous to her. Back in her youth, she couldn't recall a single occasion when her parents used the term. In her teens, immature boys always said they loved her until she slept with them often enough that they grew tired of her and sought some new conquest. During college and in her business career that followed, her clients only used the word love to describe how she satisfied their sexual desires at that moment of ecstasy. Only Howard had treated her with true compassion and passion.

Was it only he who had truly loved her? The others were merely to earn money, or get information, or survive in an unfair world. In contrast, his lovemaking had always been tender, caring, and attentive to her needs. As the magnitude of her loss registered, Janet screamed out her grief with a long and desperate howl she didn't recognize.

Then her tears flowed. As she released her pain and grief, her chest heaved, and huge droplets streamed down her cheeks. Janet didn't bother to brush them away or hold them back. Her nose filled with mucus and her vision blurred. Her head ached and her heart felt physical pain as she wrapped her arms around her chest and hung her head.

Eventually, she slowly regained her composure, and the tears reduced to a trickle. She wouldn't forget him as he instructed. Instead, she would treasure every moment they enjoyed together. And she would find a way to carry on. She always did.

Meeting up with Howard's friend in Germany held out the potential for a new beginning if Janet could only get there safely. Now, focusing on survival first, she needed to avoid those thugs. The escape plan—the one they'd rehearsed carefully more than once—called for Janet to hang out in the secluded sand dunes until darkness returned.

The lonely silence of nature, combined with her gloominess, made her uncomfortable and ill at ease. With only the repetitive crash of waves thundering against the shoreline, she needed a distraction. Years before, she'd developed a childhood habit to cope with such unease. She talked to herself to break the isolation and bolster her courage.

"As soon as it's dark, I'll make my way back toward town," she mumbled in a tone just above a whisper. "My first task will be to steal an unlocked bicycle from someone's yard. It should be easy. I'll try to find a top-end bike first but will probably need to settle for one of lesser quality. That means I'll have to pedal harder on the ride. More importantly, I'll have to be sure I find one with a working front light. But none of this can start for more than twelve hours. I need to sleep to conserve energy and prepare for the long ride. It's easy to say, but I'm still cold and have no blanket or jacket to curl up with. I'm starting to feel hungry and I'm still thirsty from both the run and dehydration from last night's wine. I really shouldn't have started that second bottle."

Even with the clouds, the light outside now shone brightly, and the tiny cavern she used for shelter was barely large enough for her to stretch out and lie prone. She crawled out of the opening and peered around. No one was in sight in any direction. A few seagulls swooped about, looking for food. Their occasional caws seemed unnecessary but presumably served as some means of communication. Maybe they realized she was there and just let each other know. Otherwise, everything outside remained still except for the undulating waves of the sea and the gentle pattering of rain on the dunes.

She crawled as far inside the cavern as possible and sat down on the coarse sand. While she was usually okay with sand at the beach, she preferred to sit on a towel and have some barrier between her and the ants and bugs. She squirmed and twitched, thinking about what might be crawling around below her. Her shoulders shuddered a final time as she breathed deeply and repetitively to relax.

It worked. Within minutes her head drooped, and her eyelids closed, with her chest heaving gently as she slumbered. Urgently needed sleep came after all.

FIVE

Howard Knight's head hit the floor and pain jolted him awake. He opened his eyes slowly but saw nothing. His captors had wrapped a blindfold around his head while he was unconscious. His hands were still bound, and he lay on a marble or ceramic floor in the fetal position. His feet moved only a few inches because they had secured him again.

They were outdoors. The air was crisp, a breeze rippled across Howard's face and he detected the salty air of the sea. His body shivered involuntarily because he was dressed only in jeans and a T-shirt. They'd removed his shoes for some reason, so his feet were bare. And the side of his head continued to throb from the whack they'd administered in the woods sometime before dropping him unceremoniously on the current hard surface.

"He's coming to life," one of them said, bored. Howard recognized the voice as Jumbo's. "Should we drag him inside or just leave him here?"

"Leave him here," the other voice said with a scornful laugh.

"Can you take off my blindfold?" Howard tried to speak, but what the captors heard was little more than a garbled grunt. They'd covered his mouth with adhesive tape, and he could breathe only through his nose. Communication was impossible.

"Should we see what he wants?" Jumbo asked.

"Yank off the blindfold but keep him quiet until we're sure the bastard's ready to cooperate."

With a quick jerk, Jumbo pulled the blindfold away, and Howard's eyes blinked rapidly in the sunlight. He slowly opened and closed his eyes until his pupils dilated and blurry objects came into focus. They were on an outdoor patio, and the sun was brilliant, even if the temperature was nippy.

Both captors sat on comfortable lounge chairs with half-smoked cigarettes dangling carelessly from their mouths. Two open bottles of beer sat on a small table between the chairs. Jumbo had a malicious grin on his face. The other guy looked bored and uninterested, while scruffy beards suggested neither had shaved for several days.

Howard tried to speak, grunt, or get their attention.

"Okay, sleeping beauty, here's the drill," String Bean said after a while. "We're on the top floor of an eight-story building. If you jump, you'll die. If you promise to keep your mouth shut—no talking at all—we'll remove the tape. You say a word—any fucking word—we slap the tape back on and it stays there until he arrives tomorrow. Got that?"

Howard nodded.

"We're going to keep you tied to the balcony, too," he continued after taking a swig from the half-empty bottle of beer. "Don't call out to people below. You can walk around on the balcony, but no funny stuff. Don't try to signal to anyone. Any noise and the tape goes back on. If you need the toilet, come to us and whisper politely. If you want a drink, take a paper cup and get water from the fountain over there. If you're hungry, too bad. Got it?"

Howard nodded again.

Jumbo approached him and roughly tore the adhesive tape from Howard's mouth, causing a squawk of discomfort he couldn't entirely contain. The fat one instantly responded with a brusque blow from his open hand against Howard's right cheek before he released the zip ties from Howard's hands and yanked him to his still-bound feet. But Howard was very unsteady. Jumbo caught him as he started to fall backward before he could shuffle his feet enough to regain balance.

String Bean returned from the nearby kitchen carrying an orange. In disdain, he tossed it on the ground in front of Howard before he sank into his lounge chair, again with a smirk punctuating his pleasure at his captive's humiliation.

As Howard's sense of balance returned, he freed one hand from the security of the balcony wall and stiffly bent over to pick up the orange as his captors snickered in the background. Peeling it was difficult with his broken finger, but he persevered and held the dripping fruit in the good hand to eat. He used the palm of his other hand for balance and looked out over the skyline.

"I know exactly where I am!" Howard whispered as his surroundings came into focus. "Ayamonte, Spain."

The pair scowled and gestured for Howard to shut his mouth. But neither made a move from his comfortable seat.

"It's Giancarlo Mareno's apartment building on Isla Canela," Howard said in defiance of their threat. "Even if I should cry out in my loudest voice, no one will hear me. There's nobody here. They're closed for the season. Every hotel is shut down and every condo is vacant. The nearest civilization is across the marina in Punta Del Moral. No sound from me would ever carry that far."

Howard craned his neck to better look across the inlet at some buildings more than a half-mile away. No activity was evident over there either. Most of the residents were probably away in their hometown villages for Christmas reunions. The thugs continued to scowl and drink their beers but seemed to concede there was no danger Howard would be overheard. They picked up their phones with vacant stares and played games or clicked "likes" on Instagram to demonstrate their disinterest.

Howard knew the building and location well. He'd bought it for Mareno during the Spanish real estate crash of 2009. The extraordinarily low price immediately popped out of his memory bank—less than a million bucks for a building assessed at more than five million. The negotiations—or more accurately the lack of negotiation—came to mind next. The previous owner found himself indebted to Giancarlo for a million bucks and couldn't keep up the interest payments. It was Howard who had to tell him to sign over legal title of the entire complex to Mareno or bad things would happen.

As though it were a dream, Howard pictured the despair on the owner's face as he signed away his rights to the magnificent property and recalled the loud blubbering tears after the man realized all was lost. Mareno later laughed about Howard's accomplishment and told him to stay on for another month and enjoy the place as though it was his own. Feeling both remorse and incredulity at how dramatically things had changed in the meantime, Howard drew an audible sigh.

Isla Canela was a beautiful spot just outside the Spanish town of Ayamonte, in Andalucía. The sun shone brightly almost every day, about three hundred and thirty days on average each year. Hotels, condos, and restaurants were all modern, and the landscaping of the massive complex was meticulous. Beaches to the west had magnificent white sand, while the scruffy wetlands to the north and east invited exploration, fishing, and shellfish harvesting.

But December was undoubtedly not a good time to be there. Hotels and condos had shut down and locked up for the winter season back in October. Almost every shop, restaurant, and form of accommodation had been safely secured. The island became a virtual ghost town until late February when maintenance workers returned to start sprucing up buildings and gardens for the annual re-opening of the island's tourist businesses.

Howard felt morose as it all sank in. His brain slowed as the gravity of his situation registered, and his hands trembled as his fearful imagination fueled images of the terrible things Mareno liked to do to punish. Isla Canela's isolation at this time of the year made it a perfect place for whatever sadistic payback the cruel crime boss might choose— even for several weeks—without any fear of detection.

SIX

After dark, Janet Weissel crawled out of her little cavern in the sand dunes, trudged back to the edge of the village, and found an unattended garden hose to quench her thirst and fill the water bottles secured around her waist. Next, she stole a functional old bike from the third yard she tried. It had a headlamp but no other accessories. The seat appeared comfortable with a chain that was smooth and quiet. She set out immediately, stopping only once at a quiet park near the last village street to make her crucial call to Klaudia Schäffer in Germany.

"Okay. I got it," the woman replied immediately after Janet explained her predicament. "Set out as we planned. But the train schedules have changed since we last spoke. Take the first two trains as we discussed and stay overnight in Oberhausen. You can't get to Angermund until tomorrow. Find a place out of sight to sleep and take the first train in the morning."

Janet rode to Utrecht during the darkness of night. Although the terrain in the Netherlands is famously flat, she quickly realized the bike paths weren't free of hazards. Clouds intermittently covered the little amount of light from the moon as she used a groomed route running cross-country from Overveen right up to the central rail station in the city of Utrecht. During daylight, she might have completed the ride on the well-maintained path in about three hours. But at night, with only a tiny dim headlamp to show the way, it took twice as long.

When they'd first talked about this kind of escape, Howard encouraged her to visualize the trail before starting out, remembering every possible detail about their research. She tried to do that as she warily pedaled and built up her speed to a steady pace.

It wasn't long before her main preoccupation became a surprising number of critters that shared the path. In the first mile or two, three rabbits and some animal she didn't recognize scooted across the trail in front of her. She managed to brake safely each time, but she feared hitting and squishing some little creature with her tires.

She remembered the several treacherous curves on the route and slowed sensibly each time. She also needed to brake again when the trail veered around protected lands and along a couple rambling creeks. Through it all, wildlife was plentiful and seemed to enjoy the darkness.

Janet was prepared for the steep dip in terrain near the lake at Aalsmeer a while before she crossed the A-2 expressway on the elevated bridge. She was ready for the sharp turn at the end of the bridge before she veered onto the path to Utrecht. She correctly anticipated the long gradual downhill slope along the trail in a southeasterly direction that let her coast for long stretches parallel to the highway.

During the day, Janet would have had no problem on the ride. But in the darkness, as she approached a curve, she didn't see the dark brown shell of a turtle crossing the trail until she hit it. Straight on.

Her speed caused the front tire to first bounce off the shell, then wobble erratically. As she instinctively braked, the rear wheel lost traction on the tiny packed stones and slid out from beneath her. She couldn't recover quickly enough, and before she knew it, found herself lying on her side on the uncomfortable gravel with her bicycle yards away, tires still spinning.

She took a physical inventory. Everything seemed to still work, but she had a half-dozen nasty scratches on her hands, knees and thighs. Slowly, she hoisted herself up from the path, retrieved her bike, and determined it was still functional too.

"Are you injured?" a booming Dutch voice shouted, breaking the quiet.

Turning toward the voice, Janet was astonished to see a tall, helmeted man partially disembarking and dragging one foot as he swung his bike in an arc, bringing it to a full stop blocking her path.

"Just minor problems," Janet replied in halting Dutch. "I'm okay, thank you. I'll just be on my way."

"The cuts do look superficial," the young man replied as he studied her legs. "But we better clean them up in the stream over there. You don't want an infection, do you?"

Hesitant, Janet tried to move her bike around him, but he gripped her handlebar firmly, looked intently into her face, then reached into a rear pocket where he retrieved what appeared to be a leather wallet using his free hand.

"I'm Marc van Albright with *Algemene Inlichtingen en Veiligheidsdienst*," he said, flashing a plastic identity card inside the leather case. The intelligence service for the Netherlands.

Speechless, Janet gasped in shock and braced herself for what might come next.

"I need to see your identity card," he said politely and with a soft demeanor.

Janet unzipped the pouch around her waist, retrieved a photocopy of her card, and presented it to the man without comment. It was better to say as little as possible to the police. That was a truism everywhere.

"So you are a three-four," he said after examining the copy for a moment. "But your name isn't really Gertrude Benevolent, is it? And you're not from Canada, are you?"

Janet didn't answer. This was the first time in almost two years anyone raised even an eyebrow about the identification card the FBI provided. Her heart was beating faster than when she ran for a half-hour back in Overveen, but she silently vowed to remain calm and took a deep breath.

"Don't worry. I'm not here to harm you," Marc offered, switching to English. "The FBI people may not realize it, but we bury a code in every identity card we give them. So I know Gertrude is not your name, and you're almost certainly an American. Why don't you tell me why you're out here riding a bike on a trail after midnight?"

Janet still froze, unwilling to divulge any information and terrified of what the guy might do next. After a moment or two, she responded feebly, "I need to get to Utrecht tonight."

"I'll need a little more than that," the intelligence officer said with a wry smile. "If you won't be forthright with me, I can always call the police in Haarlem and let them know where we're having our little chat."

Janet blanched and inhaled deeply again to get her thoughts under control before she asked, "Why would you do that?"

"Because your identity card number and physical appearance precisely match a description the Haarlem police included with their message to all Dutch police authorities early yesterday morning," Marc responded, his smile disappearing.

"I've done nothing wrong," Janet replied timidly.

"That may be the case," the agent replied. "But the Haarlem authorities are very determined to find you. The warrant they issued lists you as a person of interest in the disappearance of one, Joshua Benevolent. I believe that's the name of the man who poses as your husband since he resides at the same address and also has a three-four identity number."

Janet was speechless. *What else did they know?*

"I've done nothing wrong," she said again. "It was the police—probably the Haarlem police—who snatched my husband from our home. They wore police uniforms and threw him in a dark unmarked van. I was terrified and ran away because neither of us had done anything wrong. I'm here because I'm still terrified."

"That's what I thought," Marc said in an assuring tone. "I need you to tell me exactly what happened, and then I'll let you go. I'm not investigating you, I'm investigating people in the Haarlem police force. I was sent there today when my boss saw the alert and warrant for an arrest.

"As soon as he saw the designation in each of your identity numbers, he was suspicious that officers we've been watching for a while might be involved. I was just returning home from a visit to the Haarlem station when I saw you headed toward the trail. Your description matched the police report right down to the color of your running shoes, so I followed you. Please tell me exactly what happened."

As the intelligence agent shared the background of his involvement, he also guided Janet and her bicycle near a large rock a few yards back from the path. "Sit here and tell me everything."

For about an hour, Janet truthfully told the intelligence officer the entire story, including her stay in the sand dunes. She even confessed to stealing the old bicycle. But she still hadn't divulged where she was headed in Utrecht. Marc took notes at every stage. He asked clarifying questions and didn't entirely conceal his contempt for the police who put her in the current situation.

"Okay, that will do for now. I won't hold you in custody as it appears you haven't committed any crime except for the bike snatching. I'm not sure I'd turn you over to those characters in the Haarlem station even if I thought you might be implicated in the case of your missing partner known as Joshua Benevolent. But I'll need you as a witness if we get enough evidence to prosecute the bastards. Where can I reach you?"

She gave him the number for Howard's phone.

She'd been lucky. The minor lacerations cleaned up well in a nearby creek. The officer even offered a couple adhesive bandages for cuts that still oozed a few drops of blood. Fortunately, she had evaded serious injury and the intelligence officer had proved sympathetic and let her go as promised.

As she pedaled toward her destination and thought more about his story of coincidentally discovering her in Overveen—then following her in the dark—it seemed inconceivable. He must have tracked her for miles before her crash. That would have been impossible in the darkness. Just before she reached Utrecht, she figured it out. The phone.

She stopped and sent one more text to Klaudia Schäffer. Within minutes Janet received the woman's acknowledgment of the new issue and final travel instructions. Then, she took Howard's phone to the edge of a nearby and fast-moving river. She found a big stone, battered the device into a half-dozen jagged pieces, and threw them in the river at six different points.

When she reached Utrecht, she left the bicycle in a dark alley, found a secluded area in a park near the station and slept on the ground among bushes, bugs and who knows what else? She didn't sleep well.

SEVEN

His story wouldn't end today. Howard knew Giancarlo Mareno well. Despite all his evil, the man held a few deeply religious convictions. One of them was the sanctity of Christmas. He'd never missed a midnight mass on Christmas Eve in the more than twenty-five years Howard had worked with him.

Bizarre as it might sound, the crime boss always built his holiday schedule around the mass, then invited family to a suite at The St. Regis New York for a feast with imported delicacies, fine Italian wines, and exotic liqueurs not offered on the standard hotel menu. His family brought Christmas parcels to exchange, and Giancarlo presented an expensive gift to every guest. After their meal and celebration, they'd open the gaily wrapped packages until morning.

What Howard still found particularly strange was the man's unwavering devotion to the occasion when only a few of the participants were close relatives. Mareno's parents were killed years earlier. He'd never married. He had no siblings or children. The people who came to his annual merrymaking were all aunts, uncles, cousins or more distant relatives.

Despite the fearmongering of the two louts guarding him that morning, Howard knew there was very little chance Mareno would seek his justice on Christmas Eve. Howard also knew a bit about the personality-types of the goons Mareno usually used to perform his dirty deeds. Typically, they were guys who had drifted into the role through circumstances beyond their control and couldn't find a way out. And they were human beings who felt tugs of emotion and greed, like everyone else.

"Maybe he'll get here tomorrow," Howard speculated aloud to String Bean when he brought a tall bottle of water to the room where they'd locked him inside the condo. "It's possible Mareno will drive directly from the hotel to an airport in New Jersey and fly over here Christmas morning. At any rate, you know I don't have much time left."

"Yeah, it sucks to be you. Frankly, I don't give a shit," String Bean replied.

"Yeah. Especially since I'll never get to see that money I hid away," Howard said.

"Don't waste my time, man," String Bean replied. "If you had some money hidden away, Giancarlo Mareno wouldn't be chasing you. He only sends us to visit guys who can't pay."

"Usually that's true. I used to work for him, remember? This time, he's chasing me for some money I stole. He wants you to keep me alive so he can torture me to find out where it is," Howard said with a shrug.

String Bean set the bottle of water down on the nearby table and looked at Howard with his head tilted.

"How much money you talkin'?" he wanted to know.

"A lot. There's about ten million euros out there. I skimmed it off a deal Mareno had me working on a few years ago and buried it here in Ayamonte for a rainy day," Howard replied, his tone as nonchalant as he could manage.

"You gonna make us work hard to get the information out of you?"

"If you hold me prisoner until Mareno arrives, it'll probably get pretty nasty. I know there's no chance he'll let me live either way, and you know he likes it to be messy so you guys'll spread the word later," Howard suggested. "I'd rather share it with you than tell Mareno. If you let me dig up the money, then let me go, you can have five million and disappear too before Giancarlo gets here."

"No way! You think I want Mareno chasing my ass all over the world to get even? You think I'm crazy?"

"Fair enough. I understand. But what if you let me dig up the money now before Giancarlo gets here? I can give him five mil euros and beg forgiveness, leave two and half million in the ground, and give you and your partner the other two and a half mil to split. We all win. If he lets me go after a bit of torture, I'll still have two and a half mil. If he kills me anyway, you and your partner will know where the rest is buried."

String Bean became attentive. His eyes focused clearly on Howard looking for a problem with the scheme. His jaw tightened and back straightened, but he said nothing.

"Why don't you talk to your partner?" Howard suggested. "I can see you're both good guys. Under different circumstances, we could be friends. I know you're both intelligent, reasonable guys trying to do your job the best you can. Here's what I ask: On the other side of the harbor, there's a wetlands area with a short walking trail. It's an entirely contained area. I can show you on a map. There's an entrance right behind the village of Punta del Moral and the only exit is about five hundred yards farther down the road. The money is buried out there. There's no way I can escape from you on the trail. Bring your partner and a shovel. I'll dig up the cache and show you the money."

"I know the trail," String Bean said. "It's boring. I jogged on it once and found it useless. Too many bugs and insects. Don't bother yourself."

Encouraged the man was still listening, Howard took another approach.

"Listen, man," he pleaded. "You know I'm going to be dead a few hours after Giancarlo arrives. You know how he treats people he thinks have done him wrong. It's going to be horrible for me. Like you, I've watched it. You know tomorrow or the next day I'm going to be screaming for mercy while you and Jumbo do things to me that might make even you throw up. Talk to your buddy. Tell him what I propose. You can each guard an entrance. There's no place for me to go. And you guys can be set for life."

It took a few hours, but they came back together with another bottle of water. Jumbo spoke first. "We think you're full of shit. Why should we risk you escaping again just to see if you're lying about this money?"

"There's no risk. There's virtually no one on the island or in the village. You know that. There's no escape route from the trail. You can see me at all times. You'll be there with me all the time," Howard countered.

"Maybe you'll try to swim," he suggested.

"Have you ever been in the Atlantic Ocean this time of the year? A guy would die from the cold within minutes if he ever tried to swim any distance. Look off the terrace; you can see how far it is to the next piece of land. I'd never survive swimming that far, even if it wasn't freezing cold," Howard said.

The two captors exchanged glances, then wandered out of the room, loudly clicking the lock from the outside. Over the following dozen hours, one or the other returned from time to time, and with every visit, Howard again planted another seed to fuel their greed.

Before dusk, they both entered the room. The interval was shorter than the previous times. It had been maybe an hour since they last left, and both wore light jackets.

"We still think you're lying," Jumbo said as they entered. "But we're gonna give you fifteen minutes at the trail. If you don't show us the money by then, we're coming back here and you'll fuckin' sit locked in this room and starve until he gets here."

String Bean pulled a cap onto his head as he said, "Tomorrow's Christmas. You got fifteen minutes over there to find our gift and not give us any trouble."

Then, Jumbo slapped Howard hard on the side of the head, knocking him sprawling to the floor. On the way to the floor, Howard banged his face on a chair before he hit the ceramic tile with a thud. More pain.

"And that's just a sample of what we'll do if you even think about running away while we're out digging on the trail," he said with a malicious grin.

They left the apartment, rode the elevator down to the underground parking area, and drove less than a mile to the entrance of the trail through the wetlands. Howard wore the same torn T-shirt and jeans. When the thugs let him out of the SUV, they handed him the running shoes they'd taken away earlier. This time they didn't bind him with zip ties or shackle either his feet or hands, but the pain of his swollen little finger made it difficult for him to tie the shoelaces. Both thugs sported self-satisfied smirks as they watched him struggle with such a mundane task.

When Howard was ready, Jumbo pulled a gardening spade from the rear of the van and carried it in one hand. They escorted Howard—one on either elbow—from the parking area to the trail entrance and roughly shoved him onto the trail with another warning of severe physical punishment should he try to escape.

They walked closely on either side of Howard around the first bend of the trail, down through a hollow, and about a half mile towards the bay. Howard glanced around to get his bearings. Both men studied him intently as he swung around on one heel and held his good hand up vertically in front of his face and in line with the church at Punta Del Moral. Howard took a few more steps, then stopped and surveyed their position with his hand once again.

"It's somewhere near here," Howard said, and Jumbo passed him the shovel.

Both thugs watched Howard's every movement as he dug exploratory trenches on the left side of the trail near a protruding rock spanning about five feet in circumference. He dug deeply into the muddy soil of the wetlands and threw the heavy clay towards the rock as he backed away from it and the trench deepened. Every step backward, his captors precisely matched the distance so they were never more than a couple feet away from him.

When the trench was about six feet long and two feet deep, they all suddenly heard a loud metallic clank as the shovel encountered a hard surface.

"It's here," Howard announced with his head still down.

Jumbo leaned forward to better look into the trench. In a flash, Howard swung the spade forcefully into Jumbo's face shattering his nose and spraying blood in all directions. With a backward swing, he smashed the shovel into String Bean's outstretched arms just as he was about to seize Howard. The impact swung the thug around as Howard used one more vicious swing of the tool to topple him with a strike behind his knees.

Spinning around again, Howard raised the sharp end of the shovel upwards toward Jumbo's groin and watched the huge man fall to the ground in agony clutching his testicles with one hand and his bleeding face with the other. String Bean was outstretched on the ground clutching his knees and groaning with pain.

Still carrying the shovel, Howard ran frantically the remaining hundred yards toward the open water separating Isla Canela from the fishing village of Isla Cristina on the opposite shore of the bay.

As he ran, he unsnapped and unzipped his jeans. As soon as he reached shoreline, he used his good hand and slid his pants down his legs and pulled them off over his shoes to free up his legs as much as possible. He quickly wrapped the jeans around his neck securely, tied the legs in a knot, and looked back. Jumbo continued to writhe on the ground spouting profanities but String Bean was on his feet, running toward Howard with a severe limp but an athletic pace.

Howard scanned the horizon across the bay slowly and intently. The gap created by the bay was about a half-mile wide to the other side, but his view was unobstructed and clear. The harbor across the inlet looked like a ghost town with only the gentle up and down movement of docked vessels. Dozens of boats sat in the marina harbor, and it looked as if most were used for commercial fishing. But the owners and crews were already away celebrating Christmas Eve somewhere else.

Howard peered along the opposite shore, shading his eyes from the sun and reflected glare from the water. Boat after boat, he saw the same scene—a gentle bobbing of lifeless vessels. Even most of the seagulls seemed to be away on vacation.

When he reached the water's edge, Howard continued walking—right into the water—wearing running shoes, a T-shirt, and his underwear. At first, he recoiled and shivered in the frigid water of the Atlantic. A couple times, he lost his footing in the muddy base or caught a toe on vegetation, but he maintained his balance. When the water reached his waist, he lunged forward and started to swim at a steady pace. *Stroke, stroke, stroke.*

———•——

String Bean pulled up short of the shoreline. He couldn't swim and Knight was already beyond his reach. He turned and rushed back to the fallen Jumbo and helped him to his feet, then half-dragged him as the two injured thugs rushed back to their parked vehicle. It took more than five minutes.

As String Bean accelerated away from the curb toward the main highway, their mutual desperation was not a pretty picture. It became even uglier when they finally powered up the vehicle's GPS. Jumbo awkwardly programmed the device with oversized fingers seeking the quickest route to Isla Cristina.

Forty-five minutes, the console displayed brightly. There was only one route showing, and it wound all the way around the bay.

EIGHT

A female German voice from the overhead speaker announced Janet's train was approaching the Angermund station and stirred her to sit up alertly in her worn, leather seat. She'd been drowsy for most of the trip because she hadn't slept well the previous night.

Janet ran her hands through her hair to fluff out some of the tangles and mentally recited the text message she had committed to memory before destroying Howard's phone in Utrecht.

> *Disembark from the train using the doors in the last car. Cover the right side of your face to block the security camera's view and stand directly behind the lighted advertising sign for Ecco Verde with your back to the sign. Wait for me there.*

When the train came to a full stop, she followed those instructions and stepped down from the train into brisk early morning air. The sky was free of rain or snow, but a strong, cold breeze from the north made it uncomfortable for anyone standing on a railroad platform dressed only in slightly torn jeans and a T-shirt.

No other passengers were in sight, but Janet's field of vision was reduced by her efforts to block part of her face from the security camera mounted high on a pole to her right. She couldn't look around because she feared the camera might capture other angles of her face. She crooked her left arm over her head and used her open hand to cover as much of the right side of her face as possible. She tried to make the gesture look like she was shading her eyes, but the sun wasn't penetrating the thick clouds. Anxious, she simply stood still and listened to the chirping of a few cheerful birds in the nearby green space until she heard, "Janet?"

She nodded. The woman facing her was dressed in a Muslim-style black *abaya* from her shoulders to the ground. A matching *niqab* covered most of her face. Brown eyes sparkled welcomingly behind a narrow open slit, suggesting a broad smile on her partially hidden face as she wordlessly and expertly swirled a scarf over Janet's head and wrapped it around the lower half of her face.

"You'll need to hold it up over your mouth like this, so the security video can't capture your entire face. The railway police use facial-recognition software too. Keep your head down while we walk. But first, slip these on," the woman whispered.

From her bag, she dragged out some pieces of clothing and handed them to Janet. "Talk only if necessary," she continued. "They often record conversations, and our English will probably trigger more scrutiny by any automated monitoring systems. We're okay here but stay completely silent after we come out from behind the advertising board until I tell you we're clear."

Janet slipped on the ugly, dull gray sweatpants while the woman held her scarf. She needed both hands free to tug them up to her waist. Finished, the woman squeezed Janet's right hand and led her around the billboard toward the rail station. She kept her head down as instructed and didn't see much more than a worn concrete platform as they left the ramp.

Outside the rail station, they turned left onto a broad sidewalk and walked briskly, the woman's dark outfit swishing gently from side to side. It seemed the only sound in the tranquil village, except for an occasional passing vehicle, and they were the only people using that section of sidewalk at such an early hour.

"Okay, as you've probably guessed, I'm Klaudia. You can raise your head, and we can talk," the woman said after they'd walked a few minutes. "But keep hold of the scarf so your lower face isn't visible. It's a small town and it's better no one sees your face yet."

"Why are you dressed this way?" Janet first wanted to know.

"It's my cover. They think I'm one of the Muslim immigrants who fled wars in the Middle East a few years ago. Refugees aren't very welcome in this part of Germany so they mainly leave me alone."

The woman spoke English but not with a German accent. She used a curious inflection, and Janet wasn't sure of its origin. "Are you from Syria?"

"No!" Klaudia squealed with a tone of playful mockery. "I'm originally from Russia and used to work for The Organization here in Germany. I know Howard from his days in organized crime. We escaped their clutches about the same time. I'll tell you all about it later. But not here."

Janet took that as a signal to minimize communication and pay more attention to her surroundings. Angermund appeared to be a tiny village. They walked along the main thoroughfare. Traffic was still sporadic, but in this area a few other people now strolled the sidewalks on both sides of the street. Some carried unwrapped baguettes. Others were on their way to the tiny *EDEKA Steinert* grocery store on the left, carrying neatly folded, reusable shopping bags tucked under their arms.

The scents from the *Kamps Bäckerei* shop smelled particularly inviting as they quickly passed. Janet inhaled deeply, and the enticing aroma of freshly baked bread caused her hungry stomach to growl loudly enough for Klaudia to hear.

"Only a few minutes more until we reach my home. At the intersection ahead, we'll turn left onto Rahmer Strasse. It's only a three-minute walk until we're there," she said. "We'll get you cleaned up and give you some food right after we arrive. We can deal with all the other stuff later."

As promised, the walk was a short one, and they soon arrived at a metal gate shrouded by overgrown shrubs and evergreens on either side. The bushes looked more than ten feet high and stood imperiously behind a sturdy wood fence stretching all along the sidewalk. It was locked, and Klaudia entered a digital code into a small plastic box at the top of the gate to open it. Her first try was successful, and they proceeded along the side of a large yellow-brick house all the way to the back.

But they didn't enter the yard. Instead, they continued fifty feet or more until they reached another gate with another electronic lock.

"I'll give you the codes later," Klaudia said as she keyed in the numbers. "I chose this place because it's challenging to get into by accident. If someone should knock on the door, we know we have a problem." She laughed once, then unlocked a front door secured by three different mechanisms that all clicked loudly as she released them.

They entered the concealed house through a long hallway with painted cement block walls along each side and unusually high ceilings. The tall, unadorned walls were a soft teal color but still seemed cold and uninviting with not a picture or painting in sight.

Halfway down the hallway, they turned right at an arched opening and entered the living area. A sofa, three large cushioned chairs, and a modest wall-mounted television sparsely furnished the room. There were no end tables for the sofa, no lamps, and on the walls only the most basic of art reproductions—the type usually found in a Walmart.

In one corner, Janet noticed a large wooden table with a desktop computer, a printer, and stacks of books, magazines, and newspapers.

The mountain of clutter on the desk contrasted sharply with the barren room. Heaps of printed materials haphazardly flopped over into more piles that had sunk to the floor on both sides of the desk.

"Do you collect printed materials?" Janet asked.

"I work for the German authorities now," Klaudia stated emphatically. "They don't pay me or anything like that. But I now so loathe The Organization and what they do to women and girls, I spend all my time working with the intelligence services here to thwart their efforts to kidnap or entrap women in their despicable human-trafficking web. I'll fill in all the blanks after we get you a shower and some food."

With that declaration, Klaudia released the catch on her niqab and unwound it from her head in one smooth motion. She shook her head vigorously and released long, meticulously groomed brown hair that tumbled past her shoulders. Beautiful, with a flawless complexion, she also had an infectious smile. Janet followed her lead and freed her blonde hair from the scarf too. Since moving to the Netherlands, her own hairstyle was a much more practical length, hanging pageboy to about the bottom of her ears.

Unexpectedly, Klaudia awkwardly reached out to Janet, wrapped both arms around her, and drew her snugly into a warm embrace. Janet returned the hug but with less enthusiasm. It felt a little discomfiting. She was no prude but looked down and took a step back when they broke their hold. Naturally, she'd had threesomes with clients in the raucous days of college, but she'd never had a serious relationship with another woman. She wasn't sure about her new friend's intentions.

"Don't worry," Klaudia said, reading her mind. "I usually prefer men. But I want you to know I'll do everything I can to save you from those bastards in The Organization. I hate them. I detest everything they do to women. And I promise you they'll have to kill me to get you. But you must be careful."

NINE

It might have been Christmas Day, but Giancarlo Mareno was oblivious to the occasion. Agitated was too mild an expression to describe his current state. After flying halfway across the world, he arrived at the airport in Faro. No one met him at the private jet parked in the preferred section of the airport.

Giancarlo was tired. He and the two bodyguards had left the all-night Christmas Eve party at the St. Regis about seven in the morning and driven out to Teterboro to meet up with the jet loaned to him by a billionaire associate who liked to stroke Giancarlo's ego. The man might be a fool, but Giancarlo was happy to save a few grand and let the rich dupe think he was creating a debt Mareno would repay at some point.

The hostess was a nice touch though. The billionaire knew Giancarlo's preferences well, and the tall, well-tanned brunette who greeted them at the doorway of the aircraft wearing only the bottom of a very skimpy bikini managed to smile warmly despite outdoor temperatures below freezing.

He waited until they were in the air before he told her to take off the bikini bottom as well. She brought champagne repeatedly. Each time he declined her offer but told her to refill the glasses of each of the boys and encourage them to have a feel. She complied and the boys were soon more than a little aroused.

A couple hours into the flight, he told her to make both guys happier than they'd ever been and nodded back to his companions. Usually, he liked to watch them work over a slut, servicing them from mouth to bottom. But that morning he wasn't in the mood. He fell asleep while the guys played with their temporary toy, but his sleep was fitful.

Umberto and Adriano—the pair minding Howard Knight in Spain— hadn't reported to him in hours. They were supposed to text every two hours to confirm all was well. The last text had been just before Giancarlo left the St. Regis, and this failure to comply with instructions left him pissed. At a minimum, he'd need to teach them a lesson. In the unlikely event anything was amiss with Knight's capture, he'd take more drastic action.

When Giancarlo awoke, everyone else was asleep. The bodyguards snored loudly in their seats, still only partially dressed and apparently spent from their fun with the slut. Her eyes were closed, but she was whimpering, curled up in a dark brown blanket with a bloodstain seeping through around her buttocks.

Apparently, the boys played too rough.

Giancarlo stirred Luigi Fortissimo, his senior and most trusted bodyguard, and told him to get dressed and find out what was happening in Spain. The aircraft had all the latest technology, and he tried both texting and calling with no response to either. The failure to connect left the boss surly and unhappy for the rest of the flight.

On arrival, the pilot reported there was no car meeting them, and in a town that basically stood still for Christmas, no taxis were evident at the airport either. They had to wait more than forty minutes for an Uber driver to rescue them from the virtually barren waiting room the people of Portugal called a lounge. On top of that, the driver arrogantly informed Giancarlo he required a cash-only fare of five hundred euros more than the usual Uber fee for the one-hour drive to Isla Canela on the Spanish side of the border.

Seething, Giancarlo agreed to pay the fare, and they started toward Ayamonte. Their drive took them through the town and a few miles farther east to reach his property on Isla Canela. No one spoke. The bodyguards knew it was best to stay quiet, and the Uber driver probably felt uncomfortable for charging such a ridiculous amount.

Let the bastard sweat a little.

When they reached the high bridge spanning the river Guadiana—the body of water separating Portugal from Spain—Giancarlo told the Uber driver to stop the car. The small man with furtive eyes and a nervous twitch looked startled and didn't react immediately. Without a prompt, the bodyguard in the front seat pulled a handgun from his pocket and held it to the driver's ear until he brought the car to a full stop.

"Get out," Giancarlo commanded.

The short man complied, and both bodyguards left the vehicle with him, one from each side of the car. The one on the driver's side grasped the man in a choking headlock as soon the he stepped out of his vehicle.

"Take him to the edge," Giancarlo ordered. The bodyguards reacted immediately and dragged the resisting driver up onto the narrow walkway then shoved him roughly against the waist-high fence, staring out towards the river more than a hundred feet below.

"Pull the money out of his pocket," Giancarlo said. "And let every hundred-euro bill fall into the water. Make the bastard watch each one blow away and sink into the water."

The Uber driver started to protest but Luigi slapped his face hard and pointed the gun at him again. The whole process took a couple minutes with no one speaking as they theatrically disposed of the entire fare Giancarlo had paid only minutes earlier. Just as they finished, some vehicle headlights appeared a mile or so away on the Spanish side of the border.

"Throw him in the trunk," Giancarlo said dismissively as he marched toward to driver's seat of the car while his bodyguards wrapped zip ties around the driver's hands and feet before tossing him into the trunk.

Giancarlo drove the few remaining minutes to Isla Canela, anxious to know the status of his elusive quarry and prepared to mete out appropriate punishment for the two goons who failed to follow his instructions.

"Take the other car and this piece of crap out toward Castro Marim on the Portuguese side of the border and leave him in his trunk at the side of the road," Giancarlo instructed the bodyguards when he parked in the underground. "Remind him we have his Uber license, know where he lives, and will visit his family if he speaks a word of this to anyone."

"Shouldn't I check the apartment first, before you go in?" Luigi asked.

"No. I'll be alright. The boys are upstairs. I see a van with Dutch license plates right over there."

When he arrived at the eighth-floor penthouse, Giancarlo exploded in anger with a string of expletives and paced slowly around the parameter of the infuriating mess in his apartment. Lifeless bodies of the two thugs he had dispatched to Europe lay on the floor with brains, blood and gore splattered across the room. Umberto's rigid right hand still held a powerful gun. It looked like a weapon the Spanish national police used.

Somehow, that bastard Howard Knight had once again escaped his grasp. Furious, Giancarlo reached for his phone.

TEN

The bedside clock showed 12:07, but the room was bright. To her surprise, Janet had slept for almost twenty-four hours. Lazily, she pulled back the sheets, lifted herself from the comfort of a high queen-sized bed, and eventually dressed.

"Merry Christmas! You're looking good, sister!" Klaudia said with a huge smile and animated eyes. "I'm glad you were able to sleep so soundly after your ordeal. Ready for a festive breakfast?"

The alluring scent of coffee, scrambled eggs, bacon, and hot toast wafted temptingly through the large kitchen. In her never-ending battle to stay trim, Janet didn't eat such decadent food often anymore, but that day she caved without hesitation.

"Absolutely! It's really not necessary to go to all this trouble for me. But since you have, I'm going to indulge and enjoy. It smells great. Is it really Christmas?"

"That's what the calendar says. In Russia, we don't observe it as a religious holiday, nor do many Germans. We don't give each other gifts or things like that. But it's always nice to get a day off. Like many Europeans, back home we treat Christmas Eve as the main celebration with elaborate dinners and lots of Vodka." Klaudia smiled.

"A lot of people still treat Christmas as a religious holiday in the States," Janet replied. "But my family must have been part Russian. I can't remember getting any gifts or celebrating in any way after my tenth birthday. My parents usually left for vacation trips that day to get the best airfares. With no other siblings, I stayed with friends for Christmas a few years, then mainly spent the day alone once I reached my teens. So it's never been a big deal for me."

There was no remorse or regret in Janet's matter-of-fact tone, so her companion carried on. Klaudia checked everything cooking on the grill and snatched a piece of bacon to taste it. Satisfied all was ready, she prepared two plates and served them with German bread piled on the side. They both gulped down the food with little conversation other than about the weather and how well they'd slept. As soon as they cleared away their plates, Klaudia got serious.

"Yesterday, you told me about Howard's capture and your escape. I'm really devastated to learn The Organization snatched Howard, but he planned well for you to hide here. Now, I need to explain where we go from here." Her manner became all business. "Monday, we need to get you an identity card. You'll need to wear a niqab whenever you're out but it's not a perfect disguise. The police can still demand you adjust or remove it at any time."

"Do you mean to say I'll be staying here? With you? Long-term?"

"For the next few weeks, at least," Klaudia replied emphatically. "It would be best to stay inside the entire time, but I realize how cruel that would be. First, we'll get you the best makeover we can without cosmetic surgery. A trusted hairstylist friend will come at three tomorrow to cut your hair, change its color, and alter your eyebrows."

"Okay, I guess," Janet managed. "But what will I do while I'm here?"

"Over the holiday, we'll lie low and stay inside. Monday morning, we'll take the bus to the next village. It's called Kaiserswerth. We'll take a train from there into Dusseldorf. I have a connection who'll create your identity card. He'll take a new photo, your fingerprint, prepare a plastic card, and enter you in the German residency database. You'll be safe from nosy police."

There seemed to be little room for argument or discussion, so Janet changed her tack.

"If you're Russian, how long have you been here?" she asked.

"Let me tell you the story. You need to know where I fit in and why Howard asked you to come to me." She filled their cups again with coffee. "I left Russia many years ago. I worked in a government intelligence agency where they paid me a pittance and felt they had the right to let every agent in the outfit fuck me at will. Fidelia, a close friend of Howard's, contacted me in St. Petersburg. Did Howard ever mention her?"

"Yeah, he mentioned her," Janet responded tentatively. "They were more than close, right? Weren't they secret lovers for a long time?"

"Yeah, I learned about that much later. Anyway, Fidelia offered me a fortune to leave Russia and become a recruiter for her call-girl service in Europe. The Organization paid me five-hundred thousand U.S. dollars a year to find vulnerable young women and girls and lure them into prostitution by one means or another. That was one hundred times what the Russian government was paying me to service the horny bastards they employ. It was a no-brainer."

"So, you worked for this Fidelia and she worked for Howard?" Janet wondered.

"No, Fidelia reported to Giancarlo Mareno directly. Howard was the guy who controlled all the money for The Organization," Klaudia clarified. "But a few years ago, your Mr. Knight gave me an assignment to mind an American technology executive when the guy came to Germany. It's a long story, but I went back to the United States with the jerk and promptly got arrested when we landed in Miami! The FBI snatched us right from his private jet and hustled us into isolation! No lawyers. No judge. Nothing."

"That's horrible! How did you get out of that mess?"

"The FBI offered us a deal. They wanted this technology executive and me to use our expertise to help them track down Howard Knight and Fidelia, who had just disappeared. It seems both The Organization and the FBI wanted them, and they offered us freedom and new identities in their witness protection program if we delivered Fidelia and Howard to them first. Within a few weeks, we had successfully hacked into a couple South American telephone networks and were able to point the FBI to a house in Buenos Aires, Argentina." She paused for a sip of coffee and a deep breath before she continued.

Oh my God. This talented woman has an amazing story.

"Anyway, the FBI captured the pair and brought them to the same concentration camp where they were holding us," Klaudia seethed. "They wanted us to provide names, telephone numbers, and other information about the leaders of The Organization around the world. They promised they'd protect us if we became snitches and betrayed all our former colleagues."

"So you cooperated?" Janet asked.

"Well, not at first. Howard agreed to give them the information they wanted, but Fidelia didn't trust them. She thought The Organization would track us down no matter how the FBI tried to conceal our identities. Just like the bastards tracked down you and Howard in the Netherlands."

"So, what happened?"

"I give all the credit to Fidelia. She's brilliant." Klaudia's smile stretched across her face with pride. "Fidelia told them no deal. She insisted the only way she would cooperate was if they flew the two of us to Europe. We'd answer questions only for Interpol and only if the Americans further guaranteed Interpol would jet us to an Eastern European country that would remain unknown to either Interpol or the FBI immediately after we answered their questions."

"So they agreed?"

"Absolutely. Fidelia really was a genius. She got them to agree to everything. Then, she told Howard it was over between them. She was bailing out and had no further need for him. Within three days after they let us fly to Europe, we finished briefing Interpol about only the European contacts in The Organization. Right after that, they dropped us off at a jet in Lyon that delivered us to a friend of Fidelia's in Uzbekistan. There, the deputy minister of finance put us up in his secluded country chateau near the border with Kazakhstan."

"So, what brought you back to Germany?"

"To be honest, I wasn't happy in Uzbekistan. It's a Muslim country, and despite living in a reasonably comfortable chateau with all the modern conveniences, I felt trapped. The internet often didn't work. We had shortages of fresh fruit and vegetables. We had to dress in a niqab every time we left the chateau there too. There was very little companionship other than Fidelia. She was content to be away from civilization, The Organization, and her former way of life. And she's still there. We talk on WhatsApp once in a while.

"But, with the free time I had to think, I started feeling guilty about all the harm I had done to young women. I wanted to find a way to offset those terrible things. So, I got the deputy finance minister in Uzbekistan to help me connect with the German *Bundesnachrichtendienst*, their federal intelligence service.

"It took more than a year, but they set me up here in Angermund with all the latest technology. I now help them thwart The Organization's efforts to lure and capture young women and girls. But we must be more careful than ever because The Organization is getting very frustrated. We've kept hundreds of women—maybe into the thousands now—out of their reach."

"And you expect me to help?" Janet asked.

"I hope so, but only if you choose to and only *when* you choose." Klaudia smiled warmly.

Janet remained silent. She looked directly at Klaudia and slowly stirred her now cold coffee round and round as she tried to find the right words.

ELEVEN

Faro, Portugal, Wednesday December 25, 2019

Stroke. Stroke. Stroke.

Howard Knight forced himself forward. His muscles ached and he gasped for air with every breath. The frigid Atlantic water was more than uncomfortable; it stung. His swollen little finger, hands, and feet throbbed continuously, while a sharp pain stabbed up through his shoulders into his head. His arms twinged with cramps, but he forged forward and dared to peek back only once. He noticed nothing amiss, so he slowed his pace but continued his desperate, methodical swim to freedom.

In the final few yards, Howard's head plunged below the surface twice. He choked and spat out salty bay water. He lunged twice, trying to grip the platform at the rear, but managed to hold onto the elevated edge with his second try. With quaking arms, he slowly hauled himself upward, using his right arm for strength and the injured left hand for balance. He inched forward until he lay prone with the upper half of his body resting on the sturdy deck of a faded gray Carver boat moored at the end of a long row of docked commercial fishing vessels.

He gasped for air, his entire body trembling from cold and exhaustion. A moment or two later, he managed to get his knees on the platform. Hidden from view of any passersby, he controlled his breathing and slowed his heart rate. Out of the water, his body warmed slightly, and his quivering eased. Guardedly, he crouched, then stood unsteadily as his legs regained their circulation and strength.

He had picked out that particular fishing craft because it looked identical to the thirty-four-foot yacht he had once used in South America. This one had been reconfigured for commercial fishing. It sported none of the luxuries characteristic of Carver yachts sold in America, but it appeared seaworthy and stable enough for the Atlantic's waves. Howard had no idea what weather conditions he might encounter over the following few hours.

Looking over the top of the boat, Howard noted the surrounding area on shore remained deserted. Although it was late afternoon, a haunting quiet hung in the air like a dark cloud just before rain. Howard started his search of the boat. He knew exactly what he was looking for and was confident either this boat or one nearby would have the tools he needed to hot-wire the engine.

Commercial fishermen can never be delayed or deterred by a lost or forgotten key. They want assurance they can restart their boats even in the worst of circumstances.

Sure enough, Howard found what he needed in the forward hold, right beside the first aid kit. A piece of wood the size of a phone already had an on-off switch mounted on one side, with three long wires protruding from the other. Below the captain's wheel, he found a basic toolkit and carried both items toward the sterndrive Mercruiser diesel engine.

Howard quickly found the starter motor and connected a blue wire extending from the piece of wood to the middle contact. Then he grabbed a yellow wire and expertly made a connection to the second contact. Finally, he joined the remaining green wire and attached it to the positive contact of the battery. Expectantly, he flipped the switch. The engine groaned and showed signs of life, but it didn't start. Howard tried again with the same result. In a sudden panic, he checked all three connections to see if they were secure. They were. Once more he tried the switch, but nothing happened.

He scratched his head, frowned, and stood with his hand covering his mouth and forefinger perched on his nose. He stared at the engine and contemplated. He'd watched a YouTube video a dozen or more times to be sure he would never again find himself at the mercy of a missing key. He was sure he'd done everything right. Then Howard realized his mistake. He'd forgotten to open the fuel line to let diesel fuel flow into the engine. Adeptly, he reached around the side of the engine and opened the fuel valve. This time, when he flipped the switch on, the engine sputtered twice, then started with a deep pulsating drone.

Without a moment's hesitation, Howard untied the two retaining ropes from the dock and threw them on the floor of the boat. He quickly skipped forward to the steering wheel and controls. With his right hand, he steered the craft away from the dock and into open waters. Looking around as he headed toward the ocean, Howard saw little happening back on the docks. Checking back a final time, he scoured the horizon for life or activity but couldn't see even a stray dog or cat.

As he steered towards the harbor opening, Howard gradually increased the craft's speed with gentle pressure on the controls. Within thirty minutes, the boat faced westward across the mouth of the Guadiana River, motoring toward Portugal at half throttle. Using the vessel's Garmin navigation package that he remembered well from his previous boat, Howard chugged confidently in a southwesterly direction until he was a mile offshore. By dark, he had motored past *Vila Real de Santo Antonio, Altura* and *Tavira*. Before midnight, he had passed *Santa Luzia* and *Olhao*.

Once he was safely past Olhao, Howard veered into the estuaries at *Ilha do Farol* where the waterway was deep enough to accommodate the Faro Ferry. He shut off the GPS to avoid detection. It was a few seconds before one o'clock on Christmas morning. The moon shed enough light to maneuver in the shallow waters, and Howard took care to stay as close to the middle of the estuary stream as possible.

Everything remained deathly still. He peered in all directions to be sure he had his bearings and motored patiently until he saw the outline of an inlet before the lighthouse. A few minutes later he spotted the opening, just as he remembered it. Between the mainland and the island of *Se*, he shut off the engine and coasted close to shore. He hit the sandbank with a gentle thud before he jumped from the front, tied a rope around another nearby anchored boat, and started walking. He still had much to do before dawn.

TWELVE

"Pull out all the stops," Giancarlo Mareno commanded during the hastily arranged conference call. His gruff tone of voice left little doubt about the conviction of his order.

"Yes sir," said Juan Suarez, his leader of The Organization in Spain. "I've already had a word with the *Cuerpo Nacional de Policía* and *Guardia Civil.* The national police have set up increased security video monitoring in every city in Spain, and the Civil Guard is putting roadblocks on every highway and entrance to expressways in the west of Spain. Everywhere west of Madrid and right down to *Ceuta* in the south and up to *Santander* in the north."

"Not enough," Giancarlo replied. "I said pull out *all* the stops. It's already been three days. Knight could be anywhere in Spain or Portugal, maybe even Morocco. Get the police and anyone else who's charged with finding people in those countries stopping vehicles and boats everywhere. Get the video monitoring started anywhere they have cameras."

"I'll try."

"Estavao, what's happening in Portugal?" Mareno demanded to know.

"Not much, I'm afraid," Estavao Sereno replied with his characteristic soft-spoken tone. "My main contacts are either out of the country on vacation or they have switched their phones off for the holiday festivities. That's still very common here in Portugal."

"Not good enough," Giancarlo said. "Find a way to get in touch with them and get them moving on this immediately. Threaten them with some nasty leaks to the media, complete with graphic pictures, if they don't mobilize every officer in the country by noon today. I want Howard Knight found."

"Of course, Giancarlo, I'll make the calls right now," he said, leaving the conference call.

"Pierre, are you still on the line in Paris?"

"Yes, Giancarlo," Pierre Boivin replied. "I have much the same problem as our friend in Portugal. My guys are all out of the sandbox—as you Americans like to say—and I don't think threats of media leaks will budge either them or their subordinates. Some of those fools consider it almost a badge of honor to have pictures of them frolicking with partially dressed young beauties circulating in the newspapers."

"Well then, how about subtly suggesting the leak of some information about their illicit drug consumption?" Giancarlo scoffed.

"Maybe. But it would be much better to have a specific murder victim for us to talk about in our requests to law enforcement for such an expensive search. Won't the Spanish police provide some victim photos we can give to our people at Interpol?"

"Not possible," Giancarlo replied in a tone that suggested he was losing patience. "The guys weren't in the country legally. If we share photos with Interpol, we might create curiosity we'd rather avoid. Just find a plausible story to get their asses moving and moving right now."

"I'll do my best, Giancarlo. You know that. But Interpol's a big organization. Our guys have some influence, but they can't pull all the strings to mobilize a campaign like you want. This isn't the FBI."

"I hear you, Pierre. But this is really important to me. You know I can't have somebody whacking my people at will. Knight's really dangerous to all our interests. You know that. If he escapes and cooperates with the authorities again, how many more people will you lose? Need I remind you we fixed it to save about fifty of your associates with our influence the last time? Knight still knows those names. If he talks to Interpol people we don't control, you and your guys are toast."

To emphasize his displeasure, Giancarlo dramatically jabbed his finger on the little red "end" button on his phone, then slammed it on the table. Pierre Boivin knew very well why there could be no photos of the guys' bodies. His French contacts had arranged the false identification for them before they snuck into Europe through an obscure port in Belgium. Then the incompetent bastards created more of a mess when they killed themselves with a stolen policeman's gun. Police don't create nationwide manhunts for suicide victims. *This was the kind of shit that happened when people didn't follow orders.*

For a few days, they'd had Knight in their grasp. Interpol had discovered the whereabouts of both Knight and his whore first. For that, Giancarlo thanked them. But he needed Interpol again. If only those idiots he sent over to mind their captive for a few days had followed his instructions, they'd still be alive. It would be Knight lying on the floor with his brains blown out and missing a few body parts. When people made mistakes, it reflected poorly on their boss too, and the French bastard Boivin had callously reminded Giancarlo that people were watching. Powerful people.

"Luigi," Giancarlo called out. "Find the pilots. Tell them we're flying back to New York tonight. Find out what time we need to leave to be there by 8:00 a.m."

"Right, boss," his bodyguard replied. "They're at the hotel in Faro. I'll check, but it should be about seven hours flying time. If you plan to leave here by midnight tonight, we should be in New York with plenty of time to spare."

"Get it organized for midnight," Giancarlo said. "Then get me a phone number for that slut we planted in Pierre Boivin's camp last year, the one he's sleeping with."

THIRTEEN

Sitting on a straight-backed wooden chair and hunched over a small round table he used as an office in the back of his legitimate sightseeing tour business, Pierre Boivin stared in disgust at the silent phone. He wasn't accustomed to such rude behavior, even from Americans. To be humiliated like that in front of one of his people was simply not acceptable.

After all, he was Giancarlo Mareno's peer in France. He'd built The Organization into a multi-billion-dollar business in his homeland with currency exchange shops nationwide, virtual control of the heroin trade, beautiful women for rent in every city, and significant shares in supermarkets and food processing companies. His business model was proportionately more successful than Giancarlo's in the USA. He didn't deserve such treatment, no matter how dire the circumstances.

"Jean-Guy," Pierre said as he slowly lifted his head to meet the active black eyes of his trusted subordinate. "Do we have any sort of a lead on Knight?"

"No good ones yet. Our people at Interpol really are all away somewhere, just like you told him," Jean-Guy Gagnon replied. "We do know that someone attacked and injured a police officer in Ayamonte, then stole his gun. And the Spanish police have filed a report of a stolen commercial fishing boat from Isla Cristina. That's a village near Mareno's place where they were holding Knight, but the GPS was disabled at sea and stopped transmitting. There's no report of the vessel showing up anywhere yet."

"Stay close to that one with both Juan Suarez and Estavao Sereno's people," Boivin instructed, referring to his counterparts in Spain and Portugal. "We know Howard Knight is a seadog. He had a boat in the Caribbean while he was on the run from The Organization the last time. And he knows the area around the Algarve and Andalucía quite well. What about the girl?"

"She's vanished. One security camera in Utrecht showed blurry images of someone dressed in a T-shirt and jeans who looked a bit like her, but they didn't catch any other sightings of her on a train or in any other stations," Jean-Guy explained. "There's only one of The Organization's guys left inside the Haarlem police station. The other two had mysterious car accidents the day after she escaped."

"Yeah, Mareno acted too quickly again. It wasn't really their fault she vanished. He should have waited, at least until the guys did everything possible to capture her. We lost a lot of intelligence with their rushed elimination."

With a gentle wave, Pierre dismissed Jean-Guy, then reached for another phone on a nearby shelf. Like most people in his profession, he used multiple phones and trashed them after only a few calls to thwart effective tracking and recording by the authorities. The one he selected from the shelf was used only for texts with Nadine Violette.

There were no new messages, which was probably a good thing. She'd become higher maintenance than he liked over the past few months. Sure, she still did her job acceptably. Most of the women liked working with her, and she kept them in line most of the time. And the batch of girls she brought from Morocco last month was probably the best he had seen in several years. They were just what his customers wanted: young, nubile, and uninhibited.

But her demands had swelled recently. North Africa was becoming more dangerous. First, she needed more than one bodyguard. And travel to meet and inspect the girls throughout France was onerous. So, she wanted to use one of the helicopters from the sightseeing company. But the most galling of all was her recent request for two months' vacation like everyone else in France. That meant two fewer trips to Morocco each year.

It didn't sound like much, but the highest paying customers liked a fresh girl every month—maybe not a virgin, but one that hadn't been used excessively. Those regulars didn't take a vacation from their lust, and it would become harder to keep them satisfied if she got her time away. Since those marks were often important government officials or top business executives, customer satisfaction was a genuine concern.

Let's go to Nice for dinner this evening, he punched into the phone keyboard with his thumbs flying. Her response took several minutes longer than usual.

Sure. In Chamonix till 3. Meet you in Nice or come back to Aix?

57

Pierre thought about it a moment before he sent another text. Her tone seemed warmer and more accommodating than her messages over the past few days.

> *Come back here first. I'll make reservations. And wear your special dress.*

The dress he had in mind was virtually see-through, highlighted her gorgeous body, and would make them the center of attention at the upscale dining establishment he had in mind. To guarantee they were noticed, he'd instruct her to wear nothing under the dress. It would be good for his ego and remind her who was boss.

FOURTEEN

Düsseldorf, Germany, Monday December 30, 2019

They stepped from the train onto a platform close to the *Hauptbahnhof* exit and walked quickly, their long, black abayas swishing side to side, faces partially covered by their niqabs. Janet Weissel stayed at Klaudia's side, but a half step back. That way, she could easily adjust to any shift in direction without appearing too clumsy or disoriented in her new surroundings.

They passed a Pizza Hut, then crossed at the first intersection when the light turned green. Without a word exchanged, they continued along *Bismarckstrasse* until they reached a Europcar rental outlet. There, they crossed *Karlstrasse* when it was safe to do so. Klaudia pointed to the Café Metropol next to a large building identified as *Landesverband der Volkshochschulen*. Some sort of school.

Once they reached the café, Klaudia led them through a recessed doorway, then along a short dark corridor to a bank of elevators. She pushed a button for the fourth floor. When they stepped from the elevator, the hallway was dimly lit and strangely quiet. Janet looked around and shivered involuntarily while Klaudia motioned not to worry.

As expected, Klaudia's contacts were ready and waiting. With a minimum of talk and typical German efficiency, the intelligence service agents took Janet's photos and fingerprints. Within moments, they produced a German residency card. It claimed she was a Canadian with the right to live and work in Germany for the next two years. Finally, they invited both women into a meeting room next door.

"Hi again!" Marc van Albright of the Dutch *Algemene Inlichtingen en Veiligheidsdienst* said as he cheerfully stood and extended his right hand in greeting.

Janet was speechless. She glanced sideways. Klaudia was equally startled to see the Dutch intelligence officer.

59

"Forgive me for the surprise." He introduced himself to Klaudia before shaking Janet's trembling hand. His eyes bore into hers intently as his smile disappeared.

"You really didn't think you were going to get rid of me merely by destroying a perfectly good phone, did you?"

"How ... how did you find me? ... Then and now?" Janet stammered.

"I won't give away trade secrets, but I wasn't tracking your phone; I was trailing your bike. I knew where you were until you abandoned the bike before trying to sleep in the park. You really don't do well sleeping among bushes and bugs, do you?" he teased with a chuckle.

"Did you follow me on the trains?" Janet wondered.

"Yes. Through all three station transfers, all the way to Angermund. You really must work on your awareness of your surroundings." His tone became more serious. "I know you're not trained in intelligence, but I was never more than fifty yards away from you."

"I checked at the Angermund station. No one was around," Janet protested to both Klaudia and the spy.

"German trains usually open on both sides when the platform permits. I was in the car ahead of you. I dashed behind a tree while you waited for your friend and put on your disguise. I followed you to the house on *Rahmerstrasse* and peeked through the bushes as you made your way to the second house and went inside."

"You haven't been hanging around there since last week, have you?" Klaudia demanded with some indignation.

"No. I just came to Dusseldorf again this morning," he reassured. "Our countries still have some tensions from the Second World War, but we really do cooperate on intelligence more than many people realize. It took a single call from my boss to his counterpart in the German *Bundesnachrichtendienst*. They revealed your identity and role to us in confidence, Klaudia. And they filled us in on their strategy for you, Janet."

Three more people joined them in the meeting room. An expert used a basic detection wand to be sure none of the participants wore hidden microphones. When he found none, he poked methodically in every corner and around each heating vent and light switch. With a wave of his wand, the tech silently nodded and left the room.

"May I ask a question before we start? I'd like to know if there's been any word about Howard Knight. Have you heard anything?" Janet asked.

"Sadly, no. We've checked all the Interpol releases and communiques throughout Europe. Our colleagues there have a massive manhunt underway concentrated on France, Spain and Portugal, but all leads have proven futile so far," the leader of the group replied.

"Are you still okay moving forward with the role we discussed for you?" Klaudia sensed unease from her companion.

"Yeah. Howard begged me to start a new life if ever they captured him," Janet said. "I'm still holding out hope he'll show up eventually. But I'm ready to help you just like we talked the other night. I'm all in."

The small group spent over two hours reviewing documents, photos, maps, and unique technology as a senior intelligence officer led them through the next stages of their mission as she saw it. Janet and Klaudia listened most of the time. This session was not a discussion. Instead, the German officials clearly treated it as a briefing on a need-to-know basis. Questions were tolerated but often went unanswered when the senior intelligence officer shook her head ever so slightly.

Janet's demeanor changed gradually as the talks progressed. Early on she was passive and resigned to the coming changes to her lifestyle and work. After a while, she became more engaged, paraphrasing information they shared to be sure she got it right and caught all the nuances. Toward the end of the session, she showed determination and leadership by volunteering to do more, more quickly.

"You're best to keep the disguises and stay inside as much as possible," the female officer advised Janet. "Stay away from restaurants or bars. Shop only for food when you must. Use only the phones we've given you and only in emergencies. Stay away from all social media until we say okay and use only these iPads for now. We'll send someone around this afternoon to update the computers and routers in the house. One last thing, Janet. We need you completely fluent in Spanish.

"This new initiative The Organization has launched to recruit girls and women from Costa Rica is a serious one. Hundreds of women and girls are at risk. Please devote every hour you can to the language programs from your new best friend, *Rosetta Stone*."

FIFTEEN

Howard's earlier idea of wrapping his jeans around his neck before attempting to swim across the bay proved futile. The wet jeans became too heavy and weighed him down. He had ditched them after only a few yards and had completed his swim and journey in the Carver boat wearing only his shoes, underwear and a T-shirt.

So, the light from the moon was double-edged. The brighter light let him alternately walk and jog at a quicker pace, but dressed only in boxer shorts, his state of undress would be readily apparent to anyone he met.

Howard found a new wardrobe after scaling a four-foot-high stone wall to a backyard, where he picked out a pair of jeans and a T-shirt that looked about the right size from a clothesline. He crawled back over the wall, then crouched beside it to try them on.

The pant legs were too long, but a quick roll-up made the length acceptable. The waist was loose, but not enough that a belt was necessary. The T-shirt was a putrid yellow faded by dozens of washes. Together with his still waterlogged running shoes, he felt adequately dressed for at least a couple days.

Following the worn walking path next to the road in a neighborhood housing some of Faro's most impoverished residents, Howard felt momentary guilt as he spotted a little black Vespa scooter with keys still in the ignition. The owner probably thought he had hidden it well behind the shelter, but Howard was desperate. It took three tries fiddling with the key and playing with the fuel control, but the scooter finally started with a backfire. Howard jumped on and sped away as he noticed a light brighten the yard he had just left.

Occasional cars or bikes appeared on the other side of the road from time to time, probably commercial fishers returning to work for early-morning departures after the Christmas break. Howard accelerated to the scooter's maximum speed and bent as low to the handlebars as possible to reduce wind resistance.

He followed one paved and reasonably maintained street along the southern part of the city next to the wetlands where the fish processing industry used to be. It led to a highway. A sign indicated the 125, and Howard continued at the scooter's full speed another five minutes until he reached Highway 2. Banking to take the curve, he accelerated to full throttle again as soon as he was on a straightaway headed north.

Traffic was still light, but the first hint of dawn appeared in the east as Howard tried to coax every mile per hour from his well-worn and noisy means of transportation. His spirit soared as he saw signs alerting drivers to highway A22, the expressway that crossed the Algarve then headed north to Lisbon.

Of course, he couldn't take a scooter on the expressway, but the highway's proximity signaled he had left the town of Faro. He expected less traffic from that point on. Sure enough, he traveled more than ten miles past the village of Alportel before he saw another car. There he veered onto a secondary road and headed toward hilly farmland covered by orange and olive groves. Just as the sun peeked over the horizon, Howard heard the scooter's engine sputter. It slowed, then finally lost all power and coasted to a stop in the middle of nowhere. He was out of fuel.

Dismounting, Howard gave the scooter a mighty shove into a ditch at the roadside and watched it disappear. The trench was deep there, and no passing vehicle would see it from the road. Then he set out on foot along the country road. It wasn't far, maybe a mile or two, before he spotted an abandoned stone barn on a hill.

Small farms in Portugal were slowly disappearing as family patriarchs died, and descendants didn't want to continue farming. Other larger farmers usually bought the land from a deceased farmer's estate, but often let unnecessary second barns fall into disrepair. However, this unused shed served his purpose.

An orange grove with mature fruit grew on the other side of the road. Howard picked oranges from the tree with his right hand and carried them in his injured left while he crossed the road again to climb a disused path toward the barn. The oranges gave him enough nutrition for a few hours, and he scouted out a corner of the decrepit structure that seemed clear of vermin and insects. Within minutes, exhaustion took over, and he slept soundly for several hours.

A bright, mid-afternoon sun shining in his eyes finally teased him awake. Howard raided the orange grove again. For three days, Howard survived on only fresh oranges as he slept and let his battered body start to heal. On the fourth day, he climbed the tallest hill in the field until he reached its summit. There, he surveyed the horizon, his good hand shading his eyes from the brilliant sun. No sign of a town. But off to one side, a couple clusters of homes nestled at the bottom of a hill almost made a village.

The terrain off to the left looked more promising. There, he saw only three houses spaced about a quarter mile apart. Howard looked for signs of habitation. Smoke from a fireplace. Clothes hung outside to dry. Pets or animals. Children at play. Farmers at work in the fields. After careful scrutiny, he saw none and concluded the way was clear.

Satisfied, Howard scouted the best route. First, he needed to return to his barn shelter off the road, then continue a couple miles back in the direction from which he originally came. There, a driveway or gravel road appeared to run along the front of the houses. If he was unsuccessful at the first, he'd be able to move on to the other one or two.

It was far from a sure thing, but one of those three houses probably had permanent residents who were merely away, perhaps for the holidays. He'd make one of those dark homes his personal bank machine as soon as the cover of darkness arrived and maybe find something more substantial to eat than an orange.

SIXTEEN

Giancarlo Mareno didn't have a regular office. The heavily armed bosses' bunkers used for movies might be good theatre but that would make it far too easy for the Feds to find files or documents they might use to entrap him. It would also make it easier for his enemies to track his travel patterns and render him a more convenient target should they become ambitious or angry.

Lots of people out there fit that description. Hundreds of young bucks trying to seize their piece of the lucrative crime business surely toyed with the idea of whacking him should the right opportunity arise. Thousands of marks had lost battles with The Organization in the thirty years since Giancarlo first seized control. So, there was no shortage of people who thought unkindly about him despite his efforts to achieve business respectability.

One unit of The Organization provided "protection" to restaurants and bars. A nice piece of business, it yielded excellent cash flow by coercing fearful owners to part with a few hundred dollars a month to avoid risks like unexpected fires, customer shootings, or even personal accidents. Besides the money those businesses paid in cash every month, the owners agreed to make space available in their establishments for Giancarlo's use whenever he chose.

They didn't use a reservation system or anything like that, and the owners received nothing but insurance against undesirable events. But Giancarlo didn't take advantage of them either. Each day, he ordered his trusted bodyguard and assistant, Luigi, to pick randomly any Manhattan location they hadn't visited for at least a month.

About seven o'clock most mornings, Luigi called an owner on their private cell number and politely instructed them to open the back door to their establishment before nine o'clock and assure no one—not even employees—knew Giancarlo would occupy an office. It was a simple system and it worked.

In all those years, he remembered only one lapse. The unfortunate restaurant owner—one who let word slip to a waitress curious to see what Giancarlo looked like—died in an explosion at his business the following night. The inquisitive waitress was in the building as well. Since then, there had never been a lapse because a description of that unfortunate event was part of the orientation for every new protection recruit.

Luigi's selection that day was a busy, well-known delicatessen on Fifth Avenue and a loyal protection customer for more than two decades. Another bodyguard acted as chauffeur and dropped off Giancarlo, Luigi and another of his men a couple blocks from the deli. They walked along Fifth Avenue for about a block, then used an alley to access the unlocked back door.

The office was cramped with a single desk and chair, but it would suffice. Luigi and the other bodyguard took turns sitting on a chair outside the office door pretending to work on word games or read a book while Giancarlo worked at a tiny desk, decluttered to provide an entirely bare surface for his laptop and phone. After the third bodyguard parked the car nearby, he took his turn in the rotation from dining area surveillance to monitoring the office door. Giancarlo was able to relax and focus on his work once enough time had elapsed for all three protectors to assume their positions.

At precisely 10:30 p.m. in Japan, Giancarlo dialed a Skype number on one of the cheap throwaway phones his people in the theft unit stole by the case.

"Suji-san. Is this a good time?" Giancarlo asked to verify their conversation wouldn't be overheard in Japan.

"Yes, I'm alone," the Japanese president of Suji Corporation replied.

"My people tell me our dividend for Jeffersons Stores didn't come in last month. What happened?"

"I had to cut the dividend. Those incompetent bastards running that outfit didn't make any profit for the last quarter. I fired both the CEO and CFO and put my own people in place. They'll pay dividends again next year. They better!" Suji-san warned.

"That explanation might work for your shareholders, Suji-san. But it doesn't work that way with me. You did that deal only because I found you the last hundred million you needed," Giancarlo replied evenly.

"Yes, and I am very grateful you got me the money," the Japanese businessman said. "But we agreed I'd repay you with dividends for ten years. We're only going to delay by one year. You'll get all your money back plus a good profit. It'll just take eleven years instead of ten."

"Suji, if you wanted to change the terms of our agreement, you know you should have talked to me first. This after-the-fact shit won't work."

"I'm tight right now, Giancarlo. Those bastards at Jeffersons thought we were an endless fountain of money. I had to arrange new operating loans in the United States and send more money from the pachinko operations in Japan. I'm tapped out right now."

"Find a new source of cash and have the payment in the Macau account before the end of the week." To emphasize his point, Giancarlo slammed his fist onto the surface of the desk with enough force for the sound to carry clearly into the phone and Suji-san's ear.

"It's impossible, Giancarlo. Give me a couple weeks. I should be able to find enough to send you before Lunar New Year."

"Let me say it one more time." Giancarlo spoke slowly. "I agreed to let you retain operating control of Jeffersons Stores, provided you paid me a dividend of five million dollars every three months for ten years. If you're not prepared to honor our agreement, the next time we talk our subject will be how control of the company transfers to me. If you're going to play in the US, you're going to play by my rules. Make sure the five mil is in the account by Friday."

Giancarlo didn't wait for a reply. He pressed the "end" button on his phone before he keyed in another recently used number.

"Prepare a provisional plan for Saturday night," he commanded to the person who answered. "Make all the arrangements and get somebody into Japan. I'll give you a final go-ahead before midnight Friday. Make it a location in one of the slums. I want to get his attention, not significantly debase the value of our future investment."

After a trip to the nearby men's room and a fresh cup of coffee the restaurant owner had cheerfully offered, Giancarlo keyed a new number into yet another throwaway phone.

"Nadine Violette *ici*," she answered.

"Are you able to talk?"

Nadine delivered the required security code in English, her voice wavering. "Nine. Zero. Five. Two. Three. Zero."

"She told you why I was calling?" Giancarlo asked as gently as possible.

"Yes. You want me to travel to Martinique this weekend?"

"That's right. And leave your temporary lover at home. Tell him whatever you need to. But come alone and meet me at the place in Sainte

Anne on Friday. Leave whenever you must to get there before Friday noon. Use commercial flights. No personal jet this time. And bring the videos, all of them."

"Can't I just send them to you?" she asked with a slightly plaintive tone.

"No. I want you there, too, and for more than a good fuck. We'll discuss it all, but you'll be moving into a new phase in your relationship with Pierre Boivin. You'll like it. It'll involve lots of expensive gifts and travel."

Without another word, he pressed the "end" button on his phone again.

SEVENTEEN

A house near Alportel, Portugal, Monday December 30, 2019

The moon was brighter than Howard liked, but he had no choice. He hid away successfully for three days but survived only eating fresh oranges. He needed money to buy food and also needed to keep moving.

Using every stealth skill learned from movies or television, he gradually advanced from the hillside to a spot near the back of the target house. No vehicle had passed in the previous several hours, and no car was visible on the property. Using the shadows from large, old trees spread out around the yard, he hid behind one trunk, then sprinted a few yards to the next. The seventh tree was feet away from a large wooden door recessed into old stone masonry.

The outside walls were more than a foot thick and meticulously maintained. Someone lived there but apparently without air conditioning. However, all the windows mounted five or six feet above the ground were closed—another indication there was likely no one in the home considering the warm temperature that day. Howard stuck his nose in the air, checking for odors from cooking, and listened intently for sounds of music or entertainment. All negative.

During his reconnaissance, he spotted another scooter tucked behind the rear porch and made a mental note to check inside the house for a key. *A convenient new mode of transportation to carry on when this mission ended?*

The ground between one remaining tree and the back door was bare, without a blade of grass or stone pebbles, just well-worn, hard-packed dirt. Howard stepped out from behind his hiding spot and cautiously crept a couple steps forward. He glanced in either direction before deciding his next move. The air was still, only the humming of insects disturbing it.

Just as he took a cautious next step, a pebble suddenly bounced on the hard surface off to his right. He peeked. Then he froze. The largest dog he had ever seen tugged anxiously on a leash, its teeth bared, and a fierce, low growl suddenly broke the quiet. It was a Doberman or some similar breed with ears laid back flat and mouth drooling. Then it barked several times—loud and angry.

At the end of its leash, a woman barely managed to hold back the ferocious animal. She seemed willing to let it bark and growl a few times while its strength dragged her a few feet closer to Howard's frozen position. She called out to him in Portuguese, but he had no idea what she said.

"Who are you and what are you doing here?" she called out again, this time in perfect English, as she glanced from Howard to the rear door now within his reach.

"I'm a tourist. I'm lost," Howard answered hoarsely.

"Lift your hands above your head so I can see if you have a weapon," she demanded. "Quickly or I'll let Brutus have some fun with you while I call the police."

Howard slowly raised his arms above his head, exposing his stomach as his stolen T-shirt rode up with his stretch. He kept the rest of his body perfectly still, as though willing the massive dog to cooperate and not attack. The dog continued to bark and growl, showing a clear yearning to attack and destroy the intruder.

"Slowly, lower your trousers," she commanded. When Howard hesitated, she allowed the dog another few feet closer to him as it continued barking. "Step out of them and walk backward five paces."

Howard followed her instructions.

"Take five more," the woman instructed. "I don't want you close while I inspect your jeans. Brutus here might be impossible to stop. If he gets started with you, I don't know if I can pull him back."

Howard gingerly followed her instructions, careful to keep his balance but venturing to peek backward to be sure they were alone. She instructed him to sit on the ground. After he settled with his legs extended in front, the women told her dog to heel. Brutus immediately stopped barking and tugging on the leash, and calmly sat back on its haunches beside the woman.

She held up the jeans, turned them upside down, and then shook them. Nothing came out. Next, she reached into each pocket and swished her hand around, each time pulling her hand from the pocket empty.

"Sort of a strange circumstance for a tourist, isn't it, mister ...?" She tilted her head to one side.

"My name is David Smith." Howard chose a name he had once used on a fake passport. "I'm a Canadian."

"But we have no proof of that now, do we? It seems you disregarded the basic advice our government gives tourists. 'Keep a copy of your passport with you at all times.' Why would that be Mr. Smith?"

"I set out this morning with my companions, but we got separated during the day and they left without me and without a phone or any way to contact them. I was just about to knock on your door to see if I might use yours when you and Brutus came around the corner."

"Well, I can understand how friends might get separated, but it's curious you would leave for sightseeing with no wallet, no credit cards, no passport, and no money. Do you really expect me to believe that? And if you planned to go sightseeing, wouldn't you prefer to wear pants that weren't two sizes too large and pair them with a T-shirt two sizes too small? I'm a writer, Mr. Smith. I study people and it's apparent to me you are no tourist, almost certainly not Canadian, and likely do not have the two most common names in the English language typed on your missing passport. I'll ask you politely one more time, who are you and what are you doing here? And if I don't think you're telling me the truth, I'll send Brutus over." She gently stroked the enormous dog at her side.

Seated, it came up to her chest. The dog could easily tear him apart if the woman issued a command. Howard didn't answer immediately. His head drooped toward his own chest as he calculated next step. Nothing was coming. Fear slowed his thought processes as intensely as the huge dog imparted a sense of confidence to the woman. That sureness showed in both her words and mannerisms. With the dog at her side, she feared no one.

"You're right. I'm a fugitive. They brought me out here to kill me, but there was a freak accident and I was able to run away." Howard lied with as much conviction as he could muster.

The woman tensed and looked around carefully, perhaps to see if there might be others she had missed. Then, her narrowed eyes bored in on his as she frowned, squinted, and leaned forward.

"You're still lying, but I'm not sure what's true and what isn't. Tell me about the accident—every detail."

"I was in the back of an SUV and didn't see the collision occur. They had me tied up in the rear compartment of the vehicle where I was lying on the floor. All I know is there was a huge crash, and the SUV left the road and flipped over onto its top. It was upside down in a ditch when I first realized what had happened. The two guys in the front seat of the car didn't respond when I called out to them. I waited a minute or two, but no one answered, and no one came to the vehicle to assist. I checked myself over and realized everything seemed to be working. I found a tire iron stored under the carpet with the spare tire. I used that to break a window and crawled out," Howard explained.

"Brutus, watch," she commanded the dog in a firm voice. With two long bounds, the dog bounced toward Howard, and then danced at his feet, growling and barking, waiting for the order to attack.

"Heel," the woman said. The dog reluctantly trotted back to her side and sat again. "Mr. Smith, or whoever you are, you must learn to tell me the truth. Otherwise, I'll have little alternative but to call the police or let Brutus play with your body parts. Maybe even both. I told you before, I'm a writer. I pay attention to details. Now, you told me you were tied up in the back of the vehicle. How exactly did you become untied enough to rip up the floor carpet, find a metal object suitable for breaking a window, break that window, crawl out through broken glass, and come here without a drop of blood on your clothes or a scratch on your very handsome body?"

Howard took a deep breath and a long look at the woman. She was exceptionally tall, about his height. Younger than him by a few years, she was past her prime but still retained a youthful vigor. She looked fit, with broad shoulders for a woman. He might have guessed she was a teacher if she hadn't already claimed to be a writer. Most would consider her attractive, though not truly beautiful.

She looked back at him without malice, but her expression was stern. No smile. Little empathy. Her brown eyes had softened and no longer conveyed anger. But she appeared determined to know his real story and ready to wait as long as it took to fully understand why he was here. But was she ready to use her dog as a weapon?

From Howard's vantage point, sitting helplessly on the ground in his underwear, the dog towered over him even seated on its haunches. It kept its gaze intently on Howard without moving a muscle. In fact, on closer inspection, he saw the dog wasn't actually sitting on the ground. Instead, its haunches were taut, its bottom about an inch off the ground, thigh muscles stretched ready to pounce on command.

"You're right. I'm not a tourist," he confessed. "But I am a fugitive. I'm not running from the law. I'm trying to escape some very bad people. I made some stupid decisions and ended up owing a lot of money to a criminal organization. A few days ago, they captured my companion and me while we were vacationing at the Eva Senses Hotel in Faro. Somehow, they got into our room and drugged us. All

I remember is a big man jabbing a needle into my leg. They either carried or dragged us—both naked—from our room in the middle of the night. When they stopped for fuel, I managed to escape from the back of an SUV, but my friend was still drugged and unconscious. I had to leave her behind."

Howard's voice broke as he revealed his tragic plight and paused to take another deep breath to regain control of his emotions. The woman nodded slightly to suggest he should continue. She seemed to be buying his tale.

"Like I said, I was nude. So, I ran to a nearby fig orchard to get away and stay out of sight. I walked from a rest stop through the orchard until I came upon a farmhouse. I stole these clothes I'm wearing from a farmer's clothesline. I also stole a scooter from the yard," Howard continued, keeping his story as close to the truth as possible in case he needed to retell it in the future.

"So, why are you in my backyard, with no scooter I might add, instead of at the Faro police station reporting your companion's kidnapping?" the woman demanded in an even tone.

"The police are mixed up with these people. When we returned to our room from a late-night coffee at the McDonald's across the street, the front desk attendant jokingly asked what mischief we were involved in. He said the national police had visited to ask if we were staying in the hotel. When the attendant confirmed we were guests, they wanted to know the room number, then said they would call back later. They didn't leave a message or anything. My companion and I thought there might be some mistaken identity issue and went to bed thinking nothing further of it."

"Okay, so you're afraid of the police as well as some bad guys, plus you stole some clothes and a scooter. Now, why are you in my backyard?"

"The scooter ran out of fuel. I was riding northward to try to escape from Portugal into France, planning to contact the police there. But, when I ran out of fuel, I knew I needed to break into a home and steal some money or a credit card. As you already observed, I have no money, cards, or identification. I was going to try to steal some money from your home. I'm sorry, but that's the truth."

The woman digested his story. She said nothing immediately, but the intensity of her gaze softened, and her clenched fists relaxed. She touched the dog's head with a gentle pat, and the animal quickly relaxed into a fully seated position. Then, it calmed down enough to swipe a long tongue around its wide-open mouth as if yawning.

"You won't find any money here," the woman said. "I keep all my money in a bank in Alportel. Once a week, I take my scooter to town where I withdraw enough to buy the supplies I need until the next trip. I'm not sure I buy your entire story but suspect there's a kernel of truth buried in there. And you don't strike me as an axe-murderer. You do look very hungry. So, here's what we'll do. I haven't eaten my dinner yet, so we'll go inside, and I'll prepare something for us both. You'll sit in the needlepoint, green armchair when we go into the house, and Brutus will sit beside you. If you move from the chair, he'll attack you. Do you understand?"

"Yes, ma'am. May I put on my jeans before we go in?"

"Let's leave them where they are for now. If Brutus needs to do his work, I don't want anything obstructing his sharp and efficient teeth."

EIGHTEEN

Nadine Violette had staged a call to ring on her phone at noon on New Year's Day. She let it ring a few times before she accepted it. Shortly after she answered, she expressed horror and demanded to know what had happened. After listening for an appropriate amount of time, she started sobbing and asked for more details. At reasonable intervals, she asked where her mother was, what they were doing to treat her, and what the prognosis was. With each lapse for an answer, she wept more passionately. Finally, she said, "I'll try to come tomorrow."

It turned out her elaborate performance wasn't necessary. Pierre Boivin remained hungover from their late night of celebration. He had again instructed her to wear the white, virtually transparent dress that showed everything. Usually, when she wore that outfit, he wanted to do it two or three times when they came home. But he'd been so drunk on champagne, he hadn't even tried to seduce her.

"*Cheri*?" She shook him from a snoring slumber, still holding the phone in her hand. "I need to go to Martinique right away. It's my mother. She had a stroke and is in the hospital in *Fort-de-France*. They don't think she'll make it. It's been three years since I saw her. Please, can I go see her one last time?"

Boivin hesitated. He started to say something, probably "no," then seemed to reconsider and looked away.

"When did you hear the news?"

"Just now. My sister Josée called from a hospital in Martinique. They took my mother there early this morning. *Maman* had a major stroke and lots of nerve damage. She's not responding to the drugs they gave her. Please, *Cheri*. I really need to see her before she goes!" Nadine pleaded.

"Okay, but get someone to fill in your schedule with the women until you return. And let's make it a quick trip. Fly commercial, though."

Nadine was lucky. She was one of the few women controlled by The Organization to hold a passport. Pierre had bought her a fake one so she could travel to bring back the new girls from Africa. Every few months, Nadine toyed with the idea of using that passport to escape the clutches of Pierre and the criminal element. But her daydream always ended the same way, with a bleak realization they had the power to find her wherever she might flee. At least the passport gave her some freedom.

She left the airport in Nice early the following afternoon, bound for *Orly* airport in Paris. From there, she took a nine-hour Air France flight to *Aimé Césaire* International Airport in *Fort-de-France,* Martinique. Unfortunately, no first-class seats were available, but she managed to sleep about half the trip. Still exhausted from the New Year's celebration and the stress of deceiving Pierre Boivin to engineer this temporary escape, she welcomed the sleep. The flight arrived on schedule, and she arranged a car for the one-hour drive to Giancarlo Mareno's secluded mansion on the hillside near Saint Anne. It was in that house her current fate in life first began, and she thought back to the frightening circumstances as she traveled in the darkness with only a taxi driver and her thoughts.

——•——

It had all started so innocently. The foreign woman on the beach had complimented her beautiful tan and charming smile. They had chatted for a few minutes about the stranger's visit to Martinique and Nadine's life as a student.

She was only seventeen at the time, had never seen a city larger than Fort-de-France, and her only trip to Martinique's capital had been earlier that year when she went to check out the university she planned to attend. Her parents were poor, so she could only get a higher education with the support of the French government. With her excellent grades, she qualified for a full scholarship and looked forward to starting in the new year.

The foreigner was a beautiful woman with a Spanish accent. She returned to the beach, and they again chatted a couple times before she asked Nadine to pose for a photo shoot. The woman's boss was a famous American photographer, she said. He admired Nadine's rare beauty and was prepared to offer a contract at standard US rates if she would pose for photographs wearing a bikini. They'd pay her five hundred dollars for a half-day session and she could keep the bikini.

Nadine was used to hearing compliments. The product of a mixed-race relationship, she had a skin tone that was often admired. Her mother had often warned her against showing off her body to boys, but the idea of a harmless photo session didn't set off any particular alarm bells, and the five hundred US dollars was more than she had earned in her part-time jobs for the past three years combined.

Without telling her mother, she agreed to visit the photographer. The house looked quite ordinary as she walked up the laneway toward it that first day. Inside, she was astonished by the size, degree of luxury and decor. Magnificent furniture, sparkling modern appliances, and lavish entertainment devices filled every room. The cement block walls were painted tastefully and adorned with modern paintings and beautifully framed photographs of sights in Martinique. The house extended far toward the back, making the inside much larger than it first appeared from the roadway. It was truly a mansion!

When the woman asked if she was ready to change into a bikini, Nadine took the minuscule garment from her hand and looked at it with curiosity. She had never seen fabric so tiny.

"Don't worry." The woman smiled. "I wore it yesterday and it covered all the essential parts."

As promised, it covered her nipples and pubic area but not much else. When Nadine came out of the bathroom wearing the bikini, she saw the huge man for the first time. He was almost twice her height and certainly more than four times her weight. His hand holding the camera was so massive, the large case and lens seemed cradled in his palm.

The foreign woman reappeared, wearing a swimsuit as small as her own, and offered Nadine a Coke. She accepted it and felt better with the company. The woman chatted cheerfully and helped Nadine relax. The large man didn't say anything to Nadine. Instead, after a few minutes, he merely told the women they'd start outside.

Nadine remembered clearly only the first several poses she made for the photographer. They were unremarkable and quite repetitious until he told her to remove her bikini top. A little lightheaded, she hesitated a moment before the other woman gently loosened the strings from behind and the top floated to the ground.

She had no recollection of the other photos until they showed her the awful images and videos after she fully recovered. The foreign woman who lured her to the house was nowhere in sight when Nadine awoke. Instead, there was another unfamiliar woman. This one spoke English with a strange accent.

The new woman wasn't nearly as nice. She was all business and told Nadine to sit at a table and watch while she flashed photos and videos of her on a massive wide-screen television connected to a laptop computer.

Nadine watched herself posing nude in every imaginable position, often with her legs wide apart. She started crying when they played the video of her performing oral sex on a man she didn't even remember. The voice giving instructions on the video was the same as the woman now forcing her to watch the disgusting acts she performed. Nadine had no experience with such sexual behavior, so the awful woman coached her to massage and suck the man's penis for maximum pleasure.

When the video showed her having sex with two men—one with his penis in her mouth and the other penetrating her from the rear—she swung from the table and puked on the floor. Crying, vomiting, and screaming, she realized her plight. Shock and disgust permeated every pore of her body.

The woman changed her tack. She put her arm around Nadine and said she knew how she felt, but everything would be okay. They'd destroy the videos and pictures if she wished. They wouldn't tell her mother. The French government officials who controlled her scholarship to university need never know about her "mistake."

But the big man who took the pictures wanted to have sex with her himself. If Nadine agreed, they'd pay her three times as much and give her back all the pictures. Still not thinking clearly, Nadine demanded to have the money and photos first. Then she'd have sex with him.

The woman returned with two thousand US dollars and a small USB drive she said contained all the photos. Then she led Nadine toward the room where the huge man awaited. She trembled and the woman saw her apprehension.

"Take this." The woman handed her a pill. "It will make it easier for you and it will be all over quickly. Don't worry. He's quick."

Nadine woke up sometime later in a strange bed, in a strange room, in a city she didn't recognize. It was in a luxury high-rise condo in Naples, Florida, she later learned. They held her captive there in a massive, luxurious apartment with two other girls and the foreign woman who had drugged her. The suite was locked around the clock and could only be opened with a secret code they never shared with Nadine or the other girls.

She soon discovered their job was to service a few wealthy clients who paid large amounts for the pleasure. The girls received only food and drink, no money at all. Her captors kept Nadine in sexual servitude for two years. The big man who took her pictures came to visit only once, and the woman who minded them told Nadine to be sure she performed well because he was the big boss of The Organization.

One week after that huge man's visit, he sold her. But the crime boss made sure she understood the sale was conditional. She might not belong to him any longer, but when he asked questions about Pierre Boivin's activities, he expected her complete loyalty. The big boss's needs superseded those of her new owner, and he'd punish her severely if she ever forgot.

Pierre had treated her unusually well. He let her travel quite freely and made love to her tenderly, almost lovingly. He kept her for himself exclusively and gradually showed her more trust and liberty than she had ever before experienced. She remained his slave, but a pampered one, and she enjoyed her lifestyle of luxury and access to wealth.

It was a shame she had never again seen her family, and there'd be no opportunity to reunite with her mother. Giancarlo Mareno had reminded her more than once that both her mother and sister would suffer miserable deaths should she ever make contact with either. It was a burden she could never escape.

———•———

Mareno's demand to meet him in Martinique to discuss some new phase in her relationship with Pierre caused her concern. As they approached her old hometown, she thought about the growing conflict between the two men who controlled her life and it worried her.

Once the driver reached their destination, Nadine climbed the long steps, entered the key code Mareno had given her and opened the tall front door of his house, stepped inside, and turned on a light.

The lifeless nude body of a woman lay on the floor.

The badly battered corpse on the floor was the same woman who'd controlled her life in captivity in the high-rise condo in Naples. When her brain processed the gruesome discovery and its connection to her, Nadine screamed.

"I'm in here," a deep voice said when her scream faded. From the bedroom where her nightmare first started, he added, "Take off your clothes and come in here."

NINETEEN

Angermund, Germany, Friday January 3, 2020

"This Spanish is friggin' impossible," Janet Weissel exclaimed as she shut down from another three-hour session with *Rosetta Stone Español* on a laptop computer the German intelligence service had given her to use.

"It can't be worse than your English language with inconsistent grammar rules, weird spelling and different meanings for the same words," Klaudia replied, laughing at her roommate's frustration.

"That's true. But I grew up with English. In Overveen, I struggled to become fluent in Dutch, so it's a challenge. What I think I need is a good Spanish lover to teach me. Howard claimed his relationship with that woman Fidelia improved his Spanish measurably. And I can't remember a time since I was sixteen I've gone this long without sex. Think we could find me one?" Janet shook her head in laughter.

"I think it'd be difficult to find anyone in Angermund who speaks Spanish. If you're hoping to meet a guy, don't expect him to follow you home, panting in heat, while you're wearing your captivating black abaya and niqab that hide every one of your undeniably alluring attributes."

Janet suddenly turned serious. "Speaking of wardrobe, is there any chance we eventually get to dress normally here? Or is this what I have to look forward to forever?"

"Forever is a long time, but what are your alternatives? Do you have money stashed away somewhere like Fidelia? If not, you'll need to find a job. How will you find a job here? You speak only English. You have no experience. You have no recommendations." Klaudia stood up from her computer desk and turned to face Janet. "If you fly back to the USA, where do you look for a job? And, if The Organization found you in the Netherlands, how long do you think it will take them to track you down in America?"

"But now that I've eluded them, don't you think they'll focus their resources and attention here in Europe?"

"Of course," Klaudia replied sharply. "And that's why we have you hidden. This place is secure. If we're careful, it will stay that way."

"The *Bundesnachrichtendienst* person said they were using intelligence service channels to get me into Costa Rica. Did you hear any more?"

"I communicate with my contact every day by email. He tells me they're making progress, but they want assurances you're fluent in Spanish before they place you there. In Costa Rica, they get lots of English-speaking tourists, but they still stand out from the locals. No one can guarantee your identity won't be compromised. The assignment is already so dangerous they want you to at least speak the language with ease."

"So, all I can do for now is continue to study Spanish for eight or nine hours a day?"

"That's right. Unless you'd like to learn all about social media algorithms and spend a few hours a day with me trying to identify young girls most susceptible to human trafficking in Eastern Europe."

"That won't happen. I'm a political science grad. I have none of the math or tech skills needed to learn algorithms." Janet shuddered. "I'll keep plugging away with my friends at *Rosetta Stone*, but has there been any sign of Howard? Any indication whether he's dead or alive?"

"None. The German and Dutch intelligence services both stay tapped into the Interpol system and haven't found any entries related to Howard from anywhere in Europe. No corpse discovered matching his description or fingerprints. Nothing. I'm sorry." Klaudia pursed her lips and tilted her head in that way she did when she was remorseful.

"In my head I know they must have killed Howard and disposed of his body right after they seized him," Janet said. "But I still have this strange feeling he might be alive. I dream about him at night, and it's like he's there talking to me. Reassuring me he's okay. It's kind of weird."

"You've been through a lot the past few days. I guess it's normal to have some strange feelings. And sometimes the grieving process can do bizarre things to our minds for quite a while," Klaudia reassured.

"I know. Don't bug your contact. But do me a favor and check with him from time to time to see if anything surfaces. It would make it easier if I knew one way or the other. I think I was actually in love with the guy. We got thrown together by circumstance. I really did sleep with him initially only for gratification and comfort. But during the couple years we were together, I learned what a bright and sensitive guy he was. He truly regretted his involvement with The Organization, and I really miss him." Her voice broke but she didn't cry.

"Sure, I'll keep checking with my contact. And with Fidelia. She loved Howard at one time too, and I suspect she may still have some back-door connections to The Organization. She might be able to find out. I'll ask."

"*Gracias. Y ahora de vuelta al español.* I'll continue to study this cursed language until dinner."

TWENTY

Giancarlo Mareno's luxurious house near Saint Anne, Martinique, Friday January 3, 2020

Giancarlo Mareno turned on the lamp at his bedside and picked up a phone.

"She's here. In five minutes, come inside and dispose of the other one. Leave us alone until morning."

He left the light on while he waited and watched his penis come to life. Sometimes anticipating sex was even better than the actual act, and it had other benefits as well. This one should be particularly delicious.

When Nadine Violette entered the room at a snail's pace, she was visibly trembling. Giancarlo liked that. And she was gorgeous. The best tits he'd seen in a long time. Big, round nipples that always seemed aroused, welcoming attention. Black pubic hair, neatly groomed. Sexy black eyes with a sparkle that never dimmed. Long dark hair cascaded down her back to her waist in waves, with a few stray strands curling invitingly around her breasts. Sensuous pink lips complemented her tanned complexion and made the entire package even more alluring. Above all, her color was magnificent. Darker than women from Southern Europe and lighter than black women. A perfect combination and undoubtedly one of the best Fidelia ever found.

"Let me look," he commanded. "Pose nicely like you did for your photo shoot."

"I don't remember much," Nadine replied demurely as she coyly held her arms behind her back and straightened her shoulders to show her breasts seductively.

"Shit happens," Mareno retorted coldly. "Look how much better off you are now. Rather than being stuck here with some poor bastard fucking you every night and forcing you to take care of ungrateful, screaming little brats all day, you live in luxury. I hear Boivin even lets you use the private helicopter to make your rounds. Your life really sucks."

"I'm not complaining," Nadine protested, still trembling as he ogled her body.

"I am. This hard-on is taking much too long. Use your mouth," he commanded.

She followed his instructions and fondled, massaged and sucked his cock with her lips and tongue until he erupted a few moments later. He pushed her aside curtly.

"That was nice," he said as he left the bed and wiped himself with a corner of the bed sheet before starting to pull on his underwear. "Change the sheets, and then come to the living room. I'll wait for you there. Stay undressed."

Giancarlo took a cold cola from the refrigerator. He didn't drink alcohol, hadn't since his teens when he got so drunk friends had to carry him home one night. That night, he decided to never put himself in such a vulnerable position again. But he continued to drink Coke by the gallon, often more than a dozen in a day.

With his sparse graying hair unruly and his face sporting its usual three- or four-day growth, he cursed the aging process as he caught his image when he passed a mirror in a hallway. His huge stomach drooped below the shirt line and bulged over his shorts. His shoulders stooped as he lowered himself onto a black leather sofa and waited for Nadine to finish her chores. A tingling in his groin rekindled the anticipation. He looked forward to penetrating that sensuous body again after they discussed business.

"Sit on the carpet over here." He motioned to a spot in front of the sofa. "And spread your legs apart nicely. I like to have nice scenery while we talk."

Nadine obeyed.

"What's Boivin up to over there? What's his deal with Interpol?"

"He has six of them *dans sa poche*, in his pocket as you would say. We see them all weekly. One really likes S&M, three prefer extremely young girls and two like lots of variety, anything that moves. Pierre has videos and photos. The guys have never seen them. Pierre says all he needs to do is mention them and he gets results. The visuals are very powerful though. If the media ever got hold of any of them, the guys would lose their big titles immediately. And these guys are all big spenders. They need their jobs."

"You brought all the photos and videos?" Giancarlo asked.

"They're all on the USB." She pointed nonchalantly toward the table and the flash drive.

"Has Boivin loaned you out to any of them?"

"No. I'm his *exclusivement*," Nadine said without emotion.

"Which one has the most power?"

"Deschamps. He's apparently number three in the Interpol command structure. Pierre goes to him for the really important stuff."

"Then he's the one you're going to temporarily fall in love with," Giancarlo said without a trace of emotion. "I'll talk to Boivin this week and tell him to loan you out until we get Howard Knight. You'll do whatever the guy wants. And you'll make finding Knight the new number one preoccupation of *Monsieur* Deschamps."

Nadine gasped and tears welled as she struggled to maintain control. "You have the videos, already. Why don't you just use them to get his cooperation?"

"Sometimes it's better to use honey to attract the right behavior. You're the honey."

"But Pierre loves me. He might not agree."

"Then he'll disappear," Giancarlo said coldly. "Now do me again."

TWENTY-ONE

A house near Alportel, Portugal, Monday January 6, 2020

Remarkably, Howard was still at the woman's home a full week after she caught him intending to break into her place and steal money or credit cards.

"My name is Katherine Page," she offered that first night while she prepared a hearty spaghetti dinner. She pointed to a chair across the kitchen where she wanted Howard to sit. "I tell you my real full name. I have nothing to hide and you'll see it on the books and posters lying around anyway. I'd still appreciate you telling me your real name."

Her gaze bore into his eyes as she made her polite demand.

"It's Howard. It's better if I tell you only my given name."

"Okay, Howard the unknown. I'll leave it there for now. Sit. Brutus is a crossbreed, you know. German Shepherd and Doberman. Gentle most of the time, but vicious on demand. He will be watching and I suggest you not move more than necessary. Breathing will be okay, and it should be all right to scratch your nose if there's an itch. But any quick movement, or standing up from the chair, will immediately attract unwanted attention from Brutus. Isn't that right, my good boy?"

The dog barked once in reply and continued staring at Howard as though he was a tempting chunk of dinner meat and his owner was merely testing his patience.

Howard studied Katherine quietly while she worked. A tall, fit woman, she didn't match his stereotypical image of an introverted writer. Although she had it wrapped in a large, unruly wad at the back of her head that day, her dark hair appeared long, full and coiled for release. Her posture was good. Shoulders back and head held high even as she worked, the woman didn't look like someone who labored over a computer keyboard for long hours. The form revealed by her jeans and loose-fitting top seemed appealing.

Her demeanor exuded confidence. To some extent, her massive dog surely helped in that regard, but her overall manner and movements appeared more self-assured than cautious. Katherine looked relaxed even with a stranger giving her a once-over from across the room.

As she prepared their meal, the room was silent. Clearly, she preferred to focus on one activity at a time and first put a large pot with water on the gas range before she ignited the flame. Next to it, she set a pan to sauté the vegetables before adjusting the stove's controls.

From her refrigerator, she loaded her arms with celery, peppers of three different colors, a sprig of parsley and some herbs like chives or oregano. He couldn't tell which, but didn't intend to ask while Brutus continued to focus on Howard's upper body, swishing his tongue around the contours of his mouth every few minutes.

Chopping the vegetables seemed effortless as Katherine's hands flew across the assembled rows, the knife dicing the vegetables with her light and rapid touch. Within seconds, she put handfuls into a now warm frying pan and added olive oil with a sweeping gesture that suggested both familiarity and pleasure with the art of cooking.

Howard admired her work for the few minutes it took to boil spaghetti and sauté the vegetables. He had an appetite, and the aromas of olive oil and herbs stimulated his senses while he waited. When she spoke again, her voice seemed a little less tense.

"Okay, Brutus. Relax and come over here." The animal trotted toward her a few steps and stopped beside her legs. She rewarded it with a gentle pat on its head, a scratch behind the ears, and a treat. The dog gulped the morsel without chewing it and looked up expectantly for more.

"No, you'll eat when we're finished. Sit beside me and keep an eye on this Howard who doesn't yet have a surname. There," she pointed to a spot on the floor on the side of the table where she stood. The dog responded immediately and sat back on its haunches at the ready.

"Howard, you can sit in the chair on the other side of the table. I'll give you a fork and a spoon. Be sure you don't make any quick motions with the fork or Brutus will respond. Right, Brutus?" she asked. The dog again replied with one quick bark of understanding.

Before she sat down, she drew a pitcher-full of water from a faucet and placed two glasses and the pitcher in the middle of the table.

"There won't be any wine tonight for obvious reasons. The water is good and it's perfectly safe. I have the well tested twice a year. *Bom apetite*! Now, while you eat, tell me again how you found yourself at my back door."

Howard recounted the story once more, taking care not to change any aspect of his narrative. Again, she tested him with questions designed to get more details. But he was prepared. He respected her intellect and carefully stored every bit of information shared in his almost photographic memory. Although both seemed to enjoy the delicious pasta, she peppered him for information throughout their meal. But he rose to every challenge.

When she paused and appeared ready to clear away the dishes on the table, Howard ventured to ask a question of his own.

"What kind of writing do you do?"

"I write novels in the mystery and suspense genre. But my stories all highlight a little horror. I don't like to be shoehorned into a specific style. My favorite parts are usually descriptions of violence and physical harm to my victims. I give it a lot of thought and do it very well," she said without the hint of a smile.

"I very much appreciated your dinner, Katherine. Would you like me to leave now?"

"Where would you go?" she asked.

"Well, I have a full stomach. I can walk farther and try to steal some money from one of your neighbors instead," Howard offered. "I won't hurt anyone."

"That may be true, but it looks like you already have a nasty hand injury. What happened to your little finger?"

"One of the goons that captured us stepped on my hand. I think a bone broke. And when they threw me into the back of the vehicle, I landed on my left hand again and probably injured it more."

"The color is worrisome. When extremities of my novel characters turn to ugly blue and red hues like that, I usually have to arrange to amputate them," Katherine said with a mischievous smile. "Before that becomes necessary for you, let me see if I can arrange a splint or something to help you heal."

While the dog surveyed every movement, she first cleaned and fiddled with a sliver of wood she extracted from a kitchen drawer, then taped it to Howard's two swollen fingers tightly. The pain of forcing his fingers to straighten out against the makeshift splint seemed greater than the initial impacts, and he felt his eyes water as he grimaced in agony.

"No. I think it's better if you stay here tonight so Brutus can keep an eye on you. Some will probably consider me a fool, but we don't need you stumbling around in the dark out there and getting shot by the fellow down the road. He's not nearly as friendly," she added and pursed her lips.

"Go fetch your trousers outside before the wildlife cart them away. Then come back inside. You'll sleep over there." She pointed to a room on the other side of the small home.

Although the hour was still early for sleep, when Howard returned wearing the stolen jeans gathered up from the ground outside, he immediately headed toward the room she had indicated.

"Wait," she commanded. "Here's a glass of water and an old pot I don't use any more. If you need to relieve yourself during the night, use this. Brutus will be sleeping right outside your room. If you open the door during the night, he'll attack, right Brutus?"

The dog's ears raised straight up and he barked once again, with more conviction this time. As though punctuating the point, the canine's large mouth displayed rows of long, sharp teeth as it partially suppressed a growl.

"You better use the toilet over there if you have any other business to do before you sleep. I'll open your door in the morning. *Dorma Bem!*" she added cheerfully before she cleared the dishes and stacked them in the sink.

Howard followed her advice. That night, he slept soundly and had no need to leave his bedroom. The next morning, Katherine awoke early and knocked on his door to let him know the coast was clear. Brutus was outside doing his business, and it was safe for Howard to venture from the room.

She pointed to the kitchen table when he entered the main living area, and he took another long look around the layout as he made his way over. The concept was completely open except for the two bedrooms, one next to the other on one side of the home. Between the bedrooms was the bathroom; on the opposite side, a kitchen and eating area. The entire front wall was Katherine's working area with a long desk positioned in front of a picture window. On it sat a computer, a large screen monitor, and a compact printer. From floor to ceiling on either side of her desk, shelves were full to overflowing with books.

A large television screen was mounted halfway up the rear wall and below it an array of technical gadgets. Clustered around the television were three identical leather chairs with straight backs. In the corner of the back wall nearest the bedroom, a high-end stationary bicycle and well-worn treadmill completed the decor.

When Brutus came inside through the open back door, Katherine joined Howard at the table, poured some homemade muesli into a bowl and added yogurt in the European tradition. Howard followed her lead, and they munched in silence for a short time.

"I won't ask if you slept well, but it was a relief you followed my advice about staying inside your room," Katherine said. "I was so hoping that Brutus wouldn't wake me with the sounds of tearing skin and your screams for mercy."

"Thanks for your concern," Howard replied with a little more sarcasm than intended in his voice. "I really did sleep well. I didn't hear a hint of sound until you knocked on the door this morning. Is it always like that?"

"Unless there's a storm. As you can see, I like the quiet. I seldom play a radio or watch television. So I don't know if the police are urgently seeking you. Do you think I should check?"

"If I read you correctly, Katherine, you probably have already checked—maybe with your phone—and just want to see my reaction. Am I right?" He paused for a faint smile and resumed when she nodded with her eyes sparkling impishly. "I'm not surprised if the police are searching. The people who want me are powerful, and their reach penetrates even the highest levels of most governments and law enforcement. Would you like me to leave this morning?"

"Am I in danger by harboring you here?"

"You're in danger if The Organization finds me. That's the name of the criminal element that's after my hide. You'll know better than I how the police here might react."

"There are less than fifty homes within walking distance of the place you had your purported accident and escaped. Aren't the chances good this outfit you call The Organization will find you soon?"

"Perhaps. But the odds might be less than you think," Howard said after a short hesitation. "You're right. I wasn't totally honest with you. There was no accident. And there was no companion. There's only an old stolen scooter in a ditch about two miles from here that's connected to me. I treasure your confidence and help. Let me tell you the full story. Then you can decide if you'd like me to leave or not."

Howard revealed the entire story. He began with Janet and him plunked together in the Miami apartment and told of their journey from Miami to the Netherlands until the night they snatched him from their home in Overveen. He offered more color as he recounted his journey to Isla Canela and his subsequent escape. He didn't leave out a single detail as he recounted the saga from his arrival in Portugal and attempt to put distance between The Organization and himself. He even revealed his correct surname with a boyish grin.

Katherine listened in silence, fascinated by his narrative but scrutinizing every detail with a tilted head, furrowed brow, and skeptical eyes. When Howard finished, she asked only one question.

"That's a gripping story, Mr. Knight. It might even be better than what I create as pure fiction. So, why should I believe this version?"

"Whether you believe my story or not is entirely up to you," he replied in a tone little more than a whisper. "Like you, I think I'm a superior judge of character. You strike me as an independent, caring woman. You've already taken risks to invite me into your home to eat and sleep—even with Brutus to keep me in line. I trust you to make a decision you're comfortable with. If you'd like me to leave, I'll go right now and leave without any malice or ill-will. You owe me nothing."

Katherine didn't answer. She rose from the table, gathered up the empty cereal bowls and carried them to the sink as she contemplated his fate. She returned, picked up the container of yogurt and took it to the refrigerator. Still silent, she wiped the table with a damp cloth to collect the crumbs and rinsed it under running water from the faucet. Finally, she spoke.

"I think your story has a least a kernel of truth. If I let you use my phone, can you contact your people in the FBI for help?"

Howard tried both secret numbers without success. Unbelievably, both agents assigned to his case were on vacation and didn't have access to their voicemail according to the recorded voice messages. Their voice mail greetings gave no indication when they would return or a suggestion of other agents to contact. To Howard, it was evident someone in The Organization had found a way to penetrate the FBI telephone system and sabotage his communication channel, probably before they kidnapped him.

Katherine suggested he contact Interpol if Howard didn't trust the *policial* in Portugal. Howard differed. If the police in the Netherlands and Spain were so anxious to capture him, they would already have alerted the Interpol authorities in Lyon. They'd almost surely consider him a fugitive from justice, not a kidnapping victim.

They lapsed into silence as alternative actions dwindled and possible avenues closed.

Without divulging his thoughts to the woman, Howard weighed the pros and cons of calling his financial contact in the Cayman Islands but eventually decided the risk was too great. Should her phone fall into the hands of the authorities, they would not only know about the call, they might exert pressure on the offshore bank to withhold funds or divulge information about his whereabouts.

As he sipped a cup of tea Katherine prepared, he collected his thoughts. Howard even toyed with the far-fetched idea of contacting Fidelia Morales. He had learned the whereabouts of his long-time former lover from Klaudia Schäffer. When the pair had concocted an escape scheme for Janet in the event of discovery, Klaudia playfully divulged that she knew how to contact Fidelia Morales if ever he wanted to call her.

Howard had demurred, but Klaudia eventually read him his former lover's telephone number to file away in case he ever changed his mind. He still remembered it. Fidelia was unquestionably the most resourceful person he had ever encountered, and he wondered if she might throw him some sort of a lifeline. He dismissed that possibility within seconds.

For almost another hour, Katherine tossed up repeated suggestions about possible authorities or people to contact, but one-by-one they eventually eliminated the ideas as too risky. Finally, she threw up her arms in apparently cheerful defeat and offered to let him stay for the time being.

"If you're going to stay here a few days, get started with chores. You can clean the dishes and wash the floors this morning while I write. At noon, we'll both take a break and discuss the ground rules while you're here. In the meantime, don't go near the windows or go outside."

For a week, Howard had performed house chores under the continuous and watchful scrutiny of Brutus and stayed out of the rest of the world's sight.

TWENTY-TWO

Pierre Boivin slammed his fist on the phone, then flung it against a wall in the tiny room he used as an office behind the sightseeing business. The phone bounced off the wall and careened onto the tile floor, breaking into smaller jagged pieces.

The veins on his neck bulged and his usually tanned skin became more red than brown as his rage built. He repeatedly banged his clenched fist on the desk, causing it to bounce and teeter ominously under the attack. He kicked a trash can and spewed the contents across the floor, then punted a Coke bottle that appeared on the floor from nowhere.

Nadine cowered in a corner as far away from Pierre as physically possible. She sobbed in both fear and frustration, arms wrapped around her chest, looking downward and shaking her head in disbelief. Recovering his composure only slightly, Pierre screamed, "When did you know?"

"I didn't know," she managed between sobs. "I just heard about it. I love you, Pierre! I really don't want to do it!"

"You're lying," Pierre shouted in return. It didn't matter if the staff and customers might overhear. Then he thought better of it and lowered his voice.

"It was him you met in Martinique. I knew something had changed as soon as you came back. Now go. Do his bidding and fuck the Interpol bastard. Fuck him well, and get Mareno his satisfaction from dismembering Howard Knight," Pierre seethed through clenched teeth.

"I can't do it, Pierre."

"You will do it, and you'll start tonight. Go buy another dress that reveals every inch of your body. I want to be sure the idiot not only gets the message but instantly succumbs."

"Why can't you get someone else to sleep with the Interpol official? Mareno won't know who did the guy. As long as you find Knight, why not use one of the other girls? I've got several younger ones, just like Deschamps likes."

"No. It has to be you. There's no mistaking Mareno's intention. He insisted you had to be here when he called. No doubt about it. He wanted to be sure you knew I got his order. He did it to humiliate both of us."

"But we can tell him I did the Interpol guy and just send someone else in my place."

Calmer, Pierre pretended to consider her suggestion. He sat down, twirled a pencil in his fingers, and focused on a spot on the wall.

"Why don't we get him three or four *jeunes filles* in place of me and some meds so he really gets his rocks off?" Nadine continued.

Without raising his voice, Pierre turned to face her and coldly said, "No. Follow my instructions. Get the see-everything new dress and be ready to wear it tonight."

He scrutinized her as she took in his message. One tiny cringe escaped before she dropped her head for a moment. Then she drew a deep breath as if she might want to protest again. Instead, she suddenly raised her head, theatrically snatched her bag from the desk, and strode past him wordlessly without making eye contact.

Pierre reached for a beer and leaned back in the comfortable chair behind his makeshift desk as he hoisted both feet onto the wooden top. After thinking for a few minutes, he took a single sip from the bottle, then held that position, gazing off into space for more than an hour. Eventually he became calmer and gradually processed his thoughts more clearly. Fully recovered, he powered up his computer and clicked on Google. Then he tapped in the name Howard Knight.

About sixty-seven thousand results populated his screen. He narrowed his search by adding key morsels of information he knew about the fugitive. Knight attended Harvaard University. A possibly important detail popped up: Long-distance swimmer on the Harvaard team ranking among the top twenty-five athletes during his three and one-half years there.

Expelled in his fourth year for vandalizing a Jewish cemetery along with fellow students? How then did he get a Masters in Business Administration as some other articles claimed?

When the harvest of information on Google evaporated, Pierre pulled up the file they hacked from the FBI. The file he had used to let Giancarlo Mareno know exactly where he could find Knight and the woman seventeen days earlier. Yes, his people cracked the vaunted FBI security firewalls and shared Knight's witness protection information with Interpol and the crime boss who was now humiliating him.

Fifteen pages into the document, Pierre struck gold. When the FBI ferreted Knight out of hiding in Quepos, Costa Rica to become a state's witness against The Organization, Knight's boat was on fire in the harbor and provided cover for the FBI to snatch him. It was a thirty-four-foot Carver Yacht—the same size as the one missing from Isla Cristina and found in a quiet bay near Faro.

Pierre reached for his phone and punched the speed dial icon for Estavao Sereno, barely able to contain his excitement.

"Estavao," he said when the voice responded. "Howard Knight is somewhere in Portugal."

TWENTY-THREE

Aix-en-Provence, France, Monday January 6, 2020

"He didn't take the bait," Nadine said softly into her phone as she waited around the corner and down the street from their apartment. She was far enough away from the house it would be hard for Pierre to listen to her call, even digitally. She was also waiting for an Uber driver to take her to the dress shop.

"I think he's completely loyal to you." Nadine's tone was as cheerful as she could manage under the circumstances.

"I'll make that determination," Giancarlo said. "When will you sleep with the guy from Interpol?"

"Tonight, I think. Pierre's arranging it. He ordered me to buy a transparent dress and have it ready to wear tonight." She grimaced, but her tone didn't reflect the distaste she felt.

"Get close to Boivin's driver too. Don't do him unless you have to. But flirt with him a little and get him engaged in conversation. I want to know every place he takes Pierre for the next two weeks. Something's going on, and I want you to find out what it is. I'll call again Friday. Have something for me." The phone line died.

Nadine spent only a few minutes choosing the sluttiest outfit the shop owner had. The dress was so risqué, the woman didn't even display it on the racks out front. Instead she went into the back and rustled about for a few minutes before she returned with one that matched the description Nadine provided. She tried it on and looked in the mirror for only a few seconds before she told the woman she'd take it.

As she paid for the dress, Nadine accepted with little enthusiasm the shop owner's compliments about how well the dress fit her and displayed her best features. Her body had become little more than an apparatus for her job. Would that shop owner be as enthusiastic about a new computer or phone? To Nadine, there seemed little difference.

With her new dress in a sack slung over her shoulder, she headed toward a neighborhood gym where she was a regular. Almost every day she made time for a workout. Without those grueling sessions on the stationary bicycle and stair-climbing machine, she held virtually no hope of keeping her body trim and firm.

There was little doubt now. Any deterioration in her figure would certainly see her role with Pierre change dramatically. If he was prepared to cave in to Mareno's demands so easily, the relationship she thought they were developing would simply evaporate and she'd be just another whore he used to earn income and manipulate influential people. Except for one big change. She'd find herself relegated to the second tier.

He reminded her of that possibility occasionally. Usually, the comments were teasing, but more often lately, he'd order her to assume some provocative nude poses and take photos. Later, she'd find him at a desktop computer, comparing the photos with similar pictures taken months earlier, sometimes even asking his subordinates if they detected any differences in her body as if it was a big joke.

The planned rendezvous with the guy from Interpol weighed heavily on her mind as she worked out on the treadmill. She knew him. His name was Deschamps. They often supplied him with women and all the girls complained. At best, he was rough. A couple girls claimed his treatment was nothing short of brutality. One told Nadine the low life threatened to cut her while she was restrained in bondage.

Giancarlo's demand that she do whatever was necessary to get the bastard to pull out all the stops in the desperate search for Howard Knight left her vulnerable. She realized that. Unfortunately, the Interpol guy might eventually realize it too. She shuddered at the thought.

As she walked briskly toward their apartment from the gym, she thought again about trying to escape it all. It wasn't the first time she fantasized about leaving The Organization behind to start a new life. But all previous jaunts along that path had ended when she found no open doors.

She had a measure of freedom. People looking at her as she walked down the street would never suspect she was a slave. Her manner, appearance, and smile looked the same as theirs. But they couldn't see her desperation.

Nadine had seen firsthand how The Organization treated women who tried to escape their captivity. How they beat the one in Paris when they found her in the departure lounge of Orly Airport. The poor girl's face was disfigured forever, and they forced her to work the most dangerous streets until she killed herself with drugs a few months later.

She remembered the punishment they meted out to the teenaged girl from Africa who tried to report her kidnapping and enslavement at her country's embassy. The Organization was so powerful, someone inside the embassy called Pierre and let him know the girl was there. When she was later sent away from her government's refuge, Pierre's enforcers captured her on the street, whisked her into a waiting car, and drove her to a remote area in the countryside. Then he'd forced Nadine to watch a video depicting how his people raped and tortured the child for hours before they killed her and buried her corpse in the foothills of the Alps.

The Organization's reach was worldwide. Their influence permeated governments, businesses, and law enforcement agencies. Like all the other times, her flirtation with the idea of escape ended with a grim acceptance. She was condemned to her current lot in life. She'd just have to make the best of it.

TWENTY-FOUR

New York, New York, Sunday January 12, 2020

"Mr. Suji is in the hospital," a familiar voice whispered to Giancarlo over the telephone. It was the Japanese octogenarian's favorite Korean "comfort woman." The billionaire owner of Suji Corporation kept her in his entourage as a slave, much as Japanese soldiers had ensnared Korean women for their sexual pleasures during the Second World War. She also understood the undercurrents of power and worked for Mareno on the side.

"What happened?" Giancarlo asked.

"His heart. Last night, he experienced severe pains in his chest. I called the ambulance, and they took him to a hospital in Tokyo. After some tests they brought him by air ambulance to the National Cerebral and Cardiovascular Center here in Osaka. He's stable now but the doctors are still concerned."

"Stay there with him and keep me informed." Mareno hung up with no goodbye or other parting formality.

Giancarlo's body tensed and he drew himself upright in a chair as he looked off into the distance and pondered the implications. The news was not entirely surprising. The guy was old, after all. Everyone knew his lifestyle was not a healthy one; no one could remember the last time they saw him do any physical exercise. Giancarlo had anticipated this eventuality because that's what effective leaders do. But with all the other stuff going on, was now the right time to pounce?

Suji-san held a key to the supermarket business in the USA. His outfit in Japan engineered the takeover to seize control of Jeffersons Stores. Of course, it had only been possible with Giancarlo's last-minute help in raising the necessary funding. And everyone with leadership roles in The Organization rightly suspected Giancarlo only helped the old man because he intended to eventually pirate the prized supermarket chain from the Japanese Yakuza mogul known as the "king of pachinko parlors."

Even if Suji-san died, his subordinates wouldn't relinquish control easily. Giancarlo had thoroughly checked out the three most potent Japanese lieutenants, and none had shown signs of willingness to immediately snatch power from the old man or aid a foreigner to fold Suji-san's businesses into those of crime bosses from other countries. But Suji's health issues might change that dynamic and bring one forward.

Giancarlo punched another speed-dial number and held the phone to his ear, waiting for the coded greeting. A woman's voice came on the line. When she passed the security tests, Giancarlo got right to the point.

"I'll send you a link when we're done the call," he said. "Suji had a heart attack and is in a hospital in Osaka. Do it in the hospital before they let him out. Call that Jap we used before. Tell her to be sure to mask the drugs to avoid detection. Have her take out the Korean woman too, but not at the hospital. Then send that couple in California who speak Japanese to Tokyo to find numbers two, three, and four. Be sure they have traffic accidents just like we talked about last year."

"When?" was the only question the woman asked.

"Suji, tomorrow night. To avoid suspicion, give the Korean woman a few days, but keep her under tight surveillance until your gal does the deed."

"Are you sure you want to do it right away if he's on his way out anyway?" she asked.

"I'm sure. Tomorrow night."

"Okay. I'll get it done. Are there any developments in Europe?"

"Not really. They still haven't found him, but I'm increasing the heat on Interpol. You heard anything?" Giancarlo asked with rekindled interest.

"About him, nothing. But we may have a line on the girl. One of our informants thinks she may be hiding in Germany, but he hasn't been able to get a location yet."

"That's possible. Knight had contacts in Germany. There might be one willing to help him or shelter the girl. Which informant gave you the tip?"

"The new one in the Netherlands. The one in their intelligence service. He overheard a conversation but hasn't been able to locate a file or anything concrete. It may be a solid lead or just a rumor. I've got him checking more." Her voice carried a tone of caution with just a tinge of optimism.

"Keep me informed." Giancarlo pressed the end button.

Appealing aromas of food from a kitchen outside his temporary office suddenly reminded Giancarlo he hadn't eaten for several hours. That day's transitory location was in one of New York's finest Italian restaurants in a city filled with them. Of course, the owner claimed he would be delighted to prepare his signature veal dish for Giancarlo and the two bodyguards. He asked only for a few minutes to move the people from the private room Giancarlo always preferred.

Graciously, Giancarlo told him to take his time. He had one more call to make from the office. From his briefcase, he selected another disposable phone. He had just decided that he'd like an after-dinner treat waiting for him when he arrived home in another couple hours. He never quite understood why, but the rush of a new opportunity always left him sexually aroused. He knew the perfect antidote.

TWENTY-FIVE

A house near Alportel, Portugal, Tuesday January 14, 2020

Katherine Page heard the approaching car first and jumped up from the table where the pair were enjoying a breakfast bowl of cereal and fruit. The sound of the tires against loose pebbles suggested the vehicle was already in the driveway, and she scurried around to clear Howard's side of the table. Brutus growled, then barked once.

"Heel," she hissed to Brutus. "Hide in my bedroom, under the bed," she ordered Howard as she swept dishes and cutlery from the table in one deft motion and dropped them in a sink just a few feet away.

"Now," she commanded in a stage whisper as Howard hesitated.

As he obeyed and dashed into her room, Katherine gathered up both cups of coffee and dumped them in the sink. She rinsed everything and wiped her hands dry on a towel before a polite knock sounded at the door.

Brutus barked, then sat silently just inside the door after Katherine touched his head once. She gingerly opened the door and looked out. An officer from the local police detachment in Alportel stood patiently, hands at his side, with a slightly bored expression.

"*Bom dia, Senhora* Page," the short man greeted her with a growing smile. "I'm sorry to bother you, but I'd like to ask you a few questions. May I step inside?" He looked warily at Brutus but maintained his calm demeanor.

"Of course," Katherine replied, turning to the dog before opening the door wider. "Heel."

"Have you had any visitors or seen anyone unusual in the area?" the man asked.

"Is there something wrong, *Senhor* Delgado? Your name is Delgado, isn't it?" Katherine asked, after regaining enough composure to recall the name of a man she had met formally only once or twice before.

"Yes, *Senhora*. Your memory serves you very well," the police officer replied with a broad smile and obvious pleasure at the recognition as he scanned the entire room for clues or evidence. "We're just looking for a fugitive from Spanish justice. I doubt he's in our area, but my bosses require me to canvass every home in my territory to see if anyone noticed anything unusual."

"Oh!" Katherine replied with both surprise and a little feigned trepidation. To subtly signal Howard as he lay in darkness under the bed, she raised her voice an octave as she asked, "Is this man considered dangerous?"

"How do you know I'm looking for a man, *Senhora* Page?"

"You may remember I'm a writer, *Senhor* Delgado." Katherine gave a broad smile of assurance. "Words are important to me and I listen carefully. Did I not correctly hear you say, 'I doubt he's in our area'?"

"Ah, yes. That's right, I did," the officer replied with a casual laugh. "It seems you really do listen carefully. But you haven't yet answered my question. Are your powers of observation as strong as your listening skills?"

"I hope so. Everything has been quiet and humdrum around this neighborhood. Great for writing though, I might add."

"Good. May I just take a quick look in each of your bedrooms, *Senhora*? Just to be sure you're not answering my questions under any sort of duress?" He raised his eyebrows and added a mischievous tilt of his head.

The policeman took a couple steps into Katherine's bedroom first, then looked around slowly and carefully. Satisfied, he stepped back outside and entered the room next door. Howard, Katherine and Brutus were all perfectly still as he completed his inspection.

"The man we're looking for is an American, *Senhora* Page, and he's very dangerous. It seems he's mixed up with some very nasty people and is accused of doing some awful things to people across the border in Spain and even up in the Netherlands. They say he's killed people. So, please be very careful. I guess your dog gives you some good protection. But don't take any chances. If you see anyone that resembles this man, please call us right away." He held out a color photograph of Howard.

"Certainly, I will." Katherine's voice projected an appropriate tone of concern and interest. "Thank you for letting me know, *Senhor* Delgado."

"The pleasure was mine, as always, *Senhora*." The policeman turned to leave, but hesitated. "May I ask you one last question before I leave? Do you usually use two bowls and two coffee cups in the morning?"

"I never use two in the morning, *Senhor*." Katherine didn't hesitate. "I'm afraid you see my less than perfect housekeeping. I have a terrible habit of eating a bowl of cereal and taking a cup of tea just before I go to bed at night. Last evening, I was a little lazy. The dishes are still there for me to wash and dry. Does this raise a concern for you, *Senhor* Delgado?"

"No. My sink often holds soiled dishes for a week!" he replied with a hearty laugh. "But what would you say if I asked to check your rooms one more time?"

"Please do," she said, with a broad sweep of her arm in the direction of the bedrooms.

"No. I'm sure you would tell me only the truth, *Senhora* Page," the local police officer said with a deferential bow of his head and a touch of a finger to his cap as he backed out the door. "Perhaps we can have a coffee together when you are in town one day."

Katherine's disarming smile imparted the only answer he needed.

TWENTY-SIX

Janet finished her morning stint of Spanish lessons and broke for lunch. The online instruction with *Rosetta Stone* had accelerated, and she now had no difficulty practicing Spanish conversation for hours at a time. Her confidence grew, delivery became more fluid, and her understanding was almost perfect.

Her impressive memory had carried her through all those political science courses at Columbia with honors. Now, she found the ability to remember virtually everything she heard or read prove more than useful as her Spanish vocabulary grew, and she grasped the grammar rules with surprising ease.

Downstairs, she found Klaudia glued to her large monitor, entranced with a BBC News feature. She waved Janet over to sit on a chair beside her and increased the volume.

"… the successful operator of an empire comprising pachinko parlors and supermarkets was a bachelor and had no known family. He is survived by long-time companion Eun Ae Kim, a South Korean citizen."

"What's up?" Janet asked as the talking head paused for breath between stories.

"It's big. This guy they're talking about, Suji, just died. He was one of the richest men in Japan and part of The Organization. He ran most of the pachinko parlors there," Klaudia explained. "I heard Fidelia describe him to the Interpol investigators before they let us go. His death is almost certain to cause some upheaval in The Organization."

"Why?"

"Like the announcer said, the guy had no family to take over. Fidelia's video testimony got his most important subordinates arrested by the Japanese authorities, but they couldn't—or wouldn't—arrest Suji. So, his new top lieutenants have all been in their roles for less than two years. There's no clear-cut successor. Fidelia told me if he ever died or was killed, there would be a bitter turf war for his part of The Organization. His pachinko parlors alone generate billions of dollars every year."

"So, guys like Giancarlo Mareno might try to seize even more power?"

"Almost certainly. It probably won't reduce the number of women he's ensnaring for his human-trafficking and prostitution businesses, but it might distract him a bit."

"Speaking of human trafficking, have you heard anything from the *Bundesnachrichtendienst*?" Janet pronounced the name of the German federal intelligence service almost perfectly.

"Yeah, my contact called this morning while you were studying. The algorithms I created to monitor WhatsApp and Instagram in Latin America have established a pattern. Something seems to be developing in Costa Rica. They want you to stay focused on building your language skills, but I think they'll create a Spanish profile for you on social media platforms and get you active before the end of the month. They're sending someone over next week to test your conversation skills."

"Wow! That's sooner than I expected. Do they think I'll be ready?" Janet asked.

"You're on Level 4, right? That's already using more vocabulary than an average fifteen-year-old girl in most Latin American countries. After your tests, they want you to focus on a few dozen popular expressions used by kids today. You might find yourself trying to dupe and trap the scum that prey on these kids as early as next month." Klaudia gave a satisfied grin.

She reached for her keyboard to turn off the BBC newscast when Howard Knight's image filled the screen.

"Interpol today issued an all-points bulletin for this man," the newscaster said. "He operates under multiple identities but was living in the Netherlands for the past two years under the name Joshua Benevolent. He was last seen in Ayamonte, Spain, and is wanted in connection with the vicious murder of two Americans traveling in Europe. The man is considered armed and very dangerous. If you should see him or have recently seen him, please contact your local police with details and do not try to apprehend him yourself."

Klaudia looked at Janet with an expression of amazement.

"That means he's probably still alive!" she whispered.

Janet remained speechless, unable to believe the possibility so easily. She started to sob, her entire body heaving and shuddering as it registered that the man who had given her so much love might actually still be alive.

That he might be wanted for murder meant only that he had found a way to escape the clutches of The Organization. At least for now.

Klaudia took a deep breath and wrapped both arms around Janet's shoulders in a warm embrace.

"I'll try to reach Fidelia. She might know something, and she'll want to hear this news if she doesn't already have something," she whispered to Janet as they clung to each other.

TWENTY-SEVEN

A house near Alportel, Portugal, Sunday January 19, 2020

Howard Knight carefully hid the freshly stolen and fully refueled Vespa scooter in a large culvert beside the road about three miles from Katherine Page's house. He checked in all directions before dragging over some recently trimmed olive tree branches to hide his prize possession. Satisfied a casual walker or driver would not easily spot the scooter, and also confident he could find it when he returned, Howard set out on foot.

The sun just peeked over the horizon with faint morning light, but early indications suggested beautiful weather for his last few hours in the Alportel area. A quick glance at his watch confirmed it was just after seven. He needed only a half hour or so to cover the distance to Katherine's place where he expected she'd probably have breakfast ready as they'd planned.

As he walked at a brisk pace, Howard listened intently for any sounds of a vehicle breaking the stillness of the rural area. The last thing he wanted was someone in a car to spot him, possibly disrupting the careful strategy of deception they had developed over the past week.

At first, they both panicked for a few minutes after the policeman visited Katherine's house and inspected the rooms only feet away from Howard's hiding spot under the bed. Instinctively, he was inclined to immediately get out of the house before the police returned. It was Katherine who thought more clearly and strategically. He chalked that up to her creative thinking as a writer.

"Of course, the policeman will be back. He scrutinized every detail of my house including my unwashed dishes. Once his superiors hear about the two bowls and two coffee cups in the sink of a person living alone, they'll send him back. You'll need to leave," she acknowledged. "But I think you'll have a better chance of escape if you create a diversion."

"A diversion? What sort of diversion?" Howard was intrigued, if wary.

"If you leave now and just head out in any direction, the police resources will be spread across the country and their chances of catching you will be high," she reasoned. "If you create a diversion and encourage the police to channel more resources into one area, you can escape in the opposite direction. They'll have fewer people there, and your chances of safe passage will improve."

Howard thought about the idea for a moment, started to reply, but took another few seconds to reconsider. He saw the logic.

"So, I find a way to deflect some attention away from here—maybe to the south—then I head north. Is that what you're thinking?"

"Exactly." She smiled, content he'd grasped her suggestion so quickly. "It has risks, of course. But everything you're doing is precarious, isn't that right?"

"But you've thought about a way I can mitigate those risks, haven't you?" Howard smiled in return.

Her scheme was a clever one. She had given it considerable thought before the policeman's visit and was able to articulate her ideas and recommended actions without hesitation. She described the fields he should cross, pointed out where he should join highway 270, and suggested where Howard would most likely find scooters that were easy to steal. He found it odd she had thought through such an elaborate scheme. Was this the way minds of all writers worked?

One glaring problem remained. Even though Katherine had offered to report her mobile phone had been stolen, then wipe all her data and let him use it for navigation, Howard realized authorities could track that device easily. If they knew where to look, they'd pinpoint his precise location in minutes. So, he ran his bizarre idea by her and she bought in before he even finished explaining it.

Just after dawn that long previous day, they climbed onto her scooter in the back yard. Katherine drove and Howard held on to her waist as she steered onto the paved road and barreled back toward Faro, a scarf around her neck blowing in the wind to partially cover Howard's face. He closed his eyes and hoped for the best the entire trip. As she glided to a stop at a decrepit shack on the road to the airport, he slowly looked around the vacant parking lot and untidy exterior. A tiny Vodafone sign peeked around a doorframe that looked as though it might collapse in a gentle breeze. Perfect.

Katherine strode confidently inside while Howard stood guard over the scooter, his head down and face partially covered by a shaded helmet visor. The store was open, but just barely. No potential customers were in sight in any direction. Howard counted the seconds. Remarkably, she returned before he reached five hundred, with a broad grin and two phones in her hand.

"The clerk saw no problem selling me a cheap throwaway phone with a cheap data plan," Katherine said with a conspiratorial grin. "When I asked him to remove the SIM card from my phone and install it in the throwaway, he looked a little puzzled. So I told him I wanted a way to keep an eye on you on your weekend away. He laughed and exchanged the SIM cards in an instant."

The previous night, Howard had executed their plan faithfully. He'd drawn some attention to himself wearing the brightly colored clothes Katherine provided. Then he stole the requisite number of scooters to create a trail, each theft location a bit closer to Tavira. He harbored no doubt the police in the region would be curious about the unusual thefts and notice the pattern of activity. Finally, he carefully hid the fully charged throwaway storing her personal SIM card on an easy-to-locate fence near a cell tower. Should they trace Katherine's phone, it would bring the police right to Tavira.

As he arrived at her house that morning and drew in the aroma of freshly prepared pancakes wafting through an open back door, Howard felt a strange sensation. Was it regret? Or something else?

"Your mission was a success?" she asked brightly as Howard stood outside the door, waiting for an all-clear on Brutus. Her hand rested lightly on the dog's head while he remained seated, upright, on the floor beside her, his tail trying to wag.

"I think so," Howard replied. "I have a magnificent new Vespa GTS300 stashed away down the road, and it's full of fuel and ready to go as soon as it's dark tonight."

"I can't believe I'm saying this, but I'm actually a little sorry to see you leave." She shrugged and smiled. "It's been an adventurous few days since you've been here, but I must admit I'm quite taken by your charm."

"I was thinking the same thing." Howard felt an unfamiliar hoarseness in his throat.

They chatted amiably through breakfast. Katherine brought him up to date on the news broadcasts she had monitored on TV and radio. Reports highlighted significantly increased police activity to their south and east with roadblocks on every highway and at many main intersections in the town of Tavira. Their plan seemed to be working already.

"It's probably better for you to get some sleep, now," Katherine announced without emotion when their coffee cups were empty. "With your injured fingers, I think you may find the drive tonight demanding."

TWENTY-EIGHT

Pierre Boivin couldn't believe the stupidity of the police officer from the little town of Alportel in Portugal. He had just learned the news over his phone from his peer in The Organization, Estavao Sereno, and he needed more answers.

"So, let me get this straight," Pierre started as tactfully as he could manage. "The *policial* noticed two cups and two cereal bowls in the sink of this single woman's kitchen, but he didn't ask to look in the closets or under the beds."

"He asked, and the woman gave permission, but no. He didn't think the woman would lie to him, so he left without checking the house thoroughly. We only found out about it yesterday when we called his boss to turn up the heat even higher," Estavao explained.

"Has he now realized the folly of his decision and gone back to the house to check again?" Pierre's tone remained civil, but his voice dripped with sarcasm.

"Of course. There was no sign of anyone other than the woman anywhere around the house. He claims he checked everywhere, even while the woman's huge dog stood watching him menacingly the entire time."

"So, that was the only possible lead the Portuguese police were able to turn up? Where do you go from here? I still think the chances he's in Portugal are much greater than Spain," Pierre said.

"You may be right. The same *policial* came back with one more small detail that might have some importance," Estavao offered. "He checked with one of the neighbors to see if he had seen anything amiss since his visit a week earlier. It turns out he did. A couple days after the first visit, a neighbor two houses down from the woman saw a stranger walking away from the neighborhood."

"Did the *policial* get a description of the guy?"

"Not a good one. He showed the fellow a photo of Knight, but the

111

neighbor claimed he was too far away to be sure. He really only saw the guy's back."

"Do they have a lead on this guy who was walking away?" Pierre wanted to know.

"Maybe. It seems the *policial* received a couple reports of a stranger hanging around the village of *Santa Catarina da Fonte,* and today they received a stolen scooter report. Apparently, someone matching Knight's description snatched it from the *Supermercado Barriga* in the same village. They've ordered another fifty *policial* to immediately report for duty in Tavira. They'll use that town as their base and fan out in every direction," Estavao confirmed.

"They have fifty people involved in the search. Is that enough? Are they serious?"

"I think so. Tavira only has a population of about twenty-five thousand people. The fifty they're sending are in addition to the two-hundred and fifty already searching. There's one other thing. They're checking out a phone they just found on a fence near Tavira. Regardless, the authorities think they'll find him within a day or two if he's in the area."

Satisfied, Pierre ended the call with another reminder for Estavao and his people to find Knight as quickly as possible. Giancarlo Mareno was pushing hard.

Should I use the guy at Interpol to do one more job? Deschamps was now far more pliable than before. He capitulated immediately and came onside with barely a whimper. Nadine had performed her task with aplomb.

Of course, the guy was almost drooling when she appeared in their living room that night with her transparent dress and nothing under it. She feigned surprise and made a credible attempt to cover her exposed private parts when she first saw Deschamps. But with Pierre's coy coaxing, she was soon fully exposed and letting the guy ogle her discreetly at every opportunity.

One drink did the trick. The tasteless little something Pierre added to his guest's glass of scotch on the rocks worked quickly. Any government official with better judgment would have probably left Pierre's lair immediately after the first drink. But this guy had deep-seated problems with both alcohol and women. Everyone knew that.

When Pierre noticed Deschamps' second drink was half empty, he responded to a pre-arranged call and left them alone in the room. While Pierre was away, Nadine did her work using another tampered drink followed by ample opportunity to examine every angle of her gorgeous body. When Pierre returned to the room, the guy's face was already flush, and his pants were unable to hide a growing erection.

According to Nadine, less than five minutes after Pierre announced that he needed to go out for a couple hours to deal with an important matter, she was completely undressed, and the guy was greedily licking every square inch of her body. By then, she'd activated the cameras and captured on video more than two hours of sex acts, complete with sound effects.

Her suggestions were whispered, so the microphone didn't pick them up clearly, but they were overt invitations for him to enter every orifice of her body. The fool thought he was in paradise and stopped only when he collapsed on the sofa in a drugged and drunken stupor.

Pierre and his bodyguard, Jean-Guy, had their first conversation with Deschamps early the next morning when he awoke, naked, on the sofa. When he meekly asked for his clothes, Pierre told him he had a video to watch first. They only needed to show him the first five minutes before he was blubbering and begging. "You will ruin me! Please."

"We don't intend to show it to anyone," Pierre assured him. "We want you to keep your job, happy marriage, and growing family all intact for a long time to come. As long as you do us an occasional favor, the video will stay locked in my personal safe here at the house. And to show you we want our relationship to be a happy one, Nadine here will even arrange for you to have a session with one of her girls every week, on the house. But if you fail to cooperate even once, this video will be delivered to the president of TV-5. Do we understand each other?"

Deschamps gave no verbal reply, but the dejected nod of his head was all the affirmation Pierre needed.

Giancarlo Mareno should have been delighted with the results, but he showed no emotion. Instead, he simply ordered Pierre to use the newfound leverage to get Interpol looking for Howard Knight. Make it the agency's number one priority. To add insult to injury, and while Pierre listened, Mareno instructed Nadine to keep sleeping with Deschamps for another few weeks. He wanted to keep the scum highly motivated.

Still stung from the affront, Pierre decided to let Deschamps just do his thing for a few more days. The tip from Portugal felt like it had some promise. His intuition seldom let him down, and Pierre became more determined to find and capture Howard Knight before Giancarlo Mareno could get his hands on him. The former financial genius of The Organization knew all the secrets, and Pierre needed Knight to make his own dreams come true.

TWENTY-NINE

Early in the frigid morning, Giancarlo fumbled with his personal key to the back door of the payday loan shop in a seedier part of Manhattan while his bodyguards kept watch in all directions. The Organization controlled and managed this operation. Giancarlo liked to drop in unannounced and poke around before they opened for business. That practice started a couple years earlier when he accidentally discovered the guy he had running the place was skimming a few thousand a month off the top.

The new manager seemed to understand the lethal consequences of such foolishness. So far, he had kept the books in good order, paid Giancarlo his monthly consulting fee in cash on time, and worked hard to grow the business with more suckers paying extortion rates of interest. Giancarlo still found it surprising how many people needed instant gratification for their silly wants. How could they be so willing to pay forty or fifty percent interest to the payday operation rather than manage their income within their means?

Using his massive right hand and a violent snap of the doorknob, Giancarlo broke the flimsy lock on the fragile door to a tiny cubicle the store manager called an office. His bodyguard, Luigi, also stepped inside. With one efficient swoop of his long arms, he gathered all the stacks of paper on the desk into one pile, about two-feet high, then dropped them as neatly as possible on the floor.

Giancarlo twirled the chair on casters like a toy and set down his more than three-hundred-pound frame with caution. "Remind Pascal to get a decent chair in here before I visit again," he said in a voice that boomed involuntarily.

"Right, boss," the bodyguard replied. "Here are the phones. They're ready to go." He plunked three disposable cell phones in the middle of the cleared desk. It was his job to transfer the memory from the previous days'

114

phones to the new ones—a responsibility he took seriously. A techie on the west coast had taught him how to capture all the data from one phone and install it on the new one so Giancarlo would have access to all his speed-dial numbers. Right after he transferred the data, Luigi smashed the old phones with a hammer, then tossed the pieces in three or more trash bins so even the remnants of the phones were disposed of separately.

The other bodyguard returned with coffee, steam rising from the cup in the morning's chill. Without a word to anyone, Giancarlo picked up the phone with a red sticker affixed to its back and punched in a code with four awkward stabs of his forefinger. He took a long gulp of the coffee while he waited.

When a woman said hello, he delivered the security question, and she responded with the correct password.

"Did we get everything done in Japan?" he asked.

"Suji-san died in hospital, as you probably read. His Korean comfort woman took a horrible fall from the penthouse apartment he left her and is no longer with us. Two of the three subordinates had unfortunate traffic accidents returning from Mount Fuji. Both were in the same car when the brakes unexpectedly malfunctioned and failed to navigate a turn on a precarious curve. Their car burned entirely after violent impact with the rocks several hundred feet below the road," the woman recited in a monotone.

"And the third lieutenant?"

"We have a problem. The one called Sugimori has captured the woman we used in the hospital. She called me this morning, crying. Sugimori insists you call him today. I'll text you the number she left. Apparently, his people have all three operatives we dispatched to do the deeds and they'll each start losing body parts if you don't call him immediately." A hint of urgency crept into her tone.

"What happened?" Giancarlo asked reflectively.

"We think Sugimori has someone in Japanese immigration. You know how thoroughly the Japanese control and document every visitor. The two we dispatched were actually first detained at exit immigration. One got a text out. We had no further word until the call from our woman this morning."

Giancarlo stood up and paced in a tight circle around the chair in the tiny office, thinking.

"We thought Sugimori was the dimmest bulb among the three Japanese bright lights. What's happened with our intelligence?" he wanted to know.

"I think the bartender in Tokyo may have fed us a false narrative," the female voice replied. "He also disappeared this week."

"What other resources do we have on the ground?"

"There's still the geisha in Hamamatsu and a techie in Osaka."

"Is Sugimori still in Tokyo?" Giancarlo wondered.

"I don't know. The number she gave me is from Tokyo, but it's a cell phone. Probably disposable."

"The geisha has some history with Sugimori. She helped us once before. Get her to Tokyo as soon as possible," Giancarlo commanded. "We'll need her feeding us information. Don't take no for an answer. And get the techie in Osaka to tap into Sugimori with that software the CIA uses—the concealed worm that detects specific names or phrases, and survives with all relevant data when they wipe clean their phones. Again, he'll probably protest, but use whatever leverage you need. We have to know Sugimori's whereabouts all the time, who he's talking with, anything related to you or me."

Giancarlo pressed the end button and called out to his bodyguard for another coffee. His next call would be even more crucial. He'd need to be beyond alert for every second of that conversation.

THIRTY

A house near Alportel, Portugal, Tuesday January 21, 2020

Brutus barked loudly twice, bounded from Katherine Page's bedroom, and parked himself facing the front door with teeth bared and haunches taut. Katherine was still waking up from the commotion, but she quickly pulled a floor-length nightgown over her naked body and moved to pat Brutus once on the head before she opened the door. It was the local police officer, and he stood erect with the outline of a sunrise behind him.

"*Bom dia, Senhora* Page," he greeted with a tip of his hat as he took one assertive step forward. "I'll need to ask permission to enter your home. We must talk immediately. May I come in?"

"Of course," she replied. "May I make a coffee for us both? I'm afraid you've caught me sleeping late this morning." She laughed easily as she motioned for the police officer to enter her home with the warmest welcome she could muster at that hour.

"Coffee, no thank you," the policeman replied once he closed the door behind him. "You go ahead and make yourself a cup. Perhaps I might take another look around your home while you do that?"

Without waiting for a response, the policeman strode toward the guest room and opened the partially closed door. He put one hand on the outside of his gun holster as he pushed the door fully open. Katherine watched from the corner of her eye as she inserted a pod and activated the Keurig.

First, he peeked around the door to the room to be sure there was no one else inside. He went immediately to the closet and found it held only a few hangers dangling from a rod. He pondered the bare mattress on the bed for several seconds. Then he dropped to his knees and peered under the bed, using a large flashlight he detached from his belt.

Satisfied, he went to Katherine's room and repeated the inspection process, first checking in her closet, then looking under the bed. This

117

room took a little longer as he took a moment to admire a few of her outfits hanging on the rod before he shifted them to one side. Brutus watched warily at Katherine's side, sitting with his bottom raised imperceptibly off the floor, ears pointed upward, and ready to pounce with the right command.

"Perhaps I will accept your offer of coffee, *Senhora* Page," he announced as he returned into the living area. "I didn't want to cause you any trouble, but I see you can make a cup without too much fuss."

"Of course," Katherine replied warmly and held the cup in her outstretched hand. "Here, take this one and have a seat at the table. I'll just take a moment to make another cup. What brings you out here this morning?"

"Still looking for that mysterious fugitive from the killings over in Spain I'm afraid. My supervisors have received information he might be in this area. Have you seen or heard anything since my last visit, *Senhora* Page?"

"Well there was something curious last night," Katherine said with what she hoped was her most thoughtful expression. "I heard Brutus bark twice like he did when you came this morning. It was just after I went to bed, at about midnight. I looked out the windows but didn't see anyone. A few minutes later, my neighbor Costa called. He wanted to know if I saw someone running from my house toward the road."

"And what was your answer?" The policeman's expression was stern.

"I told him about Brutus barking, but I couldn't see anyone when I looked outside. Costa told me he had been sitting in his backyard, enjoying a beer or two, when he thought he saw a man running up the hill from my house. A few moments later, he heard a scooter start-up in the distance and roar off. He said it sounded like the scooter was traveling south as he heard it go around the curve and then fade into that direction. Maybe it would be more helpful for you to speak with *Senhor* Costa," Katherine added.

The policeman tried to digest this information. He stared at Katherine, his expression still somber. He took a breath as though about to say something, then apparently thought better of it. Katherine became uncomfortable during this long pause.

"I discovered one other curious detail this morning," she volunteered. "No matter where I look in the house, I can't find my mobile phone."

"*Senhora* Page," he said after another long pause. "How often do you wash your guest-room bedsheets?"

"I don't know," she said cautiously. "I've never really thought about it."

"Would you typically wash the linen after a guest leaves?"

"Well yes," she said after a short hesitation. "But I also wash them once a month or so to keep them fresh. They collect dust and tiny mites if they're not laundered, you know."

"And last night you decided to wash them and leave them to dry outside."

"Yes, and I forgot to bring them in again." She realized where he was headed.

"*Senhora* Page," the police officer said with a pained expression. "There has been no rain in this area, but your guest room sheets are still very damp outside. I'm afraid you'll need to come with me to the station in town. I think we should speak with my supervisor."

THIRTY-ONE

Nadine Violette probably would not have made this call even a month earlier. Back then, she accepted her lot in life. She was a slave, but a slave with some privileges. Pierre Boivin trusted her with control over the women, and she made sure they were at least well cared for, if not fairly.

People looking at her in a restaurant or store as she wore the latest fashions and luxury labels never imagined she was *une femme contrôlée*. Pierre let her use his private helicopter to travel throughout France. She felt sort of special with thirty- or forty-minute flights between most of her working stops. The bodyguards not only kept an eye on her, they actually protected her from everyone but Pierre. And the house they lived in was far more luxurious than she'd ever dreamed possible growing up in Martinique.

Until a few weeks ago, she had imagined a lifetime with Pierre Boivin. They'd never get married. She realized that. But she found his lovemaking tender and passionate in ways she only dreamed of while she serviced hundreds of men during her more than three-year incarceration. She believed things were actually changing for her, that life with Pierre was something more than merely satisfying his weird sexual desires.

The way he displayed her had always been troubling. When he demanded she wear transparent outfits that concealed nothing, it demeaned her. At social events, she watched him strut about with his chest puffed out while every male in the room ogled her and secretly craved a few minutes with her in bed. But their sex afterward was *merveilleux*. His lovemaking would always be slow and gentle after he sensuously removed what little she was wearing.

Pierre always knew exactly where to kiss and touch and when to linger. He knew just the right amount of pressure to apply to bring her to incredible orgasms over and over again. His staying power those nights was unbelievable. His penis often remained erect for hours and he too climaxed more than once. He gave her the impression she was someone special in his life.

When Pierre accepted—without any resistance—Giancarlo's disgusting order for her to sleep with Deschamps, it all changed. She knew then she was only special to Pierre as long as Giancarlo permitted it. Nadine thought it through on several helicopter flights between visits to her girls. She weighed all the factors that might influence her future. Then she decided to whom she must remain loyal in the end.

"You were right, Giancarlo," she said after the security code protocol was complete. "He's trying to go around you. I heard him speak with Estavao Sereno today. They got a tip on that guy the police in Portugal are pursuing for you. Pierre told Sereno to keep the info to himself. He didn't want you to know about the new development. Pierre said he alone would decide when to bring you into the loop."

"Okay," Giancarlo said. "And what was Sereno's reaction?"

"At first, he protested. Then Pierre shouted a little and reminded Estavao that he owed something to Pierre, something really important. Estavao caved and promised Pierre he wouldn't let you know."

"Okay. Good work." Their conversation ended. As usual, there was no goodbye. He didn't tell her what she should do next. Most importantly, Giancarlo gave no indication he might now get her out of her current position. She could feel storm clouds gathering.

Nadine had made the call to Giancarlo on a cheap disposable phone he'd given her in Martinique. She usually kept it hidden in her private locker at the gym but brought it with her today, because he insisted she use only that phone whenever they spoke. Now, she wondered why. Giancarlo was probably recording everything anyway.

Might he also have intended to learn other information about Pierre, too? Was he also trying to secretly collect other information through her? Unquestionably, with trouble brewing between the two, she was caught uncomfortably in the middle.

After making that call from a locked and secluded bathroom in one of their apartments used for prostitution, she finished her day of inspections and pep talks with the girls of Paris Nord on schedule. Then, she used Pierre's helicopter for the short flight from Orly airport to Aix-en-Provence. Her bodyguards saw her home safely with a few hours left before Pierre usually arrived. She decided to risk it. From a small envelope buried deep in her closet, she took the entire five hundred euros she had squirreled away over the past year.

She slipped out the rear entrance of their home, her head covered and wearing large dark glasses. She walked briskly down the alley next to their apartment building and came out on a different street. There, she spotted a taxi stand and got into a vacant car as quickly as possible, her head still down.

She gave the driver an address. It wasn't her ultimate destination but would be close enough to save time and avoid detection. They arrived within only a few minutes, and she paid the driver with a generous tip. Then she made sure he drove off before heading along the road to the tiny shop where she could buy her first personal phone.

Nadine bought a disposable one with a rechargeable SIM card and fifty euros of talking time. The sales guy explained how she could add additional minutes as needed. She now had the means to make private calls, and she breathed deeply as she savored the sense of freedom. But almost immediately, she worried about where she could conceal the device so neither Pierre nor his spies and cronies could find it. Somehow, she must find a way. The way things were going, her life might depend on it.

THIRTY-TWO

Valladolid, Spain, Wednesday January 22, 2020

His goal was to reach the town of Lourdes in France. When he and Katherine plotted their elaborate strategy to get him there, Howard Knight had snorted out loud when he realized the irony. His destination, just across the southern border with Spain, was the home of reputed miracles, a place where the ill and infirm came from all over Europe seeking a divine cure. For some time, he'd no longer believed a deity existed—and he surely wasn't headed there expecting a miracle—but he might well need some extraordinary help to escape his current tight spot with the police and The Organization.

Their plan seemed sound when he first set out two nights earlier. He'd steal a new scooter every night and ride in a north-easterly direction using secondary roads. Scooters were better than cars, because the *policia* focused more attention on solving car thefts than the cheaper two-wheeled vehicles. Travel time would be limited to four hours, starting in the wee hours each morning at about one o'clock and finishing by five. Katherine read somewhere that fewer police were on duty in Portugal during those four hours than at any other time of the day.

At the end of his ride each morning, Howard scouted for, then stole, a different scooter. He next searched for a secluded spot where he could hide both the bike and himself from passersby during the daylight hours. Dutifully, he selected one protein bar from the backpack Katherine had given him and ate it just before sleeping each day. He wolfed down another right after he awoke and relished one last bar just before setting out under the cover of darkness. That meant he survived on about one thousand calories a day and was hungry all the time.

He fought off the urge to eat by thinking about the pain he would have endured if he was still in the custody of Giancarlo and his thugs. For the first couple days, it was amazing how a few seconds thinking about dismemberment and torture diverted his mind from a few hunger pangs. But water was still a problem. During his waking hours, Howard carefully sought out sources of water and drank as much as possible. He grimaced and scrunched up his nose when he thought about the bacteria and other impurities he might be ingesting from the rivers and streams where he found his supply.

He had made it this far only because Katherine had been surprisingly generous after they discussed his escape plan. After extracting his promise to destroy it when he arrived in France, she deleted the small amount of data and few photos her phone contained before she handed it to a shop clerk to swap in the SIM card she'd bought. Helpfully, she had also shown him how to use the map apps.

After the phone was ready, she went to her bedroom closet where she apparently had a hidden safe. When she returned to the kitchen, she handed him fifty euros in small bills for fuel. They would attract less attention she pointed out. She also brought out a large backpack with two external pouches for water bottles. From a cupboard, she blew the dust off an entire box of protein bars she'd been saving for an emergency.

"You can repay me someday when things are a little more stable for you," she said with an optimistic grin. But her soft brown eyes betrayed her tone. They didn't seem to project fear exactly. Instead, Howard sensed apprehension mixed with a certain sadness. After only a few seconds, she had cleared her throat and quickly changed the subject back to what she called "the grand escape."

When they finished talking that day, Katherine encouraged him to get some sleep before he headed out. She touched his forearm lightly and held it there for just a second or two more than necessary. For just an instant, her eyes displayed some other emotion. Howard couldn't be sure. Was it a hint of affection?

He never found out. When she woke him up about midnight for a last meal before his departure, she leaned over the bed to shake his shoulder. As his eyes opened, it was clear she was wearing nothing on her upper body beneath her partially open robe. Howard peeked inside and saw two perfectly formed breasts with nipples aroused. When he shifted his gaze to her eyes, Katherine quickly closed the opening and drew the strap tight around her waist.

"There will be none of that tonight," she admonished and blushed as she spun away from the bed and rushed to the stove in the kitchen.

Currently, Howard was midway between the towns of *Salamanca* and *Valladolid* in Spain on a third night of riding. Bitterly cold, wet weather characterized each ride. He wore a helmet that kept the rain off his head but had only a light jacket over his shirt. Both proved to be inadequate protection from the elements. His jeans became drenched with the spray from puddles, exacerbating the effects of the miserable weather.

The cloth gloves Katherine handed him as an afterthought as she said goodbye served little purpose. At first, the material absorbed some of the scooter's vibration that sent repeated shots of pain up his injured hand. After they became soggy, the dampness seemed to intensify the discomfort in his left hand, but he continued to wear them because it made it a little easier to wipe the visor of his helmet from time to time.

The rainfall continued to pelt down on that helmet, warning him the day would undoubtedly be another saga of wet clothes and grungy shoes. For sleeping, Howard was sure he'd find another sheltered location to be out of the rain. But the constant dampness in the air meant his clothes never had adequate time to dry. He made a mental note to avoid northern Spain in January in the future.

As he motored along the deserted country road on another stolen scooter at three o'clock in the morning, he spotted flashing blue lights far on the horizon. He reflexively touched the brakes and gradually came to a complete stop. He felt an involuntary shiver as he considered his options.

He took a long look all around him in the darkness but saw no farmhouses or roadside shacks. The last crossroad was several miles back, with no sign of another ahead.

Carefully, he disembarked from the scooter and laid it flat on the ground beside the road. Then he took a few steps toward a farmer's field and noticed a wide culvert with water trickling out toward the ditch.

He checked the height. Bent over, he could wheel the scooter through the opening and by the faint moonlight he saw a tree-sheltered clearing on the other side high enough to provide some protection from the rain. He lugged the scooter through the tunnel and up the grade, then dragged his left shoe over the tire tracks to make his trail less obvious.

A pungent stench accosted his senses almost immediately. Howard crinkled his nose and sniffed to locate the offensive odor. Just feet away, he discovered the culprit. It gave off a smell so powerful he almost gagged when he bent over to inspect it. A decomposing corpse of a rodent or other small animal was covered in flies and maggots, and who knows what else? Should he simply move on to another location?

No, it was too risky to continue. He'd simply hunker down out of sight for the day and carry on tomorrow.

Looking around the site, Howard spotted a tall tree on higher ground. It had no leaves on it in January, of course, but the thick lower branches still broke the rainfall to some extent. It trickled and dripped off the branches rather than steadily pouring down. Curling up against the latest stolen scooter, Howard slipped off his backpack and reached in for his ritual protein bar.

Of course, the wrapper was wet. Rainfall had been so consistent during his ride that night, water had seeped through the protective outer shell and a small puddle collected on the bottom of the bag. Food for the next day would be decidedly soggy.

Settled in under the tree, with his hunger as great as ever, Howard tried to sleep. Despite overwhelming fatigue, and with the added distraction of the putrid odor of the decaying vermin, his mind continued to race. The unexpected change of plans and shortened ride left him with too much time to make mental notes and consider his predicament. The evolving prognosis for his eventual escape had grown increasingly doubtful.

This whole thing was a long shot, and he had realized that from the moment he plunged into the water off Isla Canela. But survival was the ultimate motivator, and Howard was determined to stay motivated. He drew on pleasant thoughts about Janet, reminisced about some of their happiest times, and dreamed of an eventual reunion. She was a keeper.

After a while, he drifted onto pleasant thoughts about cruising in the warm Caribbean again, and imagined delicious meals he'd eat in gourmet restaurants if he made it. He convinced himself that somehow he'd find a way to stay alive and beyond the grasp of those who pursued him. Eventually, mental peace returned, no matter how temporary it might be.

However, in the days to come, he expected to still harbor doubts every few hours about his ability to get to his ultimate destination. The outcome was not entirely within his control. He depended on the aid and goodwill of others, and their help was far from a sure thing. Those doubts intensified his fears about what could happen if he didn't make it.

THIRTY-THREE

Pierre Boivin regretfully hoisted himself from his side of their imported king-sized bed early in the morning. He glanced at the still-sleeping Nadine with a rueful smile. *Damn, she was good under the covers!*

Unfortunately, she was also becoming a problem. The day before, one of the bodyguards reported her taking unusual amounts of private time in the bathroom, possibly talking to someone on a phone. Covertly, Pierre had rummaged through her clothes and possessions for clues and discovered her new unauthorized disposable phone hidden on the top shelf of his little-used library.

When he confronted her with the evidence, she pleaded innocence. "I only wanted to have a phone I could call my own," she claimed tearfully. When he demanded to know who she was talking to on the phone, she maintained she hadn't used the phone yet. She was only saving it for a special occasion, maybe an opportunity to arrange a surprise for his birthday or some other special event.

He checked the SIM card on an electronic reader. No time had been used. Perhaps she was telling the truth. Regardless, he couldn't allow her to take such liberties as buying her own phone and having conversations he couldn't monitor. That could be just the opening she needed to gradually seek more independence. So, he smashed the phone to pieces while she watched, shredding the SIM card separately for dramatic effect.

Next, Pierre ordered her to undress. Then he summoned the bodyguard who had astutely reported the offense. He invited the fellow to have fun with her while he watched. To reinforce his message, he made a video of their sexual liaison and took particular delight in her performing oral sex on the over-sized member of his bodyguard. He zoomed in with the phone camera, and it served to arouse him more than usual. As soon as the guard ejaculated, Pierre dismissed him and instructed Nadine to clean up and then do him. She performed masterfully for more than two hours before they both collapsed in fatigue.

He grimaced as he finished dressing. Even while Nadine had so skillfully serviced him, Pierre had already decided to sell her. Something about her expression when he announced his discovery of her phone caused him concern.

And he knew a willing buyer. Sugimori, The Organization guy responsible for pachinko parlors in Japan, had once offered to buy her when Pierre was finished. He was always looking for more women of color for his best clients, and Pierre had recently received a message to phone him. He made a mental note to discuss the terms and timing of a sale when he returned that call.

In the kitchen, Pierre made a cup of coffee in the Nespresso machine and hit speed dial for his Portuguese counterpart, Estavao Sereno.

"Any luck finding Howard Knight?" Pierre asked without saying hello.

"None," Estavao replied tersely. "I just finished a call with my contact in the national *policia*. He checked all the local police reports during the night, but they found nothing from the roadblocks. He also said he's getting lots of heat from above about using so many resources that aren't producing any productive results. He wants to give it up."

"Too bad. I've got the Spanish guys involved now, and we're going to find Knight no matter how much it costs," Pierre vowed. "Tell me again what the *policia* got from the woman."

"Like I told you already, she finally broke when she failed the lie detector test. She cried and apologetically pleaded for understanding," Estavao explained patiently. "She claimed the guy threatened her and her dog if she told the *policia* anything, but the lie detector test showed a negative about that. She lied about her phone too. She claimed that she lost it, but they're sure she gave it to the guy. They eventually found it down near Tavira where they were concentrating their resources. The lie detector was also negative about her claim he was headed to Africa by way of Gibraltar. The *policia* are only sure Knight spent at least one night in her home and probably took off the night before they picked her up for questioning."

"So, the *policia* are following my instructions? They're focusing their search in the opposite direction, to the north?" Pierre wanted to know.

"Yeah. They took all but a skeleton staff from Tavira and moved them north to the border with Spain. They're monitoring the woman's phone twenty-four seven and they've put twenty-four-hour roadblocks on the highways to Spain. The truckers are really pissed off. Line-ups extend for miles sometimes," Estavao complained. "They're even getting calls from some politicians."

"We'll get him soon, don't worry. How about our friend in Spain? Did he get the roadblocks in place there?"

"He did and they also produced no results. There were promising reports of a couple stolen scooters near the towns of *Badajoz* and *Salamanca* near the border. But the roadblocks are down this morning. My guy doesn't have anyone in a position of power in the provincial government. The higher-ups there countermanded his orders. The barriers came down at five this morning, and he won't be able to put them up again right away. If Knight has already left Portugal—which the *policia* think is very possible—we don't have a way to trap him in Spain."

"Okay, Juan Suarez has someone in the *Guardia Civil*. We'll get the roadblocks up again in the rural areas at least," Pierre replied confidently.

"You know I'm doing everything I can to help you here." Estavao's tone hardened. "But I'll only be able to keep this search going for another day or two. My contacts are already squirming. They're getting uncomfortable questions from above. We might need to find another strategy to draw him in."

"I'll talk to Juan Suarez in Spain this morning."

But there was one more pressing call that Pierre wanted to handle first. After a second cup of coffee, he called Japan.

Initially, Sugimori expressed some interest in Pierre's offer to sell Nadine. The Japanese Yakuza crime boss liked the photos he had received by text and agreed she was a girl in her prime. They chatted casually about her sexual expertise and laughed often and easily as they drew comparisons. After a few minutes, Pierre expected his Japanese counterpart to ask the selling price. Instead, his tone turned serious and he shifted the subject.

"I'm interested, and we can talk more about your delightful little slut, but first I want you to know why I requested this call," Sugimori said. "Can I trust you to keep our call completely confidential?"

"Of course."

"We should plan the strategy for a meeting I'm going to arrange with Mareno in Germany next week. I'd like you to attend. You once told me you're not happy with the control Giancarlo Mareno exerts on your enterprises in France. I want you to know we in Japan are also dissatisfied. We pay Mareno far too much for his protection and access to American authorities. I expect you feel the same way." Sugimori paused, waiting for a reply.

After thinking about it for only a few seconds, Pierre answered.

"We all complain about sending too much money to the American boss. We pay far more than his services are worth, but he has the power. Do you think he'll willingly negotiate a change to our relationship?"

"Not willingly. But we found a gap in his usual invincibility," Sugimori said. "Despite his penchant for secrecy, multiple throwaway phones, and a different office every day, my people found a way to penetrate his invisible armor using advanced technology. We have a recording of every conversation he's had in the past two months. We know it was he who ordered Suji-san's murder, and we've also learned he has you in his crosshairs."

Shocked, Pierre managed to sputter a retort that he'd need some evidence of that. Sugimori played a taped conversation between Giancarlo Mareno and Pierre's trusted bodyguard, Jean-Guy Gagnon. The conversation was recent, and the information Mareno demanded of his subordinate seemed both intrusive and inappropriate. Further, Jean-Guy had kept the conversation secret.

Pierre's face reddened and his anger surged. His first instinct was to curse loudly and find something to break, but he thought better of it and restrained himself until Sugimori spoke again.

"Not only are you in his crosshairs, we think he's planning your downfall as we speak. Unless you and I get together and figure out how to contain him, you probably won't make it home from the meeting in Germany. I might also meet misfortune."

"What do you have in mind?"

Sugimori outlined his strategy over the next fifteen or so minutes with Pierre asking only questions for clarification. It was complicated, and the outcome was certainly not assured, but as the Japanese crime boss laid out his initial thoughts, Pierre became more convinced than ever the timing was right. They'd meet Sunday in Munich to fine tune the details.

"I'll buy your girl if you want. But I'll just send her on to the Saudis. They might pay more if you deal with them directly." To end their call, the Japanese Yakuza leader helpfully provided the private telephone number of a Saudi prince who might be interested.

THIRTY-FOUR

New York, New York, Wednesday January 22, 2020

Before he accepted the call, Giancarlo Mareno knew she would plead with him to phone Sugimori. He'd already seen the two gruesome video clips she sent overnight. They were disturbing.

Both operatives sent to deal with Suji-san's subordinates had been detained in Japan. The videos depicted a hooded person severing their forefingers. One lost a thumb as well. Both screamed in agony, then tearfully looked into the camera and pleaded with Giancarlo to call Sugimori before they lost more body parts.

"Were you able to reach him?" the woman asked without emotion after the security protocols were complete.

"Not yet. If he plans to become Suji-san's replacement in Japan, he'll need to learn patience," Giancarlo replied more calmly than he felt.

"You know best. But those injuries have finished the careers of two skillful technicians. Neither will be able to perform the delicate tasks they handled previously, and it's not easy to find new ones." Her tone grew more assertive. "The Japanese guys sent me another text message a few minutes ago, threatening to castrate the male tonight if you don't call."

"Do we know where Sugimori is or where he has the hostages holed up?"

"I received word from our plant that he's back in Tokyo mustering support from all factions," the woman replied "He's making good progress formalizing alliances and getting pledges of loyalty. Our contact thinks the others are all falling into line since his main rivals had unfortunate car accidents in the mountains. According to our spy, his torture of our operatives is admired among the Yakuza and seems to be winning over any holdouts."

"His lackeys might get some excitement from his defiance—and we probably need to keep the bastard for a while—but I want you to look for a replacement we can promote with a minimum of fuss when I decide to even the score. For now, loop Sugimori in through your location so our call won't be recorded or traced. I'll keep this number free until you're ready," Giancarlo instructed.

He focused on a computer spreadsheet for almost a half-hour before his phone rang and he heard a Japanese voice ask, "Is there anyone there?"

"It's me," Giancarlo said in the tone of voice he used to let people know he was pissed. "And if you touch one more body part of my guys over there, you'll never sleep again. Before you can blink, I'll have a swarm of guys chasing a bounty of more money than you might imagine for your dead body. Think about the take from your best pachinko parlor for a year. You think that might incent a few people to hand me your head on a platter?"

There was no immediate reply, so Giancarlo assumed his aggressive opening had served the intended purpose of unsettling the unfailingly polite fellow. He'd wait until Sugimori regained his composure. It didn't take as long as he expected.

"I'll overlook your threats this time, Giancarlo," Sugimori said quietly. "You did us a favor. We could have taken out your operative long before she administered the toxin on Suji-san if we chose to. We also know all about your relationship with his Korean comfort woman and the geisha who feeds you information too."

The Yakuza leader paused for effect and took a deep breath before he continued.

"We know the location of the woman who arranged this call. And we're watching her home right now. We also know you're taking this call from the back office of FX Global in Grand Central Station, where you arrived at 8:53 this morning. We don't fear your bold threats, and we are interested in continuing to work with you. But there will need to be some changes," he said in an increasingly confident tone.

Giancarlo processed the information, the guy's manner, and several undesirable implications. His brain worked fast to reach conclusions. He decided to de-escalate their war of words before he made a mistake in anger. Sugimori evidently expected that reaction and made no further comment right away.

"So, you're planning a rebellion," Giancarlo said.

"I'm not sure what you want to call it, but our relationship will have to change." Sugimori had returned to his polite tone. "My people are dissatisfied with the percentage we pay you. They think Suji-san made a big mistake when he agreed to it. They also think he blundered when he agreed to limit our involvement in America to a single supermarket chain. We're getting squeezed and need to be able to grow."

"Suji-san got Jeffersons Stores only because I loaned him the money," Giancarlo growled.

"We realize that. And it's precisely because we are sending too much cash to you that we have concerns. That's what we want to discuss, and we think we should have a personal meeting with you. We're not looking for a war, although we're prepared for one. Instead, I'd like to meet with you and resolve our differences."

Giancarlo gazed off into space for several seconds to mull over his options. He had a sip of coffee, cleared his throat to sound less gruff, and stood up before he carried on.

"We can talk," Giancarlo conceded. "When do you want to come to New York?"

The Yakuza leader dug in almost immediately, apparently determined to win even the small victories.

"No, not New York. Let's meet in Germany. I've never seen Munich and my people have arranged a beautiful secure spot in the mountains south of the city. Let's meet there next Monday."

The young guy was smart. He chose not only a neutral site but one far from Giancarlo's direct influence. He probably realized The Organization in Germany was one of their weakest links. Their influence with government and police authorities there was paltry compared to most countries.

Giancarlo was not only accustomed to winning arguments, he usually chose the subject. Sugimori's confident insolence tested his patience, but Giancarlo remained inclined to de-escalate the discussion for now. There would be ample opportunity to exact revenge and teach the rookie leader a lesson.

"I can clear my calendar for Monday. But why don't we meet at my place in Spain? The weather's much better there," Giancarlo replied with a chuckle to sweeten the offer.

"I prefer Germany." Sugimori's confidence was unwavering.

"Okay, enjoy Munich on the weekend and let me know where you'd like to meet," Giancarlo conceded.

"We'll deliver the details to the woman within the next fifteen minutes. Come with only three bodyguards. We expect a fruitful discussion."

The bastard gave no formal goodbye and hung up before Giancarlo could.

THIRTY-FIVE

Burgos, Spain, Thursday January 23, 2020

Howard awoke from intermittent sleep feeling troubled. It was more than a sense of malaise. For three successive nights he'd ridden the cursed stolen scooters through miserable weather. It drizzled almost constantly, and the temperatures hovered somewhere between freezing and barely livable. The chill deep inside his bones never abated. Even when he found a dry bridge to sleep under, his clothes remained damp until he set out in the middle of the next night.

Hunger and thirst poignantly focused his attention on the gravity of his situation. The carefully rationed supply of protein bars Katherine Page had sent with him was exhausted and the money for fuel gone. He hadn't eaten for almost a day. His only drinking water was carefully scooped from the cleanest spot in any moving creeks or rivers he found, and he expected any day he'd start to show symptoms of dysentery or something worse. He'd reached his breaking point. He'd had enough.

Howard hadn't shaved since his Christmas Day escape from Isla Canela in Spain. Without a mirror, he expected his unkempt beard would be more than spotted with gray and imagined his scruffy appearance might offend even the most tolerant of Spanish citizens. According to his map app, he still needed another two nights of riding to reach his target of Lourdes in France.

Admittedly, his judgment could be questioned. But that happened when any man reached his breaking point. He didn't deliberate very long and didn't seriously consider alternatives. Instead, he decided to break into another house, find some clothes, steal some food and use a razor. He considered his options. Take advantage of the afternoon light and risk discovery? Or was it better to ride the scooter to the next major town and try to get into a house at three or four in the morning when any residents would likely be sleeping the soundest?

In more relaxed times, he'd once read an article about how the Spanish lifestyle had changed with the current generation. Spain had never fully recovered from the brutal economic recession a decade earlier, but the cost of living had remained quite high. Most young couples worked long hours at two or more jobs, with both partners often away from their homes. Only fast-food and carryout restaurants had truly benefited. That quick thought process led Howard to conclude it might be better to do his break-in sooner rather than later.

He glanced at his watch, saw it was about three in the afternoon, and slung his knapsack over his shoulder. Within minutes, he wheeled the scooter up the side of a ditch from its hiding spot, hit the starter switch, and headed along the secondary roads his phone map identified as the best route to the town of Burgos. Partway there, Howard spotted the enclave he wanted. He looked down from the side of the road toward a shallow valley where he noted a half-dozen newer houses in a cluster, with modern designs and many glass windows, the kind of dwellings young, upwardly mobile professionals liked to buy.

He wheeled the scooter from the road and hid it among a grove of small trees out of the sightline of passing drivers. As he walked casually toward a band of more mature trees halfway down the gradual incline, he scoured the horizon for movement. He looked into windows of the homes for any obvious motion or sign of people or animals. When he was confident there was none, he casually slid to the ground, stretched out on his stomach, and observed the individual houses.

He more meticulously studied every window from his perch. A house at one end of the street was actually occupied. He could see that now. A television image reflected from a hallway mirror. He shifted his focus to a stone-faced home at the opposite end of the street. For more than an hour, he watched and listened for any sign of life. Satisfied no one was home, he went back up the hill and headed to a wooded area beside the road about a half-mile from the buildings.

There, Howard disappeared from view among the trees and walked for several hundred yards to position himself where he could approach the enclave without attracting attention. Before he left the woods, he spent another few minutes checking for movement in the target house.

He covered the few yards of the clearing quickly and ducked close to the building to make it harder for someone to see him from the street or another house. There, he again listened carefully for the sounds of dogs or people. He breathed in deeply, trying to detect scents that might suggest cooking or other activity taking place inside the house. Of course, he would have preferred to enter the homes by picking door locks, but the small subdivision afforded excellent visibility in all directions from either the back or front doors. Howard improvised.

With a large stone he had uncovered in the wooded area, he broke a bedroom window at the end of the house. He used his backpack to muffle the sound of breaking glass and quickly removed the remaining large shards to permit entry. He squeezed his trim frame through the opening gracefully and landed on the broken glass inside the room with care. Then he inspected the place. He checked all three bedrooms, the living area, and kitchen. All clear.

First, he headed to the bathroom and grinned at his good fortune. The guy who lived here had a beard. Right on the counter, Howard spotted an electric shaver with a row of attachments neatly arranged on a shelf above. He shaved his beard completely and rinsed the sink several times to clear the mounds of accumulated residue. It was far more gray than brown, he noted, as he wiped the appliance free of any fingerprints.

Next, he raided the kitchen and found snacks that he jammed into his backpack. Then, he rummaged through the closet of the master bedroom, found a pair of jeans that were too large but would work with a belt drawn tightly and the legs rolled up. He found a sweatshirt that was again too large but workable. He also picked out a bulky wool sweater that he pulled over the sweatshirt effortlessly.

Finally, he checked the top drawers in the main bedroom. As expected, he found a small cache of euros, all small denomination bills. A quick count confirmed they totaled about one hundred. He slipped them into the front pocket of his newly acquired jeans. A glance at his watch just before he climbed out through the window confirmed he'd been in the house less than seven minutes.

Retracing his steps to the wooded area, Howard didn't look back until he was safely shrouded by the trees and undergrowth. He stifled his curiosity to know when the residents of the house would return home and waited only long enough to let his heartbeat slow down before he headed back to the scooter. Undoubtedly, the owners would call the police and report the illegal entry and theft immediately upon discovery, so he needed to hit the road.

Within five miles, he spotted a gas station and pulled in to fill up. Clean-shaven and reasonably well-dressed, Howard was now more relaxed about making a purchase. Then he remembered the security cameras. He decided not only to keep his helmet on while he paid for his purchase but also to pull up his jacket collar to cover his neck and chin.

Inside, he spoke Spanish fluently and passed scrutiny as a budget-minded tourist. Soon, the small gas tank was full, and he was on the route toward *Burgos*, complete with a chocolate bar and bottle of water. To better avoid detection if the house-theft was reported, he changed direction at the first intersection and headed east before following another secondary road north.

Three hours later, Howard entered the small town of *Burgos* and navigated to the stately church *Arco de Santa Maria*, where he parked the scooter. He carried his backpack and helmet as he headed south along the street near the river. Next, he passed a nearby park and saw no one in the area, so he casually dropped his helmet from a bridge and watched the current carry it downstream until it sank.

At the *Plaza Vega*, Howard found a take-out restaurant selling empanadas and wolfed down three with another bottle of water. Then, he walked at a leisurely pace, as a tourist might, in the darkness for over two hours. He passed the university, went south to the Lidl store where he bought more bottled water, and wended his way back through the town to the bus station. He arrived fifteen minutes before a scheduled midnight departure, bought his ticket using some of the remaining cash, then boarded the bus along with four other passengers for the overnight journey to Lourdes.

He realized the risks he was taking. Buses carried other sometimes curious people and could be stopped easily in a roadblock. But the grind of the nightly scooter rides had exhausted his spirit. Should misfortune occur, he'd just have to find a way to deal with it.

Howard boarded last so he could get a good look at each of the passengers who boarded ahead of him. There were three men and a woman traveling together. They joined another handful of passengers already on the bus from previous stops on the protracted journey.

There would be more boarding throughout the night, so Howard wouldn't sleep. At least he would be dry, comfortable, and traveling toward Lourdes, where he hoped maybe there might be yet another miracle.

THIRTY-SIX

The first time he came by, the young man from Costa Rica was determined to trip her up with obscure phrases. As he conversed with Janet in casual Spanish, he threw in references to small towns she'd never seen on a map. He chatted about popular movies currently playing in cinemas in the small Central American country. He asked her questions about sex and relationships, using slang and expressions she'd never encountered in her *Rosetta Stone* course. She struggled.

Over and over she had to admit she didn't understand the question or simply answered his inquiry incorrectly. She became increasingly frustrated. After three hours, she jumped up from her comfortable chair, ripped the microphone from her collar, and threw it in her interrogator's face. He ducked before it struck him and switched instantly to flawless English while he pleaded for forgiveness.

"It's all right, Janet," he assured her. "I'm really sorry I made it so painful for you. You were handling the dialogue so well I didn't realize I was creating all that stress. Your skill in answering the questions showed remarkable poise and wonderful grammar. Please forgive me for making you angry!"

Janet ignored his plea and marched away from him, shaking her head in fury. The language coach's usually bright spirit and cheerful demeanor were gone, and his face looked both pale and contrite.

"What happened?" Klaudia Schäffer asked as she rushed in from the kitchen.

"It's all my fault," the Spanish tutor volunteered without hesitation. "She was doing so well with her language skills that I tried to focus attention on some lifestyle areas she needs to learn, and I did it poorly. I created too much pressure and I'm so sorry!"

With a scowl, Klaudia turned to Janet who continued to seethe, her face buried in her hands, while her shoulders heaved as she gasped for breath to suppress her anger. Klaudia took control and wrapped her arm around Janet's shoulders as she guided her from the room and in the direction of the kitchen. They left the tutor wringing his hands as he stood in front of his chair with an expression of confusion and profound regret.

"Let me get you some water," Klaudia told Janet. "Then, let's take a break and have some nice vegetable soup. I just prepared lunch."

She guided Janet toward the kitchen table and pulled a chair out so Janet could comfortably take a seat. Once she had served both the water and soup, and was seated across from Janet, she said, "Tell me what you're feeling."

"I'm sorry about that. It was just the pressure. I was trying so hard to do well," Janet explained, her tone composed. "You know how anxious I am to get started on the project. I feel badly now and wish I hadn't let the frustration overtake me and thrown a tantrum like a child. It's just that I feel a huge weight of obligation."

"What obligation?"

"Every day I watch you spend hours on your computer creating and studying algorithms. Almost daily, you save some girl from getting trapped by The Organization. You're making a difference. All I'm doing is learning to speak Spanish. I'm anxious to make an impact too and it looks like I'm screwing up my chance to do something useful."

A tear slithered from Janet's eye and she quickly wiped it away.

"I couldn't help but overhear your conversation," the tutor said from the doorway. "I can't express how badly I feel, and I apologize again. I hope you'll forgive my careless approach to our session."

"It's all right," Janet mumbled.

"No. It's not all right. You're an extraordinary student. Your vocabulary is fantastic after only a few weeks. Your pronunciation is almost flawless and your level of comprehension is unusually good."

"Then why were you making me feel so inadequate?" She raised her head and looked him in the eye with an accusing expression.

"I completely missed your signals. From your body language and responses, you masked your feelings so effectively I failed to see the effect my questions were having on your confidence until you exploded. You're really the best I've ever coached!"

"Then, why were you posing such difficult questions?"

"I was only trying to help you identify the next areas we have to focus on. You need a few days watching movies, listening to Spanish hip-hop, and simulating the lifestyle of a Costa Rican teenager. From my perspective, within days you'll be ready to start the project," he said.

"Let's chalk it up to your diligent efforts to so closely relate to Costa Rican fifteen-year-olds that you took on their penchant for anger with too much enthusiasm," Klaudia joked.

The atmosphere in the kitchen changed. Klaudia invited him to join them for soup and they strategized for about an hour. The instructor prepared a playlist of music to listen to, more than a dozen recent movies to watch, plus a half dozen Spanish young adult novels to read. By the time he left, Janet was more motivated to succeed with this project than with any other she could remember.

THIRTY-SEVEN

During their phone call, she didn't understand his *instructions* the first time, so Nadine asked Pierre Boivin to repeat them.

"Mareno wants you to join me in Germany on Monday," he said. "You need to buy another new dress because somebody I want you to impress will also be at the meeting. Make it one that's see-through, maybe like that white chiffon one. But find someone who can make you an outfit that looks like a traditional geisha style."

"Geisha?" Nadine wondered. "Why geisha?"

"Sugimori, the guy taking over from Suji-san in Japan, will be there. He wants to talk about some stuff. I need to get him onside with a few new ideas and you'll be a pleasant added attraction. Don't worry, I won't need you to sleep with him, just be some sexy eye candy." He hung up without further comment.

Nadine dropped her head in disgust. Over the past two days, life had become worse with Pierre. She noticed the not-so-subtle changes. He was more distant. He hadn't used a term of affection since their confrontation over the cell phone, and he hadn't even bothered with sex since that session after she was forced to service his bodyguard. She knew the culture of The Organization and how they often treated women as chattel and tools for bargaining and control.

Things had been different with Pierre Boivin until recently. He'd demonstrated some affection before. Clearly, things were not going well with Mareno, and this caused more than a little concern. If a confrontation between the men was imminent, where would she fit in? Mareno may have sold her to Boivin, but the powerful man had made it very clear; Boivin's property or not, she ultimately owed her loyalty to the head of The Organization. Had Pierre figured that out?

The odd request to display her body for a new Japanese mobster probably wasn't coincidental either. What kind of "new stuff" could the crime bosses from France and Japan be working on? And why would it be helpful for Boivin to show her off to the new associate?

As Nadine completed her inspection of the facilities and women in Montpellier that afternoon, she grew increasingly alarmed but arranged an appointment with her seamstress in Aix-en-Provence for that evening regardless. The woman promised to have designs ready for Nadine to choose from and saw no problem finishing the dress by Saturday. She actually expressed delight in seeing Nadine wearing a Japanese-style outfit.

"You'll be gorgeous as a geisha!" she said with a squeal. "Would you like to style your hair to look Japanese too?"

Nadine didn't think that was necessary.

Mareno hadn't ordered her to attend the get together in Germany directly, but Nadine had little doubt Pierre was merely relaying his command. Still, before she boarded the helicopter to return home, she took a few moments to refresh in the *toilette* and used her precious few minutes to dial the new secret number the powerful leader of The Organization had given her to use. He answered on the second ring, and they perfunctorily went through their security codes.

"Pierre tells me you want me to join him for a *rendezvous* with you next Monday in Germany. Is there anything specific I need to know or do?" Nadine asked.

"Oh," Giancarlo Mareno said, then paused for an uncomfortably long time. "When did he tell you?"

"He called a few minutes ago and ordered me to have a new dress made to wear at the meeting. Specifically, he wants me to buy a transparent dress in the style of a Japanese geisha. I think he wants to impress a new guy in Japan named Sugimori."

The line was silent for several seconds before Mareno finally asked, "What else did he tell you about Sugimori?"

"He said he wanted me to make a good impression on the guy because there is some new stuff they need to talk about," Nadine replied with some trepidation.

Another lengthy pause developed while Mareno processed information he seemed to be hearing for the first time.

"Go ahead and get the dress and come with Boivin. But call me again as soon as you know the details of your flights and arrival time in Germany. I imagine you'll use his helicopter, but try to pry out the travel details as soon as you can. This might be important." Mareno's tone suggested he was still thinking through all the implications, and it sent a chill down Nadine's spine.

Her situation had just become even more difficult. Not only were her suspicions about tensions between the two accurate, but a confrontation might be brewing. She would need to unearth the travel information Giancarlo wanted from Pierre with great care. And she needed to think more urgently about an escape plan. She had no desire to be caught in the crossfire between the two men.

THIRTY-EIGHT

Zarautz, Spain, Friday January 24, 2020

Howard Knight settled into the old leather seats on the overnight bus from Burgos, Spain, to Lourdes, France, as it departed the station just after midnight. To remain alert, he drank three cups of strong coffee in the two hours before departure. He knew the dangers of falling asleep. Roadblocks might occur at any time. Moreover, should he fall asleep at the wrong time, thieves might take all his meager possessions as they debarked from the bus with little fear of being detected.

He checked around for a restroom, knowing at least part of those three coffees would need to be recycled within the four-hour journey. He saw it in the back and relaxed. It wouldn't be necessary to bribe the driver to wait a few moments while he ran into a bus station for relief somewhere along their route.

Howard chose a seat in the middle of the bus. As he surveyed his new surroundings, a young couple, seated behind and across the aisle from him, were studying him and whispering. They both glanced away when they realized Howard was, in turn, observing them. However, they continued whispering. He made a mental note to check the pair from time to time in case they should make a call or attempt to take a photo.

Immediately behind Howard, two men chatted casually in Spanish. He eavesdropped on their conversation and instantly became alarmed. One had received a text alerting them to a roadblock on the highway just after the town of *Zarautz*, before reaching the border with France. According to the one who received the message, police were stopping and searching all vehicles.

Howard continued to listen as the pair discussed the merits of getting off at the stop in *Zarautz*. They might still find a place to sleep, and they could wait for the roadblock to clear away in the morning before continuing on to France. They didn't mention the reason for their concern, but Howard imagined they were transporting drugs or participating in some other illegal activity, although they were both well dressed, clean-shaven, and apparently affluent.

He continued to eavesdrop as they searched for a hotel with their phones. It seemed they had lots of choices. One traveler mentioned there were more than twenty-five hotels to choose from, and they spent considerable time discussing whether they should share a room or book separately.

Finally, the pair decided upon separate rooms. Then they discussed the most appropriate rate to pay. Rooms ranged from fifty to two hundred euros, and the price didn't seem to be a significant concern to either. They finally decided on the Hotel Alameda with a rate of about a hundred euros a night. The hotel's interesting architecture appealed to them.

When the travelers were satisfied with their arrangements, both gradually dozed off in silence. About an hour had already passed, and Howard felt grateful that extremely good luck had seemingly compensated for his bad judgment. He may have dodged a bullet. Using Katherine's phone GPS, he learned it would take about the same amount of time before their arrival in *Zarautz* and did his own research.

He no longer had any of the euros Katherine had given him, and he'd already spent part of the money he stole from the unoccupied home, so a hotel would be out of the question. Instead, he focused on city churches and landmarks. Often, a city's major attractions included balconies and other helpful places to hide out of sight for a few hours.

Within fifteen minutes, Howard identified his target destination. It would be the Zarautz Art and History Museum, the oldest building in town. Built in the fourteenth century, the building included a tower with bells, and Howard knew there must be a door and stairway to the top. Early in his days with The Organization, he'd learned virtually any lock could be opened without a key. In fact, he spent several enjoyable days with experts who cheerfully showed him many of their secrets. He had no doubt he'd be able to open the door and get a few hours of good sleep.

As the bus pulled into the old terminal, Howard waited until the travelers seated behind him disembarked. Then he quickly followed them off and headed in the opposite direction. After walking about fifteen minutes along *Nafarroa Kalea* Street from the bus terminal to the *Zarautz Tower*, he checked all around. Everything was silent at well after two o'clock in the morning.

Howard found the door to the bell tower almost immediately and yanked on the handle. To his amazement, the door creaked open without restraint. Those hard-won lock picking skills wouldn't be required after all. He leaned against and closed the large wooden door, then illuminated the flashlight on the phone.

All appeared clear. The steps, a mixture of rock and cement, were still in good repair after more than six hundred years. He shut off the light to conserve precious battery power and climbed the stairs with one hand on the wall and the other hand feeling for the next uneven step. Within a few minutes Howard reached the summit and poked his head around the corner to check with the flashlight before taking a final stride into the area surrounding the bells.

To his relief, he was alone. As he inspected his new quarters, something small darted across the floor and scurried off down the stairs. A shiver swept down Howard's spine. It was probably a mouse or a rat. Several cobwebs above the bells and in two corners looked menacing but suggested people visited the belfry infrequently. That was a good thing, but would it afford enough comfort for a decent night's sleep?

The floor was damp when Howard sat down to test its surface, but there were no puddles of water. A quick scan of the area with his flashlight confirmed no other critters lurked about at the moment. However, he decided to sleep sitting up if possible, to avoid being wakened by some undesirable vermin crossing his face. With another shudder, he leaned his exhausted body against the wall, closed his eyes and silently prayed he might sleep uninterrupted for even a few hours.

As he feared, sleep was difficult. Howard tossed and turned on the damp, uneven cement, waking often and only dozing in short spurts rather than falling into a deep slumber. That inability to sleep deeply probably saved his life.

At some point in the night, a strange sound came up the stairwell. He instantly jolted fully awake, all his senses on maximum alert. Someone was climbing the steps. Did they see him come into the tower? Was he followed from the bus? Silently, Howard used his knees to push himself to an upright position, leaning against the rutted wall for balance. Upright, he froze, then quickly developed a plan. Finally, he edged closer to the doorway.

The instant the intruder's boot crossed the plane of the opening from the stairwell, Howard kicked out with one violent motion where he guessed the person's knees might be. The timing was perfect. He caught the man from behind and he fell forward in an awkward sprawl.

A large knife clunked loudly to the floor an instant before the unkempt assailant's face hit the cement with a sickening thud. There was no time to think. He lunged forward and jumped on the outstretched hand. Fingers crunched against the unyielding surface. The man screamed in pain and tried to lift himself from the floor.

Before he could successfully plant either his hands or knees, Howard viciously jumped on both of the intruder's hands once more, then lashed out with two quick and nasty kicks to the forehead. The man collapsed, unconscious.

Howard hesitated for an instant to gather his wits. Guys from The Organization would probably finish off the intruder with one judicious slash using his own knife, but Howard couldn't do it. The way he was dressed, the fellow was probably just a homeless guy hoping for some quick money. Besides, he remembered the trauma he'd suffered when he was first forced to kill a man to earn his stripes in the criminal world. He'd vomited when the man's brains exploded from a gunshot, splattering Howard and everything else in range.

Howard left the intruder still breathing and navigated the descent of the ancient stone stairs in total darkness. Hands against the walls to maintain balance, he tested the surface with his toes before he painstakingly lowered one foot, then the other. He repeated that careful process step by step, all the way to the bottom.

It was too dangerous to stay in this town. The mysterious fellow who intended to attack him would probably regain consciousness soon, and who knew how quickly a police search might begin?

At the bottom of the stairwell, Howard creaked open the door and stepped out onto the street, checking in all directions for signs of life. Satisfied he was alone, he dashed across *Nafarroa Kalea* and strode fifty yards to a side-street leading toward the beach. Once he saw the Atlantic Ocean, Howard veered right and followed the street along the sand to its end. It took only a few minutes. There, he crossed the narrow strand to a cliff. As he hoped, it was secluded, and he plopped down on a rock at the base of the overhang to devise another plan.

A quick glance at his phone showed about twenty percent battery life remained, the time was four-thirty Saturday morning, and the temperature was just slightly above freezing. At that moment, it occurred to Howard the police might have found a way to track Katherine's phone even without the SIM card. He shut it off immediately. He'd only used the phone sparingly to conserve power, but the police would be able to pick up his trail if they could piece together the few times he had used it.

It was too dangerous to return to town to steal another scooter. He'd need to take one somewhere else, and he'd have to use the phone for one brief search. A Google Maps search showed the closest place was *Donostia-San Sebastian* following a little-used road along the coastline. The app suggested about five hours walking, but Howard always found its calculations overstated. With nothing but a gut feeling, he concluded it should take two or three hours at a brisk pace. That would get him there before light. With luck, he'd find an unattended scooter and zip through the town to find a secluded spot farther along the coast where he could take refuge for the daylight hours.

Without another moment's hesitation, Howard lifted himself from the coarse sand, slung his backpack over his shoulder, and started walking.

THIRTY-NINE

Teterboro Airport, New Jersey, Saturday January 25, 2020

Giancarlo climbed the half-dozen steps from the ground to the doorway of the private Bombardier Global 5000 aircraft his usual mark had graciously loaned him for the trip. A gorgeous new hostess greeted him at the top of the stairs. She stood coyly just inside the doorway, out of public view but directly in his sightline, as he climbed the stairs. Like the last time, this one wore only the tiny bottom of a bikini and proudly displayed her well-rounded breasts as she received him with a seductive smile and cheerful welcome.

"Put your clothes back on," Giancarlo muttered gruffly. "This trip is all business. Give the boys good service, but no sex. Not even a blow job."

Shaken, the tall brunette wrapped her arms quickly around her breasts and retreated to the back of the jet where she slipped into a short skirt and button-down shirt. She was still fastening the buttons as she approached Giancarlo a second time. He had awkwardly lowered his considerable girth into the wider leather seat at the front of the aircraft where he'd have a few feet of separation from the rest of the passengers.

"Would you like something to drink?" the woman asked, her smile tentative.

"Coke," Giancarlo replied. "And for the rest of the passengers, nothing stronger than coffee. Water, sodas, coffee. No alcohol, not even a sip of wine until we arrive. Got that?"

The hostess darted back for a bottle of cola before the rest of the passengers filed in. She had just finished serving Giancarlo when the first head popped around the corner of the door to see if it was okay for the rest of the group to enter.

"You sit up here next to me as usual, Luigi. We have some things to talk about," Giancarlo ordered. "Once the guys are all seated, read the riot act. No booze and no foolin' with the broad on this flight. If they do their jobs in Europe right, they can party on the way back. Be sure they understand that. And tell them to get some sleep too."

Giancarlo sipped his water and read that morning's newspaper as the rest of his sizeable entourage silently squeezed into their seats in the area behind him. Sugimori could just take his imposed limit of three bodyguards and shove it.

The hour was very early in New York, but already afternoon at their destination in Europe. Giancarlo insisted they leave at this ungodly hour to be sure his team would have adequate time to scour the facilities in Germany. There was good reason to be extra careful with his surroundings during the upcoming meeting. Sugimori had clearly demanded new terms and conditions for his loyalty. Boivin had something up his sleeve, possibly in concert with Sugimori. It wasn't the first time Giancarlo faced challenges to his authority, but this time it felt different and he'd take no chances.

Eleven men and one woman, Annika, formed Giancarlo's security brigade. Once they were seated, a pilot closed the door and used a PA system to welcome everyone aboard. They expected a mainly smooth flight, he assured everyone. Their flying time should be a little more than nine hours, making their arrival in Austria about nine-thirty in the evening.

Ground transportation had been reconfirmed in Innsbruck, he said, acknowledging the screwup in Spain the last time. Before he finished speaking, the other pilot had already started to taxi on the way to the runway for takeoff.

As soon as the aircraft reached cruising altitude, Giancarlo swung his luxurious leather seat around to face his most trusted bodyguard and confidant, Luigi Fortissimo.

"We can't have any screwups, Luigi. Let's review the plan again."

"Four Mercedes SUVs will meet us at the aircraft. The pilot checked. They're already there and parked discretely out of the way near the tarmac," Luigi said. "One will take you and me to our hotel in Innsbruck. The second will take our German-speaking woman and three technicians to Garmisch-Partenkirchen right way. They'll check-in tonight about ten-thirty."

"Have we found the woman's hotel contact for tomorrow?" Giancarlo interrupted.

"Yeah. Annika tracked down a night desk manager. They've already blocked the rooms we want to fix. Sometime during the night, the hotel clerk will get the room keys to Annika. She'll have the technicians finish their jobs well before we arrive."

Giancarlo nodded and Luigi continued his summary.

"The other two SUVs will transport the remaining six to their hotels. Three will go to Germany and three will stay in Austria."

For more than two hours, Giancarlo and Luigi huddled at the front of the aircraft, quietly reviewing every aspect of their plan. Giancarlo posed questions from a mental checklist, and Luigi explained every detail, referring to a massive spreadsheet on his laptop. Whenever Giancarlo identified a gap that might cause their plan to derail, he gave new instructions before Luigi typed a few notes into his spreadsheet with a promise to fix it.

When Giancarlo guessed they might be flying over Bermuda, he ended the discussion with a simple, "Good night." Minutes later, his massive hulk was heaving in rhythm to the loud snoring of a large man sleeping deeply. No plots would disturb his remaining six hours of flying time.

FORTY

The distance from Marseilles to Munich was much too long for his helicopter. The pilot pointed out the turbulence wouldn't be comfortable traveling over the Alps, and they'd need to stop to refuel twice. It would be much better to either charter a jet or fly commercial.

Since part of the discussion Pierre intended to have with both Sugimori from Japan and Giancarlo Mareno was a need for a larger share of the income generated by their illicit activities, he finally chose to fly commercial to underscore his relative poverty. As soon as he paid for his flight on a cheap fare website, he regretted the decision. His angst only increased as the actual travel began.

To meet Sugimori at the agreed hour of three o'clock, they had to catch a flight at six in the morning. That meant their alarm sounded at an ungodly hour. Nadine started complaining about how tired she was from the time the alarm rang until she fell asleep on the aircraft about five minutes after they reached cruising altitude on the Air France flight bound for Munich with a stop in Paris. She was short enough to get comfortable quickly, but Pierre's long legs never found a comfortable position during the flight.

The four bodyguards didn't complain, but each time Pierre glanced across the aisle, the expressions on their faces suggested they too weren't enthralled with either the seating or the service. Pierre's concern about their comfort was related only to his fear about how alert they'd be over the coming couple days. He needed them to monitor and study every nuance of both of the crime bosses and their entourages.

When they arrived in Paris, he first instructed Nadine to sit alone in a quiet corner of the Air France first-class lounge at Charles de Gaulle Airport for a three-hour layover before their connecting flight to Munich. He parked the security team in the opposite corner of the spacious room, told everyone to get a coffee and snack for breakfast, and then wolfed down his own croissant before he started. Patiently, he reviewed their plan with the entire team.

"Is everyone's walkie-talkie working?" he asked. From their carry-on bags, all four members of his security detail fetched microphones, which they clipped to the inside of their jackets, and inserted the earbuds for testing. Within a minute or two, everyone confirmed their set functioned. They'd have a range of about two-hundred-and-fifty yards.

"In Munich, we'll walk to the Hilton from the airport," Pierre instructed. "Space your departures from the arrivals lounge at least five minutes apart. We'll all check in to the hotel separately. You can use your waiting time to get your weapons out of your checked luggage and ready for action."

"Will we have time for lunch?" Jean-Guy Gagnon asked.

Annoyed his most senior bodyguard would be thinking about a trivial detail during this critical discussion—especially after the disturbing revelation of Jean-Guy's secret communication with Giancarlo Mareno—Pierre lashed out.

"We'll get to that in good time, Jean-Guy. Stay focused or I'll put someone in your role who has more than a few seconds to think about protecting my life." He regretted his anger immediately but thought better of repairing any damage in front of the others. "Remember, you're to get room 554. That's the room I personally arranged. Make sure they don't try to switch you to another."

That suite looked out over the massive hotel lobby and provided a clear view down to any of the several table-and-chair clusters the hotel spaced widely apart so businesspeople could conduct sensitive discussions. Gagnon was to be the quarterback of the team, watching everything and instructing the others about any action they might need to take. Pierre didn't expect violence or trickery, but he didn't know Sugimori well and would take no chances. He assumed his Japanese counterpart would do the same.

"You guys," he said, pointing to the pair seated to the left of Jean-Guy, "be sure you've got seats in the bar that are separate but with good views of this table Sugimori has arranged. Only he and I will meet here." He pointed to a specific spot on the photo of the lobby he had placed on the table.

"Will his guys all be Japanese?" one asked.

"I think so," Pierre replied. "But he's had more time to plan for this get-together. He might have been able to recruit someone who's not Japanese for the element of surprise. So watch everyone."

Before delivering his next command, Pierre took a moment for a long look at the remaining member of his detail. It was a calculated risk bringing more bodyguards than Sugimori instructed, but if the woman did her job well, Sugimori would never know. She definitely didn't look like a bodyguard.

He wasn't entirely comfortable about using a woman, but he wanted the element of surprise if necessary and this woman should work. She was fit. He'd seen her perform karate moves with Jean-Guy before they brought her on the payroll. She could be vicious if needed. After all, she'd whipped Gagnon's ass when they'd fought in the gym that day. And her marksmanship with a gun was superb. What he couldn't get entirely comfortable with was the idea that any woman might determine whether he lived or died in a nasty situation.

"Make sure you keep those nice legs and breasts well covered, Marie," he said with a twisted grin. "We don't want to attract any more attention than necessary."

She nodded without a smile, and he continued explaining her role.

"They're coming back from a sightseeing drive just before three. You should be outside, across the street from the hotel, an hour before. Be sure you let the guys know the moment you spot them getting out of the car and give a good description of everyone you see. Check where the driver parks after he lets them off and be sure you describe the driver to the guys whether he follows them into the hotel immediately or not."

Pierre continued issuing cautions and commands for most of their layover. Each of the bodyguards asked questions when appropriate and showed requisite respect for the gravity of the mission. Fifteen minutes before they planned to head to the departure gate, Pierre wondered if there were any other questions or concerns. When they all shook their heads, he finally replied to Jean-Guy's question about lunch.

"Order your lunch from room service," he said to Jean-Guy. "The rest of you should eat something at the airport. Choose separate restaurants or snack bars to avoid any suspicion if they're watching us."

Satisfied with their advance preparation, Pierre left the security team to join Nadine in the other corner. She was nibbling on a croissant with a tiny cup of espresso on the table. Before she could voice another complaint about either the early morning departure or the three hours he had left her alone in the corner, he pounced.

"Who were you talking to for so long?"

"Our *Madame* in Lourdes," Nadine replied calmly. "I promised to get back to her about the next arrival of girls from Morocco. They're scheduled to arrive by boat in *Bayonne* tonight. I wanted to be sure she had the coordinates to meet them."

Pierre looked at her intently before he asked her to give him her issued phone. "Open it with your password first."

Nadine hesitated only an instant as Pierre scrutinized her eyes for any sign of fear or deception. She quickly entered the code and passed the phone to Pierre nonchalantly. Sure enough, the last number listed was a fifteen-minute call to the house in Lourdes.

Satisfied, Pierre returned the phone without immediate comment. He decided not to waste any time charming her or trying to improve her foul mood. After all, she'd only be around for another few hours. The Saudi prince who had transferred fifty-thousand US dollars to his bank account the day before would make all the necessary arrangements to collect her from the hotel in Garmisch-Partenkirchen when Pierre was finished with her on Monday.

"As soon as we check in to the hotel, change into the geisha outfit," he ordered.

FORTY-ONE

Donostia-San Sebastian, Spain, Sunday January 26, 2020

Howard's expected three-hour hike from Zarautz took longer. First, he was astonished at the amount of overnight traffic on the small narrow roadway. He lost count after he'd been forced to seek hiding spots at least thirty times during the eight-mile trek. Every passing car cost him valuable time while he remained hidden until the vehicle was well out of sight.

Then it rained. The light drizzle hadn't been a problem initially, but when the downpour started, he took shelter under a bridge crossing a slow-moving stream. The torrential rainfall lasted more than an hour. Cold, miserable and wet completely through, Howard worried about the rising sun as he trudged toward the town. At this point, he didn't want to attract any unwelcome attention.

About a mile from his destination, Howard spotted a dilapidated, abandoned barn in a field to his right. While it was little more than a shed, he was relieved to find it vacant with a portion of the roof intact over the walls closest to the road. He banged the walls and everything seemed sturdy enough, so he cleared a space on the ground, checking the dirt floor for insects and vermin. In a matter of minutes, he slept soundly.

The sun was already setting to the west when Howard lifted his head from his backpack. He drank his remaining bottle of water and longed to have a single protein bar. As soon as darkness set in, he resumed walking and arrived in the town of Donostia-San Sebastian about twenty minutes later. Few cars or scooters passed him in the streets, but he didn't dare enter a restaurant despite their alluring aromas. He passed two. Both were busy with loud, laughing voices and good cheer.

Despite his constant hunger, Howard hid out behind the larger of the two, an establishment that served traditional Spanish foods. The pleasant spicy saffron smell of *paella* wafted in Howard's direction as he took shelter behind the trees surrounding the tiny parking area. He counted only a few cars and more than a dozen scooters.

His strategy was simple. Chances were excellent at least one of the scooter owners would have too much to drink. If Howard was lucky, that cyclist might have friends who would insist they give him a ride and leave his scooter in the lot to pick up the next day. If an inebriated rider didn't listen to his friends and staggered to the parking lot alone, Howard would hit him over the head with the four-foot-long branch of a tree he'd discovered settling into his spot in the woods.

About two hours later, an unlucky potential victim walked unsteadily from the restaurant and appeared around the corner of the building. First, he stopped to relieve himself. He was so drunk he almost lost his balance twice in the exercise. When he finished, the victim-to-be zipped up his trousers and resumed his drunken path to a scooter. It was a large one, maybe the largest parked there, and it was no more than ten feet from Howard's hiding spot.

He crept from the bushes on his hands and knees and waited until the scooter owner was straddling the cycle, ready to start it. Howard pounced. With one desperate attempt, he whacked his victim on the back of his head. The force left the man motionless on the ground, the scooter still between his legs.

Howard checked to be sure the fellow was alive but unconscious, then yanked the cycle away from his fallen victim and quickly straddled the seat. With one firm press of the starter button, he started the engine and darted off. His victim still lay motionless on the ground when Howard glanced back.

He used side streets and followed road signs rather than wasting the precious little battery remaining on Katherine's phone. There was also the issue of a helmet. Howard now had concerns about how much easier it was for police to identify him with his head bare. With the extent of the manhunt they had underway, people would be more alert, and the observant ones could become a problem.

Safety was also a worry. While many people in Europe rode without helmets, Howard had always felt exposed riding a bike or motorcycle without protection for his head. He vowed to steal one as he passed through the next town.

Of course, Howard also needed to be aware of facial recognition software. Many municipalities used electronic cameras to control speeding and other traffic infractions. Hundreds of small businesses used security monitoring devices twenty-four hours a day. He did his best to keep his head down and look away whenever he approached a likely source of monitoring. In the countryside, he might avoid discovery.

In the cities, his travel during the day became exponentially riskier.

Despite those concerns, Howard motored out of Spain and into France without event. In fact, the border between the countries was so seamless the authorities no longer bothered to post marker signs on some of the secondary roads. Visits between the neighboring countries were routine for the local population. Few locals knew where the precise borders separating the countries actually were.

If he had been able to use a highway, his drive from Donostia-San Sebastian to Lourdes would have been less than three hours. Instead, Howard noticed the sun was high in the sky as he approached the outskirts of Lourdes. He had a new quandary. He was sure the office he needed to find wouldn't be open until Monday morning. In the meantime, he needed to stay well out of sight. After the torturous experience to get this far, he planned to avoid apprehension by all means possible.

On the other hand, it would be impossible to visit that office in his current wet, filthy clothes and with his unkempt appearance. Surely, they would throw him out the door if he was even able to squeeze a foot inside. Moments later, he saw a small sign next to the road for a low-priced hostel, *Lindo Carillon*.

Howard veered off the road at the next safe clearing and checked the phone for cell reception. Relieved to see the Vodafone logo, which meant the Portugal-based phone plan was still working in France, he searched for the hostel by name and learned they had one private room; it rented for thirty euros a night and was surprisingly close to the address he would visit Monday morning.

He considered the risks. Chance of detection in hotels was generally high, but hostels usually paid far less attention to documents and personal details than higher-priced spots. Earlier in the morning would've been better. The night attendant might have been tired and paid less attention to detail. Since Howard had arrived much later, the staff would be relatively fresh, but might be harried from checkouts and cleaning rooms. Either way it was a danger, but in his exhausted state, Howard decided it was a gamble worth taking.

He checked his remaining euros. There were fifty in small bills. He would have just enough to pay for the room, launder his clothes, and eat a good meal. Within ten minutes Howard arrived at the inn and tucked the scooter in the back where it would probably be stolen. That wasn't a problem. He now had no further use for it.

Check-in was uneventful. The male attendant was engaged on the phone while he tried to sort out a problem with his computer. When he finally turned his attention to his guest, he accepted the story that someone stole Howard's passport in Paris and that he was waiting for the Canadian embassy to send him a new one this week. The clerk didn't ask for any other documents and put the cash in his pocket after giving Howard an old-fashioned metal key to the single room.

He didn't sleep immediately. Instead, Howard laundered his clothes with hand soap in the shower of the private bathroom and hung them to dry on the two hangers provided. Then he cleaned himself. Turning the shower to its maximum heat, he let the water pound against his aching body for several minutes. The ever-present chill he'd experienced for the past week gradually dissipated.

Once his body was washed and dried, he felt like a new man and not at all ready to sleep. Although he was still starving, he hadn't noticed any nearby restaurants and calculated the risking of going out to look for one too great. Instead, he wrapped himself in the functional bedsheets, threw a duvet on top and considered his options.

He couldn't call the FBI. Someone had hacked the confidential numbers, and his chances of navigating the bureaucracy without detection by The Organization weren't good at all. The criminal element had easily penetrated the shield of protection created in a foreign country thousands of miles from the USA. Surely, they could do the same at FBI headquarters.

He should also let Janet know he was alive. But what immediate purpose would that serve? If she followed his elaborate escape plan, she was in Germany under the watchful eye of an organization far more efficient than the FBI. If she didn't make it to Germany, she was probably dead, or The Organization was using her body before they discarded her like all the others.

The back and forth in his mind didn't take long. The path was clear, his first call must be to get money, and then he'd try to contact the love of his life. With enough money, almost anything was possible. He saw no practical alternative but continuing desperately to engineer an escape for as long as possible. There was more promise of a reunion with Janet that way.

FORTY-TWO

Angermund, Germany, Sunday January 26, 2020

She woke up unusually late that morning because both women drank too much the night before. After an extraordinary day and night, Janet's body felt limp and her brain sluggish. It was the fog of a hangover. Surprising as it may sound—and despite all her questionable behavior in bed with dozens of men—until the FBI relocated them to Overveen, she'd never allowed herself more than a few sips of alcohol. She had seen too often how judgment and control were easily compromised.

For all those years, Janet had mostly stayed out of harm's way by not taking unnecessary risks with her safety. But things changed in the Netherlands. Living with Howard softened her edge of wariness and his steadfastness lulled her into gradually drinking increasingly larger quantities of wine. She eventually became comfortable with the fuzziness of too much alcohol and the warm embrace of overindulgence.

As she lay on her back looking up at the bare ceiling of her temporary bedroom that morning, Janet realized it was time to do some serious reassessment. She hadn't studied political science for four years at Columbia to live as a hungover fugitive in a foreign country.

A decade earlier, back in college, she had thought of The Organization as a friend. Now it was a mortal enemy. The past few weeks with Klaudia had been instructional. Janet had learned much about the horrible way organized crime treated women and girls. Outside of her own closed world, she had discovered the unexpected and abysmal side of people she used to like and perhaps admire.

Even Howard had been complicit. He may not have done the actual kidnapping and entrapment of women, but he clearly knew about it and understood the financial benefits to the criminal bosses. Worse, he had a secret relationship with the woman reputed to have established and managed the entire labyrinth. That woman, Fidelia, was the very definition of a paradox.

The morning's thinking created moods and introspection Janet had never experienced. Oddly philosophical, she couldn't compartmentalize feelings and emotions as usual. It was perplexing.

———•———

During the previous ten days, she had watched, listened to, and practiced Spanish up to twelve hours a day. Once, she teasingly joked with Klaudia that she was actually starting to think and act a little bit like a teen. When the Costa Rican tutor returned a second time with his voice recorder and dozens of prepared questions, she aced the interview.

Like a lovelorn Costa Rican teen with exaggerated visions of life among the rich and famous, she answered questions with confidence, an occasional giggle, and Spanish language skills that felt almost natural. Of course, her cadence and accent still needed improvement, and the delivery of some answers was more halting than she would like. But for work by text and social media, she was more than functional. According to her certificate, she was fluent.

Klaudia seemed so excited by the glowing report delivered by the Spanish instructor that she broke her usual practice of wearing only the abaya and niqab to shop in the town's stores. That day, she wore a long scarf and large dark glasses with a hooded winter jacket and blue jeans. Klaudia was still mainly covered but dressed more appropriately to make her unusual purchase. She told Janet that people might find it less curious than her usual Muslim attire. After all, she was stocking up on red wine.

Right after she came home, they prepared a celebratory dinner. Janet washed and took care of the fresh vegetables and salad, Klaudia fired up a small outdoor grill with real charcoal to cook the steaks. They sipped generously from their glasses of wine as they completed their preparation. Anticipation of a private celebration left them giddy and laughing at even their most mundane comments as they moved around the kitchen, cooking and sharing stories.

Dinner was delightful. To start, they opened a second bottle of wine and then drank it as they devoured Janet's tossed salad before putting meat on the grill. They opened their third bottle of wine after the grilling started. The thick, juicy steaks were the first meat Janet had eaten since her arrival in Germany, and Klaudia cooked them with a pink interior, just the way they both liked it.

Their joyful dinner continued until they had each consumed the last morsel on their plates, and both felt more than a little tipsy as they stood to load the dirty dishes in the dishwasher and tidy up the table.

Once the minor chores were done, Janet sat down at the table and gulped more wine. She remembered the last time she drank such a large amount. It had been with Howard in the hours before that life-changing visit from the thugs during the night. Then too she felt light-headed and unsteady, but they had made love slowly and tenderly before she lapsed into sleep. The fond memory warmed her until Klaudia approached from the rear, pressed her breasts against the back of Janet's head, then wrapped her long arms around Janet and kissed her gently behind her right ear.

"I thought you preferred men," Janet said, startled but not uncomfortable.

"I do. But beautiful women come in a close second," Klaudia murmured hoarsely.

Before Janet realized it, her companion was gently stroking her neck and upper back with pressure that both soothed and titillated.

"Would you like a massage?" Klaudia whispered temptingly.

Arm in arm, they helped each other navigate the stairs, laughing and swaying to and fro with each step as they climbed to Janet's bedroom. Twice, they stopped to check their balance and giggle about their condition, but they reached the bedroom without mishap.

"Okay, off with your clothes now," Klaudia commanded mischievously. "I'll get more comfortable while you undress." She disappeared into the bathroom.

Naked, Janet turned onto her stomach and waited. In only a few seconds, Klaudia's strong hands began to knead her shoulders and upper back again. But this time, the bare skin of Klaudia's thighs wrapped casually around her hips. Her pubic hair tickled pleasingly.

Klaudia worked her way down Janet's back, teasing her with sensual touches. First, her strong hands temptingly skimmed the surface of her skin, and then she applied deep, penetrating pressure that both relaxed and energized all of Janet's senses. It was a new and invigorating experience and Janet wanted more.

After several minutes working on Janet's back, Klaudia nudged her to turn over, and she gently massaged Janet's breasts, pausing to squeeze her nipples and watch them respond. A few seconds later, she lifted her body and swung around onto her knees, facing Janet's toes, and started massaging her sensitive inner thighs.

Klaudia continued to lightly stroke Janet's legs with fleeting diversions to her pubic hair, where she applied gently increasing pressure with each visit. Then, she dismounted and ran her hands along the contours of Janet's body as far as she could reach in each direction, touching lightly then firmly, each stroke more enticing than the last.

Soon, Klaudia's hands returned to Janet's breasts. She ran her tongue along the edge of each nipple before slowly and lovingly stroking them. Skillfully, she squeezed the nipples between her fingers as she pressed in a slow circular motion. Janet felt her nipples harden with arousal, her breathing becoming shorter and deeper.

After several minutes, Klaudia returned to massage her pubic region gently, with both hands. Without warning, she tenderly probed inside Janet's moist vagina with her index finger and immediately touched the most sensitive spot. Janet twitched slightly in reflex, moaned softly with delight, and spread her legs more invitingly.

Klaudia homed in on Janet's most sensitive nerves, and her hands seemed more excited and energized. With varying amounts of pressure, she lubricated Janet's vaginal opening. Then, Klaudia altered the pace of massage, with one hand gently stroking her clitoris and the other alternately rubbing her pelvic region, then probing deep inside her trembling vagina.

Earlier than expected, Janet experienced an orgasm. Then, in an even shorter time felt an even stronger, prolonged rush of delectable satisfaction as Klaudia continued to coax her body. A stream of stronger climaxes erupted, one quickly after the other. Each left her wanting more as the intensity grew and her flush of pleasure amplified. It was all Janet could do to suppress her desire to scream.

—•—

The repeated beeps of a phone interrupted Janet's thoughts, and she shook her companion's shoulder to alert her. When Klaudia saw the message, she bolted upright, her face hardened, and her eyes squinted in disbelief.

Still naked, Klaudia reached for clothes and motioned for Janet to do the same.

"I have to call the *Bundesnachrichtendienst*. Something's happening," she said as they gathered up the garments strewn on the floor and put them on quickly. Klaudia picked up a brush to tame her wild hair.

"They want a video link right now. We may have to leave this morning," Klaudia explained.

Janet followed her roommate down the stairs two at a time and dashed to the kitchen to make coffee while Klaudia fired up the computer and waited for all the security protocols to finish. Janet sat in front of the computer just as Klaudia and their contact in the German federal intelligence service completed their greetings.

"We've got a major mission we want you both to undertake. It's dangerous and the people upstairs ordered me to assure you there will be no negative consequences if you refuse to do it. Listen to me. Think carefully about the risks. Then let me know your thoughts," the familiar face and voice assured with a soft and sympathetic tone.

"What's up?" Klaudia asked. Below the view of the camera, she reached out and squeezed Janet's hand, then continued to delicately hold it.

"We've learned a very high-profile woman in The Organization's prostitution business in France wants out. She's their main "recruiter." We know she has a ton of names and numbers. She's prepared to cooperate, but we have to act very quickly."

"Okay, what do you need from us?" Klaudia asked, with a sideward glance at Janet.

"She's attending some sort of summit the head honchos in The Organization are holding secretly in Garmisch-Partenkirchen tomorrow," the intelligence agent continued. "We don't have all the details yet, but she thinks we need to get her out tomorrow or it may be too late. Apparently, Giancarlo Mareno and a Japanese guy named Sugimori are meeting with her boss Pierre Boivin from France."

"This is the same Boivin we've been monitoring in Aix-en-Provence? The one who brings in the girls from Morocco?" Klaudia asked.

"One and the same. The woman who wants out is his chief handler of the women, Nadine Violette. A woman from Martinique. And we know she's recently been with Mareno in Martinique as well. The intelligence she might provide could be extremely valuable, but we haven't finalized a workable plan to get her out safely yet," their contact explained.

"What do you want us to do?" Klaudia's forehead creased in concern.

"If you agree to do this job, we can have a car and driver there in about thirty minutes. He'll drive you to the south of Germany to a hotel in Garmisch-Partenkirchen where they'll be meeting tomorrow. We've got a mercenary working inside the hotel. She'll get you a room near the wing the vermin are going to occupy. We'll work with our contact inside the hotel for information and keep linked to you on a secure line as you travel. We think we can develop a plan by the time you get there, but there are no promises, and we certainly can't guarantee your safety that close to The Organization."

Klaudia looked away from the camera and directly at Janet with an inquisitive arch of her eyebrows. Then, she faced the camera.

"Do you really need both of us? We're grooming Janet for the Costa Rica mission. I'm happy to go, but wouldn't it be better for her to stay here?"

"Maybe. But we have a challenge," the intelligence agent replied. "We expect Nadine to be tightly guarded, and our experts are still working on a diversion to draw away at least a part of the contingent guarding her. We may need to use Janet as a decoy to create that opening."

"That sounds awfully dangerous," Klaudia exclaimed. She turned from the camera to face Janet squarely, her eyes intense. "You've invested your soul into becoming a Latin American teenager to prowl the Internet. We need you to do that and not take unnecessary risks to save a girl who has already sold out hundreds of other women."

"You're right, Klaudia. It has some danger, but our team is devising a way to safely expose Janet just long enough for the guards to weaken their defenses," the agent explained. "It's risky, but it may be the only way we can get to the woman without endangering her life and putting our rescuers in unacceptable danger. We need to improve the chances of success. But—and I emphasize this—we'll respect Janet's decision."

Klaudia watched as Janet processed their words and her conflicting emotions. The silence lasted only a few seconds. When she spoke, Janet ignored the camera and looked deeply into Klaudia's beautiful brown eyes and said hoarsely, "If you're taking on this mission, I'm going with you. It's not negotiable."

FORTY-THREE

Innsbruck, Austria, Sunday January 26, 2020

No fan of sightseeing, Giancarlo Mareno wasn't disappointed at all to miss most of the impressive mountain views on the brief trip from the airport. He and Luigi were comfortable in the back seat of the Mercedes SUV even though it was smaller than they were accustomed to back home. They arrived in the Austrian ski-town near the German border after dark and zipped to their hotel with ease.

Despite being peak ski season, traffic was light. Climate change continued to exact its toll throughout the Alps, and Innsbruck was warmer than in years past, making snow conditions less favorable. In addition, evenings in Innsbruck were usually a time for vibrant nightlife as visitors to the scenic town celebrated their triumphant swoops down the mountainsides at breakneck speed. Most knew their adrenalin highs would compound the impact of alcohol and left their cars parked while they haunted the nightclubs and bars within walking distance of their hotels.

Giancarlo had researched the town's tendencies on Google during the flight, so he reminded Luigi to be sure they got quiet rooms when they checked in, even if the hotel had to move someone else.

"We all need to be extra alert for the entire day tomorrow." He turned to look his companion directly in the eye. "Arrange for food to be sent to every room. Tell the guys to get some sleep after they eat and to stay out of the bar. You eat your meal with me. I want to review the game plan for tomorrow again."

"Right, boss. Okay to order a glass of wine for everyone?"

"Okay. But only one each. And be sure your guys understand they're not to leave their rooms until morning," Giancarlo admonished. "Let's all meet in my room for breakfast at about 8:00. We can review the plans we make tonight with the guys in the morning. When do you expect the first report from the girl in Garmisch-Partenkirchen?"

"She'll be there in about an hour and will probably need some time with the contact at the hotel. I expect she'll be able to give me a briefing about midnight, but I asked her to call immediately if anything doesn't go according to plan," Luigi explained.

"Okay. If there's anything you can't fix immediately, let me know," Giancarlo instructed before asking his next question. "What do we know about the rendezvous in Munich?"

"Nadine seems out of the loop," Luigi said. "She knows there's a meeting at three o'clock, but she wasn't invited. She was also left out of all the planning discussions with the team. All she knows is there are four French bodyguards and they'll meet at the hotel. Boivin hasn't allowed her to hear any other details."

"It's a good thing you found that new listening technology for at least one phone. Boivin must realize she's feeding us information," Giancarlo spat out with disgust. "That one is much too careless. She might become a real liability if he starts to feed her misinformation to pass on to us. We'll need to take her with us when we go back. Figure out how you can scoop her up before we leave the hotel. Maybe put her in our vehicle."

Giancarlo took a breath and reached for a bottle of Coke from the glove compartment.

"Have we heard anything from Suji-san's geisha in Japan?" he asked.

"She's gone. Disappeared. We checked out her place in Tokyo and it's empty. Not a piece of clothing or furniture, nothing." Luigi shrugged. "We lost her after your last call with Sugimori and don't know if she just took off or was eliminated."

"Did she have any family?"

"None we know of."

"We'll need to get someone new to keep an eye on Sugimori and his crowd. Find me a likely target to approach, someone with a lot to lose," Giancarlo commanded.

"Okay, boss. I'll do that before I come to the room for our planning meeting. Anything else?" he asked as he scrawled a note on a pad he yanked from his jacket.

"Did we pay the Japanese guy? He wanted payment in advance, right?"

"Yeah. She took the money from the Macau account and transferred the funds yesterday. He's set."

"Anything on Howard Knight yet?"

"Yeah, but it sounds a little wonky to me. We're checking it out," Luigi replied. "We listened in on a conversation from Boivin's contact at Interpol. They got a tip from a hostel in Lourdes, France. Apparently, a guy matching Knight's description but with no ID checked in while we were in the air."

"Have they checked out the lead?" Giancarlo wanted to know.

"The guy from Interpol thought it was a wild goose chase. He asked Boivin what would attract Knight to a little town like Lourdes. Did he expect some sort of miracle? Anyway, Boivin finally got him to send an agent from Toulouse first thing tomorrow morning."

"Get that asshole to Lourdes right now!" Giancarlo bellowed. "I know exactly why Knight's there."

FORTY-FOUR

Munich Airport Hilton, Oberding, Germany, Sunday January 26, 2020

Pierre Boivin walked alone and intentionally slowed his pace before he entered the hotel for the second time. He and Nadine had already checked in a couple hours earlier, but he decided to go back to the airport for a few minutes, then re-enter the hotel without anyone else. He wasn't sure how closely the Japanese team monitored his actions but thought a second solo entrance might obscure the exact number of people in his entourage that day.

In genuine awe, Pierre passed through the revolving glass doors into one of the world's great hotels. Like many others, Hilton's Munich Airport Hotel was designed to impress and justify the exorbitant rates they charged, but he guessed he wasn't alone in appreciating such grandeur. They continued to invest billions in building these monuments to excess, didn't they? The majesty of the structure brought a smile to his face.

Glass walls stretched five floors upward to a glass ceiling, prompting Pierre to tilt his head upward in silent appreciation before he turned around to take in the view through the surrounding windows. The enclosed lobby area provided bright natural light even on a cloudy winter day. Spotless marble floors sparkled from every direction, and Pierre drew a deep breath of admiration for both the functional design and the builders of this masterpiece.

A few seconds passed before his mind jolted back to the immediate task at hand, chagrined that he must appear to others as a neophyte tourist. He laughed silently with that glimpse of self-recognition and looked around for Sugimori. A few seconds after Pierre stepped inside, he spotted the Japanese crime boss sitting alone at a table in a quiet corner, exactly as described in the email he'd received.

Sugimori stood up sharply, smiled broadly, and waved as soon as they made eye contact. His look was thoroughly modern. Taller than

169

average, his height equaled Pierre's six-foot frame, and he sported both a mustache and a small goatee on his handsome face. His jet-black hair was on the longer side and partially covered his ears, but where many guys might part their hair, he sported a narrow blond streak.

The new head of the Japanese Yakuza was dressed impeccably in a navy-blue blazer with gleaming brass buttons over a light blue turtleneck sweater. His blue jeans were the same luxury brand Pierre often purchased, paying a few hundred dollars for the privilege. A pair of stylish leather shoes appeared even more expensive. The guy would fit in perfectly on *Avenue des Champs-Élysées*.

As Pierre approached, Sugimori first spread his arms widely in extravagant welcome, then swung his right arm in an arch to firmly grip Pierre's outstretched hand and pump it with enthusiasm. Still gripping Pierre's hand, he wrapped his other arm around his French counterpart in an embrace of friendship typical of the Middle East or Africa. Remembering recent news reports of a nasty virus surfacing in Asia, Pierre squirmed loose at the thought and took a step back, then sat facing his Japanese counterpart with his chair a little farther back from the table.

As they exchanged pleasantries and ordered tea and coffee, Pierre casually glanced around the lobby. As expected, three other Japanese men sat at either the tall bar stools or tables a respectable distance away. A Japanese woman sat with another Japanese fellow at the table closest to them. None looked directly toward Sugimori or Pierre. Meanwhile, it looked like his own team had taken their positions precisely as they had planned.

After their drinks arrived with usual German efficiency, but astonishing good cheer from the server, Sugimori started their dialogue.

"Let's put our cards on the table right at the beginning." He flashed a charming smile and brilliant white teeth as he crossed his legs and hunched in toward Pierre. *This Japanese guy acts more French than we do.*

"None of us in Japan is happy with the current financial arrangement Giancarlo Mareno demands. It's worse than typical American arrogance. The amount of money we send him every month is crippling our ability to grow. I'm guessing you feel the same pain."

"Absolutely. His protection has value, but our intake this year barely matches last year. We've had to take on riskier stuff to keep enough coming in to support the guys and maintain their loyalty. I even had to eliminate a couple promising recruits last year when they poached on activities behind my back. As they met their maker, they pleaded for understanding. Said they were working on the side only to make enough to keep *their* people happy."

"Mareno's smart but he's become too greedy," Sugimori agreed with a nod. "Like his country, he thinks he's built an invincible wall around himself. But he hasn't kept up with technology. We now know as much about his businesses as he does. But don't ask, because I'm not prepared to give you any juicy information."

Pierre noticed the shift in tone instantly. The earlier grand gestures of welcome and relaxed humor disappeared. Sugimori's expression became stern, and his shoulders tightened as he staked out his position.

"Yeah, I guessed that from your telephone comment about Suji-san. Was it really Giancarlo who had him killed?" Pierre asked.

"No doubt. We knew about the plan the day before they murdered him in his hospital bed. We could have stopped it, but Suji-san was too old. He didn't have the will to fight Mareno, and he made some bad decisions. We let Giancarlo's flunkies do their dirty deed with the drugs so we wouldn't eventually be forced to do it."

"What kinds of bad decisions did Suji-San make?" Pierre asked.

"His big mistake was getting involved with that American supermarket chain, Jeffersons Stores. The company was a cesspool. People there had no idea how to make money, and Suji-san would have realized that if he'd done any competent research before he gained control of the company. He was too enamored with his grand ambition to outflank Mareno, who was trying to seize control of Multima Corporation at the same time. We think it was a carefully staged trap."

"Yeah, we lost a good chance in France then too. I remember, Multima merged with the French chain, Farrefour," Pierre recalled. "Mareno was pissed at that loss too."

"But Suji-san's demise is no problem." Sugimori refocused the discussion on his agenda. "I have control of Japan. Every faction has sworn its loyalty, and our technology will rout out any future dissidents before they gain traction. I've also got the Chinese and North Koreans onside. They're prepared to wage war if Mareno doesn't bend."

"I have the Spanish, Portuguese, and Ukrainians with me. The Northern European guys aren't important enough to matter, but we have the strongest factions in Europe ready to work with us. Except the Italians. Mareno is just too powerful there to risk it," Pierre countered.

"Good. We'll present a formidable front if Mareno tries to resist," Sugimori said with a satisfied grin. "He knows he'll need to give a bit.

He wouldn't have agreed to meet us if he wasn't prepared to shave something off his take. Our technology confirmed he's going to offer us about one percent and settle for two after a few hours of discussion."

"One or two percent!" Pierre exclaimed. "For him, that's pocket change. My guys want to see his commission cut in half. Five percent, minimum." Pierre slapped the table with his open hand for emphasis.

"The rest of us would like to get there too." Sugimori pushed back with both hands to urge patience. "We might not get everything in a single meeting. Let's remember, he does bring us some value. We still need his cozy relationship with the American government."

"But even that relationship appears to have its limits. Will his guy even be there six months from now? Who knows?" Pierre creased his brow to show doubt.

"You're right," Sugimori said. "Circumstances may change in the coming months, but for now, we all depend on the political clout. I propose we moderate the expectations of our supporters in the other countries now and negotiate in a way that we make progress but allow Giancarlo to save face. Here's what I suggest."

For the following two hours, the two men choreographed their coming negotiating session with Mareno with the same excruciating detail as a classical ballet.

FORTY-FIVE

Their journey from Angermund to the south of Germany started inauspiciously. As soon as they slipped into the back seat of the Mercedes, Janet noticed the driver's clean-shaven face. That posed a problem. Both she and Klaudia Schäffer wore their full, black abayas and niqabs. Their driver was a blonde Aryan. He couldn't have appeared more German if they'd asked a casting service to provide one for a movie.

Klaudia appreciated the issue as soon as Janet pointed it out. Their driver would also be their escort and protector in the hotel while they were in Garmisch-Partenkirchen. This driver would not only draw unwanted attention to them, he'd also set off alarm bells with even the most unsophisticated among The Organization. She demanded the driver wait while she spoke with her usual contact at the *Bundesnachrichtendienst*.

He too saw the problem instantly and apologized for the oversight. Because time was their enemy, and no helicopters were immediately available, he suggested they start out regardless. He'd work with his colleagues in Frankfurt to find a replacement driver and get back to her with instructions as soon as he knew more.

They set out from Angermund on a cloudy day, but thankfully no rainfall hampered their progress. The *Autobahn* routes tended to be slower when it rained because sensible German drivers prudently matched their speeds to weather conditions. The pleasantly clear motorway lured their driver to a speed greater than a hundred miles per hour within seconds of entering the A3 headed south toward Frankfurt.

They zipped past cars in the right lanes, but then their driver always moved aside to let Porsches and other sports cars pass them at speeds sometimes double theirs. Janet had never been in a vehicle traveling so fast. However, on the *autobahns* high speeds are normal with no posted speed limits for long sections.

Janet was fascinated. The large Mercedes they drove was built for high performance and its passenger security and comfort was equal to an American car traveling at half the speed. If she looked forward, she didn't realize how fast they were going until she glanced at the car's dashboard. She soon realized the reason it seemed no faster; the white painted lines and markers on the road. They were much wider and longer than lines on American roads, reducing the illusion of speed. Out her side window, power and telephone poles appeared like falling match sticks as the car passed. She drew her seatbelt tighter around her waist.

More accustomed to German driving speeds and still more than a little hungover, Klaudia dozed with her head tilted back against the passenger head restraint. As on most expressways around the world, the scenery soon became repetitious and boring with only the occasional glimpse of a castle or fort near the Rhine River on her right. Soon Janet slept as well.

They were awakened by the driver's shout that a call was coming in. Groggily, Klaudia rummaged in her bag for her phone and answered after the fourth or fifth ring.

"Is everything okay there?" the voice asked.

"Yes, everything's fine," Klaudia stammered after recognizing the voice as Agent Fronhaus, her main contact in the German federal intelligence service. For some reason, he hadn't bothered with the usual security protocol. She noticed the oversight, shrugged her shoulders, and arched her eyebrows to Janet.

"We couldn't find a Middle Eastern agent on such short notice, but we tracked down one of Turkish heritage. He's second generation and speaks only German and Turkish. You'll need to translate for Janet, which might pose some challenges in close quarters. Put me on speaker so I can talk with all of you," he said.

Klaudia pressed the button while Janet noted the driver planned to participate in the call without reducing his current hundred miles per hour speed. She tugged the seatbelt tighter again.

"Your driver, Hans, will bring you to our Frankfurt office to pick up the new agent, but he'll also stay on your mission. Although he can't serve as your escort, we think it might be helpful to have another armed agent nearby to assist with your escape once you snatch the woman in Garmisch-Partenkirchen," their contact said. "So, you'll simply make a short detour here. He'll be in our office in about twenty minutes. You can pick him up and carry on."

"Okay," Klaudia replied. "But what's the plan when we get there?"

"We're still working on that," the agent said. "We have two rooms arranged close to the wing they reserved for their grand pow-wow. I'll ping your telephone with the electronic codes so you won't need to go through check-in. I'll also send you photos and a detailed layout of the hotel. Memorize everything when you get it. We're supposed to speak with the French woman within the next few minutes. Our contact in Lourdes has found a way to link her in so she can talk to us directly."

Within minutes, the electronic messages bounced onto the screen of Klaudia's phone, and they scrutinized the map and photos until their stop in Frankfurt. As promised, their new addition was waiting in the basement of the office tower that housed the *Bundesnachrichtendienst* with Agent Schmidt. She was one of the women Klaudia frequently dealt with, and took charge as soon as the car came to a stop.

"Ahmed here will be your escort and guard inside the hotel," she said as she pointed toward a short, lean man with Middle Eastern coloring and a dark unkempt beard. Shorter than both women, he looked at ease in his blue jeans and light jacket with a scarf wound jauntily around his neck.

"Fronhaus, your main contact, wants you to know he's speaking with the French woman right now and expects to call you within the hour with detailed instructions," the woman continued.

Janet, Hans, and Klaudia all listened to the instructions without comment. Ahmed fidgeted until Agent Schmidt translated her comments into German. Then the intelligence service woman continued her orders as she handed each one a walkie-talkie. When she was satisfied they were all properly installed and working, Agent Schmidt continued.

"Neither of you is authorized to use guns, but we've got pepper spray for you. Take these and keep them with you all the time. It won't help you from a distance, but close up you just press here and point it at the eyes of your victim. It might buy you a little time."

"Do we know what the woman we are trying to rescue looks like?" Klaudia wanted to know.

"Not yet. We asked her to send us a selfie. We'll get it to you as soon as we can."

"Besides finding women and girls, what's her role in The Organization?" Janet asked.

"We're not entirely sure yet," the intelligence woman replied. "We know she's working for Pierre Boivin and is also his regular companion. But our contact in Lourdes says she also has some sort of relationship with Giancarlo Mareno. It might get complicated inside the hotel when it's time to act."

With an offer to use the toilet before leaving, Agent Schmidt handed Klaudia a thermos of hot coffee and four paper cups. The intelligence service woman's job was done.

More than an hour passed before they heard again from their usual contact. They had just passed a large roadside sign for *Karlsruhe* seconds before Klaudia's phone rang.

"We've talked to her and it won't be easy," Agent Fronhaus said with a tinge of resignation in his voice. "Mareno has told the woman she'll be leaving with him, not Boivin. Apparently, while their big pow-wow is in process, one of his people is supposed to come to her room and whisk her away to one of Mareno's vehicles. She doesn't know when, who among Mareno's people, or which of his cars. And she has no way to reach him. He ordered her not to call him under any circumstances."

"Is she committed to an escape?" Klaudia asked.

"Can't be entirely sure of that either," Fronhaus replied. "She sounds desperate. Broke down crying three times in our ten-minute conversation. Her name is Nadine. Her English is very good. And she's quite bright. But she's rattled and genuinely terrified of both Boivin and Mareno. She does believe we're her only hope, so I think she'll see it through."

The conversation continued as they sped southward. Communication took longer than necessary because they had to translate almost every sentence for Ahmed. Janet became concerned about just how much danger their inability to communicate directly might cause.

"This Nadine, what languages does she speak?"

"English and French. She's from Martinique so French is her first language, but her English is very passable," Fronhaus replied.

"Isn't there a risk if we need to translate from English to German when we actually snatch her?" Janet asked.

"Good point," a new voice on the line replied. "You've got another couple hours before you reach the hotel. Make a list of words you might need to use. Ahmed, you'll need to learn those words before you arrive."

The new voice also delivered the last part of the order in Turkish to be sure there was no misunderstanding about either the urgency or importance. With enthusiasm, the team compiled its list and Klaudia translated it into German. Within minutes, they were all playing a game with Ahmed to teach him enough words to keep themselves alive. Their game continued until Hans drove into the parking lot of the Hotel Eibsee just outside the charming southern town of Garmisch-Partenkirchen.

It was moments before dusk when they arrived, but the view of the hotel and lake at sunset were still breathtaking, even from the rear seat of the car. From the parking lot, the majestic mountains in the background of the hotel looked truly magnificent, with snow covering all but the wooded areas. The jagged granite peaks towered overhead and made the hotel seem toy-like in comparison.

The hotel was surrounded by fresh snowfall, half a foot deep on top of the peaked roof and all the surrounding area. A snow blower cleared the sidewalks. A fluffy white mass blew in the air, then settled across the ground, creating an atmosphere that seemed almost romantic while they still sat in the warm car admiring the snowflakes from a comfortable distance.

They lingered quietly for a few seconds. Everyone appreciated the magnificent sight despite their critical mission. Janet finally took the lead.

"I think we should come back when it's completely dark," she said. "I don't see many people, but it seems to me we have a better chance of avoiding detection if we use darkness for cover."

"I agree," Hans replied without hesitation. "There are actually people in two different cars in the lot."

His intelligence training clearly provided him with insights the others missed. He took charge.

"I'll drive us back into town. I saw a couple restaurants open where we won't attract undue attention." He put the car in gear and started off. "I skied here a couple times. There are a lot of tourists this time of year and a surprising number come from the Middle East."

He was right. A staff member at the restaurant *Zum Wildschütz* offered a hearty welcome as they entered, and without the group asking, ushered them to a corner where he shifted two tables together into one, positioning Janet and Klaudia facing the wall. When they lowered their niqabs to eat, only the two intelligence agents would be able to see their faces.

For a couple hours, the team ate schnitzels recommended by their driver and talked quietly about the weather, their drive, and the beauty of the area. They took pains to avoid any reference to their mission in deference to Janet's warning that The Organization was so thorough any public building in the town might be monitored.

It was late in the evening before they dared venture into the hotel. Hans left Ahmed and the women right in front of the door at the end of the building where it was unlikely someone would monitor their activity. The electronic codes worked perfectly. They used the stairwell rather than an elevator, and swept down the hallway silently until they again used the phone to unlock the room the three would share. The driver's room was right beside it with an adjoining door.

Once their vehicle was parked and Hans joined them, the men inspected their room for listening or video devices. They checked everywhere in the bedrooms and bathrooms with electronic wands. Both crawled under the beds to inspect every square inch of the floor's surface below. After almost an hour, the driver spoke.

"I think we're clear," Hans whispered. "But let's stay as quiet as possible and talk only when necessary. We'll check the hotel. You women stay here. Get some sleep. We'll wake you when we get back."

They didn't return until morning and brought with them some strong coffee and loaves of German bread with a few bananas and apples. Their whispered debriefing took more than two hours with all the translations and clarifications, but they said they felt ready. Janet wasn't quite as sure.

FORTY-SIX

Lourdes, France, Monday January 27, 2020

Just after midnight, Howard Knight awoke from a fitful sleep with a jolt. He felt around clumsily in the darkness for his phone to check the time. When the hour first registered with his brain, his immediate impulse was to roll over and get more sleep. Even though he had checked into the hostel early in the afternoon—and slept well for a few hours—he was still tired, and all of his taut muscles ached.

But he couldn't sleep more. Instead, his mind worked furiously in anticipation of the call he'd make later. For a while, his focus shifted to continued unease with his plight. After about an hour of deliberating, he concluded sleep would be elusive that night. He did the prudent thing and left.

He had draped his clothes over a radiator heater in the bathroom to dry. Silently, Howard dressed and stashed his other meager possessions in his backpack. He refilled the plastic bottle with fresh water and unplugged Katherine Page's phone from the charger. Prepared, he slowly opened the door to his room and peeked into the small hallway a short distance from the front desk.

With a first quick scan outside his room, he didn't see anyone. He glanced in the direction of the window in the tiny reception area and noticed a young man sleeping on a sofa, his back to Howard. As stealthily as possible, Howard left the room and headed for the emergency exit to his right. He checked around the doorway for alarms and was satisfied the door wasn't wired. With one last glance at the time on his phone—two in the morning—he shuddered at the thought he'd need to spend almost seven hours walking about in the cold before the office he intended to visit would open.

But he saw little alternative, and slipped quietly out the door at the side of the building, then headed west on the way to the *Ousse* river winding lazily through the center of the city. After he passed the *Musée du*

Gemmail, he crossed the river and headed north on *avenue Peyramale* toward the sacred *Sanctuaires Notre-Dame-de-Lourdes*.

As he ambled along as casually as possible on a well-lit street in the early hours of the morning, Howard thought it would probably be interesting to see the famous church anyway. He'd heard all about the Sanctuary of Our Lady of Lourdes in his youth. His mother was a devout Italian Catholic who believed in things like miracles. Her stories about the legends flooded back to him. People had once considered the water flowing from the spring in the *Grotto of Massabielle* inside the sanctuary to have holy healing properties blessed by the Virgin Mary. Thousands of pilgrims visited the site every year in the hope of cures for severe illnesses and injuries. Despite no scientific evidence to support the belief, desperate people from around the world continued to visit to drink or bathe in the water.

Howard scoffed again at the idea of real miracles as he trudged past and resolved to trust only money. With enough money, anything was possible. Without it, there could only be a futile hope for some form of supernatural phenomenon. With his penchant for numbers and facts, belief in such a spiritual possibility was not only remote, it was impossible. Nothing about the majesty of the building stirred interest in Howard. And in the end, he marched on, barely pausing to glance over as he passed.

After the sanctuary, Howard veered north and crossed the river again to follow *route de Pau* eastward on the north side of the river. At that hour, he found little to explore. Most of the shops had metal folding shutters on the outside walls to protect the windows from theft and vandalism. Even a holy city couldn't avoid petty mischief and crime.

His route continued to *boulevard du Lapacca*, then to *rue de Bagnères* on to the main thoroughfare, *avenue Général Baron Maransin*. When he returned to *rue de la Grotte*, Howard decided to pass near the hostel to start his second loop. He still had another four hours to kill before the office would open.

At *rue du Bourg*, blue flashing lights caught his attention, and he immediately ducked into a space between two buildings to survey the scene. As he peeked around the corner, he saw at least four police cars and vans parked on both sides of the street in front of the Lindo Carillon. More than a dozen *gendarmes* milled around the front of the hostel, all carrying powerful weapons. They looked threatening but didn't appear to be executing any particular plan.

With his heart beating rapidly, Howard darted off in the opposite direction. About a half-mile away, he came upon a small park with a few trees and shrubs. It seemed a shame to soil his freshly washed clothes before he visited the office, but it was imperative to stay out of sight for some time. He found a cluster of plants and bushes that blocked any view from the street and waited among the shrubs.

Just before nine in the morning, the streets around the park bustled with traffic and pedestrians. Howard could adequately blend in and thought it safe enough to venture out. He looked around slowly and carefully in a full circle after he shuffled out of the bushes, dusting off his pants and shirt as he took in his surroundings. No police were evident, and people walking in the streets avoided eye contact as they usually did in French cities these days.

Howard walked a couple blocks to arrive at the offices of *Banque TVB*. The bank's sign was a small, discrete logo mounted on a granite slab just above the upper right corner of the door. It looked impressive, even if modest in size. He tried the door and found it was locked despite the posted hours showing they should be open for business. Then he spotted a bell to the left of the door and rang it.

"*Bonjour*," a voice called out from a speaker built into the wall.

"Bonjour," Howard replied. "My name is Mr. Smith. I'm a Canadian customer and would like to use your voice recognition software."

"All right. Come in, Mr. Smith," the voice answered as a buzzer sounded and a lock clicked open. "Our software recognizes you."

Howard entered the narrow hallway and climbed another five steps before a tall French woman, dressed impeccably in a gray business suit and sensible black shoes, greeted him at the top of the stairs. She smiled as she opened yet another door with a key and motioned for Howard to follow.

Once inside, she passed him a bottle of sanitizer after squirting a dab on her own hands.

"We can't be too careful with this new virus about," she said. Then she shook Howard's hand formally with the correct amount of pressure and held it long enough to acknowledge his importance but not encourage any personal warmth or unwanted attention. The handshake was identical to Mr. Fernando's, his usual contact at the bank in its Cayman Islands headquarters. After, she squirted another dab of sanitizer.

They chatted about the unpleasant weather until they arrived at the woman's office. She had arranged coffee, and they sat opposite each other with an expansive mahogany desk between them. Her desktop was clear with only one bulky speakerphone perched on a corner, a relic from older days of technology, but still popular with business executives and bankers.

Howard explained the story he had rehearsed for hours while hiding among the shrubs in the park.

"I'm a Canadian businessman," he started with the best expressions of frustration and desperation he could muster. "Yesterday, I was sightseeing at the Sanctuary when I was robbed. They took my wallet, which had all my money and identification in it."

"Oh! I'm so sorry to hear that, Mr. Smith. Did you contact the *gendarmes*, the police?"

"Not yet. I'm headed there next. I'd first like to arrange some funds to tide me over. Can we please contact Mr. Fernando in your Cayman Islands office?"

"I'd be happy to do that, but the office isn't open yet. It's one o'clock in the morning there. Perhaps you could visit the police department to report your incident and come back about four o'clock this afternoon." Her professional smile remained fixed.

"No, thank you. I understand the hour but would still like you to call Mr. Fernando now. I'm quite sure you can reach him at 001-345-949-9823." Howard watched intently as the significance of the number registered and observed the change as her standard business smile turned upward into genuine welcome. Only the bank's wealthiest clients had access to the private number of one of the firm's most senior executives.

"Would you like me to leave the room after I dial the number?" she offered graciously.

"No, please stay. We'll probably need your help," Howard replied.

A voice answered on the third ring despite the extremely late hour in the Caribbean. "Fernando here. How can I help?"

"Mr. Fernando, good morning. It's Yvette Lachance in Lourdes. I have a Canadian customer here. A Mr. Smith. He passed the voice recognition security. Would you like to test again?"

"Yes. Give me a moment to activate it here," Mr. Fernando said. Howard meanwhile mused about the elaborate charade. He didn't believe the person he was speaking with was named Fernando any more than the man expected him to actually be a Canadian named Smith. It was the dance of illicit international finance and both were complicit partners.

"Go ahead, Mr. Smith," the voice instructed.

"I'm sorry to bother you at such an untimely hour, Mr. Fernando," Howard said and waited for the software to confirm his voice was the one associated with his account in TVB Bank.

"It's not a problem at all, Mr. Smith. It's been quite some time since we last spoke. Have you been keeping well?" Fernando was as polite and accommodating as he was every time Howard spoke with him, despite the inconvenient interruption of his sleep or whatever else he might have been doing at one o'clock in the morning.

"I'm well, but I've had some recent misfortune." Howard then spent the following few minutes recounting his carefully rehearsed explanation about his wallet and passport before he got to the real issue. "I've also had some bad luck in the stock market recently and need you to transfer the funds I deposited with you when times were better."

"Are you referring to the last deposit you made … in 2017?" he asked after apparently checking on a screen of some device. Did the man take a laptop to bed with him at night?

"Yes, the $100,000. And it's all right to speak openly in front of Ms. Lachance," Howard assured him.

"All right. Now you'll remember I must report any transfer greater than $10,000 to the banking authorities. Are you okay with that?"

"No," Howard answered. "I'd like to request smaller transfers. Can you make each about $9,500?"

"Of course. I'll arrange ten transfers of $9,500 each and one of $5,000 over the next eleven days," Mr. Fernando confirmed. "You may pick up the initial amount from Ms. Lachance after four o'clock this afternoon in Lourdes."

"I'd like to get the funds a little more quickly," Howard said. "Could we arrange for Ms. Lachance to provide me with the full amount today?"

"Of course, Mr. Smith. But I would need to transfer your $100,000 to Ms. Lachance by way of only *eight* transfers of $9500. Will this be acceptable?" Fernando asked in return.

Howard silently cursed under his breath at the man's audacity but realized he had little alternative. And he was sure Fernando realized it too. He was careful to keep his gaze directly on Ms. Lachance's eyes as he forced himself to use the most accommodating tone possible with a smile he hoped looked natural.

"Of course, Mr. Fernando. That's fair. Will Ms. Lachance be able to give me the $76,000 transfer with perhaps $70,000 in US dollars and the rest in euros while I'm here today?"

"I can do that, Mr. Smith," she replied as she hastily punched numbers into a calculator she had pulled from a drawer. "I can give you 70,000 US dollars and 4,500 euros in small bills. Will that be all right?"

This time Howard couldn't contain a wince. She too was skimming about fifteen percent more than the official exchange rate because she also realized he had no alternative. Recovering quickly, Howard smiled again and assured her that would be fine.

Less than fifteen minutes later, Howard retraced his way down the five steps from the bank with enough cash in his backpack to start the next phase of his escape. But it was still daylight. He assumed the police would maintain a presence in the area, so he darted back to his hiding place in the park and hid behind the same bushes he had used for cover earlier that morning. The space was still vacant, but a vagrant had left behind some partially eaten food and an empty wine bottle sometime after Howard left for the bank. Disgusted, Howard left the spot and found another one along the sidewalk.

The outline of his plan was coming together, but he still had to determine how he would get a fake EU passport. Clearly, he needed to flee Europe for safer environs. He would consider that in more detail in the afternoon. But first, there remained one loose end he wanted to clear up before he formulated travel plans.

As soon as he was comfortable sitting in the bushes, he pulled Katherine's phone from his backpack and sent a single text to a familiar number in Germany. He asked the party to reply as quickly as possible that day, for it would be the last day he'd have access to the phone and number. He could no longer risk the possibility the police in Portugal might find a way to track her phone despite the change of SIM card.

FORTY-SEVEN

Google Maps claimed the drive to Hotel Eibsee in Garmisch-Partenkirchen was about one and one-half hours from Innsbruck, so Giancarlo Mareno wanted to allow adequate time for the trip. He and Luigi agreed they should arrive early. Surprise was often a useful tool in negotiations.

The weather that day was cloudy, but no snow was forecast in the mountains, so they planned to leave the hotel at noon.

Feedback from the secret advance team that traveled to Garmisch-Partenkirchen was positive. The German-speaking woman, Annika, and her team had successfully hidden listening devices in the room Giancarlo would use as well as those suites reserved for Boivin and Sugimori. To be safe, they planted devices in the bedrooms immediately adjacent and opposite those of their adversaries as well, in case either decided to switch rooms with a subordinate at the last minute.

None of the groups actually planned to sleep in their rooms. That had all been agreed the week prior. Everyone would arrive for a meeting at three o'clock. They would take as long as necessary to achieve a consensus, if one was possible. Once they had an agreement, or concluded a consensus couldn't be reached, they would disband in their different directions. It would not be a social event in any sense.

Sugimori's people had already reserved and paid in advance for the entire wing closest to the lake. Last week, the hotel had sent keys for the rooms each team would use with an understanding the rooms might be occupied at any time during the twenty-four hours between nine o'clock Monday morning and nine o'clock the following day. So, Annika and her team paid for separate rooms in another wing of the hotel as a base for their clandestine activities.

But they had little sleep Sunday night, according to her reports. First, there were some technical issues with the hidden speakers. The signals faded in and out as they tested them, especially when more than one person was speaking. The audio tech on the team spent a couple hours finding and fixing the glitch.

Then a problem arose with the number of feeds they were receiving. Giancarlo had insisted the team monitor three separate rooms at once so information could be shared with Luigi. While Sugimori, Boivin and Giancarlo had agreed to surrender their weapons at the door of the meeting room—and undergo a wand sweep to ensure no weapons were hidden—all three agreed walkie-talkies were acceptable. Annika would receive all the summary information from team members monitoring separate rooms.

Her team had all the languages covered. They'd listen in on Boivin using a French-speaking resource and Sugimori with a Japanese-American. Annika would handle conversation in Giancarlo's room in the event any unplanned activity occurred. In that case, the entire team would respond. Although they still had some work to do, the sun was peeking through the clouds when Annika finally dismissed her team for a few hours' sleep.

Despite the satisfactory news from Hotel Eibsee, Giancarlo couldn't relax. He switched their focus back to the team with him in Innsbruck, those who would travel to Germany but then stay out of sight outside the hotel during the meeting.

"Who will monitor the Sugimori vehicles?" Giancarlo asked after they finished the Austrian breakfast of sausages, eggs, and mountains of crusty bread.

"Bill will handle that job." Luigi pointed to a hulking giant of a man sitting at the end of the table.

"Tell me what happens if Annika raises an attack alarm," Giancarlo demanded of the man at the end of the table.

"First, I eliminate any assets Sugimori left outside, shoot out both front tires on all their vehicles using a silencer, and then I run toward your meeting room, listening for instructions from Annika," he replied matter-of-factly.

"What if you hear gunfire from within the hotel?" Giancarlo asked.

"The same."

"What if you or our vehicles come under fire outside?" Giancarlo wondered.

"First, I alert Annika with the walkie-talkie. Then I eliminate the offenders." The man showed no emotion as he described his tasks and looked directly at Giancarlo as he spoke.

For almost an hour, Giancarlo grilled Luigi's three subordinates until he was satisfied everyone knew his individual role and responsibility. Equally important, were they ready to carry out those orders without hesitation? He devoted another large chunk of time to be sure their responses were almost automatic. There'd be no time to think if someone attacked. When Giancarlo was much younger, a near-lethal disaster had occurred, and he swore his people would never be caught flat-footed again.

"Okay, guys. It looks like you've all done a great job preparing. Now, I want you to relax in your rooms for an hour or so before we leave. I expect the meeting could be a long one. I'm prepared to negotiate, but they probably won't like the result. It may take some time to build consensus," Giancarlo warned.

Giancarlo studied each of the men carefully as they filed out of the room. He wanted to assess each guy's body language. Years ago, he'd learned how critical such troops were to his success and longevity. A mental lapse by any of them could mean his own elimination. If he detected even a hint of boredom or unease, the offender would not continue on the mission. If necessary, they'd eliminate the guy and make a new plan.

All passed the body language test.

"What happened in Lourdes last night?" Giancarlo demanded of Luigi as soon as the door to the room closed.

"He escaped again. The teenager watching the front desk at the hostel went to sleep and Knight slipped out sometime after midnight. When the Interpol people arrived this morning with local police, he'd already vanished. They dragged in the duty clerk who checked him in earlier—the one who initially gave us the tip—and showed him photos of Knight. The guy was sure the man he checked in was Knight."

"How do those people tolerate such incompetent police?" Giancarlo bellowed. "It's bad enough the bastards have no morals. But they fuck up everything they touch. The French should have another revolution and get rid of the bastards."

Diplomatically, Luigi said nothing in reply. After all, The Organization created much of that corruption and incompetence.

"Do they have any idea where he's headed?" Giancarlo asked more calmly.

"None," Luigi replied. "They put up a few roadblocks on the streets leaving town and have cars patrolling up and down the streets near the hostel. They have only one poor lead. A wino in a park near the hostel claimed he saw a new face that could have been a tourist. But he was already in a drunken stupor when they talked to him about eight this morning. The police are checking surveillance cameras in the areas around that park."

"Did they check out that TVB Bank I told you about?"

"Yes. The police were there about ten. There was a 'closed' sign in the window and no one responded when they rang the bell or tried to call," Luigi reported.

"Closed at ten o'clock on a Monday morning?" Giancarlo mused.

Luigi understood the question was a rhetorical one and made no comment. Giancarlo spent only a few minutes processing that tidbit of information before he grunted, "Get Boivin on the phone."

FORTY-EIGHT

Garmisch-Partenkirchen, Germany, Monday January 27, 2020

As Pierre had commanded, Nadine slipped into the see-through geisha outfit after they checked in. Nervously, she waited in their room until he returned from his discussions with Sugimori. Then, she felt every eye in the bright hotel atrium stare at her exposed body as they made the long uncomfortable walk across the lobby and out of the hotel.

Outside, her unease grew. When Sugimori suggested to Pierre—without even looking at her—that it might be better for Nadine to sit in the front and provide some sweet eye candy while they chatted in the back seat, she was surprised. When she looked at Pierre for a reaction, he said nothing but motioned her toward the front with a surly nod. And that's the way they started their short car ride from Munich to Garmisch-Partenkirchen.

Their driver was Japanese, but he seemed to know his way around. As they exited the airport onto the street *Zentralalle,* in the direction of the A-9 autoroute south, the driver pressed a button. A glass wall glided up from behind the front seats and closed off the car into two separate compartments. She heard the softly modulated tones of her companions gradually die as the compartment sealed tightly until not a sound came from the rear. She glanced back to see Sugimori in deep discussion with hand gestures and animation, but he didn't look in her direction at all.

She sighed, leaned her head back against the head restraint, and closed her eyes. Her knees trembled and her stomach churned, but she was careful not to display any angst with either her facial expressions or body language. She assumed the driver was part of the Sugimori team. She didn't want to attract attention that might later cause Pierre to explode and punish her again. Especially during these last few hours together.

The gruff old New York crime boss had called her again early that afternoon while Pierre met with Sugimori. She still found it amazing how precisely Mareno knew the times she was available for a call without

Pierre's knowledge. It must mean they were both under constant surveillance. A shiver ran down her spine with that thought.

Mareno was his usual abrupt self. During the meeting, two of his people would come to her room at the hotel in Garmisch-Partenkirchen. She was to go with them. They'd put her in the car he would use to return to Innsbruck, and then she'd go with him to Martinique. Say nothing to Boivin or anyone else about the plans.

Nadine remembered clearly her last trip to Martinique and the horror she felt when she arrived at Mareno's home to almost trip on the corpse of the badly beaten woman who had been her boss in Naples, Florida. Her intuition told her Mareno's plan for her was probably similar. For whatever reason, she supposed he was no longer satisfied with the value of information she provided about Boivin. She couldn't imagine him stealing her back from one of his associates for any other reason.

However, Pierre's meeting with Sugimori provided one other important benefit. It gave Nadine an opportunity to secretly call her friend in Lourdes, who connected her to the German *Bundesnachrichtendienst.* She had finally decided to take the ultimate risk and try to escape the clutches of Giancarlo Mareno and all his crime minions. They introduced themselves, but she couldn't remember their names with all the excitement. The people she spoke to seemed sincerely anxious to help her though.

They had an elite team on the way to Garmisch-Partenkirchen, the calm and reassuring agent told her. They were developing a plan to help her escape to a safe house in Germany. They'd provide all the money she needed to live and build a wall of security around her in the country of her choosing. All they wanted from her was information.

They'd need names, addresses, telephone numbers, and detailed descriptions of her activities and the people she used to round up helpless women and girls from their home countries to a life of slavery and human rights abuses. Was she prepared to provide that information? She had hesitated at first.

"I'm not sure I can remember all the details you're asking for," she tried as a first defense. They didn't accept that possibility.

"We were told you have a USB drive with you right now that contains all that information. Do you or do you not have it with you?" a woman's voice asked with a tinge of hostility.

"I do," she admitted. "But numbers and addresses change often. I don't want you to become *furieux* with me if you find the persons are no longer where I tell you."

"We understand," the calm male voice added. "We need your USB drive. If it's not one hundred percent current, we're confident the info you give us will still have some value."

"Why is the German intelligence service so interested in helping me this way?" Nadine asked.

"What you and your colleagues in The Organization and other crime syndicates do to women is despicable," the male agent said. "Our chancellor is a woman. She'll be out of office soon, but she's determined to do everything possible before then to ferret out this scum. She realizes you too are a victim. We won't harm you in any way. In fact, we'll do everything possible to help you lead a normal life after you give us your information.

Nadine finally agreed, but her anxiety only increased. They were still working on the fine details of her rescue, the male voice said. The people who would help were skilled professionals. She had to trust them.

After the female voice asked for confirmation once again that Nadine had the USB drive with all the details in her possession at that very moment, the male agent quickly intervened to give her final instructions.

"Wait in your room. We'll come to you. Trust our agents."

FORTY-NINE

Garmisch-Partenkirchen, Germany, Monday January 27, 2020

About an hour into the drive, Giancarlo's phone vibrated, and he reached for it in the pocket of the large vest he wore over a sweater and long-sleeved sweatshirt. He hated the cold and prepared himself for the worst, so the bulky wardrobe slowed down his response. The phone rang several times before he started the security verification process with the caller. It was Pierre Boivin.

"The Interpol folks questioned Ms. Lachance a few minutes ago," Boivin reported dutifully. "It took only a few minutes, and no intimidation was necessary. She confessed Knight had been there, used the bank's voice recognition tool, and she gave him about $75,000 in cash from his account in the Caymans. It seems he left the bank's office just before the Interpol folks made their initial visit, when they found the 'closed' sign on the door."

Boivin paused, probably hoping to gauge Giancarlo's reaction. It didn't work. Long before, the wily crime-boss had found he learned far more by listening than speaking. He'd grown increasingly comfortable with silence, using it to instill fear first, but also to draw out more information. After a moment or two, Pierre continued.

"She also let the police know Knight's traveling without a passport or identity card, so it's going to be hard for him to get far," Pierre continued. "They've sealed all the roads from the coast to Toulouse up north, Perpignan on the Mediterranean, and the Spanish border down south."

"What about the airport?" Giancarlo wanted to know.

"Yeah. There've been about a dozen flights since Knight left the bank, and no one matching his description was on any of them. Interpol thinks it would be hard for him to board a flight without identification. Security inside the airport is quite good."

"What kind of search are they doing within the city?"

"They brought in reinforcements and have officers knocking on every door within five miles of the bank. They think somebody must have seen Knight and will provide a lead. Nothing so far, though," Boivin answered.

"Where are you now?" Giancarlo demanded.

"We're just leaving Munich Airport. I met Sugimori at the airport, and we're sharing a car for the ride down so we can get to know each other a little better."

"Okay. Keep me posted every hour until we meet up. By the way, you have anybody in Lourdes who makes fake ID?" Giancarlo asked.

"Yeah. There's a guy. He does very high-quality stuff."

"Get to him right away," Giancarlo growled. "Find out if Knight's been in touch."

FIFTY

Garmisch-Partenkirchen, Germany, Monday January 27, 2020

The *Bundesnachrichtendienst* settled on a plan they believed involved minimal risk for the entire team. Janet would indeed become a decoy.

"Shed your Muslim disguise and put on your normal street clothes," Agent Fronhaus instructed. "We've discovered a recently installed camera hidden in a corridor near the lobby. It's monitored by the occupants of room 508 on the top floor of the hotel. When we tell you, take the elevator to the ground floor and head toward the lobby. Keep your head up and look around for the camera. It's above a doorway. Don't smile, and walk at a leisurely pace. When you reach the front desk, ask some mundane question, then turn around and return to the elevator. Pretend you forgot something and visit the front desk a second time, then head back to your hotel room and await further orders."

Next, he gave instructions to the two male agents.

"I know you guys don't like it when we have to make up our plan on the run. But we have no choice if we want to save this asset and the people upstairs think she's worth the risk. We can't get a microphone inside, so go to the fourth-floor stairwell and ping the suite," he said. "Your watch monitor will show the number of phones and countries of origin for their SIM cards. If you get at least three with three separate countries, assume they're all in the room and launch the rescue."

Fronhaus then turned his attention to Klaudia.

"Wait in the hotel room until you hear from the men," he directed. "When they call, move to the third-floor stairwell. The guys will be there waiting for you. Let them handle the attack on the room. Lie on the floor in the stairwell in case of gunfire. When they signal, enter the room and take Nadine to the SUV. Then get ready for a rapid escape."

Temporarily free of their usual abayas and niqabs, the two women waited silently in the hotel room, their anticipation growing. Klaudia appeared calm and showed no sign of the pressure she must surely feel.

But Janet felt her heart rate accelerating and found a need to visit the toilet twice after the men left to relieve her overstressed bladder. That always happened when she was fearful or under duress.

After she flushed the toilet and opened the door the second time, she heard an alert sound on Klaudia's phone as she stepped back into the central area of the room. Her friend lunged for it and gaped for a few seconds before she yelped in amazement.

"Oh my God! Howard is still alive!" Klaudia squealed as she looked at Janet. Then she handed her the phone to see for herself.

> *Howard Knight here. Borrowed phone. Respond immediately if you can. Only have number till midnight. In Lourdes, France. Did you hear from Janet?*

The women embraced as tears of joy and confusion streamed down Janet's face. She felt lightheaded from the sudden shock. How was it possible? How did he get to Lourdes? Was he all right? She had far too many questions. After a moment or two, Klaudia released her and the women sat silently beside each other on the bed to process the news.

Klaudia reacted first. "Answer him immediately, Janet. We don't know how much time we have before the action starts. Do it quickly."

Janet replied that she was answering with Klaudia's phone. She was okay and was thrilled to learn he was still alive. She used lots of exclamation points to underscore her shock and delight.

Then she started to ask her own questions. Janet keyed data into the phone with her thumbs flying continuously for a minute before she pressed the send button. Then she waited anxiously, her brow furrowed and the tightening sensation in the pit of her stomach so powerful it almost caused a cramp. A moment later, he replied.

> *Know there are many questions. Not safe to answer. Relieved to learn you're OK with Klaudia. Need to escape Lourdes FAST. Heavy police presence. Ask Klaudia if she can help.*

Janet showed the phone screen to her companion. When Klaudia saw the question, she immediately scrolled through her list of contacts and copied a number when she found it. Without talking to Janet, she pasted the number into the space on her screen for a return message, then made a comment one line below the number.

Bernadette. Call her right now. Say you're Howard. She'll help.

In another single motion, Klaudia entered that same number in a new message and sent a simple note.

Bernadette, an American named Howard will call. Pls help him with anything he asks. His lover is part of our rescue team.

Neither Janet nor Klaudia knew what to say next. The complexities caused by this astounding new development began to register. Klaudia reached over and took Janet's hand and looked into her eyes deeply as she gave her hand a loving squeeze.

The secure phone buzzed and Janet heard the command. "Right now. Third-floor stairwell lakeside. Don't use an elevator."

FIFTY-ONE

The document forger in Lourdes was reluctant to divulge that he'd made a new European ID card for Howard Knight. He pleaded ignorance and at first deflected Pierre Boivin's questions with a degree of insolence. Pierre remembered the guy. He was a hardened criminal who had served several stints in prison. Insolence was a behavior many inmates used when they felt a little pressure, so Pierre pressed more.

"I'll ask one more time," he said, pausing between each word for emphasis. "Think carefully. I'm making this inquiry on behalf of an American named Giancarlo Mareno. You know that name, right?"

"*The* Giancarlo Mareno? The guy from New York?" A little awe crept into his voice.

"You got it. Mareno has good reason to believe the guy in the picture I texted over is in Lourdes, needs an ID card, and would seek out the best ID artist in the area. Are you the best or is someone encroaching on your territory?"

"I'm the best, and now that I look at that photo more carefully, I think it may be the same guy I made a card for this morning," the forger replied. "His hair's a little longer. He has only a scruffy couple days' growth of beard in the photo I took. Not the full beard in the photo you sent me."

"Send me a file with the card you made," Boivin commanded. "And if he comes back for another one, be sure you call me immediately ... before you do any work."

Pierre pressed the end button before he opened his texts to watch for the promised file. It arrived a few seconds later with no cover note or explanation. Howard Knight was now trying to travel as Marco Romano, a Canadian citizen.

Without hesitation, Pierre relayed the file to his contact with Interpol and ordered him to circulate it across Europe without delay. He added his hope and expectation that the fugitive from justice would be apprehended within hours.

"Notify me personally, and only me, when you have him," Pierre instructed.

Sugimori heard Pierre's side of both conversations and smiled when he looked up from his phone.

"You're closing in on Mareno's greatest preoccupation these days?"

"Yeah. It looks promising, but we never know. This guy has slipped through Mareno's clutches for two years now. He's amazing." Pierre's tone was admiring.

"Why is Giancarlo so obsessed with the guy?" Sugimori asked.

"You remember Howard Knight used to be a trusted key player for Giancarlo. Some considered him the financial genius of The Organization until he screwed up on a significant investment, tried to run, and was eventually captured by the FBI in South America," Pierre began.

"Giancarlo was incensed about Howard running. He announced a million-dollar reward for his capture and return. A half-million should someone kill him instead. When the FBI offered Howard sanctuary in return for testimony incriminating Mareno and a couple hundred associates in The Organization, the bastard gave them all the evidence they needed to convict dozens of highly placed guys in the US and around the world," Pierre continued to explain.

"That's when I got my job. My boss at the time was among those imprisoned. Giancarlo, of course, found a way to elude both trial and incarceration, but he's been pissed ever since. I don't think he'll rest until he has his revenge on Knight." Pierre shook his head in feigned resignation.

"That's what I thought," Sugimori replied. "And I notice you're not relaying the news about Knight's new ID to Mareno just yet." He arched his eyebrow in expectation.

"No, I think I'll hold that new bit of information for now," Pierre confessed with a grin.

"I like the way you think!" Sugimori replied with a laugh and slap of his hands together. His laugh seemed genuine and impulsive. For the first time, Pierre also noticed a gleaming gold filling toward the rear of his row of teeth. It was curious. Older folks in Japan often used gold fillings, but it was rare among the younger generation. Did the gold carry some other significance?

He didn't have long to consider the question. Sugimori resumed discussion about how they should manage and manipulate Giancarlo

Mareno during the meeting to achieve their goals. He had several ideas and used most of the short trip from Munich to Garmisch-Partenkirchen to outline various scenarios. Pierre was surprised at the amount of detail he was prepared to share and felt uneasy.

Pierre was not nearly as well prepared, and he would be forced to follow Sugimori, not lead. As the car slowed to enter "the most famous town in the Bavarian Alps" Sugimori stopped talking for a moment to take in the sights.

"Garmisch-Partenkirchen hosted the Winter Olympics in 1936," Sugimori said. "I learned about the city in school, but I also had a grandfather who participated. My family comes from the north of Japan and my mother's dad was the best ski-jumper in the country. He didn't win anything here though."

"No shit! My grandfather was a skier and grew up in Austria. He didn't compete in any Olympics, but it's kind of cool to know we're so close to the area where he lived. Small world, huh?" Pierre laughed at the irony.

"In southern France you have the Alps as well, no?"

"Yeah. But I was really impressed with the Zugspitze back there. I heard that's the highest peak in Germany. I usually see the mountain range from the southwest. The slopes there are more gradual, and snow cover on the German side seems greater. It might also be deeper."

It helped for Pierre to shift mental gears and focus on the mountains for a while. Riding with Sugimori had been starkly revealing. As his counterpart from Japan divulged the extent of the plans he was in various stages of conniving, Pierre leaned back in his seat, took a deep breath, and let it all sink in.

Sugimori was far more knowledgeable and experienced than expected. His understanding of The Organization's operations, and its influence around the globe, was staggering. The man must have laboriously studied over several years to set the stage for his ideas and ambitions. The current crisis he'd manufactured on the heels of Suji-san's death might have been triggered by Mareno's apparent involvement in the tycoon's death, but Sugimori had obviously hatched the plot long before.

With the demands and verbal ammunition Sugimori brought to their negotiating table, how could Mareno save face and protect his aura of invincibility? Sugimori claimed he wanted Giancarlo to maintain his stature, but his words planted doubts about the ultimate head of The Organization leaving the session alive. If Giancarlo's life was in danger, could Pierre's be any more secure?

"You needn't worry," Sugimori said at one point.

"I'm not sure what I'm feeling is worry, Sugimori-san. I'm struggling a bit with the extent of your knowledge. Giancarlo spends a fortune to maintain his privacy. If you have that much information about him, how much do you have on my operations?" Pierre said.

"Enough," Sugimori replied, unsmiling. "I've made it my business to learn as much I can about every aspect of The Organization's activities around the world. As I said, you needn't worry because the things you're involved in are of little interest to me."

Was that a dismissive tone from the usually polite-in-the-extreme Japanese man? It alarmed Pierre enough that he stopped talking to again admire the Alps for a moment before he replied.

"I like the independence and larger piece of the take you think might be possible in the new order among countries in The Organization. Who wouldn't?" he said. "But what happens if we lose the protection of the United States? Won't there be chaos?"

"Maybe. But there's chaos coming anyway. It might even be better for us," Sugimori replied with quiet confidence. "This US president is already considered the village idiot by most leaders of other countries. They humor him with flattery to his face and laugh from their bellies when he turns his back.

"Governments around the world no longer rely on the Americans for either leadership or protection. Same applies to shielding our activities. We'll soon have more corrupt officials in our individual countries demanding a greater share if we don't act to 'nip that in the bud' as the Yankees like to say."

They both remained silent for a long while. As Pierre looked out the side window and took in the scenery, his Japanese counterpart glanced over from time to time. Was Sugimori taking measure of him? Deciding how much Pierre could be trusted? Wondering how much more he should share with him?

"What about the Saudi guy? He's not part of The Organization, is he?" Pierre asked after a while.

"No, The Organization has no official presence in Saudi Arabia," Sugimori grinned. "They have the royal family. The royals control everything. By definition, everything must be legal. If the royal family sanctions an activity, they get a cut. That applies to everything from human trafficking to illicit drugs. Giancarlo's been happy to leave it that way because there's always a way to get royal family support. Usually, it's just a matter of taking some troublesome women off their hands at a reasonable price. Suji-san used to work with Giancarlo on deals like that often. Then Suji-san sold the women to the Chinese. Because of the one-child policy, they have a shortage of girls in the north. Everyone cooperates to maintain the social order."

"I received the Saudi guy's wire transfer for her." Pierre nodded toward Nadine in the front seat. "But I still don't know how we plan to officially deliver the goods, so to speak."

"My guys will handle that. You just need to instruct her to stay in her room," Sugimori explained. "Once the meeting is well underway, two of my associates will go to your room to get her. They'll spirit her out of the building and take her to the Saudi's team. They're in a car following us right now, and they'll wait in the parking area for my guys to bring her out. She'll be on a plane to Saudi within a few hours. The guy intends to keep her for his harem. He likes pretty brown girls."

Pierre harbored no further doubts about the transaction. He realized it was time to be rid of Nadine. She was already more trouble than she was worth, and her lingering connection to Mareno complicated things even more. That tricky situation would grow exponentially perilous with the structural changes Sugimori was trying to implement.

From Pierre's side of the rear seat, Nadine's profile was clearly visible and her unease apparent. He was going to miss her for a while. Of all the women he had ever latched onto, she was the best. By far. He was going to miss her stunning beauty, unbelievable body, and enthusiasm for good sex. The Arab was getting a good deal.

At that point, their driver swung from the roadway into the entrance of the almost deserted Hotel Eibsee parking lot. Skiers were still out on the slopes, and it was too early for new arrivals to check in. The next two hours would be perfect for their discussions in the suite Sugimori had reserved. Pierre took a quick look back at the cars entering after them and relaxed slightly when he saw his team.

He also took a precautionary glance across the parking lot. A couple heads were visible in parked vehicles, but nothing seemed out of place or drew attention. When he looked at Sugimori, the Japanese crime boss simply smiled and nodded before he opened the door on his side and left the SUV. Without hesitation, he strode toward an entrance only feet away and far from the main lobby. No one would see their faces as they entered, but Sugimori still drew a fedora well forward to just above his eyebrows and walked with his head down from the moment he left the SUV.

Pierre didn't wear a hat, so he pulled up the wool scarf he wore around his neck and repositioned it across his nose. He kept his head down as well and followed Sugimori into the hotel as a Japanese woman opened and held the door for them. She didn't smile but bowed deeply to Sugimori and politely nodded at Pierre.

"Mr. Mareno is waiting for you in the room," she said, wide eyes looking directly toward Sugimori. "He arrived about thirty minutes ago."

Without further comment, she motioned that both men should follow her.

FIFTY-TWO

Tucked in front of a dense forest lining the roadway, a sign for the Hotel Eibsee came into view as the Mareno entourage came out of one of the dozens of curves on the winding road from Innsbruck. Five kilometers on the left, it announced.

Giancarlo's impatience and danger-antenna reared up a notch when he didn't hear from Pierre Boivin on schedule. Boivin was only a few minutes late, but he had explicitly ordered the French crime-boss to call him every hour about the Howard Knight matter until they joined up at the meeting. Annoyed, Giancarlo asked Luigi to see if he knew the name and number of the document forger Boivin had probably contacted. Luigi punched a few letters into his phone and waited for a file to populate. Then he scrolled down until he found what he wanted.

"There are two of them in Lourdes. We've used both. I think this guy is the better one, and Knight's likely to seek out the best available," Luigi said.

"Call him."

Luigi reached the forger after only two rings and was dumbfounded by the man's response when the bodyguard asked if he had been contacted by anyone to get a fake ID made that day.

"I told Boivin everything I know!" the man exploded. "I sent him the file and everything he asked for. I don't know anything more."

Luigi overcame his initial surprise and concocted a story on the fly.

"I realize that and there's no cause for alarm," Luigi said in a reassuring tone. "Boivin forwarded it on to me, but the file got corrupted somewhere. Could you please send me the file again while I wait on the line?"

Within seconds, Luigi was looking at a file that displayed a European ID card with a clear photo of an unshaven Howard Knight. There was no doubt. He showed it to Giancarlo, who motioned for him to put the call on speaker.

"This is Giancarlo Mareno. Thank you for your cooperation. I'll send you a thousand dollars for your trouble. Give Luigi here your bank details when we're done. I'll double the bonus if you can tell me where he said he was headed."

"I don't know if he was telling me the truth, but he said he needed to get to Italy and just wanted to have an ID card so he could get a flight. He said something about having family there."

"Give Luigi the bank details. You've earned another thousand." Mareno passed the phone back to his bodyguard.

As soon as the call ended, Giancarlo ordered Luigi to contact the Italians and get a team to stake out the home of Knight's maternal grandmother in Rimini on the east coast of Italy, right near San Marino. Knight's grandmother had died years before, but family members inherited and inhabited the house. The woman also had a daughter with a drug problem.

The Organization knew the now middle-aged woman and used her occasionally when her debt became too high with the guys who ran the operations in Italy. She had repaid her debt with either recruitment or sex. As she aged, it leaned more toward recruitment. Last year, they'd settled on a monthly survival allowance with the condition she'd contact them immediately if she heard from Howard. It was time to see if their investment would pay off.

Once the instructions were delivered to the Italian unit, Giancarlo focused Luigi's attention on a modification to their plan. Since the little rebellion Sugimori and Boivin were undertaking appeared more serious, Giancarlo wanted to make a couple security revisions. He explained them to his trusted colleague in precise detail and asked him to relay the instructions to the team in the car behind them.

Luigi finished relaying the directives moments before they drove into the almost deserted parking lot of the Hotel Eibsee in Garmisch-Partenkirchen. Their driver headed toward the entrance of the hotel closest to the lake and dropped them there. As the men walked through the doorway, they saw a young Japanese woman sitting quietly on the stairs, head down and playing with her phone.

She was startled when Giancarlo entered, said hello to her, and asked where the meeting room was before she could lift herself off the stairs. He planted his large frame no more than a foot from where she sat and glared down. Initial eye contact was brief, but his early arrival clearly surprised her, and her facial expression reflected it. She was terrified.

Giancarlo stepped back a foot or two, just enough to allow space for her to stand and then immediately bow so deeply Giancarlo wondered if the bottom of her jaw might actually touch the floor. In a gesture uncharacteristic of Japanese women, her sensuous brown eyes never left his face throughout her submissive bow, and an inviting smile eventually formed on her lips.

Her welcome complete, the Japanese woman promptly led Giancarlo to the meeting room and offered coffee or tea before he sat down.

While she prepared coffee for both men, Giancarlo and Luigi examined the room in detail, walking about, checking the lights, peeking into the heating vents, and adjusting the drapes of the window overlooking the lake and mountainside. Before the coffee was ready, Luigi nodded to one of the three chairs around the table. The one he indicated faced the inside wall of their suite and left the beautiful mountain scenery around the hotel at his back. Giancarlo set down his large frame in the comfortable armchair his bodyguard had suggested.

Luigi took one of the remaining three chairs positioned around the perimeter—seats reserved for only one bodyguard for each leader. He chose a corner to the left of Giancarlo, his back to the outside wall. Then, they both waited in silence for the others to arrive.

FIFTY-THREE

Lourdes, France, Monday January 27, 2020

"You're the guy they're looking for, right?" Bernadette said first when Howard called and identified himself.

"Maybe," Howard conceded. "Will that make a difference?"

"Maybe. Why are the police after you?" the woman asked with a noticeable French accent and a husky voice. She spoke into the phone as softly as Howard, just above a whisper.

Klaudia's message gave no hint but his intuition told him she was probably the madam of the Lourdes brothel. Klaudia must trust her, so he relied on her judgment.

"It's a criminal element that wants me. They're using the police to track me down. I need to escape. Can you help me?"

"It's too risky right now. They were here about an hour ago and the *gendarmes* rudely barged into every room, looking in every closet and under every bed. My customers were traumatized!" Bernadette complained.

"Can you help me?" Howard asked again.

"Klaudia asked me to assist you because your girlfriend is helping us, so I will. But not before dark. Where are you?"

It was risky, but what options did he have left? Howard told her he was hiding in some shrubs in a park behind a hotel called *La Villa du Parc*, and the woman recognized the spot immediately. It was only a few blocks from her home. But she warned him to be vigilant because the police would probably search that park using their canine team. He should leave that area right away, she said before issuing her instructions.

"I'll pick you up at seven o'clock this evening. Call me again thirty minutes before seven and tell me your location. I drive a gray *Peugeot* 108," she explained. "It's a small car, but the police find it unremarkable because it looks like a little Toyota or *Citroen*. There are thousands of them in this area."

He crept out from behind the shrubs and crawled toward the grassy area. Quietly and carefully he edged to the cusp of the lawn. It was too cold that day for children to play outdoors, and only a few hardy citizens were walking for exercise. No police vehicles were in sight, but many cars and trucks used the busy street running along the grounds. As the woman warned, it was too risky to stay where he was. In the distance, he could hear barking dogs.

With some trepidation, Howard set out toward another nearby park in the area, on the other side of the main thoroughfare. *Le Jardin L'you* according to the phone map. It was only a few hundred yards away, but Howard felt self-conscious about his appearance. Fortunately, he encountered only a couple older men as he passed them on the street. Each took a long look as they passed and grunted subdued "*Bonjours.*"

Were they suspicious? Would they see a strange homeless person? Would they detect that he was a fugitive?

Howard's clothes were relatively clean, and his beard was gone except for a few days' growth, but he still carried his soiled backpack. His shoes were again caked with mud from the mushy ground below the bushes in the park. Any casual observer could see he wasn't a local. If the police presence was as prominent as Bernadette suggested, he could easily attract the attention of any busybody looking out her window. Or anyone visiting the park. As soon as he came upon the street entrance, he found a partially secluded spot and rechecked his phone map.

He had to take cover for several hours. But where? Google Maps soon provided an answer. Less than a mile away, he discovered a cemetery. How likely would it be for the police to scour a burial ground in their search? Very unlikely.

He hitched up his backpack once more and headed north, past the primary school and toward *Cimetière de Langelle*. At a corner bakery just past the school, Howard ducked in wearing sunglasses despite the cloudy day. To show extra caution, he pulled the collar of his jacket tightly up over his lower chin before he bought a baguette and a bottle of water.

Leaving the bakery, he noticed a tiny *tabagie* across the street, the kind of place that usually sold cheap, throwaway phones next to cigarettes and cigars. He made his way there, taking care to cross at the intersection and walking back to the store. Inside, he found no customers and only one woman behind the counter, a foreigner. He guessed she was from India or Pakistan and spoke to her in English. Despite Howard's difficulty understanding her accent, she seemed to buy his backpacking-tourist-needing-a-cheap-phone story, and within minutes he was on his way again. His destination was only a few hundred yards farther.

Before entering the cemetery, Howard looked around carefully. Prying lenses of security cameras aimed in every direction he checked. He stayed on the street opposite and walked around the perimeter of the facility until he spotted one camera pointed downward, hanging by extended wires. No doubt the work of vandals, it served his purpose.

Careful not to draw attention to himself, Howard wandered along the dense ten-foot-high hedge surrounding the property until he found an opening he could squeeze through. He waited until there were no cars or pedestrians coming from any direction, then scrunched up his body and pushed through the hedge, breaking off a few dead twigs. He reached back to collect the debris from the sidewalk before he found a large tombstone to occupy for a few hours rest, well away from all functioning cameras.

The memorial was about five feet tall and so broad it spanned the entire width of the grave. The person buried there must have been a rich and influential citizen of Lourdes. However, the grass growing on the grave was tall and untended, with seed-covered weeds blotting the surface. A flower arrangement might have made it look better, but the headstone would suffice.

Howard didn't bother to check the name of the person interred. In his view of life, death was something simply to avoid and never revere. That day, he sought refuge only for a few hours, so he ignored the inscriptions carved into the polished rock's surface as he squished himself up as close to the monument as possible.

Settled somewhat comfortably behind the tombstone on the side facing the dense hedge, with his new throwaway phone, he sent another text to Klaudia's phone to update Janet on his whereabouts and plans. In his last message, he had asked her to get back to him, but it had now been more than an hour without a reply. He started to worry again. What did Bernadette mean when she said Howard's girlfriend was helping them out?

He mulled over that brief phrase and its implications for more than two hours. He weighed the risks as carefully as he could, and imagined every scenario his mind could create. In the end, his intuition told him Janet was in grave danger and he may have only one chance to do something about it.

He reached for his new burner phone, took a deep breath, and dialed the number in Eastern Europe he had memorized several months earlier.

FIFTY-FOUR

Garmisch-Partenkirchen, Germany, Monday January 27, 2020

Despite the heads-up from the Japanese woman on Sugimori's team, Pierre was immediately uneasy in the big guy's presence. He looked around the expansive suite the Japanese crime boss had reserved and saw Giancarlo Mareno seated at the large round walnut-finished table. The man acted as though he didn't have a care in the world.

Dressed casually in a sweatshirt, his beard neatly trimmed, arms crossed and resting on his ample stomach, the big boss didn't shift in the chair or show any emotions. He sipped from a cup after he scrutinized the group that had entered the suite.

Giancarlo had claimed ownership of the only chair facing the door, so his view was optimal. He waited for them all to shed their winter outerwear before he hauled his massive frame up from the leather chair by pushing off the table. A combination of his strength and weight caused the large, solid table to tilt in his direction.

The most powerful man in The Organization was unfazed by the tipping table and paid no attention as two table legs thumped back to the floor loudly when he lifted his hands. The impact caused three tall bottles in the center of the table to tip, prompting Luigi to pounce on the wayward bottles and some glasses before they crashed. Fortunately, none had been opened yet, so no damage was done.

Giancarlo circled the table and swaggered toward Sugimori to shake his hand, then turned to give Pierre's hand one powerful tug that almost threw him off balance. Pierre tried not to grimace through the pain of the handshake but wasn't entirely sure he succeeded. Mareno never missed an opportunity to demonstrate his strength. Curiously, though, he hadn't noticed Giancarlo squishing Sugimori's hand with the same intensity. Was the greeting intended to deliver some sort of message beyond his display of brute force?

As though the suite was his own, Giancarlo seized control of the conversation. With a broad sweep of his extended arm—an appendage about the size of a mature tree trunk—he gestured at the table and suggested they all have a seat.

"Let's all start with a drink to friendship before we talk," Giancarlo said.

Sugimori and Pierre exchanged quick glances but knew they couldn't politely refuse such an unexpected invitation.

Seated, Pierre noticed the three bottles were symbols of the countries from which they came. There was a large bottle of American bourbon. Beside it sat a slightly smaller bottle of *sake*, and closest to Pierre, a bottle of vintage red Bordeaux. In front of each, Luigi had rearranged the glasses that had tumbled over. Each drink had an appropriate glass style and size. Pierre couldn't recall seeing Giancarlo drink before, so he found the symbolism and invitation to drink curious.

When Sugimori and Pierre plotted their strategy, neither had foreseen the invitation or the alcohol. They glanced discretely at each other again before Sugimori laughed and said it was a good idea. Then he asked the woman on his team to open and pour drinks for everyone. She was the only female in the room and seemed quite content to become the server for the group.

Giancarlo again commandeered the conversation after she confirmed which drink each person preferred and how each would like it prepared.

"How did you enjoy Munich?" he asked Sugimori, in an unfamiliar, almost jolly tone of voice. "Did you have time for some sightseeing?"

For several minutes, Sugimori talked about the drive around the city his female team member had arranged and the sights they saw. He described, in some considerable detail, their trip past the famous Cathedral of Our Lady, the worldwide headquarters of BMW, and the *Neue Pinakothek* art museum. He finished with a laugh about the necessity of having a few beers at the *Hofbräuhaus* in the old city.

When Giancarlo asked the same question of Pierre, he was prepared.

"I visited Munich as a student and saw the sights then," he said, smiling broadly. "So my team and I went straight to the *Hofbräuhaus*. We spent all our free time in Munich doing what the Germans do. We drank beer!"

They all enjoyed a good laugh, and Pierre took some satisfaction from reducing the tension in the room. He decided to press his luck and try to engage his adversary.

"How about you, Giancarlo? Did you make any time for sightseeing?"

"None. I spent all my free time trying to figure out what you fellows hope to gain from our little discussion today," he said, the previous grin gone. "I didn't reach any conclusions. Why don't you enlighten me, Sugimori?"

The friendly discussions appeared to be over. But before Sugimori spoke, Mareno motioned for the Japanese woman to refill their glasses. The big guy had downed his entire glass of bourbon in a single gulp while they talked. Pierre took another sip of wine, and Sugimori quickly finished his sake before the woman refilled everyone's glasses. His two counterparts appeared almost grateful for the short delay, so Pierre took another mouthful of the Bordeaux while he waited for Sugimori to take the lead.

"We appreciate the value of your influence, Giancarlo. We're not opposed to paying something for your contribution to world order. It's the amount we pay. It's too much," Sugimori explained with a polite, almost friendly tone. "The Russian Mafia is stealing some of our prostitution income. The North Koreans and Indians are siphoning off millions in revenue from cyber frauds. That business used to be all ours. We've avoided war with those outfits just as you asked. But, when you combine the loss of revenue with the high percentage we pay you on our take in Japan, I'm facing a rebellion among my people. I really need to pay you less."

"It's the same in Europe," Pierre chimed in. "The Russians are getting millions from lotteries and casinos that used to be all ours. I prefer not to battle with the Russians either, but we can't rely only on prostitution and currency exchange profits to pay the bills. My guys are also getting restless, and my counterparts in Spain and Portugal are facing the same challenges. We need to pay you less for the reduced protection you're providing."

Mareno didn't address their concerns at all. Instead, he drained his glass in a single gulp and motioned for the Japanese woman to refill their glasses again, which prompted Pierre and Sugimori to quaff their own drinks quickly. Mareno was testing them, but they could never show weakness or hesitation with the powerful boss. They'd already agreed on that.

Glasses dutifully refilled, Mareno moved off in a completely different direction. How many people do the Russians have in Japan? How many in France? What's their estimated take? Were the Russians as deadly in their enforcement as rumored? The Japanese woman replenished glasses on

Mareno's command for almost an hour as he peppered both adversaries with questions that suggested he might be thinking about waging war with the Russians rather than caving in to the demands of Sugimori and Pierre.

However, over the course of their discussion, it became clear none of the men had an appetite to start a battle with the vicious Russian mafia. They all knew the thugs from the former Soviet state intelligence apparatus had far more technology and firepower, not to mention the tacit support of their president. It could become very nasty.

"I've got financial pressures too," Giancarlo finally declared.

Pierre interpreted that to mean they were finished hypothesizing about the Russians. Mareno was ready to focus on their demands. There was a long pause. Neither Sugimori nor Pierre dared interrupt before Giancarlo completed his thought.

"The politicians spend far too much on their never-ending election campaigns and expect us to funnel millions into their legalized extortion machines. If I give their PACs enough millions for them to burn through with incessant advertising, they leave us alone and do the occasional favor. If I don't give them the money they want, they waste our time with police investigations and lawsuits. We can't win." Giancarlo slugged back another glass of bourbon.

There was an unwritten code in The Organization. One must never look weak. Failure to keep pace with Mareno as he guzzled his glasses of bourbon showed weakness. Although he was feeling a little lightheaded, Pierre joined Sugimori when he swallowed the balance of his drink. Mareno ordered the Japanese woman to refill their glasses another time.

For about another half-hour, the men took turns lamenting the exorbitant expenses required to control politicians and pined for the good old days when a few dollars from petty cash for one or two local politicians were adequate to keep them out of their hair. As they talked, Mareno continued to press both men to keep pace with his abusive consumption of alcohol. Sugimori's flushed face was an extraordinary tone of red and brown, and Pierre knew he too was less in control of his faculties than desirable.

Sugimori tried to get the discussion back on track.

"We'd like you to reduce the current ten percent of our take to five," the Japanese man blurted out without any sort of preamble.

Before Giancarlo responded, Luigi stepped forward from the corner to whisper something into Giancarlo's ear. Almost immediately, the Japanese woman scurried to Sugimori's right ear.

"There's some sort of commotion on the third floor," Mareno declared. "Get some guns from the people outside."

As agreed, the crime bosses and their top security people had all come into the room without weapons. Each of their sentries kept the surrendered firearms of the meeting participants with them outside the suite. The security folks inside the room all scrambled for the door on Mareno's command. Each held a finger to his or her ear awaiting an update on their walkie-talkies, and each wore a frown of concern, if not alarm.

Luigi took control of the situation and demanded the sentries all remain in position outside the door and alert them inside at any sign of intruders. He ordered the Japanese woman to close the drapes on the large picture windows and instructed his men in the parking lot to rush to the third floor and find out what was going on.

Sugimori's security woman remained close to the drapes she had just closed and spoke into her collar microphone, then listened. Her frown intensified and jaw tightened in either anger or disgust, Pierre couldn't be sure which. She glanced sideways to Sugimori, then forward toward Pierre, before she dropped her eyes and spoke again into the microphone.

Giancarlo calmly took in the rush of activity around him with another glass of bourbon. This time he added some water from the pitcher on the table before he took a couple sips. Then he raised his massive frame from the table and moved toward the bathroom without a word to anyone. As soon as he closed the door, Sugimori's security woman rushed to his side at the table, squatted down to the level of his ear, and whispered a message in Japanese. Sugimori's flushed face blanched at the news she delivered.

He appeared to confirm her message twice and glanced uncomfortably at the closed bathroom door. They heard a flush followed by the sound of running water. The Japanese crime boss stood up at those sounds and remained standing until the door opened, and Giancarlo stepped through the doorway back into the suite. Sugimori bowed deeply and cleared his throat before he spoke.

"We have a problem," he said, looking at Giancarlo with a pained expression on his face.

FIFTY-FIVE

Garmisch-Partenkirchen, Germany, Monday January 27, 2020

Pierre had abandoned her almost immediately after they arrived at the Hotel Eibsee in the small convoy from Munich. Without so much as a goodbye, he followed Sugimori and the Japanese woman up the stairwell after they entered the side door of the complex. Without stopping, Pierre gestured that Nadine should follow a tall Japanese bodyguard waiting at the entrance. The man escorted her up the stairwell to the apartment-sized room and left her there without comment. Not a word.

First, Nadine sat numbly, almost immobilized, in the most comfortable chair she spotted. The third-floor suite was luxurious, but she didn't dare turn on any electronic devices or sample the several diversions the hotel generously provided for guests.

Then, she tried to relax with a few gulps from a bottle of water she found sitting in the center of a dining room table. After, she tried breathing exercises. Still tense, she moved onto yoga, but the tight geisha outfit restricted her movements and Nadine soon lost interest in either stretching or meditating. It didn't make her feel any better, so she tugged the outfit up above her knees, plunked down in the same large, leather chair with her feet tucked under her bum, and waited.

Le grand tumulte started with muffled sounds in the corridor outside her room. When she first heard a commotion in the hallway, she checked the time on her phone. Four-twelve p.m. the screen showed. As she lifted her head from the phone, someone jiggled the handle and Nadine drew a deep breath. The lock clicked and a voice in the corridor shouted in German. A second later, she heard a *thunk*, and a German voice cried out in shock and pain. Another *thunk*, then two more in quick succession.

The door to her room swung open slightly as sounds of footsteps running in the corridor were drowned out by shouts in Japanese and English to stop. Frozen with fear, Nadine gripped the arms of her chair like a child watching a horror show. The running and shouting stopped as quickly as it started. The new silence was even more terrifying than the disturbance, and her dread intensified as a Japanese face peeked around the doorway, followed by his hand holding a weapon.

As soon as the Japanese man located Nadine, now cowering in her chair, he stepped through the doorway and pointed a gun directly at her face. It was the same Japanese guard who had brought her to the suite.

"Remain silent," he commanded in flawless English. "Don't move."

He said something in Japanese. Then two people stumbled into the room, shoved violently from behind. One was a beautiful tall woman, the other an even taller man. The pair quickly regained their balance inside the suite and moved toward the table with their arms raised above their heads as the Japanese bodyguard commanded, still speaking English. The woman looked at Nadine and mouthed the word "Sorry." Her eyes projected pain and disappointment, but neither she nor the man appeared injured.

A moment later, another Japanese man backed into the room, stooped over as though pulling something. When his arms came into view, Nadine let out a shriek.

He was dragging a body.

The Japanese man tugged both arms of a motionless figure with blood splattered across its chest. He made no sound.

Once the corpse was entirely inside the suite, the first guard quickly shut and locked the door as his companion dragged the body into the bathroom. They spoke in tones that sounded urgent. When the second man returned from the bathroom, he carried a couple towels and a handful of the tiny shampoo and liquid soap bottles the hotel left on the counter for guests. He headed to the door, unlocking it before he left.

Meanwhile, the beautiful captive woman and her tall companion said nothing. Instead, each alternated looking tentatively at Nadine or the tall Japanese man pointing a gun at them. Both still held their arms above their heads as he had ordered.

After his companion left the room with cleaning supplies, the Japanese captor's tone became calmer and more business-like. He said nothing to his captives but carried on a conversation into a microphone attached to his collar. Nadine could clearly see the wire running from an outer pocket of his jacket to a hearing piece in his ear. His body language appeared menacing but controlled.

Her fear was so great, Nadine needed to use the *toilette*, but she didn't dare speak. Instead, she watched in resigned desperation. Gradually, she deduced the captured pair must be the German intelligence agents sent to rescue her. To be in that part of the hotel, the Japanese men must be part of Sugimori's team. Why were they anywhere near her room? What prompted their interaction with the Germans? Why were they holding their captives at gunpoint?

It took a few minutes, but the second Japanese man returned to the suite and let himself in with the plastic key. Did he have that key before? Or did he steal it from the Germans?

Nadine's questions and concerns multiplied as the taller Japanese man reached into his pocket and pulled out broad strips of zip ties.

He tossed them to his companion with a command, and the second Japanese moved toward the German male. For a second, the agent's defiant manner suggested he might try to resist, but he looked again at the weapon and slackened into submission. The man's hands and feet were not only secured but also bound together, making it impossible to move. Then the Japanese guard turned his attention to the beautiful woman.

With her companion already out of action, the woman offered no resistance. One Japanese guy worked quickly and efficiently to wrap the ties around her wrists and feet while Nadine cringed in her chair, the other man still pointing his gun at her.

The tall one who guarded her suddenly broke the silence in the room. He briefly spoke into his collar again, then stopped and listened to the voice in his ear. It was a fairly long conversation and evidently not a pleasant one for him. Nadine watched his face become first stern, then contrite. His shoulders slumped visibly while he listened. He stiffened his posture again at the end of the conversation and barked out orders to his companion.

The second man jerked her up sharply from the chair to her feet. Then, Nadine felt the strong grip of the other Japanese captor on her neck applying pressure so powerful she collapsed onto her knees. The one guarding her holstered his gun and rushed to help his companion secure her with the cable zip ties. Within seconds, her hands and feet were bound behind her back.

They left her lying on her side on the floor, well away from the other captives, before rushing into the bathroom. There, they wrestled the body from the floor into the bathtub, finishing with a loud thump as the corpse's head hit the bottom of the ceramic tub.

Before the pair came back from the bathroom, a breathless Japanese woman burst through the door, followed by yet another pair of large men who looked more American than the others.

FIFTY-SIX

Sugimori revealed that one of his bodyguards had shot a German man on the third floor. Giancarlo theatrically gave the impression he couldn't quite believe the story and was struggling to control his growing anger, a skill he had honed over many years.

It was good, too, that he'd drunk no alcohol. The bourbon bottle was fake. Nothing but colored water. He'd used that tactic with success over the years and expected to gain an advantage with it again. Giancarlo probably would have won the upper hand in their talks today anyway if this purported disaster hadn't come about, but the unexpected twist offered a promising new direction.

"My people were preparing to enter a room on the third floor," Sugimori said with a furtive glance in Pierre's direction. "Without warning, one of the Germans shouted out an order my people couldn't understand. When my guys turned to see who was shouting at them, they saw three German nationals. One of them reached for something in his jacket, so my guys reacted as trained. Without thinking, one drew his weapon and shot a German guy in the heart before anyone else could react."

Appearing incredulous, Giancarlo seethed a simple admonishment. "Either your training or your man was fucking incompetent. The German's dead?"

"Yes," the Japanese woman replied after Sugimori nodded in her direction. "They checked his pulse as soon as they subdued the other Germans. There was a struggle, but they also have a male and female secured in Mr. Boivin's suite."

"Any witnesses? Blood on the floor or walls?" Giancarlo asked the woman.

"A bit of blood apparently. I've instructed the men to clean it up as best they can. The body's in the bathtub in the third-floor suite now.

They used silencers on their weapons, and there were no witnesses. We bought all the rooms in this wing for our meetings and there were no guests around. We checked that last night and again this morning before you came. The hotel agreed to keep its staff out of this wing as well," the Japanese security woman explained confidently.

"Who are the Germans then?" Giancarlo demanded to know.

Uncomfortable, Sugimori looked again at the woman. This time he didn't nod, and she slowly hung her head in shame.

"Apparently, the dead one is part of *Bundesnachrichtendienst,* the German federal intelligence service. They found ID in his pocket. The other guy is too. We have no idea who the woman is," Sugimori answered in a subdued tone, his shoulders bent forward humbly.

"The German intelligence service? Your guys killed an intelligence agent and inside Germany no less? Is there no limit to their incompetence?" Giancarlo scornfully taunted.

Sugimori didn't reply immediately. Curiously, although he looked troubled, Pierre hadn't asked a question or expressed concern about why the Japanese men were entering his suite. Giancarlo deduced that Nadine must have been their target.

He scanned through the possibilities. Pierre had grown tired of the woman and perhaps decided to sell her to Sugimori. It would make sense for the Japanese to snatch her away during the meeting so there'd be no fuss at the end. But what was the role of the German Intelligence Service?

"This meeting is over," Giancarlo declared with a tone of finality.

Sugimori started to protest but thought better of it. Pierre looked very uncomfortable. The bodyguards remained silent but tense, waiting for instructions and looking from one crime boss to the other for a signal. Always comfortable with silence, Giancarlo took his time to mull over the next steps.

"Pierre, send two of your guys to your suite to watch Nadine. Jean-Guy can stay here," Giancarlo ordered. "Have them send up the Japanese guys with the German pair. Sugimori, have your girl tell the guys in Pierre's suite what's happening."

Sugimori nodded to his security woman, and she immediately spoke into her collar microphone. On the other side of the room, Pierre nodded after some consideration, and his trusted bodyguard spoke into his collar too.

"Luigi, have one of your guys drive into town and buy some pizzas. It might take some time to get the Germans to talk and nobody's leaving until I know what they were doing here," Giancarlo continued. Then he waited while Luigi relayed quick instructions to a remote subordinate. When he was finished, Giancarlo drew himself up from the table and chair and stood towering over everyone in the room.

"Now, all the bodyguards and weapons are going to leave the room and wait outside," he announced. "Luigi, when the Japanese guys get here with the intruders, bring them in. Secure the German pair again, but get everyone else out. Sugimori, Pierre, and I will get to the bottom of this."

Dutifully, the Japanese woman and Jean-Guy Gagnon looked first to their masters for approval, then followed Luigi out the door. When they closed it behind them, Giancarlo looked at both men and said, "Sit down. Pierre may not find it disturbing that your people were trying to break into his suite, but I'm intrigued. What were your guys doing there?"

FIFTY-SEVEN

Garmisch-Partenkirchen, Monday January 27, 2020

Janet followed the decoy instructions from Agent Fronhaus as precisely as she remembered them. It took her only a moment to spot the compact camera positioned just above a doorframe in the corridor toward the lobby. She had to suppress a smile when she spotted it because the tiny device looked very similar to the model she had used to video her clients back in her college call-girl days. But she walked slowly with her head up.

With all the excitement and stress, her mind blanked out for a moment while she struggled to develop two banal questions to ask the front desk that wouldn't create suspicion. She settled on one about the thermostat in her room for the first stop and a clarification about check-out time for her return moments later. The front desk clerk responded perfunctorily to both without showing any signals of either curiosity or suspicion.

Back in her room and still feeling unaccustomed stress, Janet couldn't sit still in a chair. It was her nature. She always liked to be busy doing something, and exercise was her go-to outlet for stress and nervous energy. It had the added benefit of keeping her figure fit and trim. Her body was her best asset, so she treated it with care. As long as she could attract men, she felt confident she could handle most challenges. This idea was considered outdated by some, and feminists probably thought her a relic of a long-gone era, but it had worked for her since college.

She began with some jumping jacks. She had no fear of disturbing hotel guests in a room below. Ahmed and Hans, the German intelligence guys, had already determined no one had checked into any rooms on the ground or second floors in that wing of the hotel. The Organization teams occupied a handful of suites on the third, fourth, and fifth floors in a separate wing. The agents had deduced there was one delegation per floor over there, based on seniority, with Mareno's on the top level.

She worked hard jumping on the spot, starting with her legs together, then spread apart with her arms following the same repetitive pattern in sync. She felt her heart rate rise and body warm, but she had no fear of becoming sweaty. The room was much cooler than she liked.

Europeans were generally so far ahead of the States on energy conversation and dealing with climate change that they willingly set thermostats lower in winter and higher in summer. Then, they complicated it by using technology to further lower the temperature when the room wasn't occupied or during daylight hours when guests were usually away skiing.

A few minutes of jumping jacks left her energized and much more comfortable as she avoided thinking about the danger of the assignment. Instead, she lowered herself to her hands and knees and did leg exercises. Leaning forward on her elbows, she raised one leg at a time to stretch her thigh muscles as far as possible and tighten the skin to keep her thighs shapely and appealing.

She had just started her sit-ups when she heard the ring of Klaudia's secure phone. Her friend had insisted on leaving it behind for Janet's use should there be an emergency or any calls from the intelligence service. Sure enough, it was Fronhaus, their coordinator at the *Bundesnachrichtendienst.*

"Is this Janet on the line?" he asked. They needed for her to say something to activate the voice recognition software. Klaudia had explained all that, so Janet spouted a sentence of nonsense about the weather. Then, cleared by the software, their discussion continued.

"Janet, I'd like you to sit down and take a deep breath," Agent Fronhaus started with deliberately calm speech and an exaggerated tone of assurance. "Please don't panic, but you need to be aware we have a major problem."

He waited for her to take the ordered deep breath and her response.

"What happened?" She willed herself to stay calm and used a tone of curiosity rather than one of the panic that was beginning to engulf her.

"Klaudia is okay, but she's been taken captive by the Japanese Yakuza at the hotel," their contact replied in a most reassuring voice. "We know she and your driver Hans are alive, but Ahmed, the agent who joined you in Frankfurt, was shot. We don't know his condition. You'll have to be very careful, but you'll also have to move out of the room."

"What do you mean?"

"If you stay in the room where you are now, they might find out about it and come for you," he said. He didn't suggest Klaudia or the agent might divulge her whereabouts if tortured or anything like that, but Janet figured it out quickly enough. She had to force herself to take several deep breaths to keep calm.

"What should I do?" she asked.

"We have some help on the way. Just before I called you, a team left by helicopter from the Munich airport. It will take less than a half-hour for them to get there, but you need to take precautions in the meantime. Are you wearing the abaya and niqab again?"

"I'm not wearing either, but I have both here," Janet replied. "Should I put them on?"

"Not yet," their contact counseled. "Take them with you in a bag or under your clothes and find a public restroom somewhere near the lobby. Our map of the facility shows one on the ground floor. You may have noticed it when you were there before. When you leave the elevator, turn left and walk about one hundred yards toward the lobby. Slip into a stall to add the abaya and niqab over your clothes."

"You want me to keep my coat and everything on underneath the abaya?" Janet asked.

"Yes, at some point we're going to need you to go outside and meet the new team. It will be cold. You'll look a little plump with the extra clothing, but that may be a good thing too. Anyone looking for you won't expect you to appear anything like an overweight Middle Eastern immigrant," Fronhaus explained.

"Okay. I get it."

"There's a bar just past the lobby. Find a seat at the back where it's darker and away from any après-ski traffic that may develop before we arrive. Buy yourself a drink you can sip with a straw to keep your face covered. Do you have euros?" he asked as an afterthought.

"I'll be okay," Janet replied. "I'll wait for you." Her voice sounded more confident than she felt. The French woman they came to rescue now seemed like a lost cause, but she was determined to do everything possible to help with the rescue of Klaudia.

She finished a bottle of water and tucked the extra clothing under the winter jacket her friend had loaned her. Then, she checked her hair, patted down the contours of her coat to look smaller, and stashed Klaudia's phone in a pocket. Finally, she took another long, deep breath before she headed out of the room.

The hallway was empty and she followed the instructions their contact gave. The restroom was precisely where she remembered, and she slipped in unnoticed. Inside, there were no other patrons, and she rushed to a stall at the end of the short row.

Within only a few seconds Janet lifted the abaya over her head and slid it down her body over the jacket. She needed to wiggle and coax it a couple times, but with a final pat smoothing her front, it fit. Deftly, she wrapped the niqab around her head and across her face. With a final glance in the mirror as she stepped out of the stall, she was ready to head for the bar to wait.

As their contact expected, she found a table at the back of the small room, against the wall, and it was vacant. With her extra bulk, Janet waddled there with a slow and measured pace. Gazes followed her path, and the watchers were neither admiring her nor envying her. She immediately felt the difference her disguise made.

When she looked up after taking a seat, a waiter had already arrived at her table. At first, she became flustered when he addressed her in German. When she hesitated, he sensed her unease and asked if she spoke English, but his tone was gruff and unfriendly. In a soft voice, she asked if he could please bring a cola. She hoped her accent sounded something other than American and watched him intently for any reaction.

As the waiter returned to the bar, he took time to wipe several tables, make a trip somewhere toward the lobby, and serve three or four customers at the bar before he delivered her cola in a glass with no ice. She forgot. In Europe, you should ask for ice or consume your drink at room temperature. It was all right because she intended to drink only enough to look like a real guest of the hotel.

Within a few minutes, Klaudia's secure phone buzzed again. It was their same contact, Fronhaus, at the *Bundesnachrichtendienst*.

"The team landed on the summit of the ski slope near the hotel," he said after the security protocols. "We arranged to start the lift running again and they'll be down in about ten minutes. Go outside. Walk to the corner of the parking lot closest to the lake and road. Someone will meet you there."

FIFTY-EIGHT

They had previously met in person only a couple times, but Pierre couldn't recall ever seeing Giancarlo Mareno so angry. After the security people vacated the room as instructed, he stood near the window with his huge frame dominating their space and waited. Taller than the others by at least a foot, he looked down at Sugimori and Pierre like they were errant children. The man was not only comfortable with silence but also used it as a weapon.

When Giancarlo was ready, he pointed to the chairs at the table and moved near his seat without speaking a word. They all sat wordlessly for another moment before he poured water from a pitcher into his glass, took a sip, and turned in his chair to directly face Sugimori.

"Tell me what your people were doing trying to enter Pierre's room. What was so important they had to kill a German agent?"

"It was a screw-up, Giancarlo. You heard that. The guy panicked when he saw the agent reaching for his pocket and shot him. I'm sure he'll tell us he never intended to kill the man. It's just bad luck the shot was lethal," Sugimori tried to explain.

"Cut the crap, Sugimori. Answer my fucking question and answer it directly," the crime boss bellowed loud enough for people in the corridor to hear clearly.

"Pierre was aware of our plan. He's selling his slut to the Saudis. We were just helping him out by handling the delivery. My people intended to deliver the girl to an SUV in the parking lot where the Saudis are waiting," Sugimori answered, gaining confidence in tone and manner.

"Which SUV in the parking lot would that be?" Mareno demanded.

"A gray Porsche. My security woman can point it out. She has all the details," Sugimori replied with an even more assertive tone.

"I see. A gray Porsche. And how many Saudis are you planning to meet?"

"I think there are two of them. I didn't ask. Where are you going with this line of questioning?" Sugimori demanded to know.

Mareno slowly raised his hand high above his head and smashed it forcefully on the table. The water pitcher bounced and tipped over, spilling water and ice across the table.

"I demanded the truth, but you feed me this bullshit you know is a lie. Leaders in The Organization don't lie to each other. It's our first code of honor, and you violated it."

His face turned red and the veins on his neck bulged erratically. Mareno leaned toward Sugimori with an intimidating stare, his nostrils flaring. Pierre squirmed in his chair.

"You must take me for a doddering old fool, Sugimori," he continued after another long, unsettling pause. "You know there are no Saudis. The only unaccounted for people in the parking lot were more of your underlings. Two more than we each agreed to bring to the meeting. Another violation of the code. They've been neutralized."

Sugimori shuddered in surprise.

"What do you mean, neutralized?" Sugimori asked, almost timidly.

"Suffice it to say they'll play no further role in your little charade. Now maybe you'd like to explain to Pierre what you really intended to do with Nadine," Mareno ordered. "Now!"

Sugimori looked sheepishly toward Pierre, took a deep breath, and then hesitantly explained.

"The Saudis didn't buy her. I did. You were talking to my guy. I sent you the money. It was a ruse because I planned to spirit her to North Korea as a gift to the Great Leader and wanted to make her untraceable. No offense intended, but our government people are trying to endear themselves to the Korean dictator. They can no longer rely on the Americans for support," Sugimori explained with a shrug.

Pierre was shocked. In truth, he was not at all concerned about the fate of the woman, and whether she ended up in Pyongyang or Riyadh made no difference to him at all. But Mareno was right. The Organization's fundamental code demanded that no leader lies to another. Though they may have differences, the understanding was always that they would respect each other with the truth.

Of course, Pierre assumed any one of them might bend that truth a bit to embellish or aggrandize. Still, it was exceedingly out of the ordinary for a country boss to lie about such a simple transaction as the one Sugimori engineered for Nadine. Doubts immediately crept into his thought process. What about all the planning in Munich? How much of it was truthful? How much was a scam?

"Your people are arriving with the Germans," Mareno announced a moment before they heard a knock on the door. "Once they secure the agent and the woman, order all three to surrender their weapons to Luigi and go with him. They won't be harmed, but they won't be available for your protection."

The Yakuza boss bowed his head in deference, then nodded. For the first time since Mareno demanded they sit at the table, he shifted his hulk and faced Pierre directly.

"Get the same message to your guys. Guns and any other weapons to Luigi. They'll be taken to another location. I'll return them all when we're done here. We've ordered food and we'll get them some water. No one will be harmed."

Pierre started to protest but caught a sharp glance from Sugimori and reconsidered. He reluctantly relayed Mareno's order to his team in the corridor and parking lot.

"Secure them on the floor in the corner over there," Giancarlo ordered as the Japanese security detail filed in with their prisoners. A quick nod from Sugimori confirmed the instruction and they followed it promptly.

Giancarlo watched the activity with a benign expression, his anger apparently under control again. He waited until Sugimori ordered his guys to give up their weapons to Luigi, who stashed the guns in a backpack brought for the purpose and then passed an electronic wand across each man to detect any hidden weapons. The proud Japanese men clearly resented the process but obliged without protest.

Pierre's guys arrived next, and Luigi performed the same ritual on his team. Jean-Guy was the last to release his weapon, and he looked at Pierre with a combination of anger and distaste. The French crime boss recognized the look and realized his decision to acquiesce to Mareno's demands created a fissure in his relationship with his subordinate that might be beyond repair should they both survive.

As they all paraded from the room ahead of Luigi, Mareno watched in silence. When the door closed, he turned to the pair of Germans sitting uncomfortably on the floor on the other side of the room and addressed them without rising from his chair.

"The food has arrived. Pierre will feed you each a slice of pizza before we have a little chat. Then you'll explain exactly who you are and what you're doing here today. Here's something you might want to think about. We may have taken away all the weapons for now, but we still have the means to make you talk, one way or another."

FIFTY-NINE

Lourdes, France, Monday January 27, 2020

Shortness of breath and the slight trembling of his hand holding the phone came as a surprise to Howard. He cleared his throat twice as the international number he dialed worked its way through a myriad of networks to finally ring.

"I wondered when you would call," she said without apparent emotion after she answered on the first ring.

"It's been a long time. How did you know it was me calling?"

"You really must learn how this technology thing works, Howard. Your life may depend on it," she scolded. "As soon as you sent the text to Klaudia, I knew your location. How's it working out for you in the cemetery?"

Howard's jaw dropped in surprise, then his shoulders slumped in despair. He gathered his thoughts.

"Have you told him where to find me?" Howard finally asked.

"No. Mareno's feud with you isn't my concern. He's probably still after me too. But you have to get rid of that phone. Bury it with one of your temporary lifeless companions if necessary," Fidelia Morales instructed. "And destroy the other one as well."

Howard shook his head at the depth of knowledge she had about him and his current whereabouts and shuddered at how many others might be equally well informed.

"How do you know all this?"

"Like you, I'm a novice still just getting by with technology, but I've got a friend who's a computer genius," Fidelia explained. "So far, we're probably the only ones who know. Once the police in Portugal reported to Interpol their suspicion that a recovered phone near Tavira was related to their search for you, my friend was able to use something called IMEI tracking to make the connection between the SIM cards and follow your progress through Portugal and Spain into Lourdes. It picked up the handset instead of the SIM chip. You've been a busy guy, and you're lucky the police in Portugal don't have the technology installed to do that."

Howard was again dumbfounded. It took a moment for him to decide what he should say next.

"You know I'm calling because I need your help, right?"

"Of course. There's not much I can do unless you're prepared to take harbor here. But I should also let you know the computer genius also performs acceptably well in bed so there's no room there.

"Message received," Howard said. "But the help I'm looking for is related to Janet Weissel. Do you know where she is?"

"She's currently with Klaudia in the Hotel Eibsee in a small town in Germany named Garmisch-Partenkirchen attempting a rescue that is almost certain to fail. Forget about her Howard."

"Rescue? What kind of rescue?"

"Sorry, Howard. That's all I can tell you for now." The line went dead.

Howard made one more call before he buried the phones—to Bernadette. Urgently, He asked her to change the charter jet flight from Düsseldorf to Garmisch-Partenkirchen. Reluctantly, he divulged his hiding spot and asked her to meet him there at the appointed hour. He let her know the phone would no longer work. In turn, she assured him there was no need to speak again and his location was safe with her.

Determined to do everything possible to connect with Janet, Howard picked up his backpack and snuck out of the cemetery and walked to the *tabagie* down the street. To his relief, a man now stood behind the counter, and he used his well-practiced tourist story to buy another throwaway mobile with a one-hundred-euro data and voice plan. He noticed more cars and pedestrians than he had in the morning, but carefully wended his way back to the cemetery and through the dense hedge with the first gap in traffic.

The remaining hours were tense, but uneventful. Three women, who all visited the cemetery to pay tribute to a departed one, seemed focused on their mission, finishing their duties as quickly as possible. Of course, he couldn't relax or sleep in such an open area, but he stayed warm by heating up his fingers in his pockets from time to time and stretched his legs as often as he dared in the shadow of the tall tombstone.

Howard's thoughts eventually drifted to Klaudia's friend Bernadette. No one had told him she was a madam at a whorehouse in Lourdes. Still, her comments about customers in their previous conversation suggested that Klaudia probably knew her from the days when Klaudia herself controlled prostitution activities across Europe and stayed in touch. Women of the sex trade were often an intriguing contradiction of character. Like Klaudia, some escaped to start new lives, but he expected Bernadette was in another camp, unable or unwilling to start over again.

Regardless, the woman was helpful beyond reproach. When Howard first texted her that he wanted to find a private plane and pilot who could discretely fly him to Germany, she replied within minutes that she had someone. It would cost five thousand euros, but he could do it that night and could be trusted to transport Howard without ID or interference. Trusting her and the pilot both involved risks. He realized that. But time and his options were in such short supply that he decided trust must trump caution once again. Who could know if it would be the right decision?

As soon as darkness fell, Howard hid in the tall hedges surrounding the facility and watched for her car. A few minutes passed before he spotted a small, gray Peugeot with a right signal light flashing. He squeezed out of the hedges and crossed the sidewalk, focused only on the occupant of the car. She waved just before she came to a full stop.

Within seconds, Howard slipped off the backpack, slid into the front seat, and plopped his belongings in his lap. The woman was older than he expected, about his age. Her hair was dyed a younger shade of brown, but her face bore the worry lines and natural scars of a life lived unconventionally. Her smile of greeting was tight and brief.

As Bernadette steered away from the curb to rejoin traffic, a police van passed them, headed in the opposite direction with blue lights flashing. The woman appeared unperturbed and maneuvered into traffic with confidence. Their drive along highway N21 to the Tarbes-Lourdes-Pyrénées Airport took less than fifteen minutes, but they still spotted three other police vehicles along the route. All were vans that could transport several policemen at a time, and it appeared they were conducting a door-to-door search.

"They'll probably check all the cars entering the airport from N21," Bernadette mused aloud when they were about halfway. "There's a separate road leading into the maintenance area. It's close to the spot where your pilot stores his plane. I think I can find it."

A few minutes later, Howard noticed signs directing traffic to the airport. Bernadette drove past that exit and continued about a half-mile farther, where she deftly navigated a busy roundabout and headed back toward the airport on a different road. After another half-mile, she left the pavement and turned onto an unmarked, unlit gravel road. Within a few seconds, they encountered a fenced area with a sliding chain-link gate and a sentry. He held his breath.

"It will be okay. I know him," Bernadette said calmly as she slowed to a stop. An armed security guard crossed directly in front of her car and looked in before he sauntered to the driver's side window, bent down and stuck his head inside the open window.

"Bonjour, Gaston, I'm bringing a passenger for Emile," she chirped in French. "He told you I was coming, right?"

The security guard grinned and glanced only briefly toward Howard. They spoke in French for a couple minutes, but their conversation appeared friendly and casual. Both laughed a few times, and the sentry finally waved her through with a grin and a grand gesture of salute.

"He'll be no problem," Bernadette said as she drove through the open gate and looked for Emile's aircraft. "He's a regular. I promised him a complimentary visit after work tonight."

Within a minute or two, Bernadette spotted the airplane and pulled up beside it. "It's a Cessna 400. Quite new, I think."

Emile stood beside his plane, undertaking a pre-flight inspection. He stopped his work and moved forward to greet Howard with a hearty handshake and a broad smile.

The guy should be happy. He's charging a fortune for the flight.

The pilot and Bernadette exchanged the obligatory kisses of greeting on each other's cheeks, then chatted in French for a couple moments. Despite reports of a virus spreading from Asia, the pair paid little attention to the concept of social distancing, and they evidently knew each other well. The pilot draped his arm around the madam's neck for their entire conversation. Conversation stopped when the woman ducked under Emile's outstretched arm before she addressed Howard.

"Best to leave now. You're in good hands with Emile, and he'll get you safely to Germany."

Howard thanked her profusely for her help and shook hands in farewell. He held her hand in both of his for just a moment longer than necessary.

"*Bon voyage* and *bonne chance!*" she called out as she returned to her car and drove off.

Emile started the engine immediately after they both climbed in and buckled up. As he prepared for takeoff, the pilot stayed focused on the myriad of controls and switches. Howard watched in silence from the other front seat of the plane. Approval to taxi and depart came quickly from air traffic control, and the aircraft was soon airborne.

"What takes you to Innsbruck this evening?" the pilot asked when they achieved cruising altitude at about 25,000 feet.

Howard was stunned. He had clearly told Bernadette he wanted to travel to Garmisch-Partenkirchen, not Innsbruck, Austria. His recall of European geography failed him, and he couldn't instantly remember if the cities were close to each other or not. Fearful of creating suspicion while he tried to sort out his memory, he simply lied.

"Skiing," he blurted after several seconds. "But I told Bernadette I want to meet some business colleagues from London in Garmisch-Partenkirchen, not Innsbruck."

"Oh, she didn't tell you? There's no airport there. Innsbruck is the closest town. But don't worry, I have a pilot friend in Austria. He'll meet us at the airport and drive you to Garmisch-Partenkirchen. It'll take less than an hour and I'll pay him from the fee you paid me. No extra costs for you."

They both laughed. Howard assessed the explanation and decided it seemed reasonable. They talked about skiing for a few minutes until the pilot realized Howard knew very little about the sport and was a novice at best. Emile then asked a few routine and non-threatening questions about working in London. They swapped stories about investing and its perils. Then the pilot switched to information about their flight and the aircraft.

"As Bernadette may have told you, our flying time will be about three hours. We'll fly about a thousand nautical miles. Normally, we'd have enough fuel for a flight of that range. But I'm always cautious when I travel over the Alps. We can get weird headwinds that consume more fuel, so I'm going to touch down for a few minutes in Lyon to top-up," he said. Then, he turned on his radio and spoke with air traffic control for a minute or so, in French.

Howard immediately experienced a sense of unease. Bernadette hadn't mentioned anything about a stop, but Lyon was about halfway and a logical place to take on more fuel. After thinking about it for a few minutes, he decided there was no clear reason for concern. He'd stay inside the plane. No one would see him. And he might have time to do some research on his new phone.

His current situation weighed heavily, and he processed it over and over in his mind as they crossed the dark expanse below. It would all sound bizarre if he were to explain his circumstances to a stranger. But the entire nightmare since they seized him from his home in Overveen a month earlier had been inexplicable and difficult to believe, even though he'd lived it. Wacky idea or not, Janet was worth the risks.

SIXTY

The dismissive manner Giancarlo Mareno used with Pierre was humiliating. The way the crime boss told the captives Pierre would feed them. The very act of holding pizza out for the prisoners to bite off and chew part of a slice while Pierre held it for them made him feel like an ordinary servant. Pierre fumed the entire time he performed the menial task.

At the table, Giancarlo huddled with Luigi and spoke in a voice no louder than a whisper. Luigi made notes and nodded his head often. Giancarlo talked, and when he wasn't talking, he was shoving large slices of pizza into his mouth and washing them down with water from the pitcher on the table. After a few minutes, Giancarlo sent Luigi away, apparently on some new mission. Meanwhile, Sugimori sat alone in another corner of the suite, nibbling on a single slice of pizza.

Pierre didn't have an opportunity to feed himself until the detainees were finished. He wolfed down the remainder of the piece in his hand just as Mareno ordered them back to the main table to "start our dialog" with the captives. He was still chewing the final bits as Giancarlo spoke to their prisoners.

"I'm not a patient man. I'm going to ask both of you some questions, one at a time," the big man growled. "When I ask a question, I'll expect an answer. Take a moment to think about your reply if you wish, but make sure it's the truth. If I don't like the answer, you'll be punished. If it happens again, the punishment will be severe. Do you understand?"

Neither captive responded.

"Pierre, get their attention," Giancarlo said in a tone he might use to ask Pierre to pass the butter at a dinner party.

Pierre hesitated a moment, looked at Giancarlo, measured his mood, and trudged over to the detainees. Without hesitation, he raised his arm above his head, swung down in a giant arc sideways, and slapped the

232

side of the face of Hans, the male intelligence agent, with his open hand. The impact was loud and so potent the agent tumbled sideways from his seated position on the floor and lay prone with his bound hands and arms outstretched.

Within just a second or two, Pierre raised his arm high again, and with slightly less force, slapped the left side of the woman's head, causing her to fall sideways. She cried out, but the male agent refused to reflect hurt, fear, or intimidation. From the look in the German intelligence agent's eyes, Pierre guessed he'd probably need to revisit the man soon.

With a penchant for dramatic pauses, Giancarlo waited until Pierre slowly walked back and took his seat again at the table. After a while, the crime boss took another swig of water from a bottle and then asked precisely the same question.

"Do you understand?"

This time, both responded. The woman's nod was quick and unequivocal. The agent apparently thought about it and decided any resistance would be more productive later. His nod was affirmative but not authoritatively so. In fact, it appeared tentative, almost daring his captors to do it again.

"Woman, what is your name and what are you doing here?" Giancarlo demanded.

"My name is Klaudia. I'm a guest in the hotel."

Giancarlo nodded to Sugimori, issuing a silent instruction to act in the manner of a gang where everyone is expected to participate in any despicable deed so all are equally guilty. They all knew the behavior was not only expected, belonging required it. Sugimori stood up without hesitation and walked quickly in the woman's direction.

When he bent over her, Sugimori's hand moved so quickly and powerfully from his side in an upward motion that Pierre didn't notice the strike until he heard the woman scream, choke several times as she spat out a front tooth covered in blood, then sob. Her anguish was palpable, her pain genuine.

Sugimori returned to his seat at the table with an entirely neutral expression, looking like he may have just picked up a morning newspaper from his doorway. Mareno used his dramatic pause again, this time cleaning below his fingernails with an instrument he had apparently pulled from a pocket during the fuss. When he finished, Giancarlo looked at the male agent again.

"What were you and Klaudia doing here in the hotel?"

"Like she said. We're guests here to ski," Hans maintained.

Giancarlo slid back his chair from the table and hauled his massive frame to its maximum height. Then, he slowly headed for the agent still lying on his side on the floor. He stopped inches from the agent's face and towered over him for several seconds.

"One last time, what are you doing in this hotel?"

"I told you, we're here to ski."

Without warning, Giancarlo raised his right foot about two feet from the floor, and with all his force jammed his booted foot down mercilessly on the outstretched hands of the male agent. Despite his blood-curdling scream, everyone in the room heard several bones in the agent's hand crush into fragments. Even Pierre felt his body shudder.

Mareno again used silence to terrify. He sauntered back to his place at the table. Soon after, three loud knocks on the door announced Luigi's arrival before they heard the lock click as he slipped into the suite again.

He motioned that he needed to see Giancarlo. When his boss nodded, Luigi moved quickly to show him something on his phone. It was important enough to hold Giancarlo's attention for a moment before he scrolled down for more information.

At that moment, Pierre felt a vibration alert on his phone and opened the message. It was from Deschamps, his mole within Interpol. They found Howard Knight and he was on the way to them! Pierre jumped up from his chair and strode toward Mareno.

"You're going to want to see this." He held up the phone for Mareno to read and watched his face register first surprise, then the hint of a smile.

"Keep an eye on things here, Luigi," the crime boss ordered with a nod toward Sugimori. The restrained captives weren't going anywhere.

Mareno plodded toward the bedroom that adjoined the living area of the suite and waved for Pierre to follow. Inside, he closed the door.

"Get your guy at Interpol on the phone. I want details."

The few minutes it took for him to respond seemed like an eternity, but eventually, Deschamps came on the line, and Mareno took control. He grabbed the phone and set it to speaker mode so they both could hear.

"Where's Howard Knight?"

"He took off from Lyon airport in a private aircraft about ten minutes ago," Deschamps reported. "We got a tip from a pilot but couldn't confirm his identity until he was airborne again. Knight's headed to Innsbruck but told the pilot his eventual destination is Garmisch-Partenkirchen in Southern Germany. The pilot's expecting instructions from us. He heard about the reward and will bring the guy back if we want."

"Who's the pilot?" Giancarlo wanted to know.

"A retired *gendarme* from Lourdes. He found his passenger resembled Knight. Snapped a picture of him at the airport when he touched down to refuel and sent it to one of our guys in Lyon. By the time it worked its way through the bureaucracy here, the guy had already left for Innsbruck. But we're sure it's Knight. We used facial recognition software to confirm."

"How long is the flight from Lyon to Innsbruck?" Giancarlo asked.

The man from Interpol needed a moment to check with someone before he replied.

"A little more than an hour. But the guy who knows the pilot says he's sure his friend will bring him back to Lyon if we ask him to," the Interpol mole said.

"No. Let him continue to Innsbruck. I have people there who can meet him. Give me the airplane details." Giancarlo waited for the aircraft description and identification markings. Once he had written the details on a notepad, he motioned for Pierre to return with him to the living area. There, he made an announcement.

"Luigi, have your guys take this pair downstairs to Pierre's suite," he said, pointing to Klaudia and the German intelligence service agent on the floor. "Secure them again once they get there. We'll give them a little more time to think about their answers. Leave one man to oversee both of them and Pierre's slut."

He waited for his order to be carried out. When the door closed, Giancarlo again spoke.

"Sugimori, they found Knight. I need a few minutes before we carry on. Luigi will escort you and Pierre to my suite. You guys can wait there for a few minutes while we take care of that matter. I'll need about a half-hour," Giancarlo said. His tone made it clear no alternative option would be viable.

With trepidation, both country bosses traipsed from the room with Luigi. They exchanged glances with each other, but neither dared to resist Mareno's pseudo invitation to leave the room. It was reasonable to believe the big man needed a little time to assure the successful capture of his long-time nemesis.

When the three men arrived in the vacant suite reserved for Giancarlo, Luigi said he'd need to keep Sugimori's phone. The Japanese country boss considered resisting, but the bodyguard's hand drifted threateningly close to the shoulder holster he wore. Sugimori surrendered the phone wordlessly.

With a light farewell and saying that he'd be back shortly, Luigi backed from the room, ever watchful of the two men he left behind.

Sugimori was first to speak. "What's that all about with Knight? Do the police really have him?"

Pierre explained the situation. Midway through his story, it occurred to Pierre that Mareno didn't return his phone after the call. Mid-sentence, he looked around the suite and realized there was no phone in the living area. He dashed to the bedroom and found none there either.

Concerned, he sprinted to the suite door and yanked violently on the handle several times, anger and desperation growing with each attempt. They were locked-in!

"What the hell?" Sugimori exclaimed in amazement. "When did the bastard find either the time or means to rig a door-lock mechanism?"

"His men must have come at least a day before us," Pierre complained. "We should have known he expects everyone else to play by the rules but ignores them completely when they're inconvenient for him."

"Why lock us in?" Sugimori wondered. Then a realization struck them both at precisely the same time.

They raced across the suite to the windows and looked out just in time to see Giancarlo sliding into an SUV while two of his men shot out the front tires of a half dozen other vehicles parked in the lot. The SUV the two men had used to travel together from Munich was the last vehicle they disabled. Within moments, four other Mercedes-Benz SUVs sped out from the parking lot headed in a southerly direction.

SIXTY-ONE

Nadine was sure her heart stopped when she heard the click of the lock at the door for the third time. There had already been two shocking visits. First, the Japanese intruders dragged in a German body and two captives, and then the Japanese woman barged in with two Americans in tow. After a heated discussion and a flurry of activity, everyone left the room except for her lying bound on the floor and the body they had dumped in the bathtub.

The instant she saw the face of the person entering the suite, her spirit dropped in *désespoir*. It was Mareno's most trusted bodyguard. She'd seen him in Martinique and Naples, and her worst fears were about to become real. The man closed the door, strode across the room without hesitation, and spouted commands as he approached her.

"Don't make a sound. Don't resist. I have chemicals and weapons if you cause any trouble." His voice was calm but assertive. Though not as big as Giancarlo, the man was tall and athletic. His temples were graying, but his body was lithe and his movements fluid.

He pulled the zip ties away from her ankles with deft motions, then hoisted her to her feet with one strong arm. His brute strength left no doubt she would be foolish to resist, particularly if he carried the weapons he claimed.

He firmly grasped her bound wrists with one hand as he released the zip tie using his other.

"Put on your coat. We're leaving. When we go out of the room, smile happily, hold hands with me and act like we're lovers. Should you open your mouth to make a sound, I'll use this," he threatened. He dangled a black cloth in front of her eyes and held it close enough for her to smell the foul odor of a chemical.

Nadine went with him without resistance. They walked to the end of the hallway and scurried down three flights of stairs. With her tight geisha outfit slowing her down, Mareno's bodyguard half-dragged her to keep up with his long stride and rushed pace. At the bottom of the stairs, he tugged her out the door. A vehicle waited at the entranceway, and he shoved her into its back seat.

Then he gripped her wrists together again. From yet another pocket, he whipped out a black zip tie and quickly tightened it. A second later, he produced another strip and wrapped it snugly around Nadine's ankles before she could resist. Last, he draped a small towel across her mouth and wrapped a third piece of cable around the towel to stifle any noise she might make. It all took just seconds to complete.

Without a word, he slammed the door and left. The man in the driver's seat of the SUV didn't move but watched her warily in the vehicle's rear-view mirror.

In what seemed like less than a minute, another bodyguard appeared at the doorway, tugging the German woman who the Japanese guys had previously forced into Pierre's suite. She held a towel to her face that appeared spotted with blood. As they approached the vehicle, she struggled before the guard slapped her a couple times and she stopped resisting.

The man pushed the bleeding woman into the back seat through the door across from Nadine. He secured her in the same way, except he first wrapped the cable zip tie around the towel covering her face, then moved to her hands and feet. Finished, he slammed the door shut, again without uttering a word in the process.

Still, they waited at the entrance. This time it took longer, but the driver remained silent and always maintained his vigilant observation from the rear-view mirror.

Nadine looked closely at the woman who returned her gaze. She saw apologetic eyes and a brow furrowed with empathy, not fear or anger. The woman must have been part of the team sent to rescue her but had become a victim too. She felt a strong, unexplained bond of *solidarité* as they looked into each other's eyes. In some perverse way, it gave her hope.

Shortly after, the driver noticed movement at the entrance and got out of the SUV. Nadine turned and saw Giancarlo Mareno on his way to the vehicle, walking at a brisk pace. Her heart dropped again.

The crime boss awkwardly slid into the front seat and ignored the women passengers entirely. On the other side of the vehicle, Luigi smoothly replaced the previous driver. Without a word, Mareno's bodyguard pressed the accelerator and sped off across the parking lot toward the exit.

"Luigi, give me Sugimori's phone," Mareno commanded the moment they started to move forward. Luigi pulled a phone from his pocket and passed it to his boss.

"What's the 9-1-1 number here?" Mareno asked next.

"1-1-2"

Mareno keyed in the number and waited for an instant for a voice to reply.

"I will not identify myself, and I won't give you any other details," he started assertively. "There's been gunfire and a murder at the Hotel Eibsee in the wing closest to the lake."

He hit the "end" button with a motion of finality, then lowered the front passenger side window, letting the cold night air rush into the back seat, chilling the women. He watched the road. When he saw a sign ahead indicating a river, he motioned for Luigi to pull closer to the side of the road. As they crossed the bridge, he slowed slightly, and Mareno heaved the phone over the bridge railing as far as possible, then closed the window.

"Give me your secure phone," Giancarlo said to Luigi.

"I'm paired to the speaker," he replied with a jerk of his head toward the women behind him.

"They won't be a problem."

Luigi continued to drive at a high speed on the winding road. Anticipating Mareno's needs at the same time, he looked for the number for Boivin's contact at Interpol, the fellow called Deschamps, on yet another phone. Mareno then keyed it into the SUV's phone system, and when a voice answered it was he who spoke first.

"I'm calling instead of Boivin. Where's our plane at the moment?"

"We've got air traffic control in Brussels monitoring the aircraft with radar," Deschamps said. "The latest info from them, about five minutes ago, puts them over the Swiss Alps with about thirty minutes flying time before they reach Innsbruck."

"Our GPS shows we need about forty-five minutes before we reach the airport there," Giancarlo said. "Tell your guy to slow down and change course just enough that Knight won't notice. Then, have him stay in the air as long as possible. I'll call you back when we're ten minutes from the airport. You can give the pilot an OK to land then."

"I thought you had people there to meet the flight," Deschamps said.

"I lied. Now follow my instructions. Call this number as soon as you confirm everything I just said with the pilot." As usual, the crime boss simply hung up.

Nadine's concern grew. It might not be odd for the crime boss to completely ignore the passengers in the back seat, but it was clearly out of character for Mareno to talk so openly. The man was notoriously secretive and demanded total privacy for phone calls and conversations. His sudden nonchalance about what the women might overhear was a terrifying omen.

She watched intently as Giancarlo punched the screen for another phone number and waited impatiently for a response. Someone answered after several rings, and the crime boss immediately demonstrated his annoyance.

"Disturb him anyway," Giancarlo said, his voice rising. It took another few minutes before Mareno spoke again.

"I've been waiting for the grand announcement," he said gruffly into the phone when someone came on the line a moment or two later.

The person Giancarlo was speaking with took some time to give an explanation.

"Working on it isn't good enough," Mareno replied. "I asked you to get the announcement out weeks ago. It's got to be done today."

There was a pause as the crime boss listened to another comment or explanation for a few seconds before he lost patience, raised his voice a few decibels higher, and gave an unequivocal order.

"Let me repeat myself. Call your people in the Justice Department. Have them announce they are immediately investigating the woman and her company before today's six o'clock news cycle. End of studies. End of our discussion."

The person Mareno spoke to apparently resisted again.

"Today. If I don't see the announcement on the six o'clock newscast, you can turn on Fox News to learn which of the fancy hotels that carry your name has an unfortunate deadly fire."

Mareno ended the conversation. The big man took a deep breath before he turned to face Luigi, still motoring at a high speed on the two-lane roadway through the mountains.

"Did the Japanese shooter get away okay?" Mareno asked as casually as he might inquire about weather conditions.

"Yeah. He took one of the SUVs Boivin's team was using," Luigi replied. "Should be about halfway to Zurich by now. The ticket we bought him was for a flight that leaves in a couple hours."

"He was smart to take out that German intelligence agent so quickly. It worked out even better than our original plan," Mareno said with a touch of admiration in his voice. "It provides strong motivation for the

German police to be even rougher on our wayward pair. Did you start the succession process for both?"

"I sent her a text right before I came back to the suite to get you," Luigi said.

"What did you do with the German intelligence guy?" Mareno asked Luigi.

"We took his ID and tossed him in the room with the Japanese and French guys. The local police will probably figure out his role fairly quickly, but we thought it might confuse the issue, for a few minutes anyway."

Luigi's face formed an impish grin while Mareno chuckled in appreciation at the clever diversion, even if it should prove to be a brief one. At the speed they were traveling, even a few minutes' delay would still allow enough time to get out of Germany and slow any communication with Austrian authorities.

With a shudder of fear, Nadine turned to face her fellow captive passenger. The woman's face was now dreadfully pale. Was it a loss of blood that caused her complexion to change? Or intensified fear?

SIXTY-TWO

Klaudia's secure phone vibrated in Janet's hand and she reacted immediately. It was Fronhaus, their primary contact with the German *Bundesnachrichtendienst,* and she spoke a few words of nonsense so the voice recognition software could do its job. Within seconds, the familiar voice was sharing some bad news.

"We couldn't get a car to the ski slope to meet your rescue team, and I'm sorry to tell you this, but you're in grave danger. We have to modify the plan." His tone suggested empathy and frustration in equal measure.

"What do you want me to do?" Janet asked.

"We asked the local police to meet the team, but they were already responding to a reported shooting and possible murder in the hotel where you're staying. If you look outside, you'll probably see several police vehicles in the parking lot. Two of those cars must go back to the ski slope for our people. But they want to check out the circumstances at the hotel before they dispatch any resources. Walk back toward the main entrance and look for a policeman inside one of the vehicles. Do it right now."

Janet took a deep breath to slow her heart rate and started walking as Fronhaus requested. Every minute or two, he asked if everything looked okay and she responded positively each time. The weather outside was bitterly cold, so it no longer mattered that her growing bulk looked the antithesis of good fashion. She smiled at the thought.

She crossed the parking lot toward the cluster of police vehicles in minutes, and the cars were all idling with their bright blue lights flashing when she arrived. The sight encouraged skiers returning from the slopes to slow down and stare as they passed toward the main entrance, so there was more activity than she expected. After looking around for a while, she spotted an officer with a walkie-talkie in his hand, standing beside one of the vehicles, actively engaged in conversation.

"When you meet the officer, say *Entschuldigen Sie bitte*, then pass Klaudia's phone to him. I'll explain everything," Fronhaus coached her.

Janet followed his instructions. The scene outside the rustic hotel was surprisingly calm despite the numbers of skiers and significant police presence. When she identified the man in charge, she politely used the German phrase to get the officer's attention, handed him Klaudia's phone, and then waited while the two conversed in German. She couldn't understand a single word nor decipher the gist of the conversation, despite some similarities between German and Dutch.

As he spoke, the officer in charge frequently glanced in Janet's direction, furrowed his brow, and appeared to resist whatever idea their primary contact in the *Bundesnachrichtendienst* was suggesting. After a moment or two, rank must have exceeded preference, and the police officer motioned for her to climb into the back seat of the car.

He finished his conversation before he leaned into the back seat, handed Klaudia's phone to her, and instructed her with waving arms and halting English to slouch down in the seat to keep her head below the rear window.

"Follow his advice," Janet heard Fronhaus at the German intelligence service say over the phone. "It's important you lie as low in the seat as possible to avoid detection. If The Organization is still inside, there may be a sharpshooter able to reach you from a window."

Fronhaus paused for a confirmation that she understood. When she gave it, he continued.

"Something's gone terribly wrong inside the hotel. The local police reported that Ahmed is dead, and the police have three Japanese nationals and three French males in custody. They also found your driver Hans locked inside the same room, but there's no sign of Klaudia so far. She may have been picked up by the Mareno faction of The Organization."

Cold enveloped Janet as it registered. The woman who had welcomed her and provided safe harbor was now herself a victim. She trembled and felt tears forming despite her best efforts to breathe deeply and maintain calm. The intelligence service contact gave her a few moments to absorb the shock and process it.

"Are they still in the hotel?" Janet managed to ask.

"We don't think so. Local police are doing a room-to-room search right now, but all the rooms they've checked so far are vacant," the agent replied.

"Do any of the people you found know anything more?" Janet knew the question sounded lame the moment she asked it but was grasping at every possible straw.

"I'm afraid not. Our team will start intensive interrogations as soon as the local police finish apprehending the participants. So far, no one has volunteered any information."

"Is Hans all right?" Janet wondered.

"He has some injuries to his hands but should recover soon. Klaudia apparently has some facial injuries as well. It seems Giancarlo Mareno was looking for information and became aggressive. Sit tight. Don't worry too much. It all gives us that much more incentive to find the bastard."

The frenzy of activity around the hotel held Janet spellbound, and her concerns grew as she sat in the back of the police vehicle. Still, she couldn't resist an urge to peek out the window, keeping her head as low as possible. More police cars arrived. Flashing blue lights, darkness, and the constant chatter of communication cluttered the night sky and added to the intrigue.

More skiers returned to the hotel, and with every few steps, curiously glanced in the direction of the wing closest to the lake as they passed the police operation. Their expressions showed concern but not alarm. The secure phone rang once more and Janet repeated the security ceremony.

"Plans have changed again," their contact with the *Bundesnachrichtendienst* said. "Our team decided not to wait at the ski slope any longer. Their helicopter has returned to the mountain and just picked up the commandos from the bottom of the hill. They are taking off now and will land in the parking lot of the Hotel Eibsee in a couple minutes. Pass me to the policeman in charge again. I'll ask him to have someone escort you to the chopper and get you out of there."

The leader of the local police acted immediately after he spoke with their contact. This time there was no hesitation or discussion, and moments after they ended their call, a new local policewoman arrived at the side of the vehicle, opened the door, and then motioned for Janet to follow her.

Half walking, half running, the women headed for one corner of the hotel parking lot. They heard the violent chopping sound of rotor blades cutting through the cold air as the helicopter neared the hotel. Both women covered their ears while the noise grew louder, then tried to wrap their coats and jackets more tightly around them to counter the bitter blasts of cold air from the relentless churning of the blades.

They stood well back from the aircraft as it touched down and waited for instructions, either from the police officer's earpiece or the helicopter itself. People on the chopper provided guidance first. Moments after it touched down, a side door opened and two men jumped to the ground, one right after the other. They ran toward the hotel and waiting women. The first to arrive stopped and bellowed into Janet's ear that she must sprint to the chopper with her head down. Someone would help.

She ran as fast as possible considering the abaya and heavy winter coat. A commando took her outstretched arm and hoisted her up the steps in a single motion, depositing her inside the doorway. Another, sitting in the front seat beside the pilot, motioned for her to sit down quickly as she felt a nudge from the man who helped her up. Before her belt was securely fastened, the chopper lifted off the ground.

SIXTY-THREE

In a small plane over Switzerland, Monday January 27, 2020

When the pilot of the small aircraft first notified Howard they'd make a refueling stop in Lyon, France, he simply nodded and accepted the man's information. The fellow was a trained, licensed pilot after all, and it was his plane. But as they started their descent into the airport, Howard began to have doubts.

Why should crossing the Alps have any particular impact on fuel consumption? They were cruising at twenty-five thousand feet. From his high school geography classes, Howard recalled the highest peaks in Switzerland were about sixteen or seventeen thousand feet, so there wouldn't be a need for fuel-guzzling climbs other than taking off again from Lyon.

If there were headwinds, as the pilot suggested might be the case, wouldn't it be better to carry less fuel weight rather than more? His rudimentary physics knowledge suggested there would be more drag and wind resistance fully loaded than with a fuel tank half empty.

Another concern popped into his brain just as the plane touched down on the tarmac. Wasn't Lyon the headquarters for the international police agency Interpol? This last thought caused a shiver to rush down Howard's spine, followed by an involuntary quiver of his shoulders. His danger antennae abruptly activated.

The pilot slowed the aircraft using a combination of brakes and engine thrust, then taxied unhurriedly toward the corner of the terminal complex set aside for private aviation. He seemed familiar with the airport. He communicated with air traffic control only to acknowledge instructions rather than posing questions. Of course, the conversations were entirely in French, so Howard couldn't be sure.

The pilot steered the plane alongside a fuel truck at the extreme end of the tarmac. An airport employee motioned to the spot where the plane should come to a full stop. Once it was stationary, the pilot disconnected his seatbelt and opened his door. He pulled a phone from his pocket and held it up as though he sought more light to get a brighter angle to read the screen. Just before he jumped out, he left final instructions for Howard.

"I'm headed to the office over there to pay for the fuel." He pointed off to his left. Then he turned to indicate another entrance in the opposite direction. "There's a tiny lounge and toilet inside. You might want to get a coffee or something. I'll meet you there in fifteen minutes."

Instead of sticking to his original plan to just stay on the plane, Howard followed the man's suggestion and activated his new throwaway phone as he walked. Inside, he found a connection to free Wi-Fi and Googled the pilot's name. Within seconds he found a match. Emile Turgeon was the owner of the aviation company that bore his name. A short biography told his story.

To Howard's dismay, in the second paragraph, he saw a notation. His pilot was a retired police officer from the city of Lourdes. He cursed his carelessness in not checking the pilot's background before agreeing to the flight, but he couldn't bail out in Lyon. That would alert the pilot to something amiss and he would almost certainly report it to the authorities. It was too late to waste time on regrets. He had to improvise.

Within five minutes, he had checked the travel time from Innsbruck to Garmisch-Partenkirchen, talked with a taxi company, and reserved a car to meet him at the exit of the private aircraft section of the terminal. He provided the airplane registration number as requested and asked the taxi dispatcher to be sure the driver spoke English. Before they arrived in Austria, he'd still need to find a way to ditch both the pilot of the small aircraft and the driver the pilot had arranged at the airport. It felt like a noose tightening around his neck.

Minutes later, the pilot came into the spartan area that passed for a lounge and suggested they both enjoy a coffee before they took off again. Emile deposited some coins in the vending machine, waited for the coffee to brew, then sat at the only table in the room.

"If you don't mind, I'd prefer to drink our coffees on the airplane after we're airborne." Howard's tone was polite but assertive.

At first, it looked like the pilot might object. He opened his mouth as if to say something but thought better of it. Seconds later, he shrugged with a friendly grin.

"Sure. The sooner I get you across the Alps, the earlier I get back home. It's been a long day already."

The pilot chatted about the weather and anticipated flight conditions as they headed back toward the plane together. Aboard, they buckled up and Emile started the engine promptly. His conversation with air traffic control took no longer than on the departure from Lourdes, and they were soon underway. Takeoff seemed ordinary with a steep, quick climb to cruising speed. Then the pair soon silently sipped their coffees from paper cups.

They were about twenty minutes into the flight when Howard noticed another anomaly. From Lourdes to Lyon, the only conversations the pilot had with air traffic control were prior to departure and just before descent into Lyon. There had been none at cruising altitude. On this segment, Emile Turgeon had two conversations. After the second one, the pilot slowed the engine slightly and veered to the left about twenty-five degrees.

"There's some turbulence ahead. We'll try to go around it, but be sure your seatbelt is nice and snug," Emile warned with a wry smile. Improvisation just gained increased urgency.

SIXTY-FOUR

Garmisch-Partenkirchen, Germany, Monday January 27, 2020

Pierre Boivin heard an aborted click as someone tried to enter the suite. It was odd. The lock tried to open, then stopped. Someone jiggled the outside handle a couple times and shouted something in German. Pierre shouted back in English.

"We're trapped in here! There are two of us!"

A German voice muttered something they didn't understand. Then, more loudly in English, told them to hold on. It would take a few minutes while they called a locksmith to come upstairs, but they would fix the problem. That was characteristic of the Germans. Rather than simply bash down the door, they wanted to neatly repair the problem to minimize both expense and clutter. The confined would just have to wait.

Sugimori realized the two men needed to harmonize their stories, so he motioned for Pierre to join him and they huddled in the corner farthest from the door and near the window. In hushed voices, they plotted their strategy.

"We'll have to pretend we know nothing," Sugimori whispered. "We don't know each other. We were just walking in different directions in the hallway when we were suddenly accosted at gunpoint. Several criminals detained us, threatening and waving their weapons. They forced us in here. Are you okay with that?"

"Sounds good," Pierre replied. "I'll tell them I'm in the hotel with some friends who were hustled off in another direction. I suggest you say the same. How do we handle questions about the dead German if they found him?"

"We know nothing. I think we should just maintain that posture with every question they ask. If the police persist, we'll need to ask for a lawyer."

They clasped hands in a firm handshake of agreement and waited. Pierre would honor their bargain but harbored doubts about their ability to make it stick. Was Nadine still in his suite with the dead body? What would she say or do? Did Sugimori forget their subordinates were supposed to be locked in the same room as the dead body as well? Would his own underlings maintain silence, or might one of them cave to pressure from the German authorities and squeal on the errant Japanese bodyguard who pulled the trigger? There were just too many variables to avoid worry.

A few minutes later, the door to the suite burst open and five or more armed police officers charged into the room with weapons drawn, all pointed directly at Sugimori and Pierre. Right behind them, two more heavily armed commandos rushed in with their weapons at the ready, and they immediately took charge.

"On the floor, face down. Both of you. Right now!" one of the men bellowed. "Stretch your hands out above your heads and keep them flat on the floor."

He lowered his voice for the second command as both apprehended men complied with his first instructions without argument. The leader issued a brusque command in German before heavy hands patted every part of Pierre's body, looking for concealed weapons. The hands started at his ankles and worked up his body inch by inch, with one sharp pinch of his testicles on the way past. Pierre dared not react to the pain or breach of protocol, fearing worse might come if he opened his mouth.

Satisfied the detained men were clear of weapons, the leader ordered them to their feet. As soon as the detainees stood, the local police officers roughly pulled their arms behind their backs and snapped on handcuffs.

After another command in German, the policemen brought two chairs to the detained men and forced them to sit. Before they realized it, police officers had deftly wrapped a single strand of cable zip ties around each of the men, binding them securely to their chair backs.

A leader issued a final command in German before the police officers filed out of the room, partially closing the door with a broken lock. Then, the German commandos huddled on the opposite side of the room in muted conversation. Twice, one of them spoke a sentence or two into his collar, then listened intently to the response.

After three or four minutes of consultation, both men turned toward Pierre and Sugimori and lowered their weapons. They approached the prisoners and towered over them, looking down in unconcealed disdain.

"We are not part of the German law enforcement and judicial system," the young leader started out in English. His heavy-set jaw protruded from beneath a helmet that made it difficult to see the color of his eyes, a broad nose overhung thick lips, and his skin was pocked with the ravages of acne. His derisive smile seemed to invite confrontation.

"Normal rules of German law do not apply to us. You have no rights, and there will be no lawyers or consultation with outside parties. If you satisfy our demands, we'll turn you over to the local police who will follow due process. If you don't oblige, we have ways of getting cooperation and won't hesitate to use them."

The leader paused and held a finger to his ear as he listened to more instructions. With a nod to his partner, the other man stepped forward with another strand of zip ties, slipped one around Pierre's legs and pulled tightly, securing him to the chair legs. Pierre waited for them to also restrain Sugimori. Instead, the man stood rigidly upright, stared straight ahead, and took one military step backward. Pierre thought he might actually salute.

"Now," the leader resumed. "For your own comfort, I recommend you cut the bullshit and answer truthfully. Mister Sugimori, don't deny you know each other. Don't give us nonsense answers.

"*Monsieur* Boivin, when we ask you questions about the dead German we found in your suite, don't plead ignorance. That man was our friend and colleague. We won't react well to such disrespect."

Sugimori appeared as indignant about his plight as Pierre felt. They were more accustomed to being the ones in control in this kind of situation, not victims. The Yakuza's black eyes flashed and his nostrils flared. He raised his chin in defiance and his tightly pursed lips signaled determination.

"Take the Japanese over to the bathroom," the commando leader told his companion. "Close the door, turn on the fan, and run water into the bathtub. Hold him in there while I ask *Monsieur* Boivin a few questions."

The leader ignored Pierre and glared at Sugimori, then watched in silence while his colleague carried out the orders. When they heard water running loudly in the bathroom, he turned to face Pierre.

"Where's Mareno?" the commando demanded. "We know you were all together earlier."

Pierre didn't immediately answer as he tried to foresee where the line of questioning was going. He was concerned that they knew about Mareno but decided not to cooperate.

"He left. I don't know where he went."

The commando took one step closer, then bent down and yanked the shoe from Pierre's left foot with one forceful tug.

"Where did he go?"

"I only saw him leaving the parking lot in an SUV before you came," Pierre said.

The commando reached forward and ripped the sock from Pierre's left foot.

"Which way did he turn when the SUV left the lot?"

"I don't remember." An instant later, Pierre screamed as the steel butt of the commando's rifle smashed against his foot. Several small bones were crushed on impact.

"I told you we have no time for games," the commando said with a cold, calm smile. "Answer the question, or more bones will break."

The searing pain was unbearable. After a short pause he mumbled, "Mareno headed south."

"How many are there in his group?"

"I don't know! I honestly don't know. Please believe me," he pleaded. "I know Mareno and his people flew into Innsbruck. A private jet is probably waiting for him there."

That seemed to satisfy the German commando for the moment. He backed away, still staring intently at Pierre as he barked some orders into his collar and waited for a response. When he received the confirmation he wanted, the man walked back toward Pierre and hovered over him threateningly when he asked his next question.

"Who shot my colleague?"

The pain in his left foot spiked horribly as he considered his response. The bastard commando wrapped both hands around the rifle. Then he raised it high above his shoulder in preparation for another vicious strike and glowered at Pierre. That was the moment he decided the Japanese shooter was dispensable.

"One of the Jap bodyguards shot him." He used the racial slur from World War Two days to distance himself from the guilty party. "It was an accident, apparently."

His resistance vanished, Pierre meekly answered questions and provided information for several more minutes, always careful to distance himself and his people from the killing. Regardless, when the commando was finished, he barked more orders into his collar, and two local policemen entered the room shortly after.

"Take him into custody," the commando instructed in English for Pierre's benefit. "I think you'll want to chat more about his role in the murder of a German citizen. You might want to get him some medical care too. He apparently took some sort of a nasty fall before we arrived."

Pierre looked down at the foot. It had turned a hideous shade of blue, appearing almost black. As he fought back tears, he felt pain, anger, and disgust with himself. When tested, he didn't have the strength he thought he would have. His followers in The Organization would not be proud.

SIXTY-FIVE

German Highway 177 toward Innsbruck, Monday January 27, 2020

Midway en route from Garmisch-Partenkirchen to the airport in Innsbruck, Giancarlo tried another phone call. He let the phone ring more than a dozen times, but no one answered. That never happened. He slammed the phone on the dash of the SUV in frustration.

"Luigi, are you sure you kept her number during the last wipe and transfer of data?"

"Yeah. Remember? You called her this morning, no problem. Wasn't she right about Sugimori and the Saudi story?"

"Perhaps. Give me the number and I'll try another phone." Giancarlo reached for another handset from an inside pocket of his winter vest. Luigi's numeric retention was legendary within The Organization. No one else could remember so many telephone numbers.

"Country code 998-71-999-32-10," Luigi recited as Giancarlo keyed the numbers into the disposable phone.

Giancarlo turned toward the rear seat as he hit the last digit. Did he just hear a muffled gasp? Both women had their eyes closed when he looked back. It must just be his growing excitement, Giancarlo thought.

The number rang but again no reply after more than twenty rings. This was not just unusual, it simply never happened. The woman kept the special phone close to her all the time. Even when she slept, she had it within reach and answered after no more than a half-dozen rings.

"What's the number for the pilots?" Giancarlo asked next.

Luigi provided the secure mobile number for the phone the pilots had with them in Innsbruck. He'd already called once to get them started on the preparations. Giancarlo now wanted to be sure they would start the engines and warm the aircraft. The SUV GPS showed less than a half-hour remaining in their trip to the Austrian ski town. He wanted their jet ready to go the moment the plane bringing Howard Knight delivered him.

The pilots said they were in an Uber on the way to the airport and assured Giancarlo all would be ready for departure. Still antsy, Giancarlo pressed the highlighted number for Deschamps, their mole at Interpol.

"Where are they now?" Giancarlo demanded as soon as the man responded.

"He's in a holding pattern near the airport. I haven't heard more since we spoke last," Deschamps answered with a hint of annoyance.

"Get air traffic control to give you an update on their location, if they're more than fifteen minutes out, get them pointed in the direction of Innsbruck, and instruct the pilot to touch down in precisely thirty minutes," Giancarlo said.

"I'll try. Air traffic control is located in Belgium. They're the most bureaucratic outfit we deal with in all of Europe, but I'll do my best." Deschamps's tone reflected less optimism than desired.

Giancarlo slipped the phones inside his vest pockets and tilted his head against the passenger headrest. He closed his eyes and his anticipation grew. Within minutes, he'd savor the satisfaction of capturing the guy who had caused him to lose more sleep the past three years than anyone in his entire career with The Organization.

Final recompense would come later. But within minutes, the man's fate would be sealed. He could allow himself a few moments to relish the victory.

——•——

Before the debacle, Giancarlo trusted no one on earth more than Howard Knight. Loyal Luigi ranked second.

Howard Knight's father had served Giancarlo's family for a generation and helped to create the massive financial empire of The Organization. Long before he wanted to retire, Knight senior introduced his son to Giancarlo and then coached him for the first few years after they welcomed young Howard into the criminal world.

From the beginning, the guy was remarkable. Gifted with an almost photographic memory, the youngster soon established himself as a powerhouse in the world of finance. He mingled easily with the heads of powerful banks, the most successful venture capital funds, and the largest stock exchanges around the globe. His strategic thinking skills were outstanding. He took ideas and crafted them into millions of dollars with both creativity and meticulous care, much like a chef preparing a gourmet meal.

When Howard's father died in an unfortunate automobile accident in Italy the week before he was scheduled to retire, Knight became Giancarlo's chief financial advisor. He convinced Giancarlo of the merits of building a criminal element that evolved into respectability like the Kennedy's in the United States or the Bronfman's in Canada. Both families became enormously rich from the illegal empires they created during the prohibition of alcohol in the 1920s, and both kept that wealth, power, and influence for generations.

Howard's record was unblemished for most of his career. For more than two decades, he guided Giancarlo to the best investments with the most consistent annual profits. As a result, he earned influence with criminal syndicates all over the world and a degree of legitimacy that gained access to the loftiest machinations of governments.

For Howard's contributions, Giancarlo rewarded him well. With every success, he paid the guy bonuses in the millions. He knew Knight had stashed away about a hundred million in the Cayman Islands, maybe even more. He surely had more than enough money to last a lifetime.

For almost twenty years, he allowed Knight to frolic with Fidelia, Giancarlo's favorite by far. The pair thought their clandestine relationship and hidden dalliances were secret, but Giancarlo always knew. He let them enjoy their sexual romps uninterrupted and thought all was well until that confounding fiasco with Multima Corporation.

The idea initially looked brilliant. They'd buy a billion dollars' worth of equities in a particular share class and eventually leverage that billion to take over and control the wildly successful multinational conglomerate. For ten years, Howard repeatedly promised Giancarlo they were close to seizing control and the crime boss patiently deferred to his judgment and waited without complaint.

Inexplicably, something happened. Without warning, Howard launched an all-out attack on the company at a time it appeared particularly vulnerable. His financial assault with complex maneuvers within the company's board of directors failed because the wily CEO and founder of Multima simply outsmarted him.

Knight apparently panicked, fleeing the country and The Organization rather than face Giancarlo's wrath for a loss in the hundreds of millions of dollars. Worse, Fidelia aided and abetted his escape. Then she vanished too.

Of course, Giancarlo was angry when he first learned of the disappearances and financial losses. That's when he first posted rewards in the underworld for their capture. Underlings should never abdicate their responsibilities and must be held accountable when they do. That's how The Organization worked.

Knight's ability to successfully evade capture by The Organization was itself a troubling circumstance. Giancarlo understood well that his peers within the criminal world closely watched his actions and achievements. They took particular interest in his failures. Giancarlo realized the longer he took to punish Knight for his misdeeds, the more emboldened his rivals would become. The Howard Knight matter had already taken far too long to conclude.

Giancarlo had little doubt the recent insubordination of Sugimori and Pierre Boivin took seed from his inability to successfully punish Knight's misdeeds. Perhaps the sticky situation he created for both men at Hotel Eibsee in Garmisch-Partenkirchen would keep them preoccupied with their own freedom and loss of face for a time. Still, others would eventually surface to challenge his authority. That reality would never end.

Those complex factors all contributed to a building sense of accomplishment, but his most potent motivation had always been more primal. Only two other people knew it was the missing money that drove Giancarlo to exact revenge from Howard Knight.

The guy who'd replaced Howard needed several months to discover it. But after he finished explaining it all to Giancarlo, there could be no doubt. More than five hundred million dollars had evaporated from Giancarlo's fortune. Embezzlement, the new guy explained.

Through complex banking transactions hidden inside The Organization's extensive money laundering activities, Howard had siphoned off a half-billion dollars over more than ten years. The dastardly dealings had nothing to do with Multima Corporation, but the losses they created were equal to that disaster Howard had both engineered and screwed up. And it looked as if Howard was the sole beneficiary of the massive theft.

Giancarlo knew it wasn't healthy to have such a fixation about exacting revenge for one wayward individual, and he hadn't really missed the money. Nor was it a debilitating percentage of his total wealth. But he liked to think long-term and imagined his eventual survival depended on settling this personal score once and for all. The satisfaction would be fleeting, but he would savor it regardless.

—•—

"We're turning onto the airport road in a couple miles," Luigi announced to get Giancarlo's attention. "Do you want me to call the pilots and make sure the engines are warming up?"

"Yeah. And tell your guys in the car behind us to stay at the tarmac entrance but out of sight. Tell them to watch for signs of interference with us or our aircraft. Should the Germans get any information out of Sugimori or Boivin, I don't want unpleasant surprises at the airport. Tell them to keep their walkie-talkies on until we're in the air."

Luigi spoke into his collar, then loosened the zipper of his jacket. If anything happened, he could reach the semiautomatic handgun in his shoulder holster more quickly.

Before they arrived at the airport, Luigi scrunched forward in his seat to peer off to his left until he found a little-used laneway. Pilots and passengers of private aircraft used the path only occasionally because the driveway was unpaved and not maintained during the winter. But, like at most airports, the perimeter was lined with high chain-link fences topped with barbed wire.

Despite the road's limited usage, a couple hundred yards in, they arrived at a small guardhouse and a barrier. When the two SUVs pulled up, Luigi jumped from the vehicle and closed the door before the guard approached them. He warmly greeted the guard in English, waving two vehicle passes in hand. Mixing German and English, the bored guard came to understand they were traveling together and let them through with a wave of his hand and some perfunctory farewell in German.

Giancarlo relaxed. The dark-tinted windows had done their job, and Luigi had done his by discovering the process for getting the passes. It was much neater when they didn't need to show passports or other documentation. There was always a chance one of the women might try to be a hero and attract attention if a guard poked his head in a window. Furthermore, the entire entourage traveled with forged passports. With so many variables, there was always the potential for a screw-up that could endanger them all. Unfortunately, only one person responding incorrectly to one question from a curious security guard could cause a messy situation.

Giancarlo spotted their borrowed aircraft parked well away from the main terminal and pointed it out to Luigi. The snow had stopped, the runway was clear, and travel to the jet took only a few minutes. Everything appeared to be going according to plan. Giancarlo turned his bulky frame as far around toward the back seat as he could manage and addressed both women.

"We're going for a little ride and you won't be harmed as long as you cooperate." He lied to win their acquiescence. "Luigi will lead you into the aircraft. Stay quiet and don't try to attract any attention. If there's any funny business, we'll knock you out."

From his vantage point in the front, he made eye contact with the German girl. He didn't know why, but something about the woman seemed remotely familiar. Even with most of her face still covered in the towel, he saw she was adequately terrified. He couldn't make eye contact with Nadine but imagined she would feel even more alarmed. She knew well how he behaved when displeased.

One pilot noticed the lights of their approaching vehicle, popped his head out the open aircraft door, then darted down the steps as the SUV pulled alongside the aircraft and came to a full stop. He moved to open the door for Giancarlo, but the crime boss waved him off.

"Help Luigi get the women into the plane. Seat them at the table, right at the back, and secure them well by their hands and feet," he instructed. "Get the bimbo hostess to give them some water and something to keep them calm."

Meanwhile, Luigi had already taken the German woman from his side and led her toward the plane, encountering no resistance. A second SUV pulled up behind the parked Mercedes and further blocked the view from the main terminal. The men bolted from their vehicle and formed a protective circle around the stairs to the aircraft, watching for any unusual movement on the tarmac.

Giancarlo waited outside the aircraft, shivering in the cold, while they boarded and secured the women. Despite their planning and no resistance from their captives, it still took five minutes to get them into the plane, seated and secured. Giancarlo muttered obscenities about the miserable weather and scanned the horizon.

When Luigi reappeared in the doorway, he bounded down the steps and started the SUV again. They had one more critical part of the mission to complete. The bodyguard motioned to the other driver and signaled for two more men to join them. Their job was to deliver their rental cars to the edge of the tarmac, close to the fence, and well back from the runway. That's what Luigi had negotiated with the Europcar manager when they rented them. There'd be no need for anyone to enter the terminal. That was important only because Giancarlo was determined to leave behind no trace of this visit to Europe.

Still standing in the frigid air, Giancarlo watched them open wide all four doors of both vehicles before the bodyguards meticulously wiped down the inside windows, door handles, steering wheel, and other surfaces that might retain fingerprints. The men needed a few minutes, but he wanted them to be thorough.

Soon, the cleaning was complete and the doors slammed shut. Luigi and the other driver sauntered back to join the rest of the team and Giancarlo. Both appeared relaxed and in no hurry to join the group gathered around the idling jet.

At the end of the runway, on their stomachs in a ditch concealed by the parked vehicles, Giancarlo knew another pair huddled in the cold, rubbing their hands to stay warm. Their weapons would be drawn and ready for any surprises.

But there was still no sign of the small private aircraft they all wanted so desperately to arrive.

SIXTY-SIX

*Approaching Innsbruck Airport, Austria, in a small plane,
Monday January 27, 2020*

Howard glanced at his watch. They were already almost a half-hour behind their originally scheduled arrival time. Increasingly, something seemed amiss. With no lights or familiar distinguishing landmarks in the dark sky, it was hard to discern, but he was almost certain they had already passed the jagged peak on the right side once before.

For the past few minutes, he had tried desperately to differentiate one mountain from another. The one on the right had a jagged outcrop near the top that looked like the outline of a head and protruding nose. He was sure he'd seen that pointy outline perhaps thirty minutes before.

"No, we're still on the same path directly in," the pilot said when Howard asked. "They just instructed us to slow slightly to ease some congestion."

The pilot stared straight ahead. Occasionally, Howard heard snippets of conversation from the pilot's headpiece, but it was never loud enough nor clear enough even to discern what language was spoken. Was paranoia taking over or was his sense of unease justified?

The turbulence his pilot warned about never materialized. Still, Howard couldn't be sure if that outcome was the result of his change of direction and piloting skill, or if it was all a ruse of misinformation for some other purpose.

While he was deep in worried deliberation, hypothesizing what possible reasons the pilot might have for creating a delay, he didn't exclude the possibility that Giancarlo might again be closing in on him. The reach of The Organization was greater and deeper than many sovereign nations.

"If the traffic is too heavy at Innsbruck, how much would you charge me to change course and fly to Munich?" Howard asked.

"We'll only be delayed a couple more minutes," the pilot reassured him. "Besides, we're too close to the airport to change our flight plan now. We'd need to land and take off again if you want to go to Munich."

What could he do from his seat in the small aircraft in the sky? He had no weapons to commandeer the flight. He had no flying skills whatsoever. His immediate future was entirely in the hands of Emile, the pilot. He shuddered at that thought.

Before his shiver was complete, Howard heard sounds from the headpiece again. The pilot listened for a moment or two. Then, using clear English for the first time, he confirmed that he understood their instructions.

"Okay, they're ready for us to descend," Emile said. Like most pilots, his tone was calm, factual and devoid of emotion. Nothing he did telegraphed anything unusual.

It took a few minutes for the aircraft to touch down on the runway, but their descent was smooth and gradual with only a slight buffeting in the breeze. Like the landing in Lyon, they felt barely a bump as Emile brought the wheels to the ground and decelerated.

Howard looked about. Curiously, not one commercial aircraft taxied out on the runways. Yet dozens were parked at the gates attached to the terminal in neat rows next to the runway closest to the main building. The pilot indeed had lied. Howard's heart rate raced upward and he took deep breaths, trying to calm his anxiety and think clearly.

At the end of the runway, the pilot veered toward the terminal. However, instead of making a sharp left turn for the shortest distance, Emile continued in a straight line toward another section of the airport. Several small jets and aircraft were parked there. Maybe the designated debarking point for all small planes like theirs?

All looked customary until he noticed one parked jet with a half-dozen men huddling around it, hands in their pockets to ward off the frigid air. To his horror, one of those men towered over all the others and had unmatched heft as well. Giancarlo Mareno.

Howard felt the blood drain from his face. He had trouble swallowing and his chest felt tight. His breathing had become irregular. His eyes darted in all directions, his frazzled brain trying to make sense of what was happening and struggling to regain control.

As the aircraft slowed to turn in a parking arc, Howard buried his face in both hands in utter despair. Tears welled in his eyes before his hands clenched reflexively in fists to do battle. From the corner of his eye, he could see the occasional accusing glance by Emile and realized his intuition was right and his worst fears had been realized.

The plane came to a full stop and Emile shut down the engine. Two of the men on the tarmac approached from the aircraft parked only a few yards away.

Without thinking, Howard released his seatbelt, pulled up violently on the door handle, and jumped from the aircraft in one desperate action. Then he ran. He ran faster and with more desperation than at any time he could remember. As oxygen surged to his brain, he began to think more clearly. It was fight or flight, and his mind had decided escape was the only hope. At end of the tarmac, a fence loomed ahead.

Despite his fitness and speed, within a minute, Howard felt two powerful arms envelop him in an iron grip, squeezing like a brutal football tackle. The weight of a body in flight hurled him to the ground. His face slammed against the tarmac. Before Howard could recover his senses, a powerful kick snapped his head to the left. Then a fist pounded his mouth and nose several times in rapid succession.

Darkness fell over him.

SIXTY-SEVEN

*Approaching Innsbruck Airport, Austria, in a
helicopter, Monday January 27, 2020*

The incessant noise surprised Janet the most when she rushed toward the helicopter. A constant whirl of the enormous blades pounded and cut through the air with violent repetitive whacks, and the resulting din was a staccato of thunder. Her heart raced. She felt disoriented and unsettled until a hand pulled her up the steps and into the chopper.

The commando who helped her into the aircraft pushed down a lever on the door, closing and securely locking it. Impatient, the pilot lifted the helicopter from the ground as the commando buckled himself into the seat beside Janet in the second row. It bounced and swayed in the light winds as he gradually lifted them above the trees and power lines surrounding the hotel parking lot until he reached a safe height.

The thrust of the jet engine pressed Janet back in her seat and she cried out in surprise as the pilot leaned forward, set for whatever they might encounter in the air.

Janet took in the banks of electronic controls, flashing lights, buttons, and switches. Her first time near a cockpit, the maze of technology astonished her, and her stomach tightened with unease. Her life depended entirely on how well the men in front of her trained for their responsibility and how skillfully they executed their knowledge. The cramped seating of the helicopter created anxiety she'd never known in the separate and comfortable passenger cabin of an airplane.

For the first few minutes, they flew over the tree-lined roadway and continued to gradually climb to higher altitudes. There was a massive mountain peak directly in front of their flight path, so their ascent would remain steep for several more minutes.

Her companion saw her unease and helpfully reached across and lowered the folding arms on each side of her seat. More confident, but not relaxed, she gripped those folding arms tightly until they cleared the mountainside and a completely new majestic horizon of mountains came into view.

With the sun setting off to her right, hundreds of separate peaks seemed to jut up in the receding light, creating a scene of both mystique and rugged beauty.

Beside her, and also in the front, the commandos seemed engaged almost continuously in conversation through their headsets, nodding or shaking their heads from time to time but never audible with the noise of the rotor blades overhead. After a few minutes, the man beside her barked into a microphone on his collar, then turned and yelled for Janet to answer her phone.

With all the motion and noise, she hadn't realized Klaudia's secure device was vibrating for an incoming call. Janet answered but discovered she couldn't hear any part of the conversation amid the cacophony all around.

The commando saw her dilemma, reached into a pocket on the seat-back in front, and passed her a headset to connect with her phone. With earphones blocking the noise around her ears, she faintly heard the voice of Fronhaus, their main contact in the German intelligence service. This time, there was no security protocol necessary.

"Here's what's happening. My superiors didn't want you to stay in the hotel. There were too many variables with the bad guys and almost certainly, the local police would insist on questioning you. We don't want them to know anything about your role in their local emergency, but you must now listen carefully to my instructions and follow them precisely. Can you hear me okay?"

Janet let him know she could barely hear him but would try to understand his message. He spoke louder when he continued, almost shouting into the phone.

"Before Klaudia and our men reached the room where the shooting occurred, they planted a special tracking device and microphone inside her bra. For some reason, we lost the signal after she was injured, but we picked it up again just a few minutes ago. Mareno has her and the woman you were trying to rescue inside a vehicle headed toward Innsbruck. Can you hear me so far?"

Janet confirmed she understood.

"We are getting clearance from the Austrian authorities as we speak. You should be at the airport in Innsbruck in just a few minutes. It's long shot but our team will try to intercept Mareno and rescue the two women.

The chopper will touch down for just enough time to let our commandos disembark. Stay inside when it touches down. Do not, I repeat, do not leave the chopper for any reason. Lie down on the floor when the team leaves the aircraft, and stay on the floor until the pilot tells you it's okay. Do you understand? Repeat my instruction."

"You want me to stay in the helicopter and lie on the floor until they come back," Janet shouted into the phone.

As the winds buffeted the helicopter, she bounced and rocked with the aircraft's motion, once again feeling nauseated and unsettled. She drew her seatbelt tightly around her waist but still found herself using the arm of the commando beside her to feel balanced and stable. In front, the pilot leaned forward as though trying to coax every mile per hour from his chopper. Clearly, he had decided optimum speed was a higher priority than passenger comfort.

Just as their contact with the *Bundesnachrichtendienst* predicted, the helicopter soon started to descend. Even as she felt the aircraft lose altitude, the pilot maintained high speed, and turbulence increased as they approached the ground. From her window, she could see lights lining a runway as they rushed downward toward the airfield.

Off to her left, she spotted another unmarked helicopter approaching them at a high rate of speed. The commando beside her also noticed and gave a slight nod. Then he and his colleague next to the pilot in front, inspected and adjusted their weapons. Their rifles looked intimidating and deadly from every angle. The men not only inspected them carefully, they also held the scopes to their eyes and checked the settings to be sure everything was ready.

As their helicopter pitched forward in a steeper descent, Janet had her first glimpse of a private jet, parked in a darkening corner. Another small plane taxied away, headed toward the terminal. It accelerated suddenly and was almost out of view when the other chopper swopped around, lined up directly in the path of the private jet and headed toward it.

Her pilot reduced speed and swung around behind the private jet. Then the helicopter started to level out for landing. Just before she lost her line of sight out the front window, Janet noticed some commotion as several people tried to rush into the private jet all at the same time, jamming the staircase momentarily. Someone unsuccessfully tried to raise the staircase and close its door. Unbelievably, the jet started to creep toward the other low-flying and incoming helicopter, the staircase flopping and bouncing on the tarmac. Then it stopped.

The commandos continued talking through their headsets. She couldn't be sure if they were communicating with one another or some remote voice. There was much nodding and their bodies tensed for action, hands nervously fingering their weapons, as their sharp descent continued.

The instant she felt the thump of the helicopter touching the tarmac behind the private jet, two commandos thrust open the doors, letting in a cold rush of air and noise as they jumped from the chopper. The one who sat beside her on the flight took a single second to cry out the order "down" and point at the floor before he slammed the door and rushed away.

The door latch didn't close and sprung open again. Terrified, Janet obeyed the command and dropped to her stomach on the frigid floor of the helicopter as chilly air poured in from the open door causing her entire body to shiver. She lay on the floor for only an instant before she heard the rapid loud pops of many gunshots.

Gingerly, keeping as low as possible, she boosted herself from the floor into a squat and peeked out the window on the other side of the helicopter. In horror, she watched as both commandos fell helplessly forward to the ground with blood spurting from multiple blotches on their backs, their weapons falling helplessly to the ground. They had run only a few steps. An ambush!

The helicopter pilot reacted immediately, revved the engine for take-off, and yelled for Janet to close the open door on her side. She pivoted and crawled to the doorway stretching her body outside the aircraft to grab the handle and pull it toward her as the helicopter started to lift.

Janet thought she caught a motion from the corner of her eye. Before she could react, a powerful hand grasped her arm and yanked her toward the open door. She looked for something to hold onto and caught her fingers briefly on the metal frame of the doorway. But her grip was no match for the strength of her attacker.

Before she could cry out, another vice-like grip encircled her chest and dragged her backward out of the helicopter in one fluid motion. She tried to resist, but the muscular arm held her head rigidly straight and arms pressed tightly against her body. She heard another volley of shots whiz past her head toward the pilot, then the sputtering choke of an engine shutting down unexpectedly.

She tried to kick her assailant, but another pair of hands restrained her and placed her upright on the tarmac. The grip over her mouth was so tight and hand so large, she had trouble breathing. One of the men pressed a gun against her head and shouted for her to come with them.

In desperation, Janet shook her head violently enough for her captive to momentarily lose his grip so she bit a stray finger with all the pressure she could muster and held on with her teeth. The captor cried out, then smashed his fist into her face shocking her enough to open the grip of her jaw.

In front of the private jet, the second helicopter hovered only a few more seconds, seemingly waiting for orders, before suddenly revving its engines and climbing off into the distance. The tarmac became measurably more quiet with only the rumble of an idling jet engine.

"Bring her aboard," Giancarlo Mareno shouted out to her attackers from the jet's doorway.

Her captors dragged her to the stairway and tried to make her stand. Once more, Janet resisted, until the one with his hand over her mouth suddenly released his grip from her face. She screamed out again.

He hoisted her over his shoulder with her head facing the ground. Then he trudged up the steps, restraining her with one arm wrapped in an iron lock around her upper legs while Janet kicked and squealed to no avail.

Inside the jet, he threw her roughly to the floor. She continued to resist, knowing her life depended on an escape. She yelled and cursed at her attacker. She kicked out in anger and frustration. She twisted her body violently from side to side. All in vain.

Giancarlo Mareno was the first person she recognized as a bodyguard tried to subdue her on the floor. He stood watching, standing menacingly in front of a huge leather seat a few feet away, his massive hulk hunched forward with his head almost touching the roof of the jet. His expression showed no emotion but his dark eyes flashed with both anger and disgust.

Still screaming, Janet managed to land one vicious kick in her attacker's groin. She scrambled to her feet as he momentarily lost his grip, and glared with unbridled hatred at the loathsome man who had caused her so much pain. Without a second's hesitation she lunged forward to gouge out the animal's eyes.

Giancarlo lashed out at her with a huge uplifted arm. She watched the giant hand rushing toward her with a clarity like slow motion. She tried to duck out of its path but failed. A searing pain shot through her entire body as her head jerked violently sideways from the impact, knocking her off her feet and backward. She glimpsed the jet ceiling for a second then it dropped from view as the dark sky suddenly appeared.

She felt her head hit the metal stair railing on one side, then bounce and bang her neck against the other railing before she smashed against the cement tarmac with a sickening thud.

Then she felt nothing at all.

SIXTY-EIGHT

In flight, on a private jet, somewhere over the Atlantic,
Tuesday January 28, 2020

At the back of the private jet, in the corner opposite the toilet and tiny food preparation area, Nadine sat facing the front of the aircraft. The thugs had tied them into two of the four anchored seats that surrounded a small functional table where a flight attendant usually mixed drinks or prepared plates of food for passengers.

When their captors first shoved them into the plane, only Nadine and the woman on her right, Klaudia, were secured at the table. Mareno's thugs had wrapped their hands and feet in the cable zip ties so tightly that it almost cut off their circulation. Next, they buckled the seat belts and pulled them tightly. Then they took a longer strip and wound it around their bodies and the individual seats. Neither woman could move more than an inch or two in any direction.

Unable to look at a watch or phone, they could only guess how long they had been detained but surely more than an hour had elapsed in the aircraft. Before that, they had traveled in the SUV from Garmisch-Partenkirchen with no stops. She was thirsty, hungry, and needed to pee urgently. She asked to use the *toilette* just before all the commotion started but everyone had ignored her pleas.

What happened next wasn't total confusion, but frenzied activity with a lot of tension and fast-moving parts unfolding surprisingly fast.

It all started when two men dragged the man they called Howard Knight onto the aircraft and through the scattered leather seats. His face was battered into an ugly red and blue color with blood oozing from his mouth and nose. They had beaten him unconscious and he had not revived. Next, the thugs plunked him into the chair directly across from Nadine and repeated the same process of tying up the wounded man with zip ties.

Nadine and Klaudia both studied Knight. His dark hair with slivers of gray was matted with blood and specks of dirt from the tarmac. Both eyes were swollen closed. His nose was crooked and drooped to the left. Dozens of scratches and bruises covered his face. His head flopped toward his chest as they gave him the zip ties treatment. He was still alive, but his breathing was worryingly irregular.

When Nadine looked up from the horrific sight, she glanced again toward her seatmate. This time, she made contact just as large tears started to flow from Klaudia's beautiful brown eyes. She didn't sob or cry out, but for several minutes a constant stream trickled down her pale cheeks.

When the ruffians left the cabin, a woman dressed as a hostess came over to the table and attended to Howard Knight with a damp cloth and towel. A few moments after she started, Giancarlo Mareno appeared in the doorway. The attendant dropped everything and rushed to welcome the huge man.

For the next few minutes, Nadine watched the jet fill swiftly with a parade of men and one woman from the team Mareno brought. They were still filing in when the next stage of the saga exploded.

A pilot rushed out of the closed cockpit door for a huddled conversation with Mareno. Before they finished their conversation, some sort of upheaval started on the steps outside the jet's door. Loud voices screamed instructions, and the plane swayed from side to side with frantic motion from the jet's stairway.

Nadine almost stopped breathing. A rescue? To her right, Klaudia also brightened. No longer crying, her red-rimmed eyes widened, and she seemed not to breathe as she crooked her neck around a seat back to see what was going on. Klaudia glanced toward Nadine and raised her eyebrows in apparent surprise, and with a glimmer of hope.

Only a moment later, the hooligans dragged another body through the doorway. A woman.

They watched intently as she resisted, kicking, screaming, biting and trying to wrestle her body free of their grip. She glared in hatred at Mareno and tried to attack him with her hands before he suddenly struck out and hit her head with such force it snapped sideways.

The impact hurled the woman backward and out the aircraft door where her head banged loudly against the metal stairs or railing. When the thumping stopped Mareno dispatched a bodyguard to bring her into the jet with a jab of his thumb.

When the man dragged her through the door, the woman's neck flopped forward like a rag doll. The bodyguard and another goon hauled her to the back and plunked her at the table. Blood oozed from the back of her head and clotted in her short blonde hair. After no more than a second's inspection of her condition, they secured her with cable zip ties like the others.

Klaudia became alarmed and looked intently at the injured woman, then pleaded for the hostess to help the woman she called Janet. The uniformed woman shook the injured female's shoulders a few times but drew no response. Janet's head flopped lazily as the woman tried to wake her. She took Janet's wrist in her hand and felt for a pulse. After a moment, she tried again on the other wrist. Nothing.

The hostess raised her head with a grim expression and slowly shook her head twice. Out of either respect or shame, she lowered her eyes and turned away.

Klaudia scrutinized the woman's examination and released a long, bloodcurdling scream.

"You killed Janet! You bastards! You killed her!"

Two of Mareno's thugs rose from their seats and stepped toward Klaudia. One grabbed the towel the flight attendant had used to care for Howard Knight and violently wound it tightly around Klaudia's mouth again to deaden her mournful screams and accusations. The other snapped a strand of zip ties snugly over the towel.

The small passenger compartment became quiet after they silenced Klaudia and the aircraft began to move while the bodyguards were still standing. In the background, the racing engines roared loudly until the aircraft lifted from the ground, climbed to cruising altitude, and leveled off high above a nearby mountain range.

A few minutes later, Giancarlo bellowed for the hostess, who quickly unbuckled and dashed forward to his seat. Nadine watched her lean in to listen to Mareno's command and saw her body stiffen. With a grim expression and pursed lips, the woman returned slowly to the back of the aircraft, unbuttoned her shirt and took it off. She wasn't wearing a bra.

Next, she slipped out of her short skirt. Again, there was no undergarment. Although the woman disrobed only a few steps away, she never looked toward their nearby table. Instead, she reached into a refrigerator and took out two bottles of Champagne. She handed an empty glass to each passenger except Mareno. For him, she brought Coke.

Completely nude, the flight attendant walked from seat to seat, filling glasses with Champagne while the passengers acted like a college football team after a satisfying victory. With elevated adrenaline fueled by alcohol, the hooligans behaved as though they lived with no limitations.

Raucous laughter grew with louder voices and hand-slapping celebrations. By the time the hostess made her second refill of Champagne glasses, the boors had devolved into behavior beyond description. They felt up her bare breasts, squeezed her nipples playfully, stroked her thighs, and poked her pubic region.

Nadine had seen it before. *Collage masculin*—a mindless ritual of male bonding meant to humiliate and degrade women—and a predictable core value of The Organization.

Soon, the hooligans passed the woman around like a doll or play toy as they took turns using her mouth or vagina at will. The debauchery continued until the men were too tired or drunk to continue. The only female bodyguard sat with her head in her hands unable to either watch or do anything about it.

After his men were satisfied, Mareno demanded a bottle of Coke before he issued another instruction to the hostess. Still naked, the attendant returned from her refrigerator with three bottles of water and placed them in the center of the captives' modest table. Before she took the cap off one of the bottles, she crinkled her nose at the odor in the area. It was the putrid smell of urine. Hours before, the hostess had begged Mareno to let his prisoners use the toilet. In reply, he merely growled, "Let them sit in their piss."

The hostess's body was bruised, with large red blotches on her breasts and thighs. Her green eyes appeared vacant and her expression grim. She cut away the zip ties and towel from Klaudia's face and held a bottle of water for her to drink. Gratefully, Klaudia gulped down the full bottle as quickly as she could.

Finished with Klaudia, the young woman removed the cap from another bottle and assisted Nadine. Drinking the water eagerly, she looked into the hostess's eyes and told her she sympathized with her *situation critique*. The woman's appearance softened as they silently connected on a level neither expected.

When Nadine finished sipping the water, the hostess moved to Howard Knight. From time to time throughout the flight, he had tried to open his eyes. With each effort, they fluttered for a moment, but gave up in exhaustion or despair. The attendant cleaned his face and cleared away the areas where blood had congealed. She shook his shoulders and tilted back his head. Surprisingly, his eyes opened slightly.

He was groggy. A few minutes passed before he focused completely, but he gradually responded to the hostess's gentle rub of his shoulder and prompt to sip some water. Finally, he looked around the table. His eyes fell first on Nadine but moved on without a greeting. He shifted back to his left and seemed to recognize Klaudia. He hesitated, unsure. She returned Knight's gaze with a morose expression but said nothing.

Next, he shifted his gaze to his right and saw the corpse of Janet, her eyes still open, head tilted askew, and her body motionless. As a grim realization slowly set in, Howard turned again toward Klaudia with a haunting look of despair.

"I'm so sorry, Howard," she said. "We tried. Take comfort. She didn't suffer long. He killed her right after he brought you onto the plane."

First, he gagged, holding back bile instead of throwing it up. Then his entire body trembled violently. Nadine wondered if he was experiencing a stroke or something and leaned forward. He began weeping in loud, uncontrolled sobs. He cried a torrent of tears until Mareno again bellowed for the hostess. She bent to hear the crime boss's latest request. Again, her body tensed before she stood up and moved to carry out the command. With a gentle nudge and a few words, she woke Luigi, asleep in the seat behind Mareno. Like the other men, he too was hungover and unsteady when she helped him stand-up to carry out the order.

Showing no emotion, the bodyguard stepped behind Howard Knight. When the hostess handed him another towel, Mareno's bodyguard shoved it into the face of the weeping man and yanked it tight, muffling the sound of his crying. Deftly, he secured the towel with a zip tie from his pocket, then pulled the strap tight. Without a word, he walked back to his seat.

With a jerk of her head, Nadine motioned to the hostess to come over to their table. In a tone just above a whisper, she asked her to clear the towel from his nose so the man could at least breathe. After glancing to be sure no other passengers would see, the naked hostess put a finger to her lips instructing silence and held it there until Knight nodded once.

After glancing to be sure no other passengers would see, she reached across the table and lowered the towel below his mouth, taking care it still appeared in place from behind his head.

In return, Nadine mouthed a *merci*. She didn't want another death. She didn't want another corpse facing her, especially a man so battered physically and emotionally.

She found it hard enough to maintain control and tolerate hours of confinement while tightly bound to restrict movement, sitting in her own urine, and with a dead woman's body propped beside her. On her right, poor Klaudia with a bloody face and missing teeth in the front of her mouth continued to sob every few minutes.

Nadine found it almost impossible to maintain calm when all around her everything seemed so insanely *bizarre*. When they arrived at the destination, would Mareno beat and attack her as well? Or just mercifully kill her?

SIXTY-NINE

Typically, Giancarlo slept only a few hours at a time. He never understood why others found it necessary to sleep for seven or eight hours, but he didn't begrudge people their choice. If they preferred to miss out on twenty-five percent of their total life, that was fine. But he was driven to use that time maintaining and exerting his considerable influence.

That was the dichotomy of power; the more you had, the more driven you became to gain even more. And Giancarlo accepted that reality.

Over the years, he'd learned many lessons and one of the most valuable was understanding how reluctantly people accept change. Creatures of habit, humans invariably resist change to their routines. They almost always prefer to maintain the known status quo and even fight against beneficial changes in subtle and subversive ways.

However, those with power understand that change is the most formidable weapon they can wield. It keeps people off-balance and unsure. It instills fear and uncertainty, and the ambiguity keeps folks pliant and submissive. The greatest irony of all was the willingness of people to believe nothing significant would disrupt their own lives. All it took was is a constant reassurance that "nothing will change."

When his men had fallen asleep after their drunken debauchery inside the aircraft cabin, Giancarlo summoned the naked and apprehensive flight hostess and told her to bring him a Coke. Her smile was gone, probably from fatigue and disgust with the way his men had toyed with her sexually in the earlier hours, but the young thing needed to learn to show respect regardless.

When she returned with his beverage, he demanded she pose for a few minutes while he enjoyed his drink and ogled her body. To be sure she understood his message, he told her she'd continue posing for him until she looked like she was really having fun. A reasonably intelligent girl, she understood immediately, flashed him a disarming smile, and assumed several provocative positions. He brushed her away after a moment or two.

From his jacket pocket, he retrieved his phone earbuds and made calls for an hour or more. He talked to associates in China, North Korea, Australia, Singapore, and New Zealand. He warned them they'd hear disconcerting news about The Organization leaders from France and Japan in the coming hours. Their accomplices were in a tight spot and would probably lose their freedom for a while. New leaders would replace the former bosses soon, but nothing would change for them.

Call after call, with a confident tone and his most uplifting words, Giancarlo reassured everyone not to worry, that nothing would change in their world. He made a mental note to make the same calls in another few hours when the Europeans woke up.

A pilot surfaced from the cockpit for a break and let Giancarlo know they were about two hours from their destination in Martinique.

"Any instructions for arrival?"

"Yeah," Giancarlo replied. "Use the same code words you use for flights from South America. And park in your usual spot."

The pilot nodded and needed no further explanation. He regularly flew the same aircraft on runs from Columbia to Martinique for the plane's owner, who imported cocaine and other drugs for distribution throughout North America and had developed an invincible network that generated billions per year for The Organization. It was one of the most creatively developed and stringently managed labyrinths they had ever produced.

Giancarlo had Pierre Boivin to thank for its creation. He had to compliment the Frenchman. His idea was brilliant and its execution had been flawless for several years. A protectorate of France, Martinique was part of its *Départements d'Outre Mer,* reporting to the secretary of state for Overseas Departments and Territories, who reported to the minister of the interior. With patience and political skill, Boivin maneuvered people beholden to The Organization into all three critical roles that governed and oversaw the beautiful Caribbean island.

Giancarlo was confident the unique code the pilots used that night would trigger a well-rehearsed chain of events he'd modify only slightly. He knew the routine well.

Recognizing the special code, sophisticated software surreptitiously embedded in the computers at Caribbean air traffic control was programmed to erase the flight from monitoring screens. There'd be no digital record of their arrival or departure. On the ground, their jet would taxi to a remote corner of the airfield where someone would open a section of the protective security fence that surrounded the airport. About a mile away, police on the idyllic island would actually close the only road into a highly fortified building in the middle of a forested area at the end of the runway.

The elaborate system had worked effectively in the past, and Giancarlo was confident that tonight would be no exception. He woke Luigi for a review of their plans.

"When we touch down, have the guys take the women—including the corpse—to the safe house. They should find a place to bury the whore, dig a hole deep enough, and get her into the ground while it's still dark. Stay behind to be sure they get it right. I'll be okay alone."

"Are you sure, boss?" Luigi questioned. "I'd feel better leaving one of my guys in charge and riding with you to the house over in Sainte Anne. We don't have time to check out the place if you leave right away."

"Thanks for your concern, but I'll be fine. We're using the usual driver?" Giancarlo asked.

"Same guy. He's trustworthy, knows the roads, and will get you there safely. What worries me is the house itself. We haven't had anyone but cleaners inside for a while. Don't you think it would be better to wait until we sweep the place for recording devices or even explosives?" Luigi persisted.

"Give your wands to the driver and explain what he needs to do. The place is well fortified and we've never had an issue before. Now, here's what I want you to do when we arrive," Giancarlo said with a wave of dismissal. "Once we touch down, unbind Knight's lower body so he can walk from the aircraft. Tie that rag over his mouth to keep him quiet. Grab a couple other guys and drag him over to the gate in the fence, then toss him into the back of the car. Be sure to wrap him up really tight once he's inside the SUV."

"You want me to use any chemicals?"

"No. I want the bastard alert the entire time. If you secure him well in the trunk, the driver and I can handle him from there. The driver will stay until I'm done with Knight in case he tries something," Giancarlo explained. "I'll send him back before morning to pick up you and the guys. There'll be enough room for you, the two other women, and a couple guys to dig their graves."

Luigi made no further attempts to change Giancarlo's mind, and for another few minutes, they fine-tuned the logistics of subsequently getting the entire team back to the USA. They decided the gravediggers would return with Giancarlo and Luigi on the private jet. For the rest, Luigi would arrange commercial flights to three different eastern seaboard cities, splitting the group up in the unlikely event they needed to clear customs and immigration at Teterboro.

As the men became satisfied all the details were clear and workable, the engines of the aircraft slowed, and the pilots began their descent. Luigi returned to his original seat behind Giancarlo.

The crime boss picked up his telephone and pressed the app for CBNN News. He didn't have to scroll down to find his story. The moment the app popped up, the headline Giancarlo hoped to see appeared, screaming its message in the largest font possible on a digital device.

JUSTICE DEPT CHARGES MULTIMA BOSS SIMPSON WITH MONEY LAUNDERING IN LATE-DAY RAID

Giancarlo sighed with satisfaction and a crooked smile formed on his lips as he read the first paragraph.

> *Acting on instructions from the Justice Department, the FBI today arrested the CEO of Multima Corporation, her Chief Financial Officer, and a Division President in Fort Myers, Florida. A spokeswoman claims the FBI received a tip leading to discovery that Multima illegally funneled billions of dollars generated by sales of opioids through its bank accounts to drug lords in Mexico. The billionaire executive and heiress of the John George Mortimer empire remains in custody until an arraignment tomorrow. The prices of Multima's common shares dropped markedly in early pre-market trading, and analysts predict further steep price declines when the markets open tomorrow.*

Giancarlo took little time to savor his delight in a development that shocked the world of business. From a pocket, he pulled out a slip of paper where he'd made a note of the phone number for a little-known financial analyst, from an even less known brokerage firm, located in a small town in New Jersey. The man responded on the second ring. There was no security protocol or other formalities. Giancarlo simply delivered his orders.

"You don't need to know who's speaking. Just understand this: I have your home phone number, know your address on West Chestnut Hill Avenue, and your wife's first name is Barbara. You helped a colleague denigrate Multima Corporation on CBNN about three years ago. Do exactly the same thing again tomorrow morning," Giancarlo said.

"I paid my debt. I did what your colleague demanded. He told me the loan was canceled," the man whined.

"I don't give a shit whether your loan was canceled or not. I'm telling you to get in front of a CBNN camera tomorrow, and tell the world what a terrible criminal that bitch is and how lousy her company is for investors," Giancarlo said with his voice an octave deeper and a bit louder. "Tell me right now you'll call tonight and book your interview time early tomorrow. And be convincing, or Barbara might have a bad accident sometime soon."

The man acquiesced as expected. A glance at Giancarlo's watch showed still enough time for one more call before the wheels touched the ground. This time she'd better be there.

The woman did answer on the first ring and immediately completed the security protocol. He launched into his instructions without any greeting or small talk.

"Call our guy at the brokerage in the Caymans right away," Giancarlo ordered. "When the Multima price drops below fifteen tomorrow, have him start buying shares with the numbered corporations. No more than eight percent of the total shares into any one company. Have him activate the software to keep the price in a range of fourteen and a half to fifteen. I want twenty-five percent of the company's outstanding shares before the markets close tomorrow."

She repeated his request, agreed to call immediately, and hung up on him before he could. He forgot to find out why she hadn't answered when he had twice tried to reach her earlier.

SEVENTY

Arrival on a tropical island, Tuesday January 28, 2020

Howard felt numb. The repulsive sight of Janet's stiffening corpse sitting across the table on the airplane—her head flopping on her delicate neck with every bump or tilt of the plane—was far more painful than the brutal beating Mareno's thugs dished out. The shock of seeing her once-beautiful face darken to an increasingly tainted shade of blue was so deep and profound it left Howard feeling like a useless vegetable.

Sobs of overpowering grief had stopped when the hostess on the jet showed a small gesture of empathy and lowered the towel below his mouth in return for his silent promise to be quiet. He obeyed. Once he had his emotions under control, his mind whirled with a powerful compulsion to exact revenge.

Not once before in his life had he felt a need for revenge. The concept seemed almost archaic and useless to him. But Giancarlo Mareno had shattered that perception with one vicious act that took the life of a woman he cared for deeply.

Their relationship had always been complicated. He was almost twice her age and first met Janet during her call-girl days at university, but never as a customer. Fidelia Morales had introduced them. Howard needed a beautiful, uninhibited young girl to sleep with special clients as favors or rewards from time to time. It's the way things worked then in the New York financial district. Fidelia told him about this ravishing beauty with extraordinary intellect, a woman who could delight any man with her conversation, charm, and sexual wiles.

"It's an unusual story," Fidelia told him at the time. "She's almost a genius and sits at the top of her class in political science at Columbia. But her parents kicked her out because they no longer wanted to pay for school. The bastards just threw her out and told her she could fend for herself like they had to. She likes sex, so she chose to service men and make good money doing it."

Howard remembered, with an intensity as though it were yesterday, the first time he met Janet Weissel. She was everything Fidelia promised. She had long, flowing blonde hair then. It bounced and bobbed from side to side, her animated conversation and youthful energy bubbling beneath the surface. Her face was among the most beautiful he'd ever seen. She could have been a fashion model.

Her smile was bright, flashing perfectly maintained teeth that seemed to sparkle when she laughed. Her always-tanned complexion was flawless. But it was her eyes that seduced. They were dark brown and seemed to draw in every man who made eye contact. Howard had watched the reaction of guys when they met her and remembered how some unconsciously leaned in to better bask in the warm seduction. Her eyes gave her a look of innocence, almost virginal purity.

But Howard had always thought of her as merely a business associate to help him get the financial results Giancarlo demanded. Until several years later. That bizarre night in a Miami high-rise condo owned by the FBI changed everything. Both had been plucked from different cities in entirely different circumstances to help the FBI build a court case against The Organization.

Janet had playfully snuggled up close to him on a sofa while they decompressed after a day of aggressive questioning by FBI interrogators. One thing led to another, and they eventually experienced a long night of incredibly passionate and mutually satisfying sex. Howard didn't even think of it as making love that first night. He remembered it more as an exquisite release of pent-up sexual desire.

However, things changed in the days and months following that momentous night. They gradually grew closer. They laughed often, recounted stories, playfully debated the ills of the world, and often touched and held each other. By the time the FBI was ready to conceal them in the witness protection program, everyone could see that they wanted to be together and enjoy their lives as a couple as long and as lovingly as possible.

During their time in Overveen, Howard steadily felt the bond of their mutual attraction grow stronger and deeper. He became a little obsessed with Janet's survival, and they designed strategies to ensure it would be her who survived to live a meaningful life should The Organization discover them. He felt a lump form in his throat again from the magnitude of her loss. He had never imagined the possibility of losing her to death first.

Now, Mareno might wait until morning to begin his dismemberment and torture, but it would almost certainly begin within hours. Running out of options, Howard still refused to give up.

"Are they all still sleeping up there?" Howard asked, with a toss of his head toward the seats in the front of the jet, after calling the hostess over with a subtle nod.

She scanned the room slowly, then stepped forward between the seating arrangements for a better view.

"They seem to be."

"Do you know who I am?" Howard said quietly, theatrically mouthing his question to be sure she understood.

"Yes. They told me."

"Did they tell you why they want me?"

"One told me you stole money from Mareno."

"That's true," Howard said. "A lot of money. Would you like to get some revenge for the way they treated you tonight?"

She nodded with hardened eyes and said, "Maybe."

"If you can find a way to get a gun from one of these goons, I'll give you some revenge and a million dollars to run away from it all," Howard said as he gauged her reaction.

The hostess looked at him quizzically, clearly weighing her alternatives. She considered the question for more than a minute while Howard watched and waited. Without a word, she went to a cupboard below the microwave oven and reached into a bag. She looked around the cabin carefully. With one hand, she pulled a cloth from a nearby drawer. With the other hand, she slipped a handgun into the fabric and wrapped it tightly.

Still nude, she stood and looked around the cabin slowly and intently, then took the three steps toward Howard, using her body as a shield from the cabin.

"Shove it inside my pants," Howard said to the hostess. To Nadine he ordered, "Tell us if anyone looks."

Using her body to block any view from the other seats, the hostess uncinched his belt and slipped the towel and gun into the front of Howard's underwear, then re-attached the belt and smoothed the pants out in one desperate sweep. It created an impressive bulge, but he doubted any of the men would notice.

Klaudia saw what was happening and jerked her head for the hostess to come over.

"I have pepper spray in my left bra. Reach in and get it for him."

The hostess slipped away and got a bottle of water. When she returned, she held the bottle to Klaudia's lips conspicuously while she reached into the bra and found a small cannister of pepper spray issued by the German intelligence service. Before she could pass it to Howard, the plane tilted gently forward in descent for landing.

"I'll try later," she mouthed to Howard as she retreated to her seat and fastened her belt.

Naturally, the crime boss was the first to disembark when the pilot opened the doors of the jet and lowered the staircase. He left without looking backward. Despite the hour, warm tropical air flooded into the cabin, its warmth soothing. Howard savored it as Luigi approached his seat at the back with two other men trailing him.

Roughly, one of them yanked Howard to his feet.

"Do you want me to cut the zip ties?" the still-nude hostess offered Luigi with a charming smile.

"Sure. Let's have one more peek at those gorgeous nipples from this angle," the bodyguard guffawed.

She expertly cut the zip ties from the rear and palmed the tiny cannister of pepper spray into Howard's back pocket as she rose from the floor with her breasts proudly extended and her smile dazzling.

They paid little attention to his welfare as they shoved him past the clusters of seats and out the door of the aircraft. He bumped against seat backs twice and grazed the railing of the staircase as they shoved him out of the jet and across the tarmac. At the end of the tarmac, they stopped and the three men lifted Howard off the ground and tossed him into the rear storage compartment of the SUV.

Luigi personally secured the new zip ties around his ankles and bound Howard's hands behind his back. Even with his new-found weapons, it looked grim. But Howard refused to give up. As soon as the door slammed shut, and the SUV started to move, Howard examined the storage area meticulously to find a sharp edge. He also wiggled and squirmed with his hands and feet. There might be some sliver of an opening.

SEVENTY-ONE

Giancarlo Mareno's luxurious home in Sainte Anne, Martinique, Tuesday January 28, 2020

"Release the zip ties from his feet," Giancarlo told the driver when they came to a stop in the driveway at the front of Giancarlo's mansion.

"Sure, boss," the driver said. "Would you like me to check the house before you go in?"

"I'll be fine. Once you release his feet, I'll take it from there. He won't go anywhere with his hands strapped like that and my grip around his collar," Mareno scoffed. "Pull the car around to the back garage. I don't want anyone to see we're here."

The nearest neighbor was a safe distance away because Giancarlo bought the properties on both sides of the road for a half-mile in each direction from his favorite residence. The chances of anyone seeing or hearing anything would be about zero once the car was tucked away in the garage.

As the driver pulled away, Giancarlo grabbed the standing but unsteady Howard Knight and shoved him toward the front door, still clutching his quarry by his shirt collar. After the beatings Howard's body had taken in the past few hours, the walk up several stairs to reach the front door from the driveway was long and arduous. Both his captive and Giancarlo paused for breath a couple times before they reached the entrance, where Giancarlo fiddled in the dark, trying to enter an electronic security code. Knight continued to wobble unsteadily on the doorstep.

When the door swung open, Giancarlo turned to Howard, intending to tug him through the doorway. Instead, without warning, Knight sprayed something that immediately blinded him. He wiped his eyes and the burning sensation intensified, increasing the pain, and leaving him unbalanced, coughing and disoriented.

Giancarlo reached out where he remembered Knight was standing and a hard metal object smashed against the back of his hand. *The nozzle of a gun!*

"Don't move, Giancarlo," Howard said calmly. "Step into the house and don't make any quick movements."

"What's going on, Knight?" Giancarlo's voice croaked.

"Your tenure with The Organization is about to end. I'll try to do it more humanely than you treat most of your victims."

"Let's try to work this out. I've always taken good care of you, Howard. You don't want to do something you'll later regret. Put the gun down and I'll forget this ever happened," Giancarlo said in the most reasonable tone of voice he could muster.

Howard tried to shove Giancarlo through the doorway, but the big man lashed out as Knight's hand touched his back. There was a gunshot, and Giancarlo felt intense pain in his left leg before both knees crumpled and he fell to the floor.

Still unable to see, Giancarlo pushed himself up and raised his head trying to orient himself and find Knight.

"Where are you, Howard? Why did you shoot?" he called out hoping to learn from what direction an answer might come. He got his answer when Knight seized his uninjured left foot and twisted his torso out of the doorway and further into the entrance of his home.

Giancarlo kicked out with all the strength he could muster and broke free of the grip. Then he swung his good leg where he guessed Knight had been standing but his leg met no resistance and fell harmlessly to the floor.

Before he could lash out again, he heard a volley of gunshots and Giancarlo's driver cried out in both shock and pain as he collapsed in a bloody heap at the front door, his weapon drawn but never used.

"Put down the gun, Howard," a woman's voice said.

"Is that you Fidelia?" Giancarlo called out.

Fidelia made no reply as she watched Howard obey her command and gingerly place the gun on the floor. She stepped forward and expertly kicked the weapon farther across the marble floor, well beyond the reach of both men.

Her eyes shifted from Howard to Giancarlo to the door and back. She did that a couple times.

"Drag in the driver," she motioned to Howard. "And close the door as soon as you get him inside."

Giancarlo twisted his upper body and searched for Fidelia through blurring, tear-filled eyes. The pain was unbearable. The stinging in his eyes, his bleeding leg, his entire lower body all seemed dysfunctional.

Where is she?

He tried again to focus and orient himself. Blurred legs appeared in front of his face about ten feet away. He lifted his head slowly, trying again to raise his upper body. With one valiant push upward on trembling arms, he raised his eyes to meet those of the woman. He could make out only her form with a weapon pointed at his head. A door slammed.

"You can't know how many times I've visualized this, Giancarlo. For your entire lifetime, you had no respect for women and a flagrant disregard for life. Now it's over. Even we who have been blindly loyal to you all these years have had enough. You've become a heartless killing machine, taking lives away on a whim. No amount of money can justify standing by while you play God for reasons only you can rationalize.

"You lost us the day you ordered me to arrange the murder of the harmless old Japanese Suji-san in his hospital bed. He was already dying and you knew it. But you weren't able to contain your ruthless ambition for only a few days or weeks, were you?

"You made it worse when you bribed the Japanese assassin to eliminate a German intelligence agent only because you needed his murder to implicate and eliminate your rivals. That sealed it for us. What about that poor man's wife and his two young children now without a father?

"It was then I realized you would eventually eliminate even me, probably the same way. It's only fitting a woman pulls the trigger now."

Before he could explain, she calmly aimed the weapon at his face. The last thing Giancarlo saw was the woman's finger gently squeezing the trigger and one bright flash.

SEVENTY-TWO

"Are you all right, Howard?" the woman he once loved asked.

He didn't know and couldn't answer for a moment. What had just happened? Was it possible the woman who had served Giancarlo Mareno faithfully for so many years was able to coldly look a wounded man in the eye and pull the trigger of the weapon that blew out his brains?

She didn't press for an answer. Instead, she laid the weapon on the floor, well away from the strewn male bodies, and strode calmly to the gun on the floor across the room. There, she bent over, picked it up and tossed it on a nearby sofa.

She checked the body of the driver to be sure he too was dead. With a half-dozen bullet holes in his shirt and blood streaming everywhere in the room, it didn't take her long. She hadn't hesitated to eliminate that young man either. The guy had no chance to react or survive.

As he slowly came to his senses, Howard looked around, but he couldn't bring himself to look at Mareno's corpse. Fragments of brain matter had spattered his own body. He'd vomit if he even peeked at the spot where Mareno lay.

Fidelia locked the front door, then turned to fetch something in the kitchen. She returned with a wet cloth and wiped Howard's face, gently and thoroughly. She cleaned his eyes first and dried them with a soft towel, then repeated the process across his face and neck. He didn't feel any more comfortable but was relieved the stench of death and human remains seemed less pungent.

"Luigi didn't think you'd be able to pull the trigger," Fidelia said. "He warned me that I'd have to finish him off."

"Luigi?"

"Yeah. He knew you had the gun and was sure you'd find a way to get out of the defective zip tie. But he was there when you killed your first man and he swore you'd never pull the trigger to finish him off," she said, her tone matter-of-fact.

"I guess we'll never know now, will we?"

"Go to the bathroom," she ordered in a calm tone. "Shower and clean yourself up. There'll be some of his clothes in the closet. They won't fit you, but you'll feel better. I'll make us coffee."

As Howard stood in the steaming hot shower, he silently tried to deal with his bewildering emotions and the stress of the past few moments. How could a guy remain sane with all this going on around him?

He'd had a secret affair with her for over two decades. They'd loved each other tenderly and passionately. She'd dumped him to save herself when she didn't trust the FBI to do it. Now—in cold blood and with no remorse—she'd killed the man who had controlled her for even longer. She was brewing coffee for them to enjoy with two bloody corpses in the same room!

Eventually, Howard felt clean enough to leave the steaming shower, dry and dress. As Fidelia predicted, the closet was stuffed with dozens of shirts, shorts, and pants about five sizes too large for him. When he glanced at his appearance in the mirror, he looked like a clown, and Fidelia couldn't suppress a giggle when he joined her in the dining room off to the right.

"Relax, Howard," she began. "You know I could never do the same to you. If I intended you harm, I'd have done it by now."

Her manner was calm. Her tone was neither gloating nor apprehensive. As usual, she had taken decisive action after careful thought and deliberation. He had never seen her show regret for a decision, and there was none evident.

"What happens now?" Howard wondered.

"I'll go back for Luigi and the guys. You know, Luigi and I have been together like we used to be for a couple years now. I've been secretly meeting up with him in New York or New Jersey every month or so. Naturally, Giancarlo's death will come as a shock to the rest, but Luigi will break the news to them and explain where we go from here. He knows them all well, and he's confident they'll start working for me. The private jet is still at Aimé Césaire International Airport and will be all cleaned up and ready for departure within a couple hours. Before dawn, we'll be en route to my new headquarters."

"How did you do it?" Howard asked with a mixture of curiosity and admiration.

"I never actually left The Organization. Once I settled in Eastern Europe, I got in touch with Giancarlo. I told him everything I gave to Interpol so he could develop a strategy. Together, we selected the guys to become The Organization's new leaders in each of the countries. Of course, every one of them was indebted to Giancarlo and loyal to him. In one stroke, I helped him get rid of a lot of potential adversaries and solidify his power. He was appreciative, to say the least."

"But how did you engineer this? This cold-blooded elimination of one of the most powerful men on earth?" Howard wanted to know.

"In the end, it was your old nemesis, Wendal. His personal judgment is still awful, but he invented a new technology we can plant undetected on anyone," Fidelia explained. "For more than six months, we've been able to monitor every conversation Giancarlo, Suji-san, Sugimori, and Boivin had with anyone. Our device picked up both sides of the conversations. We knew everything we needed to know. The only question was when."

"So now you're the head of The Organization?"

"Yeah, that will happen. I expect I'll need a couple months to consolidate everything."

"Are you still going to traffic the women?" Howard wondered.

"Traffic may not be the right term," Fidelia said. "Sadly, that nasty virus from China is spreading. Business will probably be quiet for a while at any rate. Once it settles down, will we still deal in prostitution and drugs? Of course. There will always be men ready to pay good money for sex or a few moments of escape from the realities of this world. The Organization is all about money and we'll accept it. The only thing that will change is our recruitment. We won't kidnap or force women into slavery. But for as many men who are willing to pay for sex, there will always be an adequate number of women ready to be willing participants."

Howard was dumbfounded. How could a woman who suffered so much for so many years rationalize her continued involvement in prostitution? He sat quietly and let reality set in. The woman he thought he knew so intimately for so long was evidently far more complex than he and the world around her realized.

"What's going to happen with the women back at the airport? Klaudia and the other one from the flight?" he asked after a while.

"Both are still alive and I'll bring them with me to Eastern Europe," Fidelia said. "Klaudia probably won't like to stay long and that's okay. I expect she'll start her own technology company somewhere, and I'll surely grant her wish. Nadine, the other one, will probably continue her work in Europe. She's great with the women and will probably savor her newfound freedom. Do you want to come with us?" Fidelia offered.

Howard shook his head slowly.

"No. It broke my heart when you left me in Cuba. For about a year, I thought the Argentinian police had tortured and killed you. Then I found out you had simply abandoned me to save your own skin. Now, I've moved on from The Organization, and you can put a bullet or two in my brain if you choose."

"I told you I could never do that to you. But I have a question," Fidelia continued. "You know the main reason Mareno pursued you with such anger and tenacity? No? Let me tell you. He was pissed about the five hundred million you embezzled from him. He planned to torture you until he found it. Where did you hide the money?"

Howard didn't answer right away. Despite her assurances, when there was still much about the complicated woman he didn't know or understand, who knew how much he should share?

"I can't tell you where the money is. I truly don't know. Even if you tortured me, I wouldn't be able to shed any more light on it. It's true. I misappropriated a half-billion. I used a complex algorithm developed by a gal in San Francisco. That algorithm keeps moving the money from account to account in various countries using a constant stream of digital commands randomly selected by the program."

"So how do we get it back?"

"We don't," Howard replied with a tone that left no room for ambiguity. "With the help of that very clever woman in California, there's only one trigger that stops the movement of funds. Public announcement of Giancarlo Mareno's death. The moment you announce he's dead, the algorithm moves into a new mode and will start disbursing the money."

"Disbursing? To whom?"

"Every day of every month for the next twenty-five years, the program will make an anonymous donation to two charities that specialize in education and human rights for girls and young women. The amounts will appear in their bank accounts in only modest amounts every day, but it will accumulate. They'll use the money wisely. I realize it's a piddling amount compared with what you'll make now that you control The Organization, and that sum of money won't fundamentally change the relationship between our genders in a single generation. But I think it may even out the playing field for women a bit. And that bit will hopefully offset some of the harm I've done."

At first, Fidelia didn't react. Howard watched her intently to determine her reaction. Despite her assurances, he knew the weapon wasn't far from her reach. After a minute or two, she broke into laughter.

"You are a rascal, aren't you!" she teased. "That's brilliant, Howard! I always knew there was some good reason I had a soft spot in my heart for you. Now, let's get in the car. I'll drive you to the airport."

Their drive was short and uneventful. They barely spoke as she focused on the dark, unfamiliar roads and drove at speeds well over the limits. Remarkably, Fidelia drove him right up to the main entrance of the airport and dropped him there. Before he opened the door, she leaned over and gave him a hug and a tender kiss on his cheek as though she was dropping him off for a short business trip.

"Get back in the FBI witness protection program, Howard," she whispered in his ear. "I won't chase you, but there will be others who will try. Maybe somewhere in the south of Portugal would be nice?"

She winked.

ACKNOWLEDGEMENTS

My name appears on the book cover, but I like to point out that my novels always use collaboration extensively. Once I complete a manuscript, the polishing process starts with an outstanding team of editors who provide valuable input and suggestions. With the completion of each novel, I strive to find words to adequately express my profound appreciation for the guidance each editor provides. I always come up short.

Kim McDougall, Paula Hurwitz, and Val Tobin all helped me to polish the story with critical editing and proofreading that improved my story meaningfully. All remaining shortcomings in the book are entirely mine.

Next, I asked a few select people to read early drafts and give me critical feedback on content and style. Heather & Dan Lightfoot and Cathy & Dalton McGugan all read early versions. Their incisive feedback and comments about the plot were of immense value.

Castelane performed admirably—as always! Heartfelt thanks to Kim McDougall for her patience, superb cover design, and eye-catching book layout. Most important, I truly appreciate her expertise pulling it all together with unmatched professionalism and constant good cheer.

I also want to salute my family, friends, and readers around the globe. Thank you all for a lifetime of support and encouragement. You're the ones who sustain my unwavering confidence that anything is possible.

ABOUT THE AUTHOR

Gary D. McGugan loves to tell stories and is the author of *Three Weeks Less a Day, The Multima Scheme* and *Unrelenting Peril*. Whether sharing a vision with colleagues in large multinational corporations, helping consulting clients implement expert advice, or writing a corporate thriller, Gary uses artful suspense to entertain and inform. His launch of a new writing career—at an age most people retire—reveals an ongoing zest for new challenges and a life-long pursuit of knowledge. Home may be in Toronto, but his love of travel and broad business knowledge drawn from extensive experiences around the globe are evident in every chapter.

FOLLOW GARY D. MCGUGAN

Facebook
www.facebook.com/gary.d.mcgugan.books

Twitter
@GaryDMcGugan

Gary D. McGugan Website
www.garydmcguganbooks.com

Instagram
Authorgarydmcgugan